Praise for *Unbreak Me*

"An unlikely pair take on their pasts together in this endearing contemporary tale of love through emotional hardship. Hazen writes with grace and compassion about life after trauma, smoothly addressing racism, sexual assault, and large-scale disasters without pat answers or platitudes."
—*Publishers Weekly* (starred review)

"Two trauma survivors find love and acceptance in Hazen's warm and thoughtful contemporary multicultural romance. Hazen's well-developed characters, soft and steamy love scenes, and exquisitely detailed settings make this a winning love story." —*Booklist* (starred review)

"Hazen produces solid writing that will win over readers and leave them ready for more." —*Library Journal*

"A seductive, slow-burn romance brimming with tenderness, hope, and transformation." —Tammara Webber, *New York Times* bestselling author

"From the sweeping Montana skies to the vibrancy of New Orleans, Hazen packs an emotional punch into every word of this captivating story. *Unbreak Me* is an unapologetic romance that faces controversial issues candidly and grips your heart from the first page." —Kelly Siskind

"Hazen's ability to pen sensitive and complex issues with respect and compassion made this one of my favorite books of the year! *Unbreak Me* is a must-read for anyone who believes that love can heal even the most complicated of wounds. I can't wait to see what Hazen does next."
—Tricia Lynne

"*Unbreak Me* left m███████████████████art, and I can't wait to see what's on th███████ D0974091 ███████axym M. Martineau

Jove titles by Michelle Hazen

Unbreak Me
Breathe the Sky

Breathe the Sky

MICHELLE HAZEN

Jove
New York

A JOVE BOOK
Published by Berkley
An imprint of Penguin Random House LLC
penguinrandomhouse.com

ISBN: 9781984803313

Library of Congress Cataloging-in-Publication Data

Names: Hazen, Michelle, author.
Title: Breathe the sky / Michelle Hazen.
Description: First edition. | New York : Jove, 2020.
Identifiers: LCCN 2019051639 | ISBN 9781984803313 (trade paperback) |
ISBN 9781984803320 (ebook)
Classification: LCC PS3608.A98884 B74 2020 | DDC 813/.6—dc23
LC record available at https://lccn.loc.gov/2019051639

First Edition: August 2020

Printed in the United States of America
1   3   5   7   9   10   8   6   4   2

Cover design and photocomposition by Colleen Reinhart
Book design by Alison Cnockaert

Dedicated to all my truck-dwelling bio friends.
You are a stone-cold pack of weirdos, and I love all of you.

1

The Short Straw

Mari Tucker perched on her truck's tailgate, watched her boss pick up his clipboard, and prayed.

Any crew but Wyatt's crew.

She'd volunteer for the concrete pouring team with their lecherous inspector, or the choking dust of checking in front of the bulldozer, or even monitoring the yard where they kept all the dirty porta potties. Anything.

Any foreman but Wyatt.

Mari turned up the camp stove sitting next to her so the water would boil faster. Maybe a little fresh coffee would keep her on her boss's good side. It had worked so far—she'd been on this job for weeks, passed out more free coffee than she could afford, and had somehow avoided coming face-to-face with the infamous Jack Wyatt.

"Let's stick Rajni on the porta potty yard," Marcus decided, and marked it on his clipboard. Snickers came from the other biologists all standing in a loose circle, chatting while they waited for their assignments. It always tugged like a stitch in her stomach to watch them, so she parked her old Toyota just a little away from the main group.

She shivered in the predawn bite of the air and edged closer to the warmth of her stove, where the pot was starting to steam. All the chit-chat during the morning meeting may not have been her scene, but her extra-large coffeepot was always popular.

In the next truck over, Rajni had been tightening bolts that had rattled loose on her truck's solar panel, but she stopped long enough to flip their boss a middle finger.

"Wyatt last week and now keeping critters out of the shitters? Love you, too, Marcus."

"I live to please." He laughed. "Lisa, you're with Junior's tower assembly group. Hotaka, you scored the concrete pouring crew because they get male bios only until their inspector learns to behave."

With every assignment given, Mari's shoulders cranked a little tighter. She glanced over at the construction yard, its floodlights blaring brighter than the sun that had just started to come up. Men bustled inside the chain-link fence, the reflective stripes on their safety vests flashing. The biologists always parked just outside the yard, like party guests nobody would let near the chips and salsa.

"Mari . . ." Marcus paused, tap-tap-tapping his pen, and gave her a pained look.

Nausea kicked up into her throat, and her fingers froze on the knobs of the stove. He hadn't said it. Maybe he could still mean she was on bulldozers.

"I had one more guy who was up for a rotation," Marcus explained, "but Wyatt said, and I quote, 'If you send that sunshiny mother-effer back here, he's going to end up stuck where the sun don't shine.'" A dry smile lifted her boss's beard. "End quote."

"How's the whole HR mess with those two?" Rajni asked, popping her wrench back into her bulky toolbox.

"They're still on company-mandated five hundred meters' distance from each other until the suits determine whether locking somebody in the back of a truck in the desert is assault, or if can be ruled accidental."

"It was 102 that day!" Lisa glared from the tailgate of her purple Toyota. "It could have been murder."

"Wyatt did say he left the windows cracked."

"We should change out the rotation criteria," Rajni put in. "Instead of one week at a time, it should be three strikes, you're out—if he makes you cry three times, you get to skip your next turn."

"Which would disqualify pretty much everyone," Marcus said. "Nice try."

Mari turned away so she could tuck in the end of the sheet on the bed inside her truck camper shell, and hoped everyone's attention would turn to something else. It wasn't like she couldn't endure a guy with a temper. Whatever he pulled, she'd seen worse. But these days, she'd rather just . . . not.

She didn't want much—just the chance to pull on her sun-faded safety vest and disappear into the sea of other sun-faded safety vests. Some of the biologists got bored being on the sidelines, but she sort of liked dogging the edges of the construction site while they built their power lines. It felt like playing patron saint to desert creatures, only dashing in to scoop vulnerable animals out of the way of the bulldozers and hungry truck tires.

For an instant, the memory of the little yellow cottage flashed into her mind, with buttery light pouring from the windows and its small porch beckoning. She shoved it away. This job, this *life*, was a blessing, and she wasn't greedy enough to ask for more. Not even this week, when she'd just drawn the stubbiest of short straws.

"I'll make it up to you," Marcus promised.

She nodded and gave him a quick, reassuring smile. She'd keep it polite and professional, and as soon as she could, she'd fade back into the desert. For the sake of the rare animals they protected, she could force herself not to back down. Not even from the temper of the infamous Wyatt. Her fingers tightened on the edge of the dusty tailgate.

"And if he gets to be too much, call it in," Marcus said. "I'll juggle some things and staff it myself if I have to."

"Oh, and have his crew break up another fistfight between the two of you?" Lisa gave him a pointed look. "Last time, you barely made it to eight a.m."

Marcus glanced down. "I shouldn't have tried to punch him. It was unprofessional."

"Jack Wyatt ought to be fired," Lisa grumbled. "He has a blatant disregard for the Endangered Species Act, and who gets away with treating other people that way?"

"The foreman who builds towers twice as fast as anyone else," Marcus said. "That's who. They're so over budget and behind schedule that Wyatt is the only thing saving their balance sheet from going pure red. Until he starts hitting crew members instead of just yelling at them, or kills an endangered species, he's staying."

"Which won't be long, considering he ignores half our rules," Lisa muttered.

"Coffee, anyone?" Mari called. She didn't want the debate to drag on any longer and make her look like she was trying to dodge her turn. Her coworkers crowded in and she hopped off the tailgate so they could get to the coffeepot, taking a few steps away and stuffing her hands in her pockets. The spring sun was already burning off the morning's chill, its heat ferocious even in the first moments of dawn.

Behind her was the busy construction yard full of yellow-painted heavy equipment and construction workers. But looking this way, the Mojave Desert rippled out around her in miles of empty, beautiful safety. Joshua trees waited in patient, spiky silhouettes, and creosotes stretched toward the sky, their simple leaves lacy in the low morning light.

Mari pulled her hair over her shoulder, smoothing it and beginning a braid. She needed to chop off the last few inches. They were all dead ends and two-year-old dye in a brown so cheap that it had never really matched her natural color. She preferred the naked streaks of gray. At least they were honest, and they weren't trying to please anyone.

At the thought, her fingers twitched, then slowed their braiding. After Mari's mom had remarried, she had always curled Mari's hair on the weekends. Dolling her up in her best dresses like a good little girl who wouldn't upset her stepdad. It never really worked. Her mom's personality was soothing, as creamy as her unmarked skin. Whereas Mari always set him off, and by Mondays she was usually smudged with the angry red and bruised purple marks of her failure. Still, his back-hands never hurt for as long as the tiny burns from when she squirmed in her seat and brushed her mom's relentless curling iron.

She abandoned the half-done braid and stuffed it into a careless ponytail instead, irritated to catch herself guided by the echo of her mother's desperate placating tactics from a lifetime ago.

"Ready for some good news?" At the sound of Marcus's voice, she turned around, and he gave her a hopeful smile. "Payday." He handed over her check, and her pulse jumped at the bold type across the top line.

Marianna Tucker

"Thanks." She quickly folded it in half. Seeing her real name on anything always gave her a jolt. She used a fake name for hotels to make it harder to track her down, but she didn't dare lie on legal documents that would be linked to her tax return. Still, she figured as long as the only address her real name led to was her truck and a PO Box, nothing could be traced back to her. He couldn't find her.

She must not have hidden her disquiet very well, though, because Marcus looked worried enough to attempt an awkward shoulder pat. "You only have to stick it out with Wyatt for a week," he said. "Just a week."

Jack Wyatt roared off the dirt road and onto the construction site and jammed the work truck to a dust-billowing stop. He was already in a foul mood and twenty-two minutes late, because his Cheetos-for-brains crew couldn't remember their tools from the construction yard. He needed to pack their trucks for them like a bunch of babies' diaper bags if he wanted to get to work on time.

He grabbed a metal clipboard out of the back seat, scrawled his name on the top of it, and then chucked it onto his hood with a clatter as the other crew truck crept up to park next to his.

"Sign the damn safety form," he growled. "If you're too stupid to keep yourself alive, you don't deserve to be."

That was the only safety speech his men were going to get, and he was flat serious about it. He'd seen foremen talk about every little bitty thing that could go wrong, repeating it every morning, and he'd still seen linemen plunge to their deaths off the metal lattice towers they were erecting. There wasn't anything that could keep a man from falling but his own hands and his own brains.

Talking wouldn't do crap.

He spat in the dirt, a sourness clinging to his tongue that came from more than the rapidly cooling coffee in his travel mug. A guy like him was better off alone, so it was too bad he couldn't just build towers by himself. It'd be safer, not to mention quieter. He'd never played well with other people. He'd only ever cared for two people in all his life, and one was an asshole, and the other got himself killed.

His thoughts were interrupted when he spotted something in the scene that didn't match: a slender figure picking her way around the edges of the bulldozed dirt of the tower site. She walked lightly, as if there was hardly any weight to her steps, her wisp of a safety vest lifted by the curve of small breasts.

He blinked and looked away, not wanting to gawk at her like his shitbag brother always did to women. But once he did, he spotted a parked truck that he hadn't noticed before. It was tiny compared to their work rigs, one of those foreign-made trucks with the bed of it closed in with a metal camper shell. He'd heard the desert biologists lived in them, eating and sleeping and everything in a little truck bed.

He didn't really believe it.

In the Mojave Desert, 117 degrees in the shade, where metal got hot enough to burn straight through his thick leather gloves? Nobody was stupid enough or tough enough to live in a pickup truck.

Low murmurs caught his ears, and he squinted back to find his crew done signing the safety sheet and just standing around, smirking as their eyes bounced between him and the approaching woman. Women rarely showed up on construction sites, but on this job, they had a lot of female biological monitors, so it wasn't that goddamn remarkable to see one. Even if there was something about the way this one moved that made him want to stare.

"Haven't you ever seen a biologist before?" he said, furious that they were all gawking at her. "Why don't you grab an impact wrench and act like you can do an honest day's labor around here?"

"Just wanted to watch you meet the new bio, boss." Kipp snickered from under his enormous waxed mustache.

Jack sent a furious look toward Kipp, who jumped into motion, yanking his tool belt on so fast he nearly buckled it to the belt on his pants.

Jack took off his hard hat and shoved his shaggy hair back, planting the helmet back on. "Infested with tree huggers," he muttered. "In a land with no fucking trees."

He strode forward, wanting to get this over with as soon as possible. Twenty-eight minutes late getting started now, and if they didn't get this next section bolted into place by quitting time, no way was his boss approving overtime. Which would mean his men would have to work for free to get it finished. It wasn't like they could just leave a giant tower half-screwed together like a forgotten Lego set on the living room floor.

"Um, hi," the woman said. "I'm Mari." Her quick, polite smile faded so fast he wasn't totally sure it had ever been there. "I'll be your biological monitor this week. I just need to check in with you about one or two things we have to do to keep our native endangered species safe while you work."

Safe. Jack snorted. If only this company spent half as much on its own men as it spent protecting mythical animals nobody ever saw. His safety ropes were frayed, harnesses faded and brittle, the work trucks' tires so bald and cracked they flew apart on the freeway a couple of times a year.

The corners of her mouth twitched down at his derisive sound, and he tensed, waiting for the holier-than-thou speech all these bios seemed to have at the ready.

"It's just a power line," she offered instead, her soft voice wavering a little. "Nothing should have to die for it."

The sound of cracking bone rang through his memory. Vernon had died for it. Not this power line, but another. Jack ran a hand over his face to cover the twitch his shoulders gave in response. "I ain't hurting any animals."

It was plain old desert, all cactuses and squat, ugly bushes. Wasn't like there were herds of white rhinos parading around. He'd been out here for months. You'd see a lizard, sometimes a bird, that was it. It wasn't like he was holding them down and running screws through their feathery little wings.

She took a breath, rushing out the words. "Of course, I'll be watching and moving any animals out of your way that I see. But the most important thing is, everyone needs to make sure to check under their tires before they move their trucks, because that's the best shade in the desert. All the animals are attracted to it."

"Don't they have legs? They'll run off when I start the truck."

"The species we're most concerned with out here are desert tortoises and Coachella Valley or Mojave fringe-toed lizards. Tortoises aren't known for their sprinting times, and the lizards have a trick where they shake themselves down into the sand to hide from predators. It doesn't help them much with trucks, unfortunately." She did a little wiggle, explaining how the lizards got down into the sand, and the curve of her hip caught his attention for a beat too long. He cleared his throat and jerked his gaze up.

But that wasn't much better, because the delicate lines of her face drew his eye like something he wanted to look twice at, like he couldn't catch it all with one glance. She brushed a loose ponytail of dark hair back over her shoulder, the silver strands in it catching the sunlight.

Belatedly, he realized he was just standing there like an idiot, staring at her hair. "Tortoises got shells. They'll be fine." He didn't intend to burn up any time worrying about a creature who lived inside a protective casing.

"Yes, but—" She broke off when the wind whipped up into a little dust devil cyclone that sprayed them with sand.

When it passed, she took off her sunglasses to swipe off the dust. Her eyes met his, squinting a little like she was looking for something she hadn't quite nailed down yet. "They do have shells, true enough. But animals' shells are rarely thick enough to protect them from the things that truly hurt."

Her eyes were sky-cast blue, and quiet. His pulse gave a lurch, like a truck's bumper had just skimmed too close on the freeway.

Jack scowled at her. The last thing he needed on his job site was a good-looking woman. The beautiful ones always expected attention, were used to special treatment. Not to mention his men would be tripping over their own feet, staring at her all day when they should be watching the tower they were climbing.

He had quotas to hit, never mind that they were so ambitious he'd need five more men or would have to get bitten by a radioactive spider if he didn't want to fall behind. His boss had made it clear that if Jack couldn't make quota for just one week, he'd find another guy who could. Jack hadn't clawed his way up to foreman just to become one more deadbeat Wyatt with their name scribbled across a pink slip.

And he wasn't going to let any biologist slow him down enough to lose this job, no matter how blue her eyes were.

"I don't give a shit about a bunch of turtles," he snapped. "Just stay out of our way. You come chasing lizards across my pad, and you get brained by a dropped wrench, your lawyers better not come crying to me."

A breath escaped her, like she'd almost laughed, and she popped her sunglasses back on. "As if I could afford lawyers."

A chuckle huffed out of him before he realized what he was doing.

The only people who could pay for lawyers were the ones screwing over the people who actually worked for a living. It was God's honest truth, and why he couldn't see a reason in the world for them. Lawyers swooped in to protect you after you'd already taken your beatdown. The fists had flown, the car had been stolen, the lineman had already slipped and fallen off the tower, his blood exploding out of him onto the dirt like a punctured can of spray paint. Jack shook off the memory. Lawyers came in, telling you they could pour spilled milk back into the carton and taking hard-earned money from anybody stupid enough to believe them.

Lawyers were assholes, and he had no use for them. He half liked that she didn't, either.

"Jack . . ." A whiny voice interrupted them. "The forklift won't start."

Jack turned with a ferocious scowl. "Well, dick brain, did you reconnect the battery after I had you clean the terminals yesterday?"

"Oh!" Joey's eyes brightened. "I forgot. It was quitting time, and I didn't get a chance to—"

"Well, maybe if you paid as much attention to doing a good job as you did to watching the clock, you could start a forklift without my help." Jack clapped the apprentice on the back hard enough to send him stumbling, then jerked his chin at Mari. "Get off my pad." He turned back to his crew.

Bad enough the bios had to stand there all day, watching him work and critiquing his performance just like his family always had. They didn't need to be underfoot while they did it. It's like they thought if they took their eyes off him for one second, he'd strangle a dang bunny.

They didn't need to watch—they'd hear it if he did. Bunnies screamed when you hurt them, when you sliced off their little paws. That had been his brother Leroy's thing when they were kids, not his. He didn't need a biologist to tell him he never wanted to hear that sound again.

"Wait, um, sorry, Mr. Wyatt?" she called after him.

Ugly goose bumps clawed to life all across his scarred back at the sound of his family's name tainting her light, musical voice.

Joey stopped and turned along with him, and Jack nudged the apprentice to send him on his way. Kid would pop visible wood if he looked straight at their new pretty bio. Hell, Jack was a grown man and he'd nearly needed to grab a tool belt for camouflage before he'd gotten his situation under control.

She thrust a clipboard at him, her graceful shoulders pulling back all tight and determined. "I just need your signature that you received the environmental mitigation training."

Lawyers again. Paperwork never changed anything. Just made it so the suits could claim immunity when one of his guys eventually slipped off a tower. Talking and paperwork wouldn't save her desert critters any more than it'd save his men. It'd just shift the blame off the head honchos and onto whoever's name was scrawled on that bottom line.

"Ain't signing shit." Jack spat on the ground and walked away.

2

No Glove, No Love

Later that week, Jack climbed down off the tower, the metal pegs hot through his gloves. His safety leash hung off his belt because you couldn't hitch it in while you were climbing. He didn't let himself think of anything until he got to the ground.

Hand, foot. Hand, foot. It was a quick rhythm as he descended, but solid. His own strength was the only thing holding him on to the tower and grounding him against five stories of open air below.

Hand.

Foot.

Hand.

Foot.

He'd hated heights when he started this job. Got dizzy every time his feet left the ground. But being a lineman was the most decent-paying job that they hadn't yet shipped overseas, and dizziness wasn't worth complaining about as long as it got him out of Alabama. It wore off after the second year. He still couldn't look down without feeling sick, but that just kept him honest. Kept him careful.

Hand.

Foot.

Hand.

Foot.

He didn't pause when his boots hit dirt, because he'd never let his crew see him take that gulp of relief he always, always wanted. Instead, he held his breath until the urge passed, and strode toward his truck.

"Going to the yard," he yelled over his shoulder. "If that section's not done when I get back, nobody's taking lunch."

Their new safety leashes had come in the mail today. Their old ones had finally been certified unusable, six months after he would have tossed them out if it had been his decision. Sure, he could pick them up tomorrow, but if anybody fell this afternoon, that'd be on his conscience.

He stripped off his leather gloves and stuffed them into his pocket, already calculating how much work time he'd lose by running to the construction yard. He could send the apprentice, but probably the kid would come back toting a crate of tissues or something that was clearly not what he'd been sent for. Joey was fresh out of high school, and Jack was afraid he was going to have to fire the kid. He was eager, but too head-in-the-clouds for a profession where the consequences were often a lot more dire than a bad employee review.

There was a little lump under Jack's tire. He glanced back at the crew to see if anybody was watching. The bios had said that the only way to look under his tires was to go the full 360 degrees, walking all the way around the truck and getting down on his knees to peer underneath. Well, the bad knee a half-drunk forklift driver had bumped back in his twenties wasn't going to put up with that, even if his dignity could have. But even having never seen one before, it was pretty clear that one of those freaking tortoises had cozied up under his tire.

Wasn't a big one. More like the size of a cheeseburger, and not even a double. He eyed it, glanced behind him again. The bio had walked up a wash on the far side of the construction pad, and she was peering at some weird kind of plant as she scribbled on her clipboard. Compared to his men, she moved like a creature made out of a breeze. Weightless and gentle, fading between bushes and over rocks like she never felt the roughness of the world she walked on.

He'd caught himself watching her so many times over the past four days that he was disgusted at the example he was setting for his men. It figured that the first time one of these fancy turtles decided to show up, he'd have this new soft-spoken bio instead of one of the regular smelly, bearded ones.

Protocol was to call the bio to move any "sensitive species" out of the way of his work. But if he did that, she'd probably have to do a raft of paperwork, and want him to sign even more crap. She might talk to him, *smile* at him . . .

He jerked at his pants, impatient with his own reaction. He needed to make time after work to do a little self-maintenance. In his line of work, he wasn't used to having women around, and he'd never really gotten the hang of dating.

Jack walked to his truck, his decision made, and scooped up the tortoise from under his tire. It was cool to the touch and surprisingly heavy. He cupped it in both hands, because sure as shit if he dropped an endangered species, they'd write his company a citation with enough zeros on the end that he'd be looking for new work by morning.

He strode around the back of his truck, heading out into the desert before anybody could see what he was up to.

The tortoise poked his head out, craning his wrinkled neck to see where they were going, his scaly legs paddling the air like he wanted to pretend he was in control of this voyage.

Jack huffed out a breath. "Nice try, little buddy, but you ain't steering this ship."

The shell felt different than he'd expected. Lots of little ripples and bumps, as individual as a fingerprint. And ancient, like something out of a museum case he had no business touching. He smoothed his thumb down the side of the tortoise to feel the texture, careful to keep his grip secure.

He set the tortoise down a few long strides outside the work area, then glanced toward the crew just in time to see Kipp back the forklift over an empty cardboard box he clearly hadn't seen. Jack winced, and carried the tortoise a little farther.

This time, when he bent over, a drop of sweat fell from his forehead onto the shell. Jack chewed his lower lip and picked up the tortoise a third time, stuffing him quickly into the shade of a scraggly desert bush. It was hot today. Too hot to leave it out in the sun, probably.

"Oh!" a feminine voice said from behind him. "You found a tortoise!"

He turned with a scowl. "Wasn't hurting him. Look, he's fucking fine." He gestured at the tortoise, sitting snugly in the shade and peering up at Jack as if he didn't know enough to squeeze up into his shell and hide.

"I can see that," Mari said in that gentle way she had. "But I could have moved him for you. That's my job, after all."

"Can carry my own goddamn turtle," he grumbled.

Her lips twitched. "It's just, they're so rare anymore, you need a permit to handle them. And even if it's an emergency and I'm not around, you need to use gloves." She pulled a baggie of blue latex gloves out of her pack.

He looked at the tortoise, looked at his own grubby hands, all criss-crossed with old steel burns and stained black from messing with the forklift battery earlier. "You afraid I'm gonna get him dirty?" He gestured. "Little sucker lives in a hole in the ground. Probably doesn't have a shower in there."

Her face softened, and for a second, he thought she was going to laugh, but then she seemed to stop herself.

Heat crept up Jack's collar. Why did she keep smiling when he talked? What the fuck was he saying that was so damn funny?

Pretty women were like that, though, always two steps ahead of you. So a man never had any idea what they were mad about or laughing about or looking so expectantly at you for.

"It's for disease, actually," she said. "You could be carrying all kinds of germs on your hands that might be fine for humans but affect tortoises. Or, without knowing it, you could have touched something out here that a diseased tortoise had already touched, and you might spread that disease. Tortoises were nearly wiped out from disease that we didn't have a good understanding of until just a few years ago."

"You telling me I need to use a turtle rubber?"

Her lips twitched. Trembled. And then she burst into laughter, so musical and unabashed that he saw a few of the crew's heads turn their way. His skin flared a red as deep as a sunburn.

Mari pulled off her sunglasses and wiped her eyes with the back of one hand, still grinning.

He shifted from one foot to the other, his shoulders bunching as his skin crawled with shame. It wasn't that stupid a thing to say. She was talking about preventing the spread of unintended disease and—

"You're exactly right," she said, stopping his defensive thoughts as another chuckle shook her slender chest. "I've never thought of it that way, and Lord, now I'm not going to be able to think of gloves as anything else."

He hesitated, his toes curling and fidgeting in his boots as he tried to decide what to say. She wasn't making fun of him; she really thought what he said was funny.

He wasn't entirely sure what to do with that. He'd sort of expected to be in trouble.

Seemed like, whenever he took a step outside the construction zone, the other bios were all up his butt about rare-plant this and fancy-ass-bird that, like his boots were the size of Nebraska and they'd crush everything for miles. But then the words Mari said earlier came drifting back.

Permit to handle.

Endangered species.

He frowned down at his boots. "Gonna write me up, aren't you? For turtle grabbing."

The shy smile tugged its way back onto her lips, her eyes warm before she slipped her sunglasses back on, hiding them from view. A pang echoed in his chest, and he rubbed absently at it. Probably he ought to quit this job before his stupid crew gave him a heart attack.

"I think it was consensual grabbing, considering you saved the tortoise from danger. There's a Good Samaritan law for that, though it's not usually applied on monitored sites." She cleared her throat. "I guess you were checking under your tires after all." She gave him a knowing look, the memory of yesterday's rant about "not prancing three circles before he drove his truck anywhere" hanging between them.

He grunted, and stuffed his hands into his pockets. "Don't take any brains to see a turtle under your truck. Not like I get my jollies running shit over."

He'd never forget the bump the truck made when Leroy ran over their neighbor's dog, Bart. Or the softness of the second bump when Leroy backed up "to finish him off the humane way."

He shivered.

Mari said, her voice dropping softly, "That's not what I was saying. Not at all." She reached out and touched his arm but then let go so quickly he figured she'd maybe done it by accident. "Come get me next time, okay? I'll disinfect the tortoise's shell just in case. But if you moved a tortoise and something bad happened, you could be in a lot of trouble."

His arm tingled where she touched him. "You ain't gonna write me up?" He couldn't stop frowning at her, though he probably looked like an ungrateful asshole. These bios were all like a bunch of rookie traffic cops, too quick on the draw with the ticket notepad. They didn't bother much with just talking things out.

He scrubbed roughly at his arm, trying to get his skin to quit getting all stirred up about one measly touch from a woman who didn't even mean it like that.

"You didn't do any harm. The thing is, some tortoises are more skittish than others, and if you handle them roughly, they can get scared and void their bladders." Her hint of a smile was gone now. "Out here, losing their emergency store of water can mean they might die of dehydration before the next rain."

He stared in horror at the cheeseburger-sized tortoise, sitting placidly beside the bush. He might have made the little guy piss itself to death.

"Hell." He yanked off his hard hat and turned in a circle, jerking at the knot of his hair where he kept it tied back at work. There was no shame worse than pissing yourself.

He'd started wetting the bed after his mom died when he was a little kid. Dreaming there was a fire burning in between them and if he could just put it out, he could see her again. But when he would wake with wet sheets clinging to his legs and tears salty on his cheeks, he knew it hadn't been water at all and that he hadn't saved his mother.

He'd always tried to get the sheets in the washer himself, but the one time his father woke up and saw what he'd done, he'd wrapped the soiled sheets around Jack like he was a dog getting its face rubbed in its own mess. That wet ammonia smell suffocating him, his arms pinned to his sides so he couldn't get away no matter how hard he thrashed . . .

"Mr. Wyatt? Are you okay?"

He jerked at the sound of his family's name.

"Don't call me that!" he snarled, whirling on her.

She jumped back, stumbling when her heel bumped a bush. Light on her feet as always, she caught her balance before she could fall, but the tortoise yanked into its shell at the sudden movement.

Jack felt like dog shit, his head hanging and shoulders clenching tight. He'd scared the woman and the little turtle.

"Hate that name," he muttered, trying to explain why he'd been such a jerk. "Feels like you're talking to my old man. Name's Jack."

Jack *Wyatt*. The name echoed in his head, even though he refused to say it out loud. Didn't have to. Wyatts were quick on the trigger, and women, children, and animals cringed out of their way. Thousands of miles from the Alabama hovel where he grew up and he couldn't shake the truth of that name, no matter how hard he'd tried not to be like his piece-of-shit dad and brother. This woman had known him only four days and even she could see it.

He gestured miserably to her, then to the tortoise, reaching harder for words than he usually ever tried. "I—shit, I'm sorry," he said. "Didn't know. I could scare them so bad, I mean. Didn't know. Wouldn't have . . . you know. If I did."

"That's why the training is important," she said. Not like she was shoving the I-told-you-so down his throat, but not backing down, either. Her gaze held steady, even as his flicked between her, the ground, and the tortoise that was just peeking its head out of its shell again. "It's important for you *and* your crew to hear."

The other bios had all tried to give their speech, too, but he'd never allowed them to waste working time on all that bureaucratic crap. But then, he hadn't known that they could kill the animals around here just by startling them.

He turned his hard hat in his hands, uncomfortable as all hell, but then he swallowed and jerked a nod. "We'll come in ten minutes early tomorrow. You can give them your talk. Easy on the bullshit, though, huh? I want the real deal, not a whole bunch of lawyer talk and crap."

Mari nodded. "One biological resources training coming up, hold the bullshit."

He snorted a laugh, and realized he was just standing there, his unease having drained out of him so subtly he hadn't even felt it go. Her droll humor must have tricked him into thinking he was shooting the breeze with his buddies instead of with a too-pretty tree-hugging professional interferer.

He slammed his hard hat back on. "Gotta get back to work." He stalked toward his truck.

"And, Jack?"

He turned back, liking the sound of his first name in her voice.

A sly smile lit her face. "If you see another tortoise? No glove, no love."

3

Catch More Lizards with
Honey Than Vinegar

Mari brought doughnuts to her training. It turned out to be a crowd-pleasing decision, since Jack made all the men show up early (and unpaid) to attend. Before the snacks came out, there had definitely been some grumbling. Jack had also smacked a lineman upside the hard hat for talking during her speech. Jack, on the other hand, had listened so intently that the training went on six whole minutes into their working time before he'd noticed.

During the part about baby desert tortoises, he looked like he wanted to ask a question, but when she offered him the chance, he denied it with a grunt.

Once he realized the training had gone late, he cut her off and harangued all the men to get moving with his usual lack of tact. She packed up the scraps of the doughnuts and carried the pink box back to her truck while, out of the corner of her eye, she watched Jack herd his workers toward the tower. He wasn't what she'd expected, from all the rumors. Not cruel, or even cocky.

He was a rough-looking man, with impenetrable dark sunglasses, nearly black hair he kept yanked back in a high knot, and a growling southern accent so harsh it could have scared Rhett Butler straight.

Even at the best of times, he was gruff, but he mostly only lost his temper when somebody had screwed up enough to put themselves in danger.

Slamming her truck door, she left the doughnut box in her Toyota and strolled out beyond the bulldozed area. For the first two days, she'd tensely walked her monitoring laps around the construction site, twitching every time she heard Jack's voice raised in anger.

She knew how quickly a certain kind of man's temper could flame, and she seemed to have a talent for setting people off. She'd stayed at a shelter while she saved up to buy her truck, and the social workers told her that her husband's behavior hadn't been her fault. He'd been out of line, to be sure, but it was a problem that had dogged her long before her marriage, and as easy as it would be to blame everyone else, she knew she wasn't entirely innocent. Her stepfather had been perfectly sweet to her mother. It was just Mari who couldn't get along with him, which was why she'd been so happy to get married fast and out of his house.

After her divorce, the open desert became her sanctuary. When she was alone, there was no one to get upset at her. But alone wasn't an option at work, and she needed to eat. Needed to pay the old medical bills that kept coming to her PO Box printed on brighter and brighter colors of paper, as if dye alone could make her more able to come up with the obscene numbers they represented.

Despite his temper, she knew Wyatt couldn't touch her at work, and whatever abuse he tossed her way would be laughable compared to what she'd already lived through. But it wasn't easy, being around another guy with a temper. She even thought of telling Marcus why it was so hard for her to work on this crew, but didn't want to ask for special treatment so soon into taking a new job. That one bill for the dislocated jaw that she'd gotten right before her divorce . . . it was painfully past due and racking up more interest by the week.

So she took deep breaths and stuck it out, and the more she watched, the more she realized Jack Wyatt wasn't the thoughtless bully everyone made him out to be.

Right now, Jack was pointing at the tower, then jabbing a finger toward the plans, glaring at the confused worker in front of him. After nearly a week on this crew, she could predict exactly what was going on. She'd always watched the world around her, and so she knew that a lot of men yelled because they were trying to cover up how stupid they were. But Jack yelled because he was too smart.

He saw every mistake before it was even made. He had strategies two and three steps more efficient than all the other men, and he got so frustrated with them when they didn't automatically get the best way to do things. It wasn't hard for him, and he never understood why it was so hard for his crew. Why they needed him to explain every little thing he just *knew*.

Of course, that was no excuse for his being such a jerk about it. If her people skills were shaky, his were terrible. The man had no idea how to teach, and even less of an idea of how to communicate.

But on the third day, the apprentice's shoe had slipped because he was distracted and talking while climbing. Jack had grabbed him, both of them clinging to thin tower struts several stories off the ground. The whole tower had shaken with how hard Jack slammed Joey into the metal when he caught him. That day, his yelling had hit new decibels.

After that, Mari noticed how closely he watched the other men when they were doing dangerous things. How his eyes missed nothing their hands and feet did, but slid away from their faces like he was afraid to know them, to even get used to seeing them around. How he locked himself away in his truck at lunchtime while the other workers all grouped up in the shade of their one tattered EZ-Up awning. Free of their grouchy boss, they laughed and passed their food around. It reminded her of herself, brewing coffee in her little pot, just outside the circle of the Monday morning meeting.

Then, yesterday, she'd caught Jack carrying that tortoise. So gently, in both his big hands. Moving it twice when he wasn't satisfied with its placement, and even thinking to put it in the shade so it would be comfortable. He'd made her *laugh*, which had surprised her almost as much as it had him. He'd been dismayed when she told him the dire consequences of frightening the shy little desert creature. And there was no mistaking his shame when, for an instant, he'd frightened her, too.

After all the stories, she'd expected Jack to remind her of her ex-husband, Brad, but he didn't. He reminded her of herself.

She tucked her hands into her pockets, pretending to check a bush but actually peeking past it to steal a glimpse of him.

They were watchers, both of them. But where she tried to stay out of sight and away from all the things that might hurt her, he puffed up bigger and plowed straight toward them as if to bluff his own fear into backing down. She noticed his steps hitched every time he approached the tower to climb it, like he wanted to take a moment and a breath to steady himself but wouldn't allow himself the luxury.

After he had apologized, gesturing to her and to the tortoise like he was equally upset about having scared both of them, she simply couldn't be afraid of Jack Wyatt.

Unfortunately, that did not mean they were friends.

"You telling me I can't use my own goddamn forklift until a fucking lizard gives me permission?" Jack howled. He couldn't believe this crap. "Desert's chock-full of lizards, woman! You gonna tell me I can't use my forklift when sand touches it next?"

Mari scooted back from where she'd been crouched under the giant tire of the forklift, her hard hat falling off her head and landing with an annoyed plop next to her. She gave him a determined look.

"When it's a lizard that only has a handful of sand dunes left to live in, yes, as a matter of fact, I am."

Her cocoa-brown hair was wet with sweat as she ducked and crawled farther under the forklift. "I saw him dart under here. I just need to . . . catch him." She squeaked as she made another grab, then sighed when the little thing scampered away toward the back of the forklift. "Darn it." She came out and sat back on her heels.

Jack's boss was so not going to care about some lizard when he had to explain why they weren't done with this tower site today.

"What the hell am I supposed to do, lift these struts myself? I need my lift to put this shit together!"

Mari winced. "Sorry. I've always been terrible at catching the animals. Too slow."

Hearing her say that made his older brother's voice echo in his head. *You slow or something, kid? Why the fuck can't you hit a target?*

Leroy had been angry that his little brother had been practicing with a rifle for a full hour and hadn't yet learned to hit the bull's-eye.

"You ain't slow," Jack grunted, not liking the unhappiness in her face. "Lizard's always gonna be faster than your hand."

He spent his whole childhood catching animals. Lizards, toads, squirrels . . . whatever he could grab, and then whatever he could trap or shoot. At first, for pets. Later, for when Leroy forgot to buy groceries. He learned how to cook them over a campfire, too, when his brother went on a bender and forgot to pay the electric bill.

"Here, I'll catch it."

He stalked over to his truck and jerked the straw out of yesterday's soda cup.

"Dick brain!" he hollered. "You still got that box of goddamn jewelry in the truck?"

"Yes, boss." Joey came at a trot and grabbed out the tackle box, offering it with a puzzled look but smart enough to know he'd catch the rough side of Jack's temper if he asked.

Jack jerked the box open. Kid was always messing with it on the long drives to and from work. Making leather necklaces and stringing up ugly beaded chokers like that was somehow a dignified kind of doodad to wear around one's neck. Kids these days were so weird. He took some thin fishing line out of the kit and pushed a loop of it up through the soda straw, working as he walked back toward where Mari was waiting next to the forklift.

"All right, where is the little bugger?"

She pointed toward the back tire, eyeing his fishing-line-and-soda-straw contraption.

His face twitched with pain as Jack bent his bad knee, dropping to the sand with an audible *oomph* and then getting all the way down on his belly in the hot sand, elbow crawling forward into the marginally cooler shade of the forklift.

"Thing with lizards is, they don't really pay much mind to things coming up behind them," he said, keeping his voice pitched low. Steadying himself on his elbows, he eased the soda straw up behind the lizard. To its tail, then up over its back. The loop of fishing line poking out the front dropped down over the lizard's head without it so much as twitching.

At his side, Mari was watching so intently he couldn't even hear her breathe.

Jack pulled the fishing line at the back of the straw, the noose going tight around the lizard's neck. It jerked, flipping as it tried to run away. Mari gasped but his hand snapped forward as fast as her breath, cupping over the lizard and scooping it up. He held it gently against the palm of his hand as he pulled the noose free.

"See? He ain't hurt. It's just to slow him down enough to grab him." He used his free hand to stroke the lizard's scaly head, the texture weird and cool against his fingertips. Funny how that was exactly the same as when he was a kid, though so much else in his life had changed.

He glanced up to find Mari watching him. "Ah, shit," he said, remembering. "I didn't use a rubber."

Her laugh got the whole crew's heads turning their way. He wriggled out from under the forklift and thrust the lizard into her hands.

"Keep him away from my lift," he grumbled. "Got work to do." But as he walked away, her shy, soft laugh warmed the back of his neck.

4

The Boss

At the Monday morning meeting, the bios all stood in a loose circle while Marcus eyed his clipboard and Mari brewed coffee and tried not to fidget.

Any crew but Wyatt's crew. Anybody but Jack.

After the tortoise, she had started to warm to him. After he caught the fringe-toed lizard for her, she figured they'd had something of an understanding. A cease-fire, at least. But on the sixth day of the week, she'd had to ask him to keep secondary containment under his forklift to catch leaks. And the volcano blew.

"I move my damn forklift three hundred times a day! How am I supposed to keep a container under it every time it's parked?"

"Well, it's important because you never know when a leak is going to occur, and out here, those toxic fluids sink fast into the sand, which poisons the watersheds that animals—"

"You think I take such shitty care of my forklift that it goes blowing hoses left and right?"

"No, of course not, but you can't predict—"

"You can *predict it! That's the whole fucking idea behind properly*

*maintaining your shit! Only assholes who can't predict leaks are the ones
who are too lazy to do things right!"*

By the end of that fight, Jack's face had turned a brash red, and
Mari had retreated into the desert, guilty and upset all at once so even
the silence couldn't soothe it away. The drip pan, however, had been
firmly placed under the forklift.

No matter how much she hated it, she couldn't hide from conflict
if it meant animals might be hurt. Jack didn't scare her, but even so, a
week of having to stand her ground in constant confrontations had left
her exhausted.

Marcus sighed. "Mari, is there any way you could put up with him
for another week? I hate to do it to you, but Jorge's the only one who
isn't spoken for and he's still on HR restraining order from Wyatt."

Lisa winced in her direction.

Hotaka shook his head. "I'll take him. There's no reason to feed our
nicest bio to the meanest foreman."

Mari blinked in shock, and then half laughed and shook her head.
"That's ridiculous. You're way nicer than I am!"

"I'm a complete dick and I never stop talking about plants," Hotaka
said. "You just like me because I made you a cutting board."

She sputtered a laugh, but wasn't sure what to say. They'd worked
together a lot on the last job, and even though the Japanese wood-
worker and botanist was half her age, he didn't seem to mind her.
Mostly because she would listen to him talk about plant speciation for
hours without interrupting, since she didn't want to upset him by mentioning it wasn't quite as interesting as he thought.

When he saw her chopping vegetables on a flattened cereal box,
he'd made her a beautiful hand-sanded cutting board, sized to fit perfectly in her box of cooking utensils. Though Mari still always put a
cereal box on top of it when she cut things so that she wouldn't mar its
surface.

"Sorry, Hotaka. I need you on the east end of the project, finishing the rare-cactus survey." Marcus fussed with his clipboard a little more. "Maybe . . . but no, then . . ."

Shit. But then, if she didn't take Wyatt, someone else would have to, and he'd made most of the female bios—and Jorge—cry.

Mari put on a placid smile. "Of course, Marcus. Don't worry, I can handle him."

That was not, as it turned out, strictly true.

On Monday, it was about his crew checking under their tires.

On Tuesday, they got into it because he was driving too fast. He claimed his eyes weren't so damn slow that he couldn't see a tortoise when it was right in front of his face, no matter how fast he was going.

On Wednesday, the drip pan under the forklift cracked, he refused to pause work to get a new one because his boss was "all up his ass to get this tower done," and she had to write him up for a secondary containment violation.

On Thursday, his crew read the plans wrong and put part of the tower together backward. And, of course, they hadn't yet gotten that fixed when Jack's boss showed up.

Mari hated the big boss on sight. He parked in the middle of the road and left his truck running for an hour and a half. He had shiny boots that kept scuffing Jack's already-scuffed ones when he got up into his space, forcing Jack to back away time and again. Calling him "son," repeatedly reminding Jack to call him "sir."

She overheard the words "lazy" and "slow" and "half-assed," and it made her cringe.

It was cruel, and it didn't even make any sense because the only other tower assembly crew on this section was still working on the same tower while Jack's crew had finished several. Lisa was the other crew's monitor, and she always joked that it took them until eleven thirty to get warmed up enough to pick up a wrench and then they needed a two-hour lunch to recover from the trauma of doing actual work. Mari didn't understand why they weren't getting this chastising from the big boss. Or at least she didn't until she got a close look at the boss's face.

He had a slab of a jaw and heavy brows, like an older version of the foreman in charge of the slower crew. Ah. Well, now she got why Junior was getting special dispensation and Jack was being lectured despite picking up Junior's slack and then some. They'd been getting the tallest tower assignments, the ones that started in low-dipped washes and had to be built higher and with more-complicated shapes so they could get up high enough to draw even with the towers built on high spots. They still built three of those for every one of the other crew's shorter ones. And yet this jerk seemed determined to make Jack apologize for it.

The next time the word "lazy" drifted over to her, Mari had had it. Her mother had always warned her that if she didn't learn when to hold her tongue, it'd cause her a world of trouble. Mom sure hadn't been wrong, but right now, Mari didn't care.

She marched right up onto the pad, the crew stopping to stare because she was always so careful to stay out of their way. She went up to the boss and inserted herself into the conversation, even though he didn't even turn to acknowledge her when she approached. His shirt buttons nearly brushed her breasts before he finally, grudgingly, gave way and stepped back—from both her and Jack.

"Can I help you?"

"Your truck is parked in the road, and if it's going to be stored onsite, it needs to have secondary containment underneath to catch any engine leaks," she said crisply.

"Uh, sorry about that, little lady," he said, sounding anything but. "I don't happen to have a pan with me to put under the truck. Wasn't expecting this crew to need so much supervision."

She wasn't looking at Jack, but she could feel his chagrin at this latest passive-aggressive swipe. It was probably taking a lot for the normally explosive man to keep from defending himself. She'd already heard the supervisor suggest to Jack that he use a particular method that Jack had discarded last Monday as being too slow.

"In that case," she told his boss, "I'm afraid you're going to have to go. We don't have extra containment pans on-site."

Jack shifted beside her, and she hoped he wouldn't blow her cover. He knew all too well she had three shiny new pans in her truck, because she'd shown them to him this morning. She brought them from the yard after the forklift argument, explaining that now they wouldn't have to lose work time to get a new pan if one of theirs broke, because she'd keep extras on hand for them.

"Listen, darlin', if you could just look the other way just this once, that'd be real nice. I need to stay and talk to my crew a little more."

She didn't smile. "I'm sorry. State and federal regulations don't have leeway for that. You're welcome to come back after you get a pan from the construction yard."

"Well, somebody's got a stick up their lady parts," he muttered, and Jack took a sharp step forward. The boss's eyes widened and Jack reluctantly backed off, his jaw clenching. Something in her stomach curdled at him being forced to back down, like she'd seen something private and too vulnerable.

Mari turned and walked away, not dignifying the boss's comment with a response. Men like him wanted you to laugh off their poor behavior, and she'd be damned if she would. Behind her back, she heard the supervisor growling something to Jack that sounded like "keep your bio bitch on a leash."

She walked out toward the road, stooping to check under his tires for animals. Which turned out to be a good thing because the boss didn't check at all when he jumped in and screeched away a second later, leaving them all to choke on his dust.

She tucked her hands in her pockets and forced herself to keep casually strolling along, even though she wanted to crawl into her truck

and gobble the last of her brownies just to wash the taste of that en-
counter out of her mouth. Why didn't she call him on that "lady parts"
comment? She ought to report him to HR. Darlin' indeed. What a
jerk. Telling Jack to "control" her like she was his property instead of
an educated professional.

Jack barked something to his crew and stalked back to his truck.
She watched out of the corner of her eye as he pulled his dusty lunch-
box cooler out of the back seat. Good. He'd worked through lunch
again, and he was even grouchier when he was hungry. She pulled her
shoulders back, taking a deep breath. Somehow, she'd slouched right
into her old posture from when she was married, her back already aching with the unfamiliar curl of it.

But she'd stood up to that man. She hadn't just folded up and let
him abuse Jack when he'd done nothing wrong. She had no reason for
the shame that clung dark and sticky in her belly. No reason to feel like
that supervisor had touched her in a place where she couldn't push his
hand away.

That guy put her on edge in a way that none of her clashes with Jack
ever had.

Jack ripped his sandwich out of its bag with such force that the
meat flew out of the center and landed on the ground, the mayonnaise
immediately going black with dirt. "*Fuck!*" he hissed, looking at the
bread in his hand, then into the cooler, which seemed empty from her
angle. He balled his fist, crushing the bread into a doughy ball, and
dropped it on the floorboard of the truck, chucking the cooler back in
after it.

Mari ducked her head. Did he feel the same shame after the en-
counter as she did? Probably worse, since it was his work the man had
criticized. His livelihood.

Jack yanked the tower blueprints out of his truck and laid them on
the tailgate, dropping a hammer on one end and a chunk of discarded
metal on the other to hold them down in the wind. Then he went still

and glared at the paper, no doubt trying to decode the fastest way to transform his crew's backward-tower fuckup without having to take every last screw out and start from scratch.

A faint growl traveled her way on the wind, and she wondered if it came from his stomach or his mouth.

Mari turned and slipped away, retreating to her Toyota. Even two long years after her divorce, she still wasn't the best at making friends. But she did have one trick that never failed to soothe people.

Jack slapped a hand down on the tower plans. That piece. They could leave that whole section intact if they just took off the struts to the east and north and rotated the shape 240 degrees, then reattached—

His thought broke off half-formed when a small shoulder nudged his arm. He flinched away, a curse rising to his lips before he recognized the faint vanilla scent of Mari. She was the only thing in a world of sweat and sand that smelled good. Or maybe that was just the brownie she was holding out to him. She tried a smile, but it looked a little weak today.

"What an asshole, right?"

He choked, coughed, then laughed. "Yeah. Yup, he really is." He stopped laughing. "Sorry about what he said." He nodded to her to indicate which comment, not wanting to repeat the man's filthy remark.

She shrugged. "I've heard worse. Brownie?" She offered it again.

He took it hesitantly, not sure why she was being nice to him.

She nodded at the plans. "You know, I'm not totally clear on what you're doing here, but this piece"—she pointed at the section in the middle that he was going to leave intact—"looks like that piece up there." She pointed up at the partially finished tower. "Maybe you could leave that piece and just take off the stuff around it, and still use that part?"

He slanted her a sideways look, trying not to look impressed. All lattice towers looked the same to greenhorns, but there were actually thousands of permutations of metal bars to match the towers to the contours of different landscapes. It had taken him years of reading the land and the towers to figure out how to fit them to each other without just following the plans blindly.

He grunted. "Yeah. Maybe we might do something like that."

She passed him another brownie. He popped it into his mouth and chewed. No idea where she bought these things but he ought to track it down, because they tasted homemade. Which just made him feel worse about what had just happened.

"You shouldn't have done that." He jerked his chin toward the road. "Threatened to write him up like that. Rod holds a grudge. He'll take it out on you any way he can." His lips twitched. "Was ballsy, though. Damn. Lying about those pans."

She made a small, disgusted noise, her pert nose crinkling. "Fuck him."

Jack damn near grinned.

"Huh" was all he could manage, looking at her with new respect. Some part of him really wanted to watch her chew out Rod. The rest of him was worried his fist would find his boss's mouth fast enough to get himself fired if Rod talked to Mari like that again.

She tossed him a protein bar, and he barely managed to catch it before she strolled away. "Better get started. Looking like it might be a late shift for us tonight."

A moment ago, he hated his job and everything about it. And now, he didn't want to admit it, but he was almost looking forward to working overtime.

5

The Cottage

The horned lizard tickled Mari's palm as she carried him away from the construction site. Jack's men were making good time disassembling the backward tower, and his grouching had eased considerably after he'd eaten the protein bar she gave him. She made a mental note to add snacks to her biologist's tool kit. Whatever she could do to make the crews more cooperative, it only benefited the animals.

"Find your way home, little guy," she whispered to the horned lizard as she stooped to let him scurry off her hand. It was a baby, no bigger than a quarter, and it stopped to cock its little head at her when her phone rang. "It's not for you," she informed the lizard, a hint of a smile curving her mouth. She was riding high after chasing off Jack's terrible boss.

She straightened and checked on her workers before she answered the phone. It was Lisa, from the other tower assembly crew.

"How did you not tell me you got the biologist-in-residence job?" she half shrieked.

Mari flinched, pulling the phone a little away from her ear. "Hold on, it's loud here." She walked a little farther from the workers so that the blast of impact wrenches and beeping of the forklift wouldn't interfere. There was no background noise coming from Lisa's end, though.

"Is your crew at lunch?" she asked, checking her watch. Two o'clock, far too late for lunch. "Or is it just mine who can't do a thing without making enough noise to wake the Yellowstone supervolcano?"

Lisa snorted. "On Junior's crew? They started lunch at ten forty-five and haven't managed to put in a single bolt since. Though he did lose about two hundred bucks on some kind of tailgate dice game. And don't think I didn't notice you changing the subject."

Mari kicked at the dirt. "It's not final yet, so I can't say I *got* it."

"Bullshit. Hotaka interviewed for the botanist-in-residence job, and he said the national park staff mentioned your name and said they'd offered it to you, so there's no need to be modest. Don't worry, I'm not jealous at all. Even though it pays better. And goes year-round. And comes with free freaking housing."

Mari almost smiled, even though her stomach still squirmed. "If you're so not jealous, why don't you apply yourself? The program doesn't officially roll out for three months, so they don't have to make a final decision until then."

"Well, they weren't exactly looking for *two* biologists in residence, and I'm not sure Marcus would appreciate me dumping him for a job. Even one that comes with an adorable little cottage. Did you see the houses when you were there? Hotaka showed me pictures on his phone. I guess it was some kind of postwar religious commune that was donated to the park system, and they remodeled them for the interpretive team."

"They might have mentioned something about it." Mari stopped to pick up a scrap of trash so it wouldn't attract the ravens that preyed on the hatchling tortoises.

"So?" Lisa practically squeaked. "You're single. You need the money—I'm sorry, I know I'm not supposed to know about that, but come on, Mari. This power line will wrap up before June, and I haven't heard of any work coming up after that. No work means no rent money, which means no AC. It's gonna be a long, hot summer in the truck. Again."

Her fingers tightened on the phone. Lisa had come by one time when Mari had papers all spread out on her tailgate under rocks, trying to reconcile her health insurance statements with the amounts on the medical bills. In the moments before Mari had managed to snatch up all the papers from their makeshift paperweights, Lisa had gotten an eyeful of all the injuries Mari was paying off. Which meant she knew more about Mari's past than Mari ever would have shared, and she didn't exactly appreciate Lisa's bringing it up now.

Her voice was a little sharp when she said, "Well, maybe I didn't think Marcus would like me taking it, either. This job came up at the same time, and he said he was really short-handed. He was so sweet, taking me hunting last year, and I didn't want to let him down."

"You mean *you* were so sweet, going hunting with him when everybody else bailed, even though you don't even hunt. Marcus would have understood if you turned this gig down for permanent work."

She fought the urge to make an excuse and hang up on the other woman's prying. Lisa had her faults but she'd been friendlier than any of the rest of the bios, and Mari didn't take that lightly. Her friends had never stuck. Not the ones from high school, and not the ones from her old job in an insurance office, who used to avoid her with such discomfort every time she turned up with long sleeves in the middle of the summer.

After her car accident, when Brad wanted her to stay home and let him take care of her, she'd been happy not to go back to their stares and awkward silences. By the time she reinvented her career as a biologist, she'd been too worn out to try again, and Lisa was the only one who continually tried to drag her off the sidelines.

Mari took a breath and tried to explain, without getting too personal. "Turned out in the interview they're not just hiring a bio. It's a full interpretive team: botanist, artist, writer, and historian in residence, all living side by side. 'Interpretive team' meaning they expect me to give speeches and interact with tourists, which would mean I would have to be good with people."

"You're great with people, when you're not avoiding them."

"Oh yeah?" Mari turned back to sweep the construction site with her gaze, ignoring the workers in favor of searching for the telltale coil of a snake or the bump of a tortoise. "Who was it who had to write their crew up yesterday because she couldn't get them to follow one of the simplest rules? And who took a week to get the crew to accept the training we're supposed to carry out on the first day? Because as they say, I had *one* job . . ."

"Wyatt doesn't count. I've met badgers with sweeter personalities. We've all had *months* to work on him, and he's never let us give the environmental awareness training before. Seriously, though, Mari, the park asked Hotaka to put in a good word with you. I think they really want you to say yes."

"Seriously, though, Lisa," she echoed, trying to keep the annoyance out of her voice. Lisa may have been the friendliest of the bios, but she was also the nosiest. "I didn't specialize in the most remote species in the lower forty-eight because I wanted to settle down and have neighbors."

What she did want was that sunshine-yellow cottage, with vanilla-creamy trim, and a little porch with its own rocking chair. A table just big enough for a paperback and a sweating glass of iced tea.

Even though she'd told them she probably couldn't take the job, her interviewer had insisted on showing her inside. The kitchen was perfect, with counters so much wider than the tailgate she was used to cooking on, and walls so she could make pumpkin pancakes without dust blowing into the batter, or could even bake a cake. The whole thing would be perfect, if it had stood alone instead of arced along a circular driveway with four other cottages.

It wasn't just a house, it was a home, and as soon as she had seen that, she'd turned it down.

When she'd left Brad, she promised herself everything would be different, that she could have a whole new life. Freedom, space, quiet. But not a marriage, or a home. There was peace in knowing and accepting your own limitations, and those were hers. The wind and the open land were where she'd found her place, and fantasies of soft throw blankets and cozy rocking chairs were just that: fantasies.

"Are you sure you wouldn't like to settle down?" Lisa asked softly. "I mean, all of us dirtbags have lived in our trucks for years, but you were the first to sew curtains for the windows of your camper shell instead of taping up newspaper to keep out the sun. You were the first to put a little mat under your tailgate so you wouldn't track in dirt. You were the first to hang Christmas lights so you'd have more light inside than just a headlamp."

"Just because I fixed up my truck a little doesn't mean I want to sign up for a whole house." Or a permanent, traceable address.

Lisa was quiet for a beat longer. "Okay."

Mari found herself scowling and tried to smooth her face.

"Well, anyway, a bunch of us are going to the Barn for beers after work tonight, if you want to come."

"No, thanks," she said automatically. She liked beer, though Brad always teased her that she looked masculine when she drank beer. He thought it was more attractive when women drank wine from delicate little glasses. But it was too easy to screw up in a group, especially if they'd all been drinking, and she didn't want to be the pity invite.

She heard the sigh Lisa tried to stifle. "I'll wear you down one of these days. Anyway, good luck with Wyatt. Only a few more days left on your sentence and I bet you can get Marcus to let you skip your next turn, since you held out for two rotations."

They hung up, and Mari just stood there, holding on to her phone. She felt off-balance, and she checked her safety vest and hard hat, scanned the site for any animals she might have missed during her call. But still the feeling persisted. She'd been trying so hard not to think about that damn cottage. It had teased tears at the corners of her eyes to leave it, even during the interview. But she couldn't risk Brad finding her, and she didn't want to live with other people ever again. Not even in separate cottages, because they'd all have to work together as part of the park interpretive team, and she couldn't stand seeing the looks on their faces when she disappointed them but they were still stuck with her. She'd seen it too many times.

But there was a pain in the center of her chest, sharp like a stab, when she thought about it.

Jack looked up from the tower plans on his tailgate, and caught her staring at the site. She blinked and started to look away, but before she could, he gave her a little nod.

She nearly dropped her phone. Jack Wyatt had *nodded*. At a *biologist*.

It was hardly the Nobel Peace Prize, but as far as she knew, he'd never said a single word to one of the bios that hadn't come out as a shout or in four filthy letters. And she'd lasted more than a single week.

Her toes curled inside her shoes, holding on hard to the warmth of the desert sand beneath her. She felt a little dizzy, or maybe sick. Or hungry.

What if she *could* take that other job?

Move into that cottage and sew new curtains, close the front door and have a quiet place all to herself, where she didn't have to worry about her habits annoying anyone else. Be part of a team. She really loved the national park that was hiring. They had the habitat for all her favorite animals, and the most beautiful cactus.

If she could get Jack Wyatt to let her train his men, and earn a nod from him, was it so crazy to think she could get along with live-in co-workers?

Her heart raced, even though she was only standing still with the sun pouring heat down on her suddenly heaving shoulders. Here was the perfect place to practice. None of her coworkers on the interpretive team would be as hard to please as Wyatt, and if she stumbled like she always used to, no one would even notice if she ticked him off. The man existed in a perpetual state of ticked off.

She could even, maybe, try a little with her fellow biologists. It was a small group, the only odd ducks who were rootless enough and tough enough to live in the desert year-round, with only the fragile protection of a hat brim from the sun that ruled brutally over everything. They all had their secrets and reasons why they drifted from one temporary assignment to another. It was why, she'd always suspected, they gave her space.

Rajni never talked about why she left the marines, and there was a rumor she'd lived in a cave in Italy once, for four straight months. Jorge slept on the ground in every kind of weather, because the back of his truck was stuffed full of bike parts and different copies of Shakespeare plays, even though she'd never seen him bike, or read. Hotaka refused to speak of anything but plants, and he whittled. Ferociously. All the time.

They certainly weren't ordinary, well-adjusted citizens, and maybe they could be the training wheels she needed. After all, if she fell flat on her face, the job would end in a few months. She'd see most of the same people again on the next job, but she could get certified for different species and try to get work outside the desert if she had to.

That yellow cottage burned in her memory. Yellow had always been her favorite color. How could the park employees have known that?

Mari flipped her phone over and texted Lisa before she could lose her nerve.

Too busy to make the Barn tonight, but maybe we could do coffee sometime?

As soon as she sent it, she felt ridiculous. The other woman was so nice, she'd probably feel obligated to say yes even if she didn't want to. What would they even talk about? How many lizards they'd seen that day? Thirteen side-blotches, eight whiptails, and a double handful of zebra-tails.

Thrilling.

Her phone dinged and the message flashed before she could even decide if she had the courage to look.

Absolutely! Just tell me when.

6

Animals

Jack's crew had been pulling overtime shifts for two days, trying to catch up after the tower-put-together-backward disaster. Which of course meant Mari was pulling overtime, too, walking endless laps around the construction pad to make sure animals wouldn't get in the way of their work.

Today, they were doing crane work, which was terrifying to watch, even though they'd done it a million times and it was probably no more scary to them than changing lanes. They would put together a section of tower, all the metal lattice pieces bolted together, then the crane would lift that piece and set it atop the existing tower they'd already built.

The catch was that four living, breathing men had to perch atop the tower to guide the corners into place.

If Ricky, the crane operator, slipped or even moved too fast, the new section started to swing. That could impale a man, or knock him off the beam. They had safety straps to tie them in, but she could see that those would catch them at just the right height for them to swing face-first into the metal struts below them.

Four men climbed the four corners of the structure at the same time: Jack, Toby, Kipp, and Gideon. Joey the apprentice had begged to be allowed to help, and Jack had turned him down so loudly she was pretty sure the next crew a mile down the road had heard. For all the truly filthy names he called that apprentice, Jack watched out for him very carefully. But then, that seemed to be his way—he always scowled the darkest when he was being kind, like he was afraid someone would catch him at it.

Hand over foot, the four of them swarmed up the tower so fast it looked like they were on an escalator. All they had to climb were fat metal bolts sticking out on both sides of the supports, and when they got higher than twenty feet, Mari had to close her eyes to keep her stomach from churning. They couldn't clip their safeties in until they stopped climbing, and she didn't want to see any of them slip.

When Jack's gruff shout rang out, she opened her eyes again. She should do a sweep for tortoises, but instead her gaze glued itself to the sky, where Jack straddled a thin metal strut as comfortably as if it were a La-Z-Boy recliner. The crane swung the metal lattice of the new section over the top of them and started to lower it toward the waiting men. It was swaying so much in the breeze that the operator, Ricky, had to reel it in and try again on the approach.

"Damn it, Jack," she muttered under her breath. The guys had argued about whether there was too much wind today to use the crane. It was two miles per hour below the safety cutoff . . . until it gusted. And it was the desert, so it gusted whenever it pleased.

But Jack thought they needed to push it to finish at this site today, so here they were, four tiny men on top of a tower, trying to catch the swinging metal thing that outweighed them by several thousand pounds. On the third try, Jack got impatient and stood up, balancing on a piece of metal narrower than an Olympic balance beam. And then he leaned out to grab the swinging piece.

Mari sucked in a breath, her hands flying to her mouth, but Jack caught the metal beam and locked on. His body stretched taut as he muscled the tower piece into place, the other men catching their corners now that he'd steadied the whole. It seemed impossible that they could fit something so huge into such an exact spot that the bolt holes would line up, but a moment later, it was done. The compressor blared as they slammed bolts home, and Mari shoved her gaze back to the ground, trying to remember how to breathe.

When they climbed back down, tossing taunts and insults jovially back and forth, she stepped forward to meet them.

Jack stopped, the slant of his eyebrows puzzled. "We fuck something up?" He glanced around. "Dunno what we could have hurt from up there."

"No, no. That was incredible!"

His brow furrowed, like he thought she might be making a joke at his expense, so she cleared her throat and reeled in her tone a touch.

"Good work, I mean."

She'd been determined to try to speak to the crew a little more, not just hide out with the lizards and the creosote, and yet Jack seemed more thrown off by her attempt than she was.

"Uh, right." He glanced away toward his men, uncertain. She supposed compliments from the bio weren't exactly part of their normal routine. "Ricky's one of the best crane operators around. Asshole, but good at his job." He paused. "Guess I'll, um, get back to it then."

"That's not all," she hastened to add, scraping up her courage. "I just wondered . . . you guys want to see something?"

Mari seemed excited, and his guys really had kicked ass today, so Jack went along with it, letting her lead his whole crew like the Pied Piper away from the construction pad. Leaving their tools behind and crunching over rocks, dodging cactus. Her loose swirl of a bun peeked out from under the back of her hard hat, exposing her long, slender neck. His gaze kept being drawn to it like it was a gap between her buttons, something he wasn't supposed to see. And he kept reminding himself it was just a neck. Nothing sexual about that.

He cleared his throat and refocused his eyes on the sandy gravel under his boots. She stopped next to a hole in the ground and dropped to her knees, and he blinked with renewed interest. Was this one of those holes the turtles lived in? He bumped Toby out of the way, trying to see better. Was one in there right now? He wondered what had happened to the little cheeseburger-sized one he'd moved.

Mari bent forward, her head low to the ground and her bottom in the air as she flicked on a flashlight and peered down the burrow. Her jeans stretched taut across her hips and he was hit with a bolt of hard, fierce lust. It was basically a sex position, so he couldn't help but imagine her bent forward like that for him, his hands clenching the pretty curve of her waist . . .

He choked and looked away, shifting his weight around before he remembered the burrow and looked to see what her flashlight revealed. There was an animal inside, and it was . . . fuzzy?

"You see them?" She looked back with a smile so bright he got distracted all over again. "Kit foxes. They're about the size of a house cat, but with great big ears so they hear everything. You won't often spot them out during the day, so it's really cool to find them in a den like this. Can you see?"

She shielded the beam of her flashlight with her fingers so it wouldn't blind them, but Jack could still make out the eye shine of three creatures, their sharp, furry faces poked inquisitively out toward the entrance. They did look like big-eared cats. Little buggers were kinda cute, actually.

"Why don't you look deeper, sweetheart?" Ricky said. "Think I see something way back there."

"What?" Mari unshielded the flashlight, craning her cheek closer to the ground. He could see the moment she got what Ricky was really saying, because her shoulders went stiff and she sat back on her heels, suddenly awkward.

Jack slapped a hand against Ricky's chest, cuffing him toward the worksite. "Why don't you shut the fuck up and go back to work?"

Ricky smacked his hand away. "What? We were just looking. Weren't we, boys? At the fox."

Itchy heat flushed up Jack's neck. Those fox kitten things were cute, but they didn't hold a candle to the allure of Mari all bent over like that. And he hated like hell that he'd been gawking at her just like this idiot.

Jack glowered, but when Ricky didn't retreat, he gritted his teeth. Stupid cocky crane operators. But hell, if he wanted to play it like that, Jack was game. He stepped up into his face, the other man two inches taller but Jack moving with the absolute confidence that he could punch harder.

"Think you can wave your big paycheck around and stop taking orders? You're working on my crew, and if you wanna be here, that's what you do. *Work*."

Jack saw the retreat in the crane operator's face a second before he stepped away. But Ricky tossed out a parting shot, his eyes flashing with the humiliation of being forced to back down in front of an audience. "Better watch your mouth, Wyatt. Might be one day my hand slips."

Jack scoffed but the other men on the crew looked pissed. It wasn't the kind of thing you said on a job site. Fucking ever. But he'd deal with that later.

He didn't look at Mari as he herded his guys back to work. He didn't want to see how she'd shrunk into herself at his stupid crew mouthing off like he couldn't control them. He didn't want to see the disgust written in every line of her body because that was her real, undisguised reaction to guys like them wanting a woman like her.

He might have been the one smacking Ricky for opening his mouth, but he was no better than him, and he knew it. He just wished Mari didn't know it, too.

7

Good Samaritan

At the end of the day, Jack normally headed back to the construction yard with his crew, swapped his work truck for his motorcycle or personal truck, and went back to the motel from there. But tonight, something about the tower plans kept bugging him. He couldn't think with all those guys jawing around him.

So he stayed late, plans all spread out on the tailgate and weighted against the wind, and went over them until he was absolutely sure they were drawn wrong. Then twice more, because he really didn't want to fight this. He'd have to put any changes through Rod, who'd have to battle with corporate to get a revision from the engineering department on the word of Jack, who didn't have an engineering degree. Hell, he barely had a high school diploma.

They were going to make it out like he was the one who was wrong, but numbers were numbers. Maybe in a court of law you could make it sound like two plus two equals seven, but when you had a bunch of tower pieces, those bolt holes just weren't ever gonna line up.

He rolled up the plans and chucked them back into the truck. Better get home in time for an extra beer tonight. When he had to call

Rod in the morning, he was going to wish he had had one more, whether it ever made it from his mouth to his stomach or not.

He glanced under his tires as he rounded the truck, thanking the God of Bad Knees that his work vehicle was jacked up high enough that he didn't have to bend down to see underneath it. He kicked some dirt at a lizard to get it to run off. Didn't know if it was a fancy lizard or a plain one, but better safe than sorry. He didn't want to see Mari's face fall if she found its little squished body on the job site in her morning rounds.

He'd seen her find the corpse of a mouse that got hit by one of the water trucks that kept the dust down on the roads. Didn't say a word, just took her shovel and buried it out in the desert, like it deserved a burial, mouse or not.

He guessed that, to Mari, it probably did. She was the kind of woman who had enough in her to care about even mice.

The work truck coughed and sputtered, then roared to life when he gave it some gas. He pulled out, wondering what it said about him that he wouldn't have buried a damn mouse. Maybe kicked some dirt over it, if it was fresh. Maybe not. He hated mice.

On his way out, he spotted another truck pulled off the side of the road. He squinted against the setting sun. Everybody should have been off the dirt access road by this time of night.

It was a truck the color of dust and old metal, scarred down both sides with scratches. He knew that truck. Every day, he watched a graceful, light-footed woman retreat to it for food and water and the refuge of shade, like it was some kind of surrogate mother. A desert oasis formed of steel and gasoline.

Jack pulled over behind her. Probably she was just stopped to text, or whatever young people did on phones these days. Mari's hair had more threads of silver than his, but her face looked younger. He had no idea how old she was, and he may not have known much about women, but he knew enough not to ask that. Still, thirty-five or forty-five, she was likely more interested in technology than he was, because who wasn't? But just in case she had broken down and wasn't just on her phone, he might be of a little use. Besides, it'd bug him all night if he didn't check on her before he drove on by.

His crew had gone home, but there were probably worse men than Ricky roaming this open desert. He wouldn't leave any woman there alone, much less his biologist.

His door popped open with a creak and he frowned at his own thought—*his* biologist? It was ridiculous to think of her that way just because she lasted two weeks without crying or disappearing midday to be replaced by her judgy little bearded boss. That guy always came to fill in when Jack chased off another biologist, and he hated him. Seemed like the type who knew the "right" way to do everything and couldn't wait to tell you all about it.

Fortunately, he was distracted from that uncomfortable internal debate by the jack under the truck and the array of tools spread out around Mari in the dirt.

"Got a flat?"

"Two flats." Mari huffed a sigh and sat back on the ground, draping her black-streaked hands over the knees of her jeans. She was wearing a cute little admiral's cap instead of her normal hard hat, and Jack caught himself staring and pulled his gaze back to the tires lying next to her.

"Spare gone bad?" he grunted. It happened a lot in the desert, where the dry air gnawed away at rubber things until they cracked and died like just another kind of corpse.

"Yup." She popped the *p*. "Should have checked on it before I needed it, but it's too late now. And at six days a week of ten's, we're at work every hour the tire stores are open for business." She glanced up at him. "My cell doesn't work out here, so I was getting ready to hike it to the highway."

He frowned. "You don't want to thumb a ride out here. Mostly crackheads and desert rats."

"Well, I probably should have thought of that around the time I was forgetting to check my spare." She slapped her hands down on her pants and shoved to her feet.

He scowled. "Get in. I'll give you a ride to town."

She looked faintly surprised, and he scowled harder. Probably she'd rather not be alone in a truck with an asshole like him, and he couldn't half blame her, but he also couldn't leave a beautiful woman stranded like a target for whatever perverts and deviants were passing through.

Strangely, his scowl brought a tiny smile to rise on her face. "Um, okay. If you're sure you don't mind. Here, I'll be quick." She hurried to put away her tools in the bed of the truck. She had a slick little setup in there: a bed stand built of two-by-fours with a big drawer underneath, a mattress tucked in with flower-print sheets on top, and matching curtains hung with a string over the long windows. Next to it lay a lineup of dusty water jugs and a milk crate full of cracker boxes and granola bars.

Jack frowned harder. "You living in this thing?"

"I wish." She closed the camper shell and locked it. "Normally I do, but there's too much privately owned land around this project. Nowhere to camp, so I had to pay for a motel in town."

"Never heard a woman complain that she'd rather live in the dirt than stay in a motel."

"Probably never heard a man say it, either." She grabbed a small backpack from the front seat. "But come on. A motel can't match this for square footage."

She swept out an arm at the whole Mojave. Tinged with sunset-pink light, it spread out for miles. The mountains in the distance reminded him of Mari's face. Unadorned by anything, the pure lines of them were more beautiful than anything else he could remember seeing in his life.

He nodded, not quite able to remember what he was agreeing to, but agreeing all the same. "You need me to help grab your stuff?"

She waggled the backpack at him. "Got it. I travel light." He lifted both her flats into the back of the truck while she knelt to check under his truck for tortoises. He frowned, because it felt like he was making her work when she should have been off the clock, but he supposed turtles didn't ever clock out.

"You don't have to take me all the way to town if it's out of your way," she offered. "If you just get me into cell service, maybe I could—"

"No."

She glanced over at him when he cut her off, and he chewed on the inside of his lip. Probably his own fault she thought he was such an asshole he couldn't even be bothered to drive her all the way to some-place safe.

"It's fine," he grunted, not quite sure how to apologize, and she nodded and shrugged.

She didn't force him to make small talk as they drove toward town, but the cab of the big truck felt more intimate than it ever had. He was uncomfortable enough that he didn't stop at the yard to swap out this work truck for his personal one. It ran better but had a long strip of duct tape holding the seat together—courtesy of last year's hunting season when he'd thrown his compound bow carelessly into the truck and one of the broadheads had slit the upholstery.

Inside the truck, the radio didn't fill the silence but somehow just managed to underline it. Every song that came on felt too loud and too awkward, as if by being on in his truck, it was saying something about him. What kind of music did treeless tree huggers listen to? Probably drums or chanting or some shit.

Mari only piped up to give him periodic directions. *Turn here, don't go down this road there, it's got road construction.*

When they pulled up at her place, he frowned at the motel's pot-holed parking lot and broken sign.

"This where you're living?"

"Aren't you staying in a motel, too?" She dug her key out of her backpack.

"Yeah."

"Oh, which one?"

"Best Western," he said grudgingly, feeling like he was one of those rich blowhards, bragging about their stuff. "Company pays for our housing. Guess yours doesn't?"

He eyed the tape holding a cracked windowpane together. The two-story motel had beige paint that was peeling in the heat. The metal railing on the upstairs story was bent outward in one spot, like somebody had been thrown against it in a fight. A fast-food cup rolled slowly through the parking lot, shoved by the gusts of wind huffing in from the open desert.

"Best Western, huh?" She gave a slow whistle and a teasing grin. "Does it come with all the free six-shooter movies you can watch? Is that what makes it the best?"

"It's got all its windows," he said bluntly. "That makes it best enough in my book." He shoved the back of his hand across his nose and nodded at her motel. "It even safe here?"

"It's better on the inside, has fridges and microwaves and everything. And it was safe enough until Creepy Ricky moved in." She rolled her eyes and laughed, but it must not have been a joke, because his gaze lit on Ricky's Chevy pickup in the corner of the parking lot. Bright red and a brand-new tint job on the windows, truck balls swinging from the chrome trailer hitch. "Funny he's staying in this dump if your company pays for a Best Western."

"Yeah. Funny." Jack was frowning so hard he thought his face might kink. The doors on this place looked flimsy, and he didn't see any other cars in the parking lot. What if it was just Mari and Ricky in here? All night, every night? It wasn't his business, but he couldn't help asking. "He give you any trouble?"

"No. Not . . . really." She smiled, but there was an odd line to it. "Nothing I can't handle."

The steering wheel creaked under Jack's tightening grip. He needed to get a decent crane operator in so he could fire that asshole. There had to be a non-asshole crane operator somewhere in the union without a job. Well, maybe.

"Thanks again for the ride," she said, pulling open the handle.

"What are you gonna do about tomorrow? You coming to work?" It put a little drop in his stomach to ask, like everything was about to change. But she was just a bio, and there were others. Probably that bearded hippie would show up. With his clipboard.

Jack hated the clipboard.

"Sure I am. Now that I have cell service, I'm sure I can call and get a ride into the site tomorrow with one of the other bios." A shadow crossed her face, and he wondered if she hated to ask for help as much as he would have. "No idea when I'll get a tire, though. Guess I'll have to take a day off work to get to the shop when they're still open." She winced a little at the thought. "Wonder if Marcus would give me a half day?"

She couldn't afford it. He knew she couldn't. It wasn't just the scratched truck with its sun-rotted tires, or this dump with its garbage-strewn parking lot. It was her face, the way she didn't *say* she couldn't afford it. Only people who had money complained about how they didn't.

Everybody else kept their mouths shut so their pride didn't fall out.

He nodded. "Give me a call if you ain't going to make it."

She gave him a funny look. "You don't have to stress—Marcus will make sure your crew is covered so you can work. And I don't have your number, anyway." She hesitated, her fingers curling around the edge of his door.

He didn't want to leave her here. Not in this place. Not with Ricky.

Before he could decide if he should give her his number, or really any good excuse for why he'd do that, she smiled and said, "Don't worry, I'm sure the other bios will help me out."

Of course they would. Most of them were scruffy twentysomething hippies who would probably give their last chia seed to get their hands on a woman like her. But who knew if any of them could even change a tire without checking YouTube?

Mari closed his truck door—quietly, like somebody who took care of their stuff—and it was too late to say anything, even if he'd known what to say. He watched her walk up to the motel, and wondered if she wanted him to drive away. She probably didn't want a guy like him knowing what room she was in. But he was also totally fucking incapable of leaving her before she had at least a locked flimsy door between herself and this seedy parking lot.

He didn't put it in reverse until she unlocked her room and gave him a half-awkward, half-cheery wave before shutting the door behind herself.

He hoped she'd turned the dead bolt.

He wished he'd given her his number.

The banging sound interrupted the night in a way she hadn't heard in years. Mari jerked awake, bracing against pain. *Brad.* It must be Brad. Awake, angry, breaking something. What had she done? What had she forgotten to do?

When the sound came again, she recognized it. Knuckles against a door: a knock. Her fingers sagged in the tangled sheets. She didn't have to escape all over again; she was already gone. But there really was someone at the door.

She groped on the nightstand for her phone but there were no messages on the screen to hint at what emergency might send somebody to her motel in the middle of the night. She didn't have any family left. She didn't know anybody except bios, and tortoises weren't nocturnal, so that couldn't be the emergency.

She dragged herself out of bed and staggered across the room.

Maybe it was just somebody looking for their drug dealer. It had happened in this motel before.

Mari pulled open the door the three inches allowed by the chain, even though the fixture was only held on by a single crooked screw and a layer of sloppy paint. She blinked, wondering if it was the flickering light bulb outside or her sanity that was failing her.

"Jack?"

He jerked an irritated nod, his work boots mumbling against the gritty concrete when he shifted his weight from one foot to the other.

"What are you doing here?" She wasn't awake enough to be more tactful than that. Throwing a glance at the alarm clock beside her bed, the numbers 4:12 gaped back at her, as if even they were incredulous at this turn of events.

Belatedly, Mari thought to tug down the hem of her oversized T-shirt. She really hoped she hadn't just flashed her panties.

"Got you a tire," Jack said. "Figured we'd better put it on before work, so you'd have your truck today." He paused. "So you could get stuff out of it. Drive places. You know. Don't want you stranded." His face twitched and he looked away, like he was already regretting the last statement.

"You . . . got me a tire?" Her brain cranked over as slowly as a cold engine. "And you're going to drive me out there to put it on? Right now?"

"Not thinking you could walk," he snapped. "It's forty-odd miles."

"Right. Give me a minute to get dressed." She closed the door, throwing another wide-eyed look at the clock. Four fourteen.

She hit the button on her tiny coffeemaker, already primed the night before, and threw on a pair of cargo pants and a thrift-store cotton button-down to protect her from the sun. She snatched up her backpack and poured the coffee before it was all the way done brewing, the stray drips hissing as they fell on the burner.

She yanked open the door and it hit the end of the security chain, probably jarring its single screw even further loose. Closing the door with a blush and wince—Brad hated it when she did thoughtless stuff like that—she unhooked the chain and tried again.

"Sorry, I'm ready."

Jack turned around from the spot he'd taken up next to her door, frowning. It seemed to be the only expression his face could form, in varying degrees. Frown, scowl, glower, and *oh my Christ how dumb are you?*

"Why are you apologizing? I didn't tell you I was coming, so how the hell could you know to be ready?"

She hesitated for a second, her now-practiced Jack brain sorting out his tone from his words and registering that he was embarrassed to have roused her and a little defensive about being there at all. So instead of getting offended, she just changed the subject.

"Want some coffee?" She held up her cup. "I've got enough for two, assuming we're both child-sized and got a solid eight hours of sleep."

"Which we ain't."

"And we didn't," she finished for him, leading the way to his softly rumbling truck. "So maybe we should hit a gas station for a refill on the way out?"

"Got coffee," he said shortly. "We can stop, though. You need more?"

"Nah," she lied, wishing like hell he didn't already have coffee. The maker in her room was teensy and the ready-packaged filter pods they left seemed recycled out of tires and ashes. And caffeine. She hoped. There had to be at least a little caffeine in tires and ashes, right?

"You make that motel shit?"

"Yes," she admitted, staring at her cup with a level of regret that she hadn't felt since her wedding night. She'd spent too much money she didn't have on making fair-trade coffee for all the bios on Monday mornings, so when it was just her, she had to skimp.

But at least drinking free motel coffee saved her a dollar toward her hospital bills, and now that Brad was gone, there would be a lot more of the former and no more of the latter. There was a silver lining in everything, even motel coffee and divorce.

Jack nodded toward her door. "Pour it out. I've got a thermos." He stretched out an arm. For a breath-held second, she thought he would touch her, but instead he reached behind the seat.

And she was definitely not disappointed. Because that would be crazy.

Especially not after he brought out an old Stanley thermos roughly as wide as her leg.

"God bless you," she breathed, and dumped her motel coffee onto the pavement without a second thought.

He refilled her cup, then started driving. She sat curled with one foot tucked up underneath herself in his giant, warm truck, breathing in the steam off the delicious coffee he'd given her. And then she finally remembered.

"How did you get a tire? They were closed when we got off work last night and I know they don't open at four in the morning."

"Knew a guy."

"You don't even live here. How do you know a guy at the tire store?" She eyed him. "I've seen the ancient tires on your work trucks."

He let out a pained grunt. "Used to work in a tire shop, back in high school. Know the type. Guys would do anything for an extra buck."

"So . . . you bribed them?" She slanted him a curious look. "How much do I owe you, anyway?"

He named a price.

It was her turn to snort, turning to look out the side window at the night and nothingness beyond. "Uh-huh. Cheapest tire I've ever heard of."

"Saw your motel. Figured you wouldn't want premium brands. They couldn't patch the old tire, but since I had to buy a new one, I got them to throw in a new spare, too. Well, it ain't new. It's used, but it's got good tread left and it ain't one of those bullshit doughnuts that'll only get you twenty more miles."

She considered how to handle this new debt she owed him. Weirdly, she got the idea that he'd be more uncomfortable if she tried to pay him back. Most guys couldn't wait to get you to owe them something, however imaginary, so they could cash in. She'd probably end up leaving an envelope full of cash in his truck, but she wasn't going to make a big deal out of it right now.

She sipped her coffee. Delicious. "Where are you from?" she asked instead. "You've got kind of a drawl going, at least on certain words."

"Alabama." He changed lanes, threw her a glance. "Redneck backwoods Alabama, so it probably sounds worse than what you're used to."

"Or better," she said, then tensed.

That was maybe too friendly for the endless sexual minefield of life on a construction site. Or too much like flirting. Neither of which she should be doing with a guy who was kind of her boss and kind of had to take orders from her that he didn't want to take. It was a precarious situation without adding any sexual tension to throw off that tightrope walk.

He hadn't answered, and she couldn't tell in the low light, but something about his awkward posture hinted at a blush.

"I like it, I mean," she said. In for a penny, in for a pound. "Your accent. It's kind of growly and soft and . . . I'm going to shut up and drink my coffee now."

He did not respond. And she did not allow her pre-caffeine self to make any more conversation until they swapped out the tire and put away the new spare using her headlamp and his gajillion-watt flashlight. When they were done, he refilled her coffee cup and gave her a rag to clean her hands on, just as the sun started to peek over the horizon.

She shivered, and he twitched. "Ain't you got a coat or something in that truck of yours?"

"It'll pass in a minute." She shrugged, unconcerned. "It gets colder just after sunrise, you know."

"Humph. That doesn't make sense. Sun ought to warm things up."

"It does, though. Pay attention, at dawn tomorrow. Happens just like that every day, whether it makes sense or not." She ducked her head, hugging her arms across her chest with her travel mug digging into her ribs. "Thank you for all this. I'll pay you back, but you didn't have to help me, and it's . . . really nice of you."

He glanced at her, then away. "Ain't nice. Didn't want you to slow down my whole crew waiting on the damn hippie car pool." He stuffed the rag they'd dirtied into his back pocket and didn't wait for her to respond. "There, tire's on. Now get your ass to work."

8

To Make an Omelet

The day went quickly despite her super-early start, and Creepy Ricky was waiting for her when she got back to the motel. He tried—for the third time—to invite himself into her room. She managed to dodge both his hands and his implications with grace, so she was feeling pretty darn good about herself by the time she finished the mac and cheese she'd made on her camp stove. She washed the dishes in her motel room, and was headed back outside to grab a new book out of her Toyota when she stopped at the sight of an unfamiliar truck parked next to hers.

The motel didn't get much nightly traffic: it was too seedy to appeal to anyone who didn't need the discount of weekly rates. The truck was tall and dark green, with new tires and a black motorcycle strapped into the bed that looked fast enough to be as expensive as the truck itself. She glanced at it as she passed, and unlocked her own vehicle. It was odd that the motel staff had put the overnighter in the room right next to hers, when she knew good and well most of the rooms were vacant.

She grabbed a book, turned around, and immediately froze, her brain glitching as it registered a familiar sight in a very unfamiliar place. Namely, the man standing in front of her, at a motel she knew he didn't stay at.

"Jack?" Then it clicked why he would be here, and she relaxed. "I still need to pay you for that tire," she said, before he'd have to fumble his way into how to bring it up politely. "I was going to hit an ATM when I got gas in the morning, but if you'd like, I could make a quick run down to the cash machine right now." Thank goodness she hadn't yet mailed most of her last paycheck to the medical bill collections agency. She'd just have to tear up that check and make only the minimum payment. Again.

"Ain't here to visit." He edged past her open truck door and reached into the green truck, hauling out a suitcase.

She glanced from him to the open motel door next to hers, and back. "You're . . . moving in?" Her lips twitched. "Couldn't resist all this luxury, hmm?"

He scrubbed his free hand over the back of his neck, his expression darkening from Resting Scowl Face to Embarrassed Glowering Face. "I can save more money if I stay in a place like this. Probably that's why Ricky's here."

"Uh-huh." She did not try to hide her smile. "That's probably why you're *both* here, huh?"

She was pretty sure he'd said his company paid for their rooms, which meant they didn't get a per diem allowance he could save by staying somewhere cheaper. But she still remembered how hard he'd shoved Ricky for making an off-color comment at her. How self-consciously he'd scowled when he brought her a tire he'd magically procured in the middle of the night. And for the first time, she thought maybe she wouldn't mind having a neighbor.

He ducked his head to look at the ground, cleared his throat. "Anyway, I'm not gonna bother you. You're not at work, and you don't need to look after me. But if you need something, just knock. I won't yell, or nothing like that. You won't bother me."

The warmth in her chest was growing and growing, until she thought he must be able to see it lighting her eyes. "Okay," she said, very softly. "I understand."

Mari kind of loved that Jack had moved into her motel to look out for her. Grouchy as he was, sometimes she felt like he was easier to understand than any other person in her life. He was so uncomfortable around other people it almost made her feel confident by contrast. But seeing each other more often had only seemed to make him close up tighter. She thought she might know why—whenever he was near, her skin prickled with an awareness that made it hard to focus on anything else. But she wasn't sure if he was feeling any of that, or if he was just shy about getting caught doing something nice.

For the next few days, when they crossed paths, he'd jerk a nod without making eye contact. Unless Ricky approached her, trying to chat her up when she was cooking on her tailgate, or attempting his usual method of trying to invite himself in when she was going back to her room. Then Jack would appear within seconds, either to pull Ricky aside to snap something work related or—rather less tactfully— to bark at him to stop bugging the bio in her off time.

It was nice, and it felt like he was on her side.

Except that nesting season was starting.

"It's covered under the Migratory Bird Treaty Act and state law," Mari explained, for the third time that week. "Every bird's nest with eggs in it gets a buffer zone, and we can't work inside the buffer."

The first nest she found meant they couldn't drive by on the road, and had to take an hour-long detour to get to their tower site. The second nest that appeared meant they could only use one half of the normal construction site to put their tower together. That required a whole lot of gymnastics to make it work and, she was pretty sure, took two years off Jack's life expectancy. At least if the shade of purple his face turned was any indication.

The third nest, however, was going to block out this entire tower site.

"Damn nest ain't even on the site!" he protested. "Eggs are fine. Ain't touching the fucking eggs!"

Mari glanced away, wetting her lips. The first two nest arguments had been stressful enough, but now his volume was really starting to climb.

The rest of the crew was grouped up on the far side of the trucks. On the other side of the construction pad. Very pointedly not getting into the discussion. She wished she could join them.

"The birds get disturbed by the noise and activity on the site, and sometimes the parents will abandon the nest," Mari explained, hoping more information would win him to her side, like it had before.

"How the hell long do birds nest for, anyway? When can we work?"

"A few weeks, maybe more. Until the babies can fly."

"Christ." Jack stalked away a few steps, whirled back around, and surged back toward her.

She didn't flinch, not like she once would have. Jack wouldn't hit her. But his anger was a palpable thing, beating at all the edges of her. She hated upsetting people, hated not being able to find a compromise to smooth over the fight.

"What the hell kind of bird is it, anyway?" He flung a hand out toward the nest she'd found in a low-slung bush. "A golden-plated peckerbill?"

She winced. "Black-throated sparrow."

"A fucking *sparrow*?" he exploded. "There's a million of those in the desert! I hear them all morning long."

For once, she wished he knew a little bit less about animals. She took a breath and tried to think of another approach.

In the early years of her marriage, she'd argue with Brad when he blew up at her. The first time he hit her, she'd slapped him right back. But the harder she fought, the angrier he became, and after a while, it was easier to just give in. To get small and quiet and go away in her mind until it was over.

This nest thing had Jack worked up worse than she'd ever seen him, but this was the *law* and she simply wasn't allowed to give up.

"Do you want to talk to my boss?" Her throat was ratcheting ever tighter. Her whole life, she'd been making people lose their temper. Her stepdad, Brad, now Jack. She just wanted to disappear somewhere in the middle of the desert in her truck, alone, where she couldn't set anybody off. "Maybe you and Marcus could work something out."

"Don't want to talk to that asshole with his fancy clipboard." Jack turned his head, spit on the ground. He glared at the empty concrete anchors where the tower was supposed to go.

Mari glanced out toward the nest. It was impossibly tiny from this distance, just a bundle of sticks the size of an orange. She thought of the little eggs inside. She had to stand her ground, no matter how furious Jack got at her. No matter if he moved out of the motel and left her alone with Ricky, no matter if he complained to Marcus and demanded a different bio. Those birds didn't have anyone else to fight for them. Rajni or Hotaka would both be better at it, but all these birds had was her. She drew in a breath.

"Look," she said, her voice as steady as she could make it. "I understand that you're frustrated, but it's not a negotiation. We can't work here. So call in and get a new tower assignment and we'll move on to there."

"I don't think you get it," Jack said. "This is the last tower in this section. If we can't build this tower, they can't string this line. They've already got wire-pull crews coming from the union, helicopter time booked for the pull. You know how much that shit costs? All those people, all those budgets, they're waiting on one thing. Me." He smacked a hand against his chest. "Trust me, one foreman ain't worth shit when you stack me up to the bunch of zeros on that bottom line. If I can't build it on time, they'll get somebody who can."

Anger sparked in her chest, breaking through the aching fatigue that had been dragging at her through this whole argument.

"No, they can't. It's the law, Jack. It's not *your* fault, and not even your boss could blame you for this, because it would be the same for any foreman trying to build a tower here."

He stared at her, his eyes harder than she'd seen them since they first met.

"You don't know my boss."

Her lips tightened. "Well, tell your boss he can call me directly if he thinks he can just assign another crew to this tower and ignore state law."

She didn't care how many nerve-racking arguments she had to force herself through. That jerk Rod wasn't going to kill baby birds on her watch.

Jack scoffed. "Yeah, right. I'll give him Marcus's number, maybe. Gonna be a bloodbath."

Her back snapped straight and she took a breath to insist that she could handle it, but it was already over. He was walking away, dismissing her. And why wouldn't he? She'd spent half that argument wilting into the ground. Until the very end.

She swallowed and headed back to her truck to get flagging so she could mark the new buffer zone around the nest. At least she'd done her job. Probably all the other bios could have done it better, but for now, the birds were safe.

Even if it might have cost her whatever fragile friendship she and Jack had begun to build.

Jack had a hard time going to sleep. Rod had been all over his ass about the nest, just like he expected. He needed to find a way to build that tower, and his boss had made it clear that it was Jack's issue to solve.

It's just a fucking bunch of eggs, Wyatt. What's your problem? You and

the girl are the only ones who've seen them. So if they just . . . go away . . .
it's your word against hers. And who's going to believe some bleeding-heart
environmentalist bitch?

That would have been enough to make him lose a night of sleep any-way, but there was also the matter of Mari, who was avoiding him after their argument. She'd stayed well away the whole rest of the day, like he'd strangled her puppy. Or like she knew what his boss had asked him to do about the nest problem and she already hated Jack's guts for it.

He couldn't remember exactly what he'd said during their argu-ment about the nest buffer zone, but he'd probably been an asshole. He wondered if it would help to apologize, or if she'd still be mad.

Probably she'd still be mad. Leroy used to apologize, after he'd break Jack's toys during his sleepless drug benders. As a kid, Jack hadn't hated him one bit less after those apologies.

Mari didn't understand, though. All she saw were those eggs. She didn't know that Rod was buddies with every major contractor in the industry and had a couple of union reps in his pocket, too. If Jack got fired from this job, it'd be his last job. Back home in Alabama, there were plenty of guys like his daddy who lived in busted-down trailers, bitching about how there wasn't any work.

He was painfully aware that this job was the only thing keeping him from being just another one of those guys.

He'd lain awake until two or three a.m. and barely dozed after that, so when the scream sounded, he bolted out of bed without a hint of confusion. He knew where it came from, and he figured there was only one thing in this world that made a woman scream like that.

Another scream ripped apart the silence, coming through the wall between his room and Mari's. The doorframe of his motel room cracked dangerously as he jerked open the door before the dead bolt was fully retracted. He charged out to Mari's door and hit it with both fists.

"Ricky, YOU SACK OF SHIT!" he bellowed. "OPEN THIS FUCKING DOOR RIGHT THE FUCKING HELL *NOW*!"

Rage blasted up through him like wildfire smoke, the sound of his yelling hurting his own ears. He'd never hit that volume in his natural-born life, but right now it felt like her whole door might shiver and wilt away just from the force of what was inside him.

"NOW, DAMN IT!"

This was Ricky's last chance to surrender, or Jack was putting both fists straight *through* that door, and screw the consequences.

"Boss?" The crane operator's voice was both quieter and farther away than he'd expected. Ricky stepped a little farther out of his door at the end of the motel row, rubbing his eyes and wearing nothing but a yellowing, sagging set of tighty whities. "What's going on?"

Jack did a double take. If it wasn't Ricky who'd gotten into Mari's room and was making her scream like that, who was it? He changed gears in an instant.

"Ricky, get your ass over here and help me break this door down!"

He rammed it with his shoulder without waiting for his employee. The weak wood shuddered and made a satisfying cracking sound, but didn't give way.

He backed up to take another run at it, Ricky coming to stand confusedly next to him. Before they could coordinate their efforts, the door swung open to reveal a wild-haired Mari squinting out of her dark room.

"Jack? What on earth?" She tugged at the bottom of her T-shirt, like that would cover the miles of long, toned legs and the flash of deep blue that must be her panties.

He felt light-headed with relief that her panties were still on. Maybe he'd gotten there in time.

He darted past her and into the room, throwing on the light and already winding up a punch, his muscles flexing with a battering thirst for violence.

The room was empty, but the sheets on the bed were a storm that made him sick to look at. Literally sick, so the nausea choked greasily up into his throat. He slapped open the door on the bathroom—the only other place in the room for a person to hide—and wondered if he'd have to stop his search long enough to puke into the conveniently located toilet. After which he'd use its porcelain lid to smash out the teeth of whoever had made Mari scream.

But the bathroom was deserted.

He threw back the shower curtain with a rattle of rusted metal rings. Nothing. Turning around, he came back into the main room, his eyes narrowed, sweeping every corner.

Still no attackers in sight. Ricky loitered in the doorway, stealing glances at Mari's legs in between eyeing his boss with more than a little wariness.

"Get the hell out of here," Jack growled at him.

"The fuck, man?" Ricky said under his breath, but turned to leave, scratching his butt through his threadbare underpants.

Jack looked at Mari. "Where'd he go?" The bathroom window was too small. There was no way anybody could have gone out the back.

"Oh my God, Jack. I'm so sorry."

"Are you hurt? Why are you apologizing?" His stomach flipped over again. "Do you need . . . I don't know, a doctor or a . . . another woman or something? I could call . . ." He tried to remember the names of any of the other female bios. There was one who worked with his crew before Mari came. Dark hair, skinny. Cried all the time. Jack had no idea what her name was, much less her number.

"It was nothing. A nightmare." She pushed her hair back and gave him a weak smile. "It's fine, really."

A nightmare? She'd screamed like . . . He hadn't heard full volume like that, not ever.

What had happened to her that was bad enough that even the *memory* could make her scream?

He stared at her, his fists slowly uncurling as it dawned on him that there was nothing he could do to save her. And more, that he had no business being in this room at all. He wasn't anything to her. She wasn't even speaking to him right now.

Her eyes were sad beneath the strangely beautiful spray of her chaotic chocolate-and-silver hair.

It wasn't until the cold air of the AC brushed his chest that he remembered he was naked. Or near so, wearing old black boxers gone gray with washing. He blinked. "I'm sorry."

He meant for himself, for yelling at her so she wanted to avoid him. For being in only his drawers in her room when she wanted to be sleeping. And being an asshole when she probably wanted him to care about baby birds more than his job, the way she did. Mari would have stood up to being fired to protect those birds, he was sure of it. He was a coward for not doing the same.

But that scream . . . that scream was straight out of the hellhole trailer park where he grew up. It quivered in the marrow of his bones now, like he couldn't scrub it out of the air.

He couldn't go back there. He needed this job.

"Sorry," he said again, talking over more of her apologies. He edged toward the door and let himself out. Rattled the knob to make sure it could still latch safely after the damage he'd done to it.

And then he stood there and stared at the blank side of her door, with her on the other side. She'd looked so small and scared, and all he'd done was frighten her more. Hadn't been able to do shit for her.

She was alone in there, behind that crappy door in that tiny room, thinking God knew what about him. Whatever it was, however bad it was, she was probably right.

After Jack left, Mari half fell, half sat onto her bed and tucked her shaking hands under her legs. Embarrassment squirmed up her body, and she could still feel her husband's hands from the dream, holding her down until the rough fibers of carpet rubbed the skin off her back.

Ex-husband.

She swallowed, listening to Jack going back into his room next door. He nearly broke down her door because he thought someone was hurting her. And they weren't even really friends.

No one else had cared that she was screaming. If she ever wondered if the motel management would respond in an emergency, this was her answer. All those years with Brad, even when he cracked the front window with her head . . . no one had come. People called the cops sometimes, but they never came themselves.

She crawled up onto her bed and pulled the blankets over her, folding them so she could have more layers between her and the world. The lights she left on, but it didn't matter because all she was seeing were the moments when Jack had been there.

How frantic his voice had sounded. The embarrassment in his face when he'd realized he was in his underwear, and how upset he must have been not to notice for so long. The way his hands curled at his sides. From fists into something . . . gentler. Something that made her ache.

The way his eyes flicked from her face to the floor like he wasn't sure he was allowed to look at her. The way the door had shuddered and nearly given way under a single blow from his desperate strength.

She stared at the wall with him on the other side, and thought about what kind of man would do all of those things. Or why he would do anything at all for her, a virtual stranger. After a while, she stopped wondering about why and just thought about the way his eyes looked when he realized she was safe.

And she fell into a deep, soft sleep.

Mari piloted her truck along the dirt access road just as the sun was barely peeking over the horizon, backlighting all the cactus so they glowed with prickly golden halos.

She should have felt odd or off-balance after last night; it was an embarrassing thing, after all, to have disturbed everyone and been seen in her scant pajamas. Not to mention seeing Jack's bare chest when he was clearly not comfortable with that. She should be feeling guilty at the fresh reminder of why she shouldn't have neighbors.

Instead, she felt centered and . . . warm. Like she'd just woken from a nap in a beam of sunlight, someplace very safe.

Her hands twitched on the wheel, though, when she saw Jack's truck. His personal one, not his work truck, and not at the job site they were supposed to meet at. Instead, he was parked at the tower site she had closed because it was too close to the bird nest.

Even stranger, he wasn't supposed to be there before her. She always got to work before the crew so she could make sure to move any animals out of the way that had burrowed into the tower pieces or pallets overnight.

Mari blew out a slow breath. "Oh, Jack. What are you doing? And why are you doing it *today*?"

She parked next to his green truck and walked out to meet him with a sinking feeling in her stomach. He was standing well inside the flagged buffer zone, right next to the delicate little nest.

If he'd destroyed it, she'd have to report him. She had no idea what the penalty was, but it was a state law. Worry tightened her throat.

When she reached his side, he was just staring down at the nest, hands hanging at his sides. She had to drag her eyes from his face to the small hollow of the nest.

The eggs were untouched.

Perfect, tiny little speckled eggs. He hadn't hurt them. Her heart jagged as she realized it would have changed something in her if he had.

"Fuck." He whispered the curse word so heavily that it felt like it sucked all the hope out of the dawning sunrise around them. "They're so . . . little."

"They are." She waited, not crowding him because she knew he wasn't going to make a move on the nest. The possibility of that had come and gone far before she got here.

"It's just a sparrow," he said, but without much conviction. "You know, my boss is gonna raise hell about this tower. Not now, not direct like. But he will."

She touched his arm. They needed to go, before the mother sparrow tried to return, or more of their scent tainted the nest site. "Everyone deserves a chance, though, don't you think? Even the creatures who aren't the flashiest, or the most popular."

He turned at her touch. His head ducked, looking deeper into her than he usually did. She held his searching gaze. He looked tired, and maybe even a little afraid.

But he nodded, and he let her lead him away.

9

Silver Lining

The bios all stood in a circle for their weekly meeting, shoulders hunched beneath hoodies against the predawn bite of the crisp desert air.

"First," Marcus said, "I think we ought to have a round of applause for Mari, who survived not one, not two, but *three* weeks on Wyatt's crew. Without medication. Or illegal drug abuse."

"That we know of," Hotaka added.

Everyone laughed as they began to clap. Lisa slung an arm over Mari's shoulders and gave her a little side hug.

"Lisa . . ." Marcus tugged at his beard. "Sorry, but it's your turn."

She nodded. "I swear that Wyatt won't make me cry this time."

There was a conspicuous silence.

"At least not more than twice," Lisa amended.

Marcus sighed. "Well, that would be an improvement."

Something dark twinged in Mari's belly, and she couldn't quite bring herself to join in the laughter. It wasn't fair of them to talk about Jack that way. It wasn't that he was mean, like they were making him out to be. He liked animals, and he watched out for his men. Granted, he did have a tendency to raise his voice more than strictly necessary, but everyone was acting like he was going to lay into Lisa like he *wanted* to make her feel bad. Jack wasn't like that.

She took a small step forward. "Lisa doesn't have to go. I'll stay with Ja—with Wyatt's crew."

Hotaka frowned. "You know they drug test on this job, right?"

"You don't have to," Marcus said. "You've proven you're willing to do more than your share of the dirty work around here."

"I'll be fine, honey," Lisa said as she touched Mari's arm. "It's sweet of you to worry."

Mari shrugged. "I really don't mind. Wyatt and I have come to an understanding." She did not feel that was the strict truth, but it was at least in the same zip code as the truth.

She was getting better at figuring out the right approach to take with him, and the shouting matches were getting a little shorter, perhaps losing a decibel or two. She didn't shrink these days when he got mad.

Marcus made a mark on his clipboard. "Well, I'm not going to stop you if you're offering. Next up, I need volunteers for monitoring the helicopter crew."

After the meeting, Lisa tagged along with Mari when she headed back to her truck, her sparse eyebrows low over narrowed blue eyes. "I appreciate you trying to save me, but I don't know how you can stand it. He's so loud and mean, I just get all flustered."

That dark feeling twisted in her stomach again and she resisted the urge to snap at Lisa. Instead, she shrugged. After all, she couldn't claim he hadn't flustered her a time or two. Or twelve.

"He's just under a lot of pressure from his boss. That's why he gets impatient with the slowdowns from following the environmental mitigation measures."

Lisa took her arm and turned Mari so they were face-to-face, lowering her voice. "Listen, I know you don't like to talk about it, but I know you're divorced, and I've seen the medical bills. It's not healthy, you thinking you have to take it from another guy who yells and screams at you. I don't know if I'm comfortable with you volunteering to take that on for the rest of us."

Mari stiffened, but it wasn't like the other woman was wrong, even if it wasn't her business. "Hey, at least I'm used to it," she joked, trying to lighten the mood a little.

"That's my point. You shouldn't ever get used to that, from men. You don't deserve to be treated that way. You know that, don't you?"

"It's not like that."

Lisa looked unconvinced, so Mari took a breath and tried to explain.

"Jack's not cruel. He wouldn't hurt me. And when he yells at me, I don't feel like he ever really means it."

Lisa sighed. "Oh, honey, they always say they 'didn't mean to' and 'don't take it like that' and whatever they have to say to get away with doing exactly as they please. But the proof is in the pudding."

Mari's skin prickled with annoyance. It wasn't like she couldn't tell the difference between a guy like Brad and a decent man. And it wasn't as if Lisa would know the difference, when her main complaint about her boyfriend, Marcus, was that he was too nice to argue with her. She squinted against the rising sun, taking a long breath scented with creosote and the hint of dew.

"Jack never yells at me when we're not at work," she said. "That's how I know he's not really like that. He just gets stressed out, because of his jerk boss and the responsibility of all his men's safety."

Lisa had started to braid her dark hair over one shoulder but she paused at that. "Um . . . when exactly do you see him when you're not at work?"

She paused, feeling vaguely guilty. "We stay at the same motel. And he helped me out, when I got that flat tire the other day. So you see? He's not as bad as all that."

Lisa snapped a tie onto the end of her braid. "The construction company bought out a block of rooms at the Best Western. If he's staying elsewhere, he's doing it on his own dime."

Mari glanced away. Apparently he'd lied about doing it to save money. Once he'd seen Ricky's truck at her motel, he didn't even wait for the next day off to move, when he would have had more time.

She looked down to hide the warmth that suffused her. He was paying out of pocket to live in a far crappier place, all so he could be there if Ricky harassed her.

Not to mention he'd nearly broken down her door to get to her when he heard her scream. She couldn't remember the last time anyone had gone to such lengths to protect her.

But he also flew off the handle and cursed a blue streak whenever she told him he couldn't do what he wanted on the job site, and she remembered the look in his eye when he'd stepped toe to toe with Ricky at the kit fox burrow. Jack clearly wasn't a stranger to using his fists.

She'd found him at that roped-off bird's nest, too. What would he have been there for, alone and that early, if it weren't to destroy the nest? Maybe she'd been wrong, and he would have smashed the eggs if she hadn't shown up just then.

Mari tugged at the ends of her sleeves, hiding her hands inside of them.

"I don't like you making excuses for a guy who treats you bad," Lisa persisted, apparently taking her silence as tacit agreement. "Especially if he's following you after work, to your motel no less. Mari, you know you can move into the house a bunch of us are renting. If it's about money, you can have the couch for free."

She'd worked on other jobs with Marcus and Lisa. When they all got hired on here, Marcus had offered to let her move in with them, renting one of the smaller rooms at a suspiciously discounted rate. Mari shook her head, just like she had then. If she really wanted a chance at that biologist-in-residence job, she should take the practice living near coworkers, but the idea of being in the same house with so many other people made her throat go tight. It felt safer to stay at her seedy motel, with Jack next door. He hated all people equally, so she couldn't really disappoint him.

"I, uh . . . snore." She smiled ruefully. "I wouldn't have many friends left if you had to put up with all the noise I make at night." She gave Lisa's arm a gentle squeeze, equal parts annoyed and touched at her new friend's misplaced concern. "Listen. I know abusive men. Jack isn't one." She took a breath. "And I'm equally aware of my many shortcomings, one of which is—clearly—my taste in men. I'll be careful, both of him and my own instincts. I promise you I won't take any crap from him, at work or otherwise."

Lisa hesitated, then nodded, and Mari tried not to be offended at how unconvinced the other biologist appeared. But no matter how calm she kept her face, her stomach was churning as she got into her truck.

Mari's strides were pensive as she made her laps around the construction site. The sun warmed her back, and the sharp scent of creosote made everything smell fresh and interesting. The birds were active today, calling to each other as they flitted from bush to bush. She absently dodged the reaching spines of cactus, too many things on her mind to pay them much attention.

She kept thinking about the concern in Lisa's expression, and how when Jack lost his temper about the bird's nest, she'd shrunk down to a smaller version of herself. And then how she'd been able to straighten and hold her ground, when it was to protect the eggs.

Then again, it hadn't been the first time. She went up against Rod to protect Jack. She could be tough, if she had someone to stand up for.

Mari paused a moment, staring out at the construction site without really seeing it. Even though the nest argument with Jack had kicked loose one of her old nightmares, when she woke back up, she felt different. Not helpless like the woman in the dream. Something in her had shifted in a tiny and fragile way that she wasn't ready to talk about to anyone yet. Just in case she was wrong.

But then again, she'd felt like that before. There had been so many times with Brad when she was sure that things had turned a corner, and this time he'd really resolved to change.

Lisa was concerned, and she had a much better track record with choosing men than Mari did. Was facing Jack's temper doing her good, or exactly the opposite?

The crew was climbing off the tower, streaming out toward the trucks for lunch, and Mari watched Jack unbuckle his tool belt and shuck it off by the base of the tower.

He'd seemed so sad since that morning she'd found him alone inside the bird nest buffer. She'd second-guessed a hundred times why he'd been out there by the nest. He hadn't said, and she hadn't asked, but whatever it was, it had left his shoulders dragging and heavy for days.

Despite her worries about him, it was hard to see him unhappy.

Even now, the rest of the crew was grouping up under their EZ-Up awning, laughing and giving each other a hard time, but Jack was headed off to his foreman's truck without a word to any of them.

He shouldn't be alone, not when he was already feeling low. But she just so happened to have something stashed in her truck that she hoped would fix both those problems.

Jack was halfway through wolfing down his dry bologna sandwich when he sensed that something was wrong.

He checked the tower, but everybody was already down and on break. Checked behind him to make sure Rod hadn't snuck in without his noticing. Nothing. Huh. But then, slowly, it sank in what was different.

It smelled . . . good.

Nothing ever smelled good on a job site. They smelled like sweaty, ugly men and hot metal. Sometimes like animal shit, because so many of their power lines went through pastures. Right now, it smelled like a bakery, all vanilla with a tang of melting chocolate.

What the hell?

He got out of his truck, half convinced he was having a brain aneurysm, or one of those seizures where you smelled oranges and jet fuel right before you fell down and started flopping like a trout. But no, it smelled like brownies. About forty miles from the nearest kitchen.

He nosed around, checking where his guys were eating lunch—and not failing to notice how the conversation faltered and died when he got close—and then over to Mari's truck, just for lack of anywhere better to look. She must have heard him coming, because she abandoned her chair in the shade and came around the truck with a smile.

"How's it going? Lots of progress on the new tower this morning."

He nodded, and shoved the back of his hand across his chin. "Hey, you smell . . . something?" He didn't want to get specific. If his brain was finally breaking from all those years of inhaling Leroy's secondhand crack smoke, he'd rather his pretty bio didn't know about it.

"Something like brownies? Sure. They should be done baking in about three more minutes."

His brain was fucked for sure. She had definitely just said she was baking brownies in the middle of sandblasted nowhere. "But, um . . . how?"

Her smile turned knowing and she cocked her head toward the far side of her truck. He followed her to a propped-up box with a Plexiglas front and angled tinfoil-bright wings sticking out the sides. They reminded him of the reflective panel his mom used to lay out in her lap when she was suntanning in front of their old trailer, back when he was a kid.

"Solar oven," Mari said. "I like to bake, but living in my truck for the past couple of years made that a little tough. I made the batter last night and brought it in my cooler this morning."

"You been living in this thing for two *years*?" He stared at her tiny pickup.

"It's got everything I need. Bed, water, stove. Especially when we're doing remote research jobs, it just makes more sense to camp. It's fun, like summer camp."

"Summer camp with no AC."

She laughed. "I have missed AC."

She moved back to her chair and he came around into the shade, too, the relief of being out of the sun immediate. He leaned one shoulder against her truck and folded his arms, tucking his hands against his sides. "Used to camp a lot, back in Alabama. In a tent, though, not a pickup. I go back for bow-hunting season, usually."

As soon as he said it, he wanted to bang his head against the truck. The last thing you wanted to tell a nice tree hugger lady was that you killed cute, furry animals for sport.

"You're a bow hunter?" She let out a low whistle. "Wow. I'd like to try that someday, but I don't think my stalking skills are up to getting that close yet. I'm lucky if I don't scare them off even at rifle range."

"You . . . hunt?" He perked up.

"Deer hunt. We tried elk, but didn't get anything." She peered in the window of her solar oven. "Just last year. Marcus taught me when he needed someone to go with him, because Lisa hates to hunt. He's a great shot, but he's even louder on the stalk than I am." She smiled at Jack. "Don't tell him I said that."

"But you—" He gestured out at the desert, at all the creatures hidden in shadows and burrows that she had dedicated her life to protecting.

"Sure, but these are *endangered* animals. I'm not a vegetarian. There are plenty of deer. What sounds more fair to you, eating an animal that's been stuck in a tiny, manure-filled pen its whole life, eating food that makes it sick to fatten it up faster? Or eating an animal that lived its whole life roaming free, that you stalked and shot in a fair fight. That had a good life and a quick, humane death?"

She warmed to her topic, gesturing passionately.

"How about an animal that's native to the landscape rather than one we introduced in unsustainable numbers and whose hooves destabilize streambeds? Besides, since we killed off a lot of the natural predators like wolves and cougars, deer have proliferated in numbers that can send the whole ecosystem out of balance. Culling a few through hunting can help keep the population to healthier numbers that the grazing can support and—" She paused, her cheeks pinkening. "Oops. I'll just tuck my soapbox away, then."

"Nah." He couldn't stop staring at her. "Nah, you're right. Deer are like rats in some parts of the country. There are too many of them and they're good eating. Just didn't think a bio would hunt, that's all." He glanced down and back up, hoping he hadn't offended her.

"Maybe you need to get to know more bios. There are a few down here from Alaska who could give you a run for your money in the bow-hunting department. Hotaka makes all his own sandals from elk leather he tans himself, and he could build you a beautiful coffee table, too."

"I'd like to learn how to tan hides," he said. "My older brother didn't know how, so I never learned."

She got up to open the solar oven. "I can introduce you to Hotaka, if you like. If you haven't worked with him already, I mean. Hey, can you help me with something?"

"Sure, what do you need?" He stepped forward. "I could take one or two of those brownies off your hands, if you needed me to."

She grinned, way brighter than he expected for his lame little joke. "Hold up your hands."

He hesitated for a minute, his stomach clenching. Whenever Leroy said shit like that—*Close your eyes, little brother. Hold out your hand*—it never went well. But Mari wasn't Leroy. Didn't have that mean streak down deep in her. So he held up his hands, feeling stupid but doing as she asked anyway.

She slid oven mitts onto his hands. The one on the right had sunflowers on it. The one on the left read "Live! Love! Dance!"

He scowled at them.

But then she put on her own oven mitts and placed a pan of brownies in his hands, and he felt a little better about things.

"Fu—I mean, damn these smell good."

"I use my mother's recipe with very dark chocolate, and a touch of hazelnut flour, plus some secret stuff you'd have to torture me to get me to tell you. Come on, help me make friends with your crew." She led the way toward his men. He grimaced, following a reluctant step behind.

"They all already pant after you like a bunch of puppies. You don't need to feed them."

"Maybe not. They're already following me home," she teased, but her voice was so light he could tell she wasn't trying to say she didn't want him in her motel.

Though he really couldn't figure why she was letting him carry her brownies after he'd busted through her door in the middle of the night like a crazy person. Bad enough that he had, as she said, followed her home without an invitation.

Some home it was, too. Tape on the cracked windows, and the bedspreads pocked with cigarette burns and musty with dust, just like his daddy's trailer. This morning, he'd almost shut off his alarm without getting up, with just the hazy thought that he'd lose this job anyway, the next time Leroy went on a bender and wrecked Jack's work truck, or Jack had to ditch a shift to bail his brother out of jail. Why get up when it was only a matter of time?

Good thing he blinked himself awake and remembered he'd left Alabama and that life, even if right now he was in a motel that felt like he'd never even made it across the state line.

His steps faltered at the memory, but once you had oven mitts on your hands and a pan on top of them, there really weren't too many choices about what you could do next. So Jack kept following Mari.

The men perked up when Mari came into sight, and they all sat up a little straighter when they saw Jack behind her.

"Dessert, anyone?"

"Wow, are you serious? Don't mind if I do," Kipp said.

Toby pretended to consider. "I don't know . . . are these fat-free?"

"Better not be," Mari said, and the whole crew burst into laughter.

"Didn't know you made deliveries, boss," said Joey, the only one who dared to approach Jack's pan.

"Don't get used to it," he snarled, dropping the pan with a bang on the nearest tailgate and shucking off the oven mitts. Mari pulled a pie server out of her pocket and busied herself cutting and passing out desserts. He threw a longing glance at the peace and quiet of his truck, but the aroma of chocolate was too enticing to ignore. He grabbed one, blowing on his fingers when it burned them. Besides, he didn't trust these idiots not to say the wrong thing to Mari if he wasn't around to chew them out for it.

Silence descended on the rowdy bunch, but he hardly noticed because the batter of these brownies was like . . . He gobbled a second one, then a third, trying to pin down what it was about them that hit the spot so directly.

"Whew-ee!" Kipp said finally. "Sure is a hot one today."

Jack snorted, his mouth still full of his fourth brownie when he grabbed a seat on the tailgate. "You think this is hot, you never been to Alabama."

"I worked in Alabama once," Gideon said. He was a quiet lineman and only had a few friends on-site, but Mari couldn't tell if the others avoided him because they didn't like that he was gay, or because he could climb nearly twice as fast as any of them. "So humid you needed to dry the air off with a towel before you could breathe it."

Jack chuckled. "Damn straight. Lungs like to shrivel up like burnt paper, coming from there to here."

"Yeah. Miss the grits, though."

"Mmm-hmm. And the fried chicken." Jack glanced at the half-empty pan, feeling bad he'd eaten so many of Mari's snacks.

"Go ahead," she said, intercepting the glance and airily waving a hand. "My hips don't need them anyway."

"Your hips are fine," he grunted, then flushed when he realized he'd commented on her figure in front of all his crew. "I, uh—"

"Whew, these are about the best brownies I've ever had," Kipp jumped in, and Mari smiled. "Don't you boys think?" he prodded the others, and a few more voices piped up in agreement.

Jack kept his eyes on his brownie, not wanting to admit that the annoying, chatty lineman had just rescued his ass. Maybe he wouldn't fire him this week. Next week was fair game, though.

"You know, the desert has a silver lining," Mari said. "Watch this." She took one of the brownies that had cooled in the shade and cupped it in her slim palm, extending it out into the direct sun again. While they all waited, the chocolate chips went shiny and started to melt, so that by the time she pulled her hand back in, it was as warm as fresh baked all over again.

Jack just watched her, the light in her smile drawing every eye while she stood in a circle of dirty old construction workers who he'd never once seen watch their mouths for this long at a stretch.

This desert had indeed come with quite the silver lining.

10

Hello, Neighbor

The week had gone by slowly, and mostly in silence. Mari felt weird about talking to Jack, their every interaction seeming fraught with implications once she'd analyzed them through the filter of what Lisa would think. Whether he was being nice, or maybe just acting nice to get close to her, or being the kind of nice Brad was when he felt bad for a fight they'd had.

She wasn't sure about anything anymore, and it left her feeling dizzy, so she just kept to herself. Which wasn't hard. Jack didn't exactly seek her out to engage in small talk. When they crossed paths at the motel, he'd just duck his head and mumble something that sounded like a gruff, rumbly Alabama version of hello. Or maybe just hi. Or maybe some kind of nonsyllabic acknowledgment that they vaguely knew each other in a professional sense.

It was entirely possible he was simply living there out of thrift, and Lisa was wrong about how the linemen's housing allowance was paid. He certainly didn't seem to have any interest in her or in being near her any more than necessary. The only exception had been when she made him brownies at work, but what man didn't like brownies?

On their one day off, she dreamed of the roar of motorcycles, and when she woke up, his bike was already gone. Jack didn't return until sunset, his hair tangled when he took off his helmet before he shoved it back into its normal knot—too rough to be called a man bun. And Mari let the curtain fall before either one of them had to acknowledge why she had been peeking out the window.

On the first day of the fifth week, everyone had waited when Marcus brought up the assignments for Wyatt's crew. She felt odd and squirmy, unable to hold eye contact with anyone. She wasn't entirely sure Jack wanted her on his crew after the whole bird's nest argument, but she didn't want to make anyone else go when they'd be uncomfortable and probably upset Jack in the bargain, when the last thing he needed was more stress. Except she also knew Lisa would worry if she went back to Jack's crew.

She felt like there was no right decision that wouldn't backfire on her, and that made her feel so caged it was like being married all over again. So she volunteered for Wyatt's crew twice as loudly just to drown out all the competing voices inside of her.

Then she spent all day regretting it, because the only words Jack said to her weren't even *to* her. They were just in her general direction, when he was blasting one of the guys for chatting her up when he was supposed to be stacking the wooden pieces of cribbing into the work truck.

The evenings, though, were different.

It started weeks ago, the first night after he moved in, when she was watching HGTV. It was fun to have TV again after so long in her truck. Her favorite guilty pleasure was a zombie show, but it came on only once a week, and HGTV had programming all the rest of the days. Simple, sunny shows about house buying and remodeling that appealed to her so much that she, perversely, didn't want anyone to know she watched them.

But that first night, the sound on her program was weird. Echoey, or hollow sounding. She eventually shut the TV off in frustration, only to get a chill when the sound kept going after the screen went blank. It took her a second to work out that it was coming from the room next door. Jack's room must be a mirror image of hers, his TV mounted on the other side of the same wall as hers. He was watching HGTV, too.

That made her smile. She had cozied back into her pillows, and flipped the TV back on.

The same thing happened the next night, and the next. The echoing sound became a comfort, as if she wasn't watching alone for once, even though being alone was what she'd long since decided she wanted. On Sunday, when her zombie show came on, she felt a pang when she flipped the channel. Like she was abandoning him.

He probably hadn't even noticed. She was just being silly.

That Monday, after she volunteered for a fifth week on his crew, she felt lonely all day . . . until she got home and turned the TV on. Not three minutes later, she heard his come to life, and it made her laugh out loud. They must have been working together long enough to be on exactly the same schedule, as predictable as an old married couple. Or maybe, did he look forward to the echo of that sound just like she did?

She quieted, thinking about it. He was awkward, in his own snarly, terrifying way. He still ate lunch alone on most days. He hadn't seemed to know how to act when she thanked him for helping with her tire, and he was even more uncomfortable when she paid him back the money for it.

What were the chances he was sitting on the other side of that wall, feeling stupid, like she didn't want him at her motel? But also unwilling to move as long as Creepy Ricky still occupied a room down at the end of the row. What if he'd come here at least partially because he wanted to talk to her, but he didn't know how?

She sat with the thought, staring unseeingly at the TV until the show switched and the theme music of her favorite house-shopping show started, on both sides of the wall.

And then she pushed off the bed. When she left Brad, she swore she'd change, let herself have a new life, be the opposite of everything she'd been before. It was easy when it came to picking clothes she actually liked, getting to wear earrings now and again. It felt a lot harder when doing the opposite meant being egotistical or cocky, or putting herself out there to try to make friends. Because what if people weren't interested, but they were just too polite to turn down her invitations?

Mari stopped to smooth her hair in the bathroom mirror. "What's the worst that can happen?" she asked herself. "You embarrass yourself?" She snorted. "Been there, done that."

The minifridge was her last stop before she let herself outside. She didn't realize her feet were bare until she felt the heat of the gritty sidewalk. Looking down, she winced as she registered her yoga pants and ancient "Geology rocks but biology grows on you" T-shirt. Too late to change, and it didn't matter anyway. Seduction wasn't her aim here.

Breaking a cycle. It was as giant and minuscule as that.

She threaded the long necks of the two glass beer bottles through her fingers and rapped the bottom of one on his door.

Jack opened it, his man bun a little mussed and shirt crooked like he'd just pulled it on, a pair of thrashed old jeans hanging low on his hips. Without his sunglasses, his eyes were a deep, dark green, like the color was a secret you only got to see if you looked closely enough. She pulled in a steadying breath and smiled.

"Hello, neighbor. Figured if we were going to watch the same show every night, we might as well save electricity and do it on one TV. Can I come in?"

11

A Fixer-Upper

When Mari showed up at his door, Jack's first thought was, *Thank God I wear headphones when I watch porn.*

He hadn't been sure until just now if she could hear his TV as well as he could hear hers.

His second thought was more incoherent. Mostly four-letter words jumbled up in his head while he stared at the woman in his doorway. Her hair was back in a loose, messy bun, her breasts soft and round under an old T-shirt, and yoga pants smoothed lovingly over her strong legs.

All that hiking must be dang good exercise.

He cleared his throat, wanting to ask her to repeat herself because no way had she just asked if she could come in. To *his* room.

Except she was holding two long-necked beers hooked through her agile fingers, and she didn't seem like the kind of woman to double-fist her drinks. He stepped back, figuring if this was some alternate universe, it wasn't a half-bad one.

"Yeah, sure. Course. You can, uh . . ."

He glanced back at the room, and all the things he hadn't noticed before were glaring at him. His open suitcase, vomiting boxers out onto the floor. A take-out container from last night perched on top of the microwave. His French press sitting prissily by the sink, making him look like a city boy who couldn't even drink plain coffee without whining about the brand.

Something cold pressed against his chest and he took the beer automatically. Mari breezed past him and hopped onto the bed, nodding at the TV.

"You ever notice how the guy on this show uses the same three things to describe all his favorite houses?"

The corner of his mouth lifted. "*Expansive.*"

"Sunny."

"Feels like home," they finished together, and Mari laughed.

Distracted by looking at her, he tried to crack off the beer cap and nearly ripped his palm open when it wasn't a twist-off. Fishing his keys out of his pocket, he used the opener on his keychain to pop his cap. He threw away the take-out container and kicked the lid of his suitcase closed on his way over to open Mari's beer for her. Once he did that, he was already mostly onto the bed, and it seemed like it'd be weird for him to sit in one of the chairs by the tiny table. Especially since they were tucked into the wrong corner to see the TV and had preacher-straight uncomfortable backs.

He let his weight settle gingerly on the bed, one leg still slung over the side and his bare foot brushing the hard carpet, waiting to see if she'd protest.

She didn't.

"You think they always pick the third house they look at," she asked, "or do you think they edit it to look that way?"

He took a sip of the beer. Good. A solid porter, none of that pretentious, fruit-infused shit he'd seen the bios drink sometimes.

"Edited," he said. "Leroy dated a girl one time who sold houses. She said people'd look at every damn house in their price range, then 'just peek' at the more expensive ones, then end up offering on one of those. She'd have loved if it only took three houses to get them to buy."

Great. Put a girl in his room for five seconds and he suddenly couldn't stop running his mouth. Telling her the life story of a girl Leroy had fucked a grand total of maybe twice, and she didn't even know *Leroy*.

"Sounds about right. Is Leroy that mustache guy on the crew, the one who thinks he's a smooth talker?"

"Nah, that's Kipp. Leroy's my brother. Back home. Well, I think he's still back home. Haven't heard from him in a while, so I ain't sure."

Why had he added that? It wasn't like she cared where Leroy lived, or that he wasn't exactly the kind of family that remembered to send birthday cards, or even text messages, really. Jack changed the subject.

"Figured you'd know Kipp by now. Practically have to put him on a leash to keep him on the job site instead of off talking to you."

"He does a lot of talking." She cut her eyes his way as she took a slow sip of beer. "Doesn't mean I'm listening."

Jack snorted out a laugh. "That's the best way to be when it comes to Kipp. Not listening."

She held up her beer without looking over, and he clinked the neck of his to hers.

A surge of something weird and unfamiliar swept through him. Like pride, or . . . something. He wasn't that good at talking to women, usually. Too rough, so they took everything he said the wrong way. Or he didn't have anything to say because he spent most of his time working.

Then again, Mari spent every day out on the job site with him. She wasn't working steel, no, but she was in the same dust and ruthless sun as the rest of them. Sweating through her shirt just the same. Maybe it made a difference.

He sat a little more squarely on the bed. Tried leaning back against the wall next to Mari but keeping her in the corner of his eye so he could read if he was crowding her. She didn't budge, just pointed the neck of her beer at the screen. "Oh my gosh, the porch on this one? I could live on a porch like that. Forget the house."

Jack did not know what to do with a woman on his bed, watching his television.

However, she didn't seem to be unhappy, so he figured it was easy enough to sit and throw out a comment or two on the show they were watching. He started to fidget when the credits rolled, but Mari stayed put like she didn't mind watching the next one, too. Besides, the next show was a fix-it-up, which were his favorites. Quickly, it became apparent that the snarkier comments that slipped out were the ones most likely to get a laugh out of her.

He didn't quite relax, not really. He got her a second beer from his own fridge when hers went dry, but he never got past the neck of his own, too nervous that he'd catch a buzz and say something to make her tense up, the way she had that day at the fox burrow with Ricky.

Besides, he could already feel every inch of his skin that was on the Mari side of his body, ripples and tingles running up him that he couldn't seem to squash. So he was plenty busy trying to keep his hard-on from growing to noticeable levels.

After the third show, she set down her empty beer and swung her legs off the bed. He jumped up to walk her out, even though it was only a few steps. His mama hadn't lived long, but long enough to teach him a manner or two.

Also, something was bothering him, and he hadn't had enough time to figure out how to phrase it the right way. She reached to open the door and he was out of time.

"Hey, uh, Mari? Don't do this with the other guys from the crew, okay? Might not be a good idea, you tapping on their door with a couple of beers."

Her face fell. "My ex always said I was too much of a flirt, and it's been a long time since I had any neighbors. I'm probably going about this all wrong. I'm sorry, if I—"

"Hey, no. Not what I meant. All the guys on the crew would be happy as pigs in shit if you wanted to spend time with them. Probably even the married ones. Just ain't sure if you were alone with them, if they'd mind their manners. Is all."

She looked at him oddly. "But not you?"

He shoved his fists into his pockets. "Hell, I know you didn't mean it that way."

She just kept gazing at him, like she wasn't sure what to think.

He was pretty sure he had messed this all up and made her feel bad, so he swallowed down a big gulp of nerves and pride and said, "Was nice. Having the company. Even if you were wrong about the tiles on that countertop."

"They looked pretty!"

"Wouldn't look so pretty after the first time you got hot sauce in the grout and it stained for good."

"That's what Comet is for."

"What's a comet? That a housecleaning service?"

She laughed. "And *that's* why you can't get the hot sauce out of your grout." She turned back to her room. "See you in the morning."

"Yup." He kept leaning against his doorframe after she was gone, and it wasn't until his cheeks started to ache in an unfamiliar way that he realized he was smiling.

12

An Issue of an Adult Nature

Jack had a problem with his erection.

He'd seen the commercials for those pills, sure, but he was having the "other" kind of trouble. Namely that the sumbitch wouldn't lie down when Mari was nearby. Something about the warmth of her presence and how it settled over him like the soft touch of hands. And his dick, dumb handle that it was, didn't know the difference between that and actual hands.

Probably because it had been too long since it felt the touch of anything but his own rough palm.

He'd been watching a lot more porn to combat it, but at this point, he wasn't sure if that was part of the solution, or part of the problem.

He always watched on his laptop with headphones on; everything else felt too exposed. The best were the videos with locker rooms. Something about the idea of walking in on an undressed girl and have her not be disgusted or shrieking for him to get out, but excited and happy to see him. Welcoming. It turned his crank something fierce.

That and cars.

He loved everything about sex in cars. And, lately, trucks.

Me and Mari alone on the worksite, in my foreman's truck. Laying her across that big bench seat . . .

He tried not to fantasize about her that way. Knew it wasn't right. It felt invasive. Like he could see right through the wall between his motel room and hers.

When he heard her shower turn on, sometimes he had to leave the whole damn motel to keep from thinking about her undressing so near to him. And once—a shameful, exciting once—he got in his shower at the same time and let his imagination run wild.

He came so hard he hit the shower wall with his response. Afterward, blushing, he'd cleaned it up with his own rags that he then threw out. Driven to the store and found that Comet stuff to make sure he got it all out of the grout. Not because he was really worried the half-hearted cleaning staff at the motel would be able to tell what he'd been doing in there. But more because he didn't want to be the kind of guy who didn't know about cleaning products.

Mari had laughed off his lack of knowledge at grout-cleaning methods, but she hadn't been surprised, either. Jack had an idea that the ex who'd called her a flirt probably had left most of the cleaning to Mari. He didn't want to be like that.

Hell, he didn't want to be like *this*. Horny as holy fuck, just, all the time. His eyes straying to Mari's ass when they were at work. Her hips, the little inward nip of her waist. The line of her throat and the shining silver threads in her chocolate-dark hair. It was getting so bad that even her small footprints in the dirt could get him excited.

He was disgusting.

She'd visited his room once. *Once*, and probably only sat on his bed because the chairs were less comfortable than a sidewalk. She'd casually watched a little TV with him and he was returning the favor by imagining her in every steamy locker-room or classic-car fantasy he'd ever had. Mari deserved better than that.

She was so effortlessly elegant. Despite his utter lack of social graces, she might somehow even be willing to be friendly with him, if he could keep the situation in his pants under control for five frigging minutes.

Even then, he knew she'd never be on his bed for anything more than sitting to watch TV.

There were 86,400 seconds in a day, and he was spending about 85,000 of those thinking of her. But Jack was not so stupid as to believe that Mari was spending any of those seconds thinking of him.

Mari had a problem. And the problem was Jack's arms.

It had gotten very hot that week, topping 105 more often than not. Most of the guys wore long sleeves to protect their skin, but once it hit the triple digits, Jack didn't seem to be able to stand those and went back to short sleeves. The arms thus revealed were shiny and sweat slicked, the sharp muscles soon slashed with burns from where he brushed against the metal of the tower. And it was probably really twisted of her to find that sexy, but the sheer manliness of it, the way he just didn't even bother about the pain . . . well, she'd probably stepped on four endangered species just that morning, watching his naked biceps.

She couldn't stop thinking about how she'd gone to Jack's room, bold as anything, and he hadn't thrown her out. She'd had to clench her hands around her beer to hide their trembling, making the silliest small talk about the TV show so she could appear confident and casual. It had been a risk, just a guess, and if she guessed his feelings wrong, she would have been crushed. Instead, she'd dispelled the awkwardness of both of them feeling unwanted.

Brad had not been right about her.

Her instinct for years had been to keep to herself and spare others her company. Brad loved her, and even he could barely put up with her. He was, he'd told her time and again, the only one who would ever want her.

Jack had jarred her out of that mode of thinking because she could see him feeling unwanted in exactly the same way. And he was *wrong*. She knew it even if he didn't. Even when he was shouting or in a towering rage, it was because he had integrity and wanted to do the right thing, in his work and for his men. And when they were off the job site, out of his element, he was quiet. Always hesitant to speak or impose himself on anyone, even though she could tell his men idolized him and were bowled over and terribly nervous the one time he'd deigned to have lunch with them. Maybe that lunch had helped, too, because he didn't seem upset with them as often as when she first started.

She glanced over to where they were all standing around the tower plans, Jack's shoulders wide under his plaid work shirt. He flipped a hammer absently in his hands while he talked.

He hadn't thought she was too forward to come to his room. Hell, he hadn't even thought she was flirting. *I know you didn't mean it that way.* The problem was, when he'd brought it up, she felt an odd little pang and she couldn't have said whether she wanted him to interpret her visit "that way." She hadn't thought that far ahead.

Then again, if he wanted her that way, it seems like he automatically would have assumed she was flirting. So many men did, if she so much as smiled at them. Her head began to hurt trying to decode it all, and she winced as she wandered a little farther from the site.

She chewed on the inside of her lip, sneaking glances back toward him. He was moving across the site now, his muscular strides gobbling up ground. His nervousness around her, the way his eyes would catch on her and then flick away . . . she'd thought maybe he was interested in her. Sexually, at least, if not in her personality. But perhaps that was just her libido's wishful thinking.

She tugged at her sleeves, squaring her shoulders as she resolved not to lose the thread of her good mood. He'd welcomed her into his room, and platonic or not, he hadn't been aggravated by her company. That was the main thing. A solitary life was the safest choice for her, she knew that.

But it didn't mean she didn't wish she could have more sometimes. Didn't mean that every HGTV show featuring a house with a porch didn't fill her with longing. Didn't mean she wasn't curious to try to determine what those looks meant.

And in the meantime, she'd just have to try to ignore the spark of heat deep in her belly every time her eyes strayed back to his bare, glistening biceps.

13

Ground Squirrel Orgy

Mari stepped up into the weekly bio meeting circle, humming a little Josh Ritter song under her breath. Most of the bios' assignments got swapped around by the week, but she had to admit, it was kind of nice to know where she was headed. No one else wanted Wyatt's crew, and so Marcus had fallen into the habit of just glancing at her for her nod, then assigning her to him.

This week, Marcus glanced up from his clipboard with his faux serious face, his cheeks hollowing slightly beneath his beard as he squinted to hold back a smile. "The apprentice from Wyatt's crew stopped by last night. Apparently the crew took up a collection to bribe me to keep putting Mari with them. Seems she has an effect on the boss's mood that they're in favor of."

Snickers broke out around the circle. She flushed, avoiding meeting anybody's eyes. It didn't have anything to do with her; it was most likely that he wasn't as awkward around his crew now that he'd had lunch with them once. Which was probably nice for them since Jack covered his nervousness with ferocious shouting.

"Pretty healthy bribe, too, and we all know what that means . . ."

He pulled out an envelope and started around the circle. "Trader Joe's gift cards for everyone."

The snickers turned into cheers and even Mari laughed now. Trader Joe's was the universal drug of choice for biologists, who were all obsessed with healthy snack food.

Hotaka grinned. "It was her solar-oven brownies, right? I swear those brownies made me find religion."

"Nirvana," Lisa agreed. "One step above heaven, those brownies."

Rajni poked Hotaka. "Mari doesn't need brownies to charm anyone. Girl's plenty sweet on her own."

Mari rubbed at her arm, uncomfortable with the other woman trying to make her feel better. "You guys . . ."

Fortunately, Marcus stopped in front of her at that moment and gave her a reason to look away.

"I needed to speak with you about something else," he said. "Wyatt's boss, Rod, stopped by to lodge a complaint. Said you were being too hard-assed about enforcing the rules."

Her blood clamped to a stop in her veins. "I can explain—"

"No need." Marcus passed her not one but two Trader Joe's gift cards. "Keep up the good work."

And slowly, cautiously, a smile began to creep onto her face.

A low hum of conversation welled up from the coffee shop around Mari, the air-conditioning a blessed relief. She sipped her chai and half groaned at the explosion of spicy, creamy flavors on her tongue.

Lisa laughed at her reaction. "They make it from scratch here. Better than sex, am I right?"

About a thousand times better, in Mari's experience, though she would have expected the other woman's experience to be a bit more positive. "I'm telling Marcus you said that."

"You do and I'm never bringing you here again."

"Okay, I take it back." Mari snuggled into the deep, worn cushions of her armchair.

"You better. This place is my favorite." Lisa relaxed into her own chair and exhaled. "What does it say about us that a coffee shop visit is the most luxurious thing I can remember doing in, like, forever?"

"That we enjoy the simple things," Mari said, because she knew it would make Lisa feel better. Privately, she wasn't sure a drink that cost $3.87 a cup counted as a simple thing, especially not when it tasted like something fit for sultans and fairy tales. She really shouldn't have spent the money, but after the other bios were so nice to her the other morning, she was riding high enough to follow through on her long-ago coffee date invite. Lisa always made such an effort to include her and ask her out to do things, and it felt like turning a corner in her life to have a sort-of-almost friend again. She hadn't had close friends since she and Brad moved away from the town where they'd grown up, when he took that job in Wisconsin.

"Well, we'll have to think up something even better than coffee shop time soon, because you deserve a treat after all those weeks on Wyatt's crew." Lisa shuddered.

Mari took another sip to cover her frown, and her complicated feelings. She hated Lisa thinking that Jack was some kind of cruel beast. But at the same time, she got a little guilty-selfish thrill from the idea that someone—that anyone—would be concerned about her. Enough to worry that she was being treated well at work.

And a very practical, secret part of her was aware that it would be easier to continue to get assigned to Jack's crew if everyone thought she was doing it out of pure generosity. It would hardly be professional if people knew she didn't just get along with the foreman she was supposed to be monitoring, but that it was starting to be . . . more. At least on her side of things.

In a lot of ways, it would be to her benefit to let her coworkers see him as a villain, but it sat all wrong to let Lisa insult Jack. After all, who would stand up for him, if she didn't?

"Lisa," she said, putting down her drink. "He's not like you think. Really not at all. Outside of work, he's quiet, a little unsure of himself."

"And how much are you seeing of him outside of work? Is he following you around at that motel?"

"No!" Mari snatched up her drink again, annoyed with herself. She could never manage to express herself right. With Brad, she'd always managed to say things just the way that would upset him. Now, she couldn't even explain to her coworker that a man was good, not bad. Maybe she should give up on English and learn sign language.

But no, that wasn't entirely right, because she did seem to be figuring out the key to communicating with Jack when no one else had. He didn't just follow the rules now, he watched his own men for her. God help the one who forgot to check under all sides of his tires for a tortoise. She'd seen the men check their tires three times in a row, just because they weren't sure if Jack had seen them doing it the first two times.

He just hadn't understood the reasons behind the rules before. Once he'd seen the animals, how hard they were to find, how they really were everywhere out there once you knew how to look . . . she suspected he might like animals even more than the biologists did. He was certainly good at catching them. The other biologists had just approached him wrong, throwing out orders that made no sense to him and backing them up with citation tickets.

Of course, she couldn't say that to Lisa, who had been one of the biologists who had failed to get through to him.

Mari took a breath, determined to try to be better at communicating. "It's not that he's following me around at the motel, at least not unless that stupid crane operator is bugging me."

"Creepy Ricky?" Lisa curled her lip. "Hate that guy. Rajni swears she's going to kick his ass someday. I really don't like that he's living at your motel."

"I know. But if he comes within half a mile of me, Jack runs him off. Anyway, you know I cook on my camp stove in the parking lot most nights, and Jack sometimes works on his motorcycle after work. So I see him there."

She let it stand at that. It had only started happening after that night she came to watch TV with him. And she didn't mention that she usually pulled her truck out and angled it so he and his bike would have a little shade to sit in. Or that he seemed to enjoy the scent of her cooking so much that she fed him most nights. For all his protesting that he'd already eaten and he'd just have "a little bit if she had too much," he gobbled up whatever she gave him. Usually so fast that she thought maybe it had been a long, long time since he'd had a home-cooked meal.

"He knows how to work on motorcycles?" Lisa winced. "Damn it, that should not be sexy."

Mari wasn't sure how it could *not* be sexy. Especially with that careless man bun of his, and how a strand always fell loose over his face when he was concentrating. And how when he swiped it back, sometimes he left a dark streak of grease over his cheekbone or his brow. It was hard not to notice, sometimes, that under the scowl and the hard hat, he was ruggedly pretty. Could that be a thing, rugged *and* pretty? Maybe he'd invented it.

Either way, it was good for her health because, lately, Mari cooked a lot more often than she microwaved ramen.

"He's pretty funny, actually. He'll catch himself swearing sometimes now, when he's around me, and he'll substitute it, but it's still totally hopeless." A smile tugged at her mouth and she leaned forward and lowered her voice. "Like the other day, he banged his knuckles when he was tuning the bike and shouted, 'c—' well, you know, the C word. And then he broke off halfway and said, 'Fuck, I mean. Sorry.'"

Lisa burst out laughing. "That's Jack Wyatt for you. Even his clean version is dirty."

"I know, right? And he blushes." Mari knew she shouldn't be saying all this, but it was too cute, really, not to share. "I think he's the only man I've ever met that gets *more* shy the more you get to know him."

"Shut the front door." Lisa shook her head. "I don't believe it. Blushing?"

"Yeah, when I say anything that could be taken as dirty. Or if I say anything nice. Or—" She stopped, because there were a ton more times when he blushed, but if she listed them all, she worried Lisa would read too much into it.

The other biologist leaned forward, amusement playing around her eyes. "That is completely adorable. I never saw him blush any of the times I worked on his crew. C'mon, give me more dirt on Wyatt. I love it."

Mari bit the inside of her lip, debating. It was risky, but part of her was bursting with stories about him, especially the one from last week.

"Okay, but you have to promise not to tell Marcus, or anyone where it could get back to Jack, because he'd be mortified."

Lisa nodded, sitting back in her chair. "Men hate it when they're cute."

Mari paused for the scream of the espresso maker to quiet, then said, "Anyway, so we got to talking about hunting the other week, because he's a hunter, too, I guess. Bow hunting, even," she couldn't help but add, but then rushed on because the pride in her voice was too apparent. It wasn't as if she had anything to be proud of there, since it was his accomplishment. "And he's a tracker, too, a damn good one. Remember that juvy I found two weeks ago, the forty-five millimeter?"

"That *was* a crazy-good find."

A forty-five-millimeter juvenile tortoise was smaller than the size of a ChapStick, and harder to locate than a unicorn, since they lived in a desert riddled with thousands of rat-sized burrows they could disappear into.

"It wasn't my find, though, because Jack found it. Well, kinda."

He'd noticed her frowning at some eggshell fragments on the

ground and said, "Somebody peeled an egg for lunch, big fucking deal. Biodegradable, ain't that what you call it?"

But when she'd explained the difference between the fragments of a chicken egg and a tortoise egg, how one was matte and one was a touch shiny, and the curve was different, round not ovoid, he'd looked thunderously impressed.

"You can tell all of that by a piece of shell?"

She'd ducked her head, feeling odd about the praise, but had to nod. She had followed it quickly with the confession that she couldn't find the hatchling tortoise who'd crawled out of the egg, but was worried that it must be nearby.

"The soil was rocky around the burrow," Mari explained to Lisa, "so there were no tracks and I thought it was hopeless. Except he just started looking around and didn't stop." It was the only time she'd seen him get off task at work, and after ten minutes, she felt really bad about distracting him. But he had picked up the tiny tracks a shocking distance away, and followed them to a bush, where he proceeded to scowl himself half to death because they seemed to vanish into thin air.

"But you found the tortoise?" Lisa asked when she got to that part of the story.

"Yup. Deep in a rat hole, could just see one tiny foot around the corner with a flashlight. I had to dig him up to move him because he was right on the edge of the site." Mari flushed with pleasure at the memory.

Jack's face when she'd held up the baby tortoise on her gloved palm . . . she'd never seen reverence like that outside a church. She had felt like the world's worst villain when he asked, in a halting whisper, if he could hold it, and she had to say no, since he didn't have the proper permit.

She should have just let him. She had extra gloves and no one would have known. Jack wouldn't have hurt the newborn, no matter how soft its little shell was at that stage.

"How did he know how to track a tortoise?"

"Just by watching one walk, *once*," Mari scoffed, and shook her head. "Anyway, that wasn't the story I was going to tell you—that happened on another day. Get this."

It had been the tracks that started it. She'd noticed him staring down at the ground, and had come over to see what had caught his attention.

"The hell kinda tracks are those?" he had asked, still frowning.

She'd glanced down, and froze. The tracks in question were a round, slight depression, like someone had taken a large serving bowl and pressed the bottom maybe an inch down into the sand. Except, of course, for the texture, which was more like hammered copper. At one side was a dash of darkened earth.

She had understood his confusion. The first time she'd seen one, she didn't know what to think of it, either.

She'd glanced away and cleared her throat. "They're tortoise tracks."

"Don't they teach you tracks in biologist school? It's all about how they move, what shape of foot they've got. Turtles don't walk nothing like that."

"I didn't say they were walking."

He had looked at her.

To the ground.

Back at her.

"You saying they was fucking?"

Even now, just at the memory, Mari couldn't contain her laughter. "He just couldn't get it," she gasped out, stifling her giggles into her hand. "How the tracks ended up making a circle."

"Oh God," Lisa said.

"So then, of course, I had to explain. That tortoise shells are so rounded that when you balance them on top of each other, they get a little, well, wobbly."

Lisa covered her face, blushing and half laughing, half moaning. "You didn't. Did you have to do the dance?"

"Well, no one ever gets it if you don't do the dance!"

They both knew exactly what she meant. How every thrust unbalanced the male tortoise and he'd stagger to the side, scraping for purchase with his back legs while the female staggered along with him, both their feet stomping down the ground as they went round and round, trying to get the deed done. The thrust-and-stagger dance was a hilarious staple of the public education portion of explaining mating circles.

"Tell me," Lisa gasped, both of them laughing so loud now that the other coffee shop patrons were turning to stare. "Tell me he didn't notice the wet spot."

"Oh, he so did." Mari choked on her laughter, remembering.

Jack had eyed the patch of wet dirt at one end of the mating circle. "Uh, that ain't . . ."

"Oh," Mari had said, her face red with the effort of restraining her giggles, her voice a little strained as it threatened to burst free. "It definitely is."

"My God," Lisa wheezed, holding her stomach. "You've got to trade me assignments next week. I *have* to see his face when I tell him about ground squirrel orgies!"

Mari poked her in the arm, whispering, "Why don't you say 'ground squirrel orgies' a little louder, Lisa, my goodness, we're in public!"

But a smile still brightened her face. Because maybe, just maybe, she'd won Jack another ally.

14

Ain't Clumsy

"Hello, stranger." Mari looked up from the camp stove she was setting up on her tailgate, and smiled at Jack as he got out of his truck. "I was starting to think you had a hot date tonight and you weren't coming home."

He ducked his head, scratching the back of his neck. "Ran by the store," he mumbled.

"Well, you missed a lot of good stuff. Room 102 came out, realized the vending machine was out of cheese puffs, and kicked a couple of new dents in the bottom." She pulled her cutting board out of one of her milk crates, flattened a cereal box on top, and lined up her vegetables on it.

"Ain't pot legal in California now? How does that kid still have a job?"

"I get the idea he's a little cheaper than the dispensaries." Mari started chopping, a smile teasing at her lips at the memory. "After the vending machine, one of his customers stopped by and 102 apparently forgot to collect money for his, um, goods, so he chased the car out to the road. The running, of course, would have worked better if he'd tied up his pajama pants first."

Jack looked disturbed. "Fall clean off?"

"Yup."

"Kid ever buy him some drawers after the last time?"

"Thankfully, it appears he did."

Jack's mouth lifted at the corners. "Did he fall?"

"Nah, just stumbled a little. Does it make me a bad person that I was hoping for a full face-plant?"

"Nope. Idiot deserves it, if he can't keep his damn pants up. Or get money for his drugs." Jack grabbed a piece of carrot and popped it in his mouth, then froze. "Shit, you probably needed that, huh?"

"I think one slice of carrot probably won't be the gateway to starvation. Hungry, huh? I was going to pull the truck out so you'd have some shade to work on the bike, but I can just start cooking, if you'd rather."

"Don't have to feed me." His boots scuffed at the parking lot. "I don't need any shade, either. Be fine."

"What, did you finally run out of things to fix on that bike? As long as you've spent working on it, I was starting to think that thing was one step away from the grave."

Jack glanced at the motorcycle in its normal spot between their trucks. "Ain't nothing too wrong with it. Just gives me something to do after work that ain't sitting on my ass."

She peeked up at him, a smile playing around her mouth, but didn't tease him further because she didn't want him to think she didn't like him keeping her company while she cooked dinner. She looked forward to that more than she probably should. Not that it was official, or a plan or anything. They just sort of . . . naturally ended up there. Every day.

It was nice for her because she didn't have to define it or think about what she wanted, when their paths just accidentally crossed. Besides, somehow it was easier to talk to Jack when her hands were busy. Better than at work, when he always had a hundred things to do and her eyes needed to be on things that weren't his bare arms. Even now, the sun-browned muscles stretched the short sleeves of his shirt and . . .

Mari cleared her throat and banged a frying pan onto her camp stove, then grabbed an olive oil bottle out of a milk crate and dashed a bit over the bottom of the pan. "So how'd it go with Joey? How badly did he fail his first apprentice evaluation tonight?"

"Bad."

A laugh slipped out of her at his staccato answer, but then it turned to a frown as she turned on the burner. "Oh no! He's not fired, is he? He's been trying so hard to impress you this week, I'm surprised he hasn't brought you flowers yet."

"You think he's *trying*?" Jack crossed his arms and leaned against her truck.

She told herself a dry mouth was normal in the desert.

"I think that kid would drive the forklift better if he was drunk," Jack said. "He climbs like he just got those feet put on his legs last week, and he damn near bolted Kipp to the tower on Tuesday."

"Yes, but he's getting really fast at organizing the tower pieces."

"You on his side or what?" Jack scowled at her, his Good Mood Scowl.

"I'm just the bio!"

"Uh-huh."

"Don't have an opinion at all."

"Right."

"I mean, it's not an *opinion* to point out that he's an apprentice and he's there to learn and of course he wouldn't be perfect yet. Those are just facts."

"Facts."

"In *fact*, one could even argue that a lot of mistakes made at this point might help him later, because he'd know exactly what not to do." Mari leaned over the tailgate to reach into the drawer under her bed.

"Exactly, because he already did everything you ain't supposed to do. He fucks up any harder, those towers are gonna start unbuilding themselves."

She frowned at the contents of the drawer, then sighed.

"Quit. I didn't fire him."

She glanced up. "Quit what?"

"Sighhhin'." His accent drew it out into three long-suffering syllables. "Didn't fire the kid. Gave him another damn chance, so don't even start about it."

"No, it's not that." Though "that" was enough to make her bite the inside of her lips against a smile she knew would make him blush and grouch even harder. "It's just that I forgot to get more curry powder, so this stir-fry is going to be really bland, and I know you're hungry, and now I feel bad."

"Ain't gotta feed me," he protested, turning to his truck.

"What, and bear the guilt of eating delicious stir-fry while you microwave three packs of ramen noodles in your room? Well, semidelicious now that I was an idiot and forgot to buy spices and—"

"Ain't an idiot!" The bark came out a little louder than their conversation, and her brows went up a touch.

"Okay, sorry."

He came back from his truck, frowning harder. "Don't apologize. Didn't mean to snap. I'm just saying of course you don't wanna go to the store for one thing after a long day of work. Doesn't make you an idiot, makes you human. Store's twenty extra minutes up the dang road. Here." He passed her a little paper sack that rustled as the wind caught it.

"What's this?" She waggled her eyebrows. "You been buying from Room 102?"

He snorted. "I keep giving that apprentice one more chance, people gonna think I'm smoking something for sure."

She laughed, opening the bag. "They'll think you have a big heart and he has a lot of promise and you're *training* him, which is what apprenticeships are all about." She took out a little plastic spice shaker. "Curry! Jack, how did you—"

"Said last night you used the last of it and needed more." He shoved his wrist across his mouth, still mumbling. "Had to go to the store anyway, so I just got some. Sorry if it's the wrong kind. It's yellow, like the other one you had. Might not be the right yellow."

She squeezed the little spice container, her vegetables starting to sizzle in the skillet as she smiled at him, unable to help herself. "You bought me spices."

Now he was really blushing. "Ain't a big deal. I'd better go shower. I've got plenty of food, don't make any for me." He was already hightailing it for his room before he finished grunting the last sentence.

"Too late!" she called after him. "I'm afraid I've gone and spilled too many vegetables into the skillet already. I'm so clumsy, you'll just have to take some off my hands."

His door was already closing, but she grinned when she heard the last words he shouted over his shoulder.

"Ain't clumsy!"

The wind was hot today. Blasting and scouring everything it slapped past. Sucking all the life and moisture out of the whole damn world. Even so, Jack had lingered outside with Mari as she cooked, polishing his motorcycle while the wind coughed dirt all over it.

He didn't mind. Gave him more to do.

He'd eaten two helpings of whatever sweet-spicy vegetable curry thing she'd made, too. After she told him she'd made too much and that sort of thing didn't keep well, and she really had plenty to spare. He'd have gobbled it off a sidewalk without a spoon, it tasted that good, but he asked for seconds partially just to buy time. They ate dinner together just about every night now, but she hadn't yet been back to his room. They just watched the same shows on two sides of the same wall.

He was hoping she'd ask first.

But she hadn't. Just smiled and cooked and listened to the little he had to say. Didn't even seem to notice the wind.

And then dinner was over, they were standing in front of their side-by-side doors and he was out of time.

"Do you wanna . . . I mean . . ." He reached up to yank at his hair, some of it already blown out of whatever thing he'd stuck it back in. He was gonna have to hack it off soon.

At the moment, though, it wasn't his hair he wanted to take scissors to. More like his own fumbling tongue.

"Think you might wanna—"

"Stop listening to your TV through the wall?" She brightened. "Absolutely I would. My place or yours?"

He'd already unlocked his room before she got to the second sentence. He stopped, the door hanging open just enough to see the socks that he'd forgotten about on the rug. "Maybe yours'd be nicer."

He hadn't been sure she'd want to come back, after how awkward he was last time. But she was already following him, so he had to open the door the rest of the way, kicking the socks behind it as she flipped on his light.

"Pfft. I'm sick of my room. I like visiting yours. Unless you left your pornos out."

He choked. Twitched. Recovered. His pornos couldn't be out because they were hidden on his ancient laptop in a folder entitled "Tax Paperwork Shit."

"They still make pornos that come on tapes? Or DVDs, I guess?" Fuck, he felt old. He was on the light end of his forties, but the first porno he'd ever seen was one of those booths where you plugged in a quarter for a peep show. He and Leroy had snuck in and got it started with stolen tokens from an arcade.

Tokens were worth nothing, pretty much just like the pair of brothers had been, too. Shit, he didn't even know where his brother *was* these days. He'd show up again sometime, though, probably talk Jack into doing some stupid shit like he always did. It was hard to say no to the big brother who'd taught Jack how to use a can opener so he wouldn't have to stay hungry until his dad remembered to come home.

Jack stopped, realizing he hadn't heard whatever she'd answered about pornos. He rattled the key in his palm, the plastic diamond-shaped marker on it loud against the brass key. This motel was as old as he was. Everyplace else had switched to those credit card keys.

He thought he heard Mari suck in and let out a big breath, but she plopped on his bed all casual like they'd known each other since they were twelve. "You want fix-it-up or buy-it-new?"

"Fix it," he said, pulling the rubber band out of his hair and fisting it back into a fresher kind of wad.

Mari's eyes flicked toward him once, then twice.

He frowned. "Can watch the other channel, if you'd rather."

"No, this is good." She grabbed a pillow and stuffed it behind her shoulders, cozying in. "I like seeing all the old, broken places made nice again."

"Yeah." Something in his gut lifted when she said that, and he tried to remind himself that he wasn't one of the broken things she liked.

No matter how much he was starting to wish he were.

15

Homemaker

If someone had asked him a year ago, Jack would have said he didn't have a thing in common with a tree hugger. But a year ago, he didn't know Mari.

It turned out that Jack and Mari both liked to hunt, loved the smell of the wind, and finished the day at the same embarrassingly early bedtime. He figured out the last of these after a week of TV nights together, when she fell asleep sitting up next to him at seven p.m.

He dialed down the volume on the television and held very still. He wasn't certain what he was supposed to do. She'd be easy enough to lift, but he didn't have a key to her motel room. He could take the floor, but he didn't think she'd want to actually *sleep* in his room. Even if, arguably, that was what she was currently doing.

Pretty much everything he could do seemed like it was assuming too much, so Jack just sat next to her, too nervous to even get up to piss, until he dozed off, too.

Not that he knew that's what he was doing until he blinked awake again sometime probably hours later.

She was already awake, looking at him with her head tipped his way and resting against the wall, her eyes so, so serious that he had to ask, "What?"

He didn't clear the sleep out of his voice, so it came out all husky and rusty as fuck, and then she started to cry.

Not all the way. Just tears glittering over the surface of those crystal-blue eyes enough so he was horrified, ready to apologize for anything and everything, before she started to explain.

"I just . . . fell asleep."

"Uh-huh," he said. Dumbly, but he wasn't sure what else he could say about it. That he didn't mind? That he *liked* it? He couldn't imagine much that'd sound creepier to a woman.

"I, um . . ." She cleared her throat, gave him a wobbly smile. "Haven't been very comfortable around other people, most of my life. Especially since my divorce."

He didn't know what he could have possibly done to make her feel *comfortable* around him. He'd yelled his fool head off at her a few dozen times. Changed her tire, as if that counted for shit. Ate up all her brownies. Overall, he thought, he had a pretty crappy score. He hadn't even given her the good pillow to lean against tonight.

"Probably just because I'm being boring company," he attempted. "Tired tonight, ain't got much to say."

She shook her head, blinking the tears away as a smile spread brilliantly across her face. She looked radiant, even half-asleep after working long hours in a filthy desert with an even filthier crew of guys.

"I don't mind," she said. "I guess I just like this." She gestured between the two of them, then at the TV, playing another ridiculous home improvement show he probably shouldn't even like but did.

"Yeah, me too," he admitted, feeling like he was shucking off his pants right in front of her but not knowing how else to answer the confession she'd just trusted him with. Not sure how to believe she'd entrusted herself to him, in some small way. He smiled sheepishly. "Guess we're pretty lame, huh?"

She snorted a laugh and smacked him on the arm. "Speak for your-self, buddy. I'm enjoying my glamorous and cosmopolitan evening of Budweiser and HGTV."

"Nah, I just mean it's funny that I build shit all day and then come home and watch people build shit."

"I'm even worse," Mari said. "I *watch* people build stuff all day, and then come home and do more of the same."

He liked the way her eyes crinkled at the corners when she smiled. Liked it so much he forgot to answer. Why would women get Botox to get rid of wrinkles when they could be so damn cute?

"Why do you like them?" she asked softly, and he startled, afraid he'd spoken aloud. "The shows, I mean?"

The shows, right.

"Guess I like the houses. Better than anywhere I've ever lived." And now he sounded like the penniless redneck he'd been for most of his life. *Way to flirt, Wyatt.* "What about you, why do you like them?"

"They look like places where families could be truly happy. Like homes. I was a homemaker, you know." The smile that flickered across her face didn't last. "Back when I was married. That's just what they call it, when you don't work. But to me, it meant something." Her fingers picked at the blanket between them. "Brad had a bad child-hood, with a dad who was drunk on religion and mean with it. He never felt safe or relaxed at home, and I wanted that for him. Wanted to make a nice space for him, but I failed." Her voice cracked a little and her lashes swept down.

"How'd you—I don't think you—" He was pretty fucking sure it wasn't her who'd messed up, but the words tripped out of his mouth too fast, not in the right order.

"No, I did. I tried, really, my hardest, but I couldn't." A tear slipped down her cheek, and she dashed it away. "I'd always forget something or screw something up, upset him. I didn't have any other friends, couldn't seem to make any after we moved. Brad was the only one who would stick with me. He loved me and he'd forgive me, every time. He hated his temper but . . . when he lost his temper, it was really *lost*. He couldn't find it at all, never could rein it in." She took a long, quavering breath. "I left because I realized he was going to kill me, and I didn't want him to go to jail."

She leaned back against the wall and looked up at his ceiling. The tears kept falling from her eyes, but she'd wipe them away as soon as one escaped. She was even an apologetic crier, like she was afraid it might bother someone.

"Sometimes I wanted to live, sometimes I didn't," she said matter-of-factly, "but I didn't want him to go to jail just because I couldn't make home a nice place for him."

The room was so quiet that the sound of commercials playing made him want to crawl out of his skin. He smashed down the button on the remote, turning off the TV.

"What are you . . ." He stopped, sputtered, tried again. "You can't think that—that it was you. Who made him do those things. You didn't make him do shit."

"I know, I know." She glanced at him sideways with glittering eyes and a self-deprecating smile. "But I didn't understand then. Not until after the divorce when the medical bills kept coming. Kept coming and coming for all the things he did to me. When he was right there in front of me, telling me he'd always forgive me, no matter what I did . . . I was so twisted up then that I couldn't see the truth. It wasn't until he was gone and I saw the numbers that I realized he was wrong. It wasn't my fault. I wasn't a perfect wife, not even close, but he didn't *have* to hurt me like that. He . . . shouldn't have hurt me." Her voice faltered, like even now she had to force those words out as if she were lying.

She dried her tears, dropped her hands back to her lap.

"Anyway. I guess that's why I'd rather live in my truck now. I could never make a home, but in a truck, nobody expects that. Can't have roommates or even neighbors because I wake them up screaming." She dodged a rueful glance at him. "Sorry."

Jack swallowed several times. His throat was thick, and the inside of his chest felt black. It hurt, like the bruises he'd worn all his life—as much a part of him as his hair color. But this wasn't his story. It was hers.

Still, he knew a thing or two about it, because that story had been told in a lot of places. For a lot of years. By a lot of different people.

"Mad guys are always mad," he said. "Ain't you. Ain't nothing. Just is. Best thing to do is get the hell out of Alab—get outta there, I mean."

Her eyes paused on him for a moment before she nodded. "I know. I did. Just . . . sometimes it feels like I'm still making the decision to leave, all the time. And sometimes"—her voice dropped to a thread barely above a whisper—"I forget and I stay. In that place where it's my fault, because it feels too much like a lie to believe anything else."

His hands shook and he pressed his fists into his thighs to keep them still, searching for some way, any way, to make this better for her.

"You make that job site more like a home than anyplace I ever lived. Baking everybody brownies." He tried to smile at her but it was a small, shy thing. "Think the guys try to get me to yell at them lately because they know you'll feel bad. Give them brownies."

She laughed. "Oh dear. I'm sorry."

"What? Why are you sorry?" It came out louder than he meant it to. "All those times I yelled at you, at work. Wasn't because you made me mad."

"I think I did," she said drily.

"No. Just a habit I got into." He ground his teeth, his fists pressing hard enough into his legs to bruise. "Shouldn't have. Not to you. Not to a woman."

She tugged at her wrinkled pants, and Jack tried to ignore how the digital numbers on the clock across the room stared them down. They had to be up again for work, too soon.

"My foreman when I started out. His name was Vernon." He hadn't known he was going to tell her until he was already speaking. "He always spoke real quiet. Didn't tell people what to think. Got them to figure it out themselves. Died, uh—" His voice disappeared on him and he had to cough and start again. "Fell. Slipped trying to save an apprentice who was fucking up. Safety rope was old. Gave out." He looked at the ceiling, pinching his fingers over his eyes savagely when he realized they'd begun to water. "His way was good, for making you a man. Turning your brain on. But for a lot of guys, they didn't learn fast enough. Got Vernon killed."

He dropped his hand, looked at Mari.

"When I got my own crew, I didn't speak quiet. I told them when they screwed up instead of waiting for them to figure it out; didn't have any patience because Vernon had too much. Quiet and gentle don't get shit through thick skulls, and thick skulls is all we've got, out on the job site."

"Oh, Jack," she whispered. "I get it, okay? I've known for a while why you are the way you are at work, and I never thought that—"

"No," he cut her off. "Wasn't your fault. Wasn't ever your fault when I yelled at you. That was me, being stupid. Letting my temper lead me around just like my brother used to let his. Ain't gonna happen again." His face twitched into a grimace. "You probably heard that a lot from your ex, but there ain't nothing else I can say now. Just got to show you I mean it, and I will. I will."

She laid her fingers on the back of his wrist, her touch like cream in a way he could never have explained but felt perfectly.

"Jack," she said, and her voice made his name sound so damn good. "You're nothing like my ex. And I'm not afraid of you. I never would have come to your room if I was. And I never could have fallen asleep beside you."

He reached for her, but halfway there he faltered, not sure where he'd intended to touch her. Where it would be good, gentlemanly. He wanted to comfort, not to push his luck or make her uncomfortable, but nothing in his life had trained him how to comfort.

Mari rescued him seamlessly, leaning just a little forward so his fingers slid along her neck, cupping the slender base of her head. His thumb just brushed her earlobe, and it was so soft it made him tremble with the responsibility of being allowed to touch something so precious.

He bent forward, his heart thundering in his ears, and touched his lips to hers. Soft, because that's what she made him feel. Safe. Like everything, with her, was different.

And it must have been, because she kissed him back.

16

New Leaf

It could have been very awkward. When Jack got done kissing a woman light-years out of his league, at the workingman's midnight of ten o'clock, and they were alone in his room with no distractions to break the ice.

Taking it further than a kiss wasn't an option, not that she knew that.

But Mari made a joke. She made it easy. She made it okay.

Long after she went back to her room, Jack stayed awake, thinking about Vernon. About Leroy and Brad. About Mari.

Mostly what he decided was that she deserved better than what he'd been.

"We're having a meeting."

It was what Jack grunted the next morning at work when the men piled out of their trucks. Mari's eyebrows shot up. A meeting? Jack didn't believe in meetings. He said if there was anything that wasted more time than meetings, it was managers. And if there was anything that wasted more time than meetings and managers, it was probably a politician.

As if that weren't weird enough, he looked at Mari after he said it. "You can come, too. If you want."

"Let me just get my umbrella for the rain of frogs," she said, but he didn't hear because he was already striding over to a spot in front of his truck's bumper. Joey and Gideon heard, though. The apprentice snickered, and the older lineman gave her a quiet smile that somehow made her feel understood. She'd talked to him only a few times but he'd always been kind to her, and she got the idea that he saw a whole lot more than he ever let on.

Mari hurried to get into the circle of men, because Jack was already drawing a breath to speak.

"I been a dick."

He faced his crew squarely.

"It's dangerous work out here. You ain't pushing pencils, and ain't nobody there to catch you if you fuck up. I buried two men in my years on this job, and I ain't looking to bury more." He cleared his throat. "I don't need to tell any of you the other reason I push you so hard, but I will because y'all know it anyhow. I want you to understand that I know it ain't right. Rod's son, Junior, is running the crew down the row from here, and he's so lazy he'd hire somebody to lift his own peck—" He glanced at Mari and broke off. "His daddy wants us to pick up all his slack because he's slow. But y'all ain't slow, for as much as I've ragged on you. Shouldn't have done that. You're good, hard workers. 'Cept for you, Kipp, and you're out on your ass next week if you don't shape up."

The mustachio'ed man made a squeak of protest, and Mari held her breath so she wouldn't start laughing. He really did spend more time talking than he did working, but she got the idea that none of his other foremen had ever called him on it.

Jack pointed at Ricky. "And you're fired."

Mari blinked, swapping a stunned look with Gideon as Jack walked away, then tensing when the crane operator chased after Jack.

"What the hell, man? You can't fire me without cause. I'll have the union all over your ass."

Jack didn't stop until Ricky grabbed his shoulder, and then he whirled, throwing the other man's hand off and backing him up with one, ferocious movement. "You been inappropriate with the women, and I've seen you do it myself. Already lodged a complaint with the union this morning. Now, you can get off my job site, or I can do what I should have done before and punch the shit outta your face. You pick."

Jack glared, his face so close to Ricky's the other man was forced to breathe only the air that had already been expelled from Jack's lungs.

"The ladies didn't mind, or they would have complained, not you." Ricky smirked. "Maybe you're jealous of my effect on the fairer sex, hmm, Wyatt?"

Jack was going to hit him. It was absolutely clear in the shift in the air, even before she saw his biceps flex and his arm draw back. And she leapt forward to stop him.

In her mind went the lightning-fast debate of *They're not talking about me, I'm not important enough for men to fight over but who else could they be talking about and how many women are on construction sites anyway?*

"I minded," she said.

Breathlessly, uncertainly. She sensed something behind her and glanced back to see the whole crew had moved in. To back Jack up, or her? Somehow, it felt like both, and it steadied her.

She met Ricky's eyes, and his additional inches of height somehow felt puny. "I minded," she said again, calmly.

"Well then, you should have said something. I was just joking around, didn't mean anything by it, didn't know you'd be so uptight and—" Ricky started sputtering, and Gideon stepped forward and took his arm. It looked gentle, but he must have thumbed a pressure point or something because pain spasmed across Ricky's face and he rushed to keep up with the pace Gideon set when he led him away.

"I'll give him a ride back to the yard" is all Gideon said.

"Lose him off a cliff before you get there, if you want," one of the other men muttered.

Mari flushed, the hairs on the back of her neck rising in a rush of goose bumps. She hadn't known any of the men objected to Ricky's behavior. What he'd said in front of Jack, and the other things he'd tried or said, when no one else was looking, she thought the other guys just sort of . . . agreed. Or didn't care. Or a mix of both. She hadn't thought they might be keeping silent for the same reason she had, which was that she was shocked and wasn't sure what to say, and then the moment had passed.

Only when Ricky was most of the way to the truck did Mari think to let go of Jack's arm. He scowled at her. "That idiot needs a decent punching."

"And I think you would have delivered a more than decent one," she said, smoothing his sleeve. "But for today, you're his boss, and if he has a violence complaint against you, it will undermine any complaint you made against him. Tomorrow, you can punch him."

She tried to keep her hands from shaking at the thought of going back to the motel today, when Ricky might be moving out, or might not move out at all. Jack would be there, and Lisa and Marcus, if she asked them to. She swallowed down the tightness from her throat.

She wasn't alone. Not today.

Ricky's truck was gone by the time Jack made it back to the motel, and he wasn't sure whether to be disappointed or relieved the crane operator hadn't stuck around to pick a fight. Mari was quieter than usual through dinner, and they watched one and a half renovation shows together before she glanced over at him and said, "It was brave today, what you did."

He tried to think what she might be talking about, so the silence lagged long before he said, "The meeting?"

"Yeah."

He snorted. "The hell is brave about how long I been running my crew like some kind of asshole? Like Rod."

"*Not* like Rod."

The show came back on and they subsided, letting the screen soothe the crackle of tension between them. The couple on the show were installing some exotic stone counters, which were blue.

Jack could not see the sense in blue counters.

When a Swiffer commercial blasted on, Mari's hand covered his on the remote control and pushed the mute button.

"It was brave," she said, "because most people can't stand admitting when they're wrong."

Swiffer gave way to Brawny paper towels.

Brawny to Home Depot.

They were halfway through a Mr. Clean animated commercial when he said, "Your ex was an asshole and a coward, yeah. Still don't make me brave for trying to turn around before I end up anything like him."

His thumbnail picked at the rubber buttons of the remote, accidentally changing the channel so he had to change it back.

"My daddy—" A tickle came into his throat so he had to cough before continuing. "Daddy had the same temper. So did my brother, who mostly raised me. Ain't no excuse." He turned to her, and she was already looking at him. "If I can't hold it together—if I don't get better from here, I want you to change crews."

By the time they looked back to the screen, the show was on again, and it had moved from countertops all the way to bathroom mirrors.

———————

Mari stayed late that night, all the way past the new episodes and into the reruns. Well past the point when they could get a full night's sleep before work the next morning.

They didn't talk much, though their glances bumped into each other more and more. He brought her a plastic cup of tap water, because neither of them seemed much in the mood for beer.

When she finally scrubbed her hands down her jeans and forced herself up from the bed, he was off the mattress after her in a second, walking her to the door like he always did.

She wanted this night to end differently. For something, *anything* in her goddamn life to end differently. It made her ache to think of his words earlier, the determination still so palpable in the room that she could feel it quivering in the air.

He wanted to be someone she could trust.

Not someone who lost his temper, or lashed out in anger. Except in the short weeks she'd known him, he'd already done both. He'd hinted just enough at his history that she knew it was like hers, like Brad's. She was drawn toward him like he was something she'd been craving, but she knew better than to trust her instincts, because she remembered.

She remembered the intensity with which she'd loved Brad in high school.

She remembered the night they got engaged, when he came to her with a tiny diamond ring, tears glittering in his eyes and a knees-bent vow sworn on all the years that diamond had existed that he'd never be like his father, or her stepfather. They would make a life away from all that violence and drama.

She wished she could say the diamond had been a cubic zirconia, only a year or two old, but it had been real. As had been his vow, every day until he broke it and probably even after. He'd *meant* it, and she'd known him well enough both then and now to realize that.

It's what made it so hard to leave him. He never meant to hurt her, but he always did. He wanted, so badly, to stop. And yet he couldn't. Hadn't. She still wasn't sure which.

It was part of the reason all her mail went to a PO Box and she lived in a truck. She knew Brad. He wouldn't let her go. As long as she rejected him as unfixable, he'd hate himself for it and her, too, and he'd look for her. And if he found her, he'd kill her.

Mari reached out, her heart in her throat, and her reckless hand landed on Jack's chest, crinkling his T-shirt when her fingers clenched.

"You're a good man," she said hoarsely.

In his eyes, it was clearer than words that he didn't believe her.

She wanted to be right about him, that he was a good man. She wanted to shake the part of her that warned that a guy with a temper and an abusive father was a risk she couldn't afford to take twice.

She wanted, just one time, for things to be different.

17

Pizza Doesn't Lie

Mari did not like this coffee shop as much as she remembered liking it when she'd come here with Lisa. The chandelier draped with Mardi Gras beads seemed kitschy instead of funky. The air scented with vanilla and freshly roasted espresso was heavy and cloying instead of delicious. The chairs looked butt-sprung and sagging instead of soft.

It might just be her. Even her clothes itched today, like nothing in her life fit the way she wanted it to. Not long ago all she wanted was to be left alone, and now she wanted so many things. A job that didn't change every few weeks. A home and friends. And a man who unfortunately didn't mix with a single one of those other goals.

A man she wasn't even sure she should want.

She caught Rajni checking her expression and she threw what she hoped was a reassuring smile at her companion as they waited in line. It was the first time she'd invited the other woman to do something outside of work. She was relieved Rajni had agreed, and was hoping that buying her a coffee would at least somewhat make up for the fact that she needed a favor, even though she and Rajni weren't really close enough for her to justify asking.

Mari couldn't stop thinking about last night. That awful, sick feeling in her gut when she met Jack's eyes at the doorway of his room. He had looked ashamed and maybe even guilty. Even in the midst of that, she'd loved the way his eyes always came back to her face, as if there was nothing else worth seeing in the room. He was like that when they were outside, too, with the whole sky and world rolling out around them for miles.

She trusted Jack. She would have sworn on her life that no matter what the situation was, he'd only move to protect her, not hurt her. Except that the reason she was hiding here, with no permanent address and a motel room under a fake name, was because she'd trusted another man with her lifelong vows. That one couldn't even obey her restraining order, much less resist his compulsion to break her body into pieces.

She knew, as deeply as you could know anything, that she made the wrong choices when it came to men.

Which was why she was here.

She and Rajni both ordered the homemade chai, and she slid her card across the counter to steal the tab while controlling her own grimace, because Rajni had ordered the medium, which was an entire $1.20 more. Her budget was pitiful enough that even that was a blow, but it was worth the investment to get her advice. Making the right choice now might save her from a new medical debt to duplicate what she already owed.

"Thanks for the chai, but what's the deal with the coffee date?" Rajni asked, grabbing their cups and giving her a sideways look as she led them to a table by the window.

Rajni was an ex-marine that Mari had worked with on two or three other jobs. She had her Toyota truck rigged to the hilt, with solar panels to run a little refrigerator, and custom cubbies built in under her bed to hide both weaponry and more outdoor gear. She'd done the wiring on the fridge herself, and customized the .45 pistol she hid beside her bed. Most people would say that was too high a caliber gun for a woman's small hands, but they hadn't seen the custom grip, or the steadiness of her siting gaze when she practiced on targets way out in the desert.

Mari was a lot more interested in Rajni's history with boyfriends than guns, at the moment, but both were informed by the undercurrent of efficiency and utter lack of bullshit that always characterized Rajni.

"Well, I probably owe you a drink for something, and this chai is something special."

"That's no lie. For a free cup of this, I'd date plenty gnarlier people than you." She winced. "Not that I don't like you. I just meant, I'm not usually your first choice."

Mari shifted, at a loss. Had Rajni wanted to spend more time together? They got along, yes, but Lisa was the only one who sought her out. She just assumed no one else really wanted to get closer, but maybe they were assuming the same thing about her.

"I'm . . . almost as rusty at the friendship thing as the dating thing," she said. "But not because I wouldn't like to spend more time with you when we're not digging up burrows or scrambling around on scree slopes."

"Understood." Rajni smiled, her smooth, light brown skin setting off the red of her tank top so the simple cotton looked runway-flashy.

The other biologist had never had a stitch of trouble getting a boyfriend, which was part of the reason Mari had chosen her to ask for dating advice.

"Lisa told me you had a pretty rough divorce," Rajni said. "Takes time to get back to real life after all that."

Mari's fingers twitched. She had suspected Lisa wasn't the best at keeping secrets, but it still hurt to hear that she'd been telling her private business to the other bios.

"Yeah. It does." She toyed with the sleeve on her cup, shifted in the too-soft armchair. "I need some advice, actually. And Lisa . . ." She tried to think of a kind way to say that Lisa was a little gossipy, and more than a little judgy when it came to the construction workers, who she mostly saw as Ford-truck-driving, climate-change-denying jerks.

"Let me guess, Lisa hates the guy."

Mari stopped, her eyes widening. "How did you know it was about a guy? And how did you know—"

"Lisa hates all the guys. She's got a real good one, and somehow she still manages to be cynical." Rajni crossed her legs, amusement playing around her lips. "And you're all fidgety today. It's-about-a-guy fidgety. Color me officially curious." She leaned forward. "C'mon, please tell me you need advice because the sex is too kinky or something."

Mari smiled. "Would I need advice if we'd gotten to that stage?"

"Depends on how kinky is too kinky."

She broke out laughing. "Well, let's hope I'm having those problems next week."

"What problems are you having this week?" Rajni's face was still alight with amusement, but her eyes were kind, and Mari realized the other woman had been trying to break the ice.

"How much did Lisa tell you about my ex?"

"Enough that if I see him, he isn't going to walk away in one piece." Rajni smiled. With a lot of teeth. "There's a whole lot of desert out there. A man could get lost."

Mari glanced down. She was warmed by the reaction, but at the same time, she felt off-balance knowing other people knew.

A hand gripped her arm, and she flinched before she realized it was Rajni. "Don't do that," the other woman whispered. "Please. Don't look down like it's you that should be shamed by what happened."

Mari cleared her throat, covered Rajni's hand with her other one. "I know. I do. I'm still figuring out all the space between knowing and *knowing*, though. It's hard. That's why . . . this new guy."

She looked up, all her fear flooding into her face. The lack of bullshit in Rajni's personality was a blessing and a curse, because she wouldn't lie to you, but you couldn't hide anything from her, either.

"I don't know if I should do this. With him, I mean. I can't tell, for sure, if it's a good idea."

Rajni squeezed her arm one more time before she sat back. "And you were hoping I might know?"

Mari nodded, wincing, but sort of smiling. "It's a lot to ask. And I know you don't know him, but you . . . All your boyfriends have been so great. Jorge's the sweetest, and Leo—he looks intimidating and he can seem crude, but truly he's got a heart of gold behind that mouth. You must have better Man Radar than I do to have dated both of them."

Rajni shrugged off the compliment and fell silent for a moment, appearing to really think it over as she toyed with her chai. When she finally looked up, her gaze was steady. "I know this. A man never slaps you just once. He might say it's once, but if it's once, it's all the times."

"I don't think he would hit me," Mari backpedaled, "but—"

"But you didn't think your ex would, either."

Mari exhaled a laugh at Rajni finishing her sentence. It wasn't funny, but there was something relieving about being understood so thoroughly. Even if it was humiliating, too.

Rajni crossed her legs. "One and done, that's what I say."

"But you just said they never hit you just once."

"They don't. Once and I'm done," she clarified. "I'm gone before they get to twice, no matter how much they beg."

Something changed in the other woman's expression and Mari struggled not to let her surprise show on her face. She could hardly believe something like that had ever happened to tough-as-nails Rajni, but there was a time when people would have said the same about her. Bad relationships could happen to anyone, she supposed.

She cleared her throat. "But what about until then? Before the once, I mean. I don't want to . . ." She trailed off. "I can't go through all that, not again. Just to end up in the same place."

Brad and Jack both came from violence, both raised their voices when they got angry. But surely not everyone with a temper was dangerous and not everyone from a rough childhood became violent. She hadn't. Rajni seemed to be saying that there were warning signs that could go either way, but the line got drawn at hitting. Mari remembered arguments when Brad would throw things at her, and decided that the line got drawn before intimidation, too. It was violent, doing something like that, even if the lamp didn't hit you. But there had to be more, a way you could tell without just waiting for the first slap.

"What does your gut say about Jack?" Rajni asked.

"That he's right." Mari looked up, her answer having come out before she thought it through. "Not just that I trust him but that something about him . . . is just right for me."

Rajni smiled, and didn't say a thing.

"But what if I'm wrong?" Mari asked again, her chai slowly going cold between her palms because her stomach was in too many knots to drink it.

Rajni sipped hers, unperturbed. "All right. Let's say you two lovebirds get a pizza, but you ordered the medium, not the large. You get to the last slice of pizza and you're both still real hungry. What does—"

"He'd pretend like he didn't want it so I could have it," Mari answered before Rajni even finished the question. It was no test at all, considering how many times Jack had lied over the growl of his own stomach about not wanting to have any of whatever tailgate meal she'd cooked that night. He was never hungry until she'd eaten her fill. And then he'd say, "I'll just have a little if you're gonna throw it away otherwise."

"Then he's a good man," Rajni said simply. "Pizza doesn't lie."

The next day, Jack did not show up for work.

This wasn't just a first, it was sort of like a seismic event. According to the biologist grapevine, it had never happened before in project history. At lunchtime, Mari had asked the crew what was going on. They had spent the morning stumbling along under the guidance of Gideon, who was the second-in-command but knew nothing because Jack had trusted him with nothing. The crew looked around at each other with a lot of wide eyes and guilty looks and didn't say a word. Joey opened his mouth and got an elbow to the ribs for his trouble.

Mari didn't know what the heck was going on.

Rather unfortunately, she'd had a breath-holding, courage-scraped-up plan for tonight that involved a pizza. She was pretty sure the plan wouldn't go so well if Jack had the puking flu or something. She was also pretty sure that if she didn't do this tonight, she'd die alone with thirty-two cats because she'd never have the confidence to make a move on a man again.

Which is why she found herself knocking on Jack's motel door that night with a cardboard box in hand that had shot her food budget for the whole week, freshly showered with her good jeans on.

He opened it with his man bun swinging crookedly, his T-shirt inside out and all twisted from where he'd just thrown it on. A change in his scent hit her, bringing with it a flinch of memory, and it took her an extra second to identify it and blink in surprise.

"Are you . . . drunk?"

He leaned against the edge of the door, stumbling a little when it swung farther open. "It's what Wyatts do," he growled, voice as dark as his bloodshot eyes. "Can't hold a job, can't hold our liquor. We fuck up, we get drunk, we do it all over again."

She stood there, as off-balance as if she'd stepped into a dream. He had a beer sometimes, but never two, even on the rare times when she'd gone for a second. She'd never seen him drunk, or hungover, or even heard him talking about being either. "Except . . . you never screw up at work. And you don't get drunk."

"Is that a pizza?" He frowned at the object in her hands. "Why do you have a pizza? You never buy anything."

"It's a long story," she mumbled, hesitating.

She wasn't sure if she should invite herself in and try to sober him up, or stay well away from whatever train wreck suddenly had him missing work in favor of the half-empty bottle of Jack Daniel's on the table behind him. But instead of shouting or throwing things, he gave her a mournful look.

"I got you something," he announced. "Prolly shouldn't give it to you now, though, because I'm wasted."

That tickled a corner of her mouth into turning up. "Is that so?"

He dropped his head against the door and groaned. "Stupidest, saddest present in the world. Jesus."

"You got me the saddest present in the world?"

He opened one eye. "Why're you smiling?"

"Because that sounds kinda cute, is all."

He closed his eye again. "Ain't cute. Ain't fucking cute." He groaned again, deeper and rougher. "Stupid. Shoulda drank myself to sleep before you got back."

"Then I wouldn't get my present."

He didn't move. She made her decision, sweeping past him into the room. She deposited herself at the table and plunked the pizza next to the whiskey. Brad had done a lot of things when he was drunk, but he'd never bought her a present. Those had only usually shown up . . . after.

"Better give it to me now," she announced. "You'll just be more embarrassed once you sober up."

He gave her a narrow look. "Why aren't you yelling?"

"Maybe I'm working up to it."

He looked at her.

She folded her arms and looked right back.

He shut the door, staggering a little. "Okay, I'll give you the present. But only because I'm drunk. And if you don't like it, you gotta get drunk, too, so you forget about it."

"That seems fair."

He rummaged around in the nightstand beside the bed and came up with a plastic bag, hesitating. "Ain't wrapped."

"I imagine I'll live."

He crossed the room with three too-quick strides and shoved it into her hands, grabbing up the bottle and twisting off the top, then giving it a side-eye and setting it back on the table, untouched.

Brad never would have left a bottle of whiskey alone until every bit of liquid was wrung out of it. Her shoulders eased a little more.

Mari unwrapped the bag, taking out a textbook-sized paperback. On the cover, it read *Treatment Workbook for Survivors of Domestic Abuse.* Her fingers tightened, and a shiver worked itself through her whole body.

"Said you didn't have no friends, back home when you was married," Jack said abruptly. "Said you couldn't make no home for your husband. Ain't you. Says right here in the book."

He leaned across the table to tap it with one thick finger.

"People married to assholes that thump on them, those guys always tell you it's your fault, not theirs. Keep you home so nobody sees what they did, tell you they'll take care of you so you don't have to work. My mama didn't have any friends, either. Nobody to take her to the doctor when she started having fainting spells, nobody to find her when she passed out and hit her head too hard. That's how my daddy wanted it. Didn't want nobody to see the things he did to her."

She looked up at him with her eyes starting to water. "You read all that in the book already?"

He snorted. "Fuck, I had all day."

She watched him, trembling as she tried to decide if she should say anything about the terrible way he'd lost his mother.

Jack slung himself back into his chair, his arms loose and carelessly hung over the armrests as his eyelids drooped. "You should have seen the guy who sold me the book. Skinny little asshole, glared a hole right through me. If he could have found a reason to take my book in the back so he could spit in it, he would have."

"Why would he think that you'd buy that book if you were the one hitting people?"

Jack reached over and rapped the book with one knuckle. "Chapter seven, that's why. Apologizing. They're always sorry after what they did. Real sorry, too, not even lying. Doesn't change anything. Just like a drunk, gives up drinking every morning and takes it up again every night."

He looked at the bottle on the table and seemed to remember he still held the cap. After a moment, he leaned forward and screwed it back on with slow, clumsy fingers.

"My daddy was like that. Bad enough that when my big brother was eighteen, he left and took me with him." Jack grunted. "But Leroy had my dad's temper. At least he just used his fists, not whatever else happened to be lying around."

She winced. No wonder he had such trouble trusting anyone. He had thought his brother was taking him away from all the violence, only to find out he turned on him, too. She waited, hoping the silence was gentle enough that he knew he could tell her more, if he wanted to. But she wasn't exactly surprised when he didn't go on.

Mari laid the book down in her lap. Careful with the pages, because she suspected that if he'd needed understanding so badly he'd skimmed half of it in a day, she probably needed to read it cover to cover. "You want to tell me why you weren't at work?"

"Don't worry about it. Just temporary suspension, anyway. Boss won't fire me, or he won't have anybody to do his boy's work. He just wants me to know his dick's bigger, that 'no' ain't a word I get to say to him."

Mari stiffened, ugly goose bumps running up her spine.

Jack sniffed carelessly, half-asleep already. "This docks me a couple days' pay. It's what he was after, costing me money. I don't give a shit."

"Is this about the bird nest?" She remembered Jack saying his boss wouldn't forget, that he'd find a way to get even with Jack for disobeying. "Rod told you to do something to it, and you said no—that's why you were there, wasn't it? So early in the morning." His boss couldn't do that, could he? It was against the law. But of course he wouldn't say the suspension was because of the nest. He'd make up some other excuse to punish Jack. Her face fell.

Jack frowned at her. "Don't look at me like that. Didn't hurt any baby birds."

"I know you didn't. You wouldn't."

"Humph," he grunted. His eyelids slipped down again, and she realized he was going to fall asleep right in his chair and leave the entire pizza for her to eat herself. While she read the book he'd bought her because he didn't know how to heal her but wished he could.

Mari set the book aside and slipped to her knees in front of his chair. She touched his hand. "Can you do something for me?"

"Yeah. Whatchu need?" He yanked himself straight, blinking sleep out of his eyes. "Sorry, got jawing on, didn't ask if you came by because you needed something."

She patted his knee. "Drink some water, have something to eat. And get some sleep, okay?"

He nodded, but just to be sure, she went to the bathroom and put some water in his travel mug. She filled it all the way to the brim, her chest feeling just as full.

She brought the cup to the nightstand and then extended her hand, pulling Jack to his feet when he took it. Without much fuss, she maneuvered him to the bed and left him sitting on the edge, blinking up at her when she retreated to pick up her new book and his bottle of booze.

"You gonna pour it out?" he asked, not sounding like he cared one way or another.

"Nah. I'm going to drink it." She smiled. "I love whiskey, and from the looks of it, I handle it better than you do."

Jack rubbed his hands over his face, sending his hair even more chaotically askew as he mumbled something that sounded like "fuck, that's sexy."

"I'll see you in the morning." She flicked off the light as she opened the door. "And, Jack?"

"Mmm?"

"Thank you for the present. I like it, more than you'd probably believe." She hesitated for a second, and then closed the door.

She left the whole pizza behind.

18

Tomorrow

It was still early when Mari got to her room, with a bottle of whiskey in one hand, and the *Treatment Workbook for Survivors of Domestic Abuse* in the other. She took off her shoes, poured herself a drink—paused, then poured it a little stiffer—and began to read.

On the other side of the wall, Jack was quiet. She wondered if he'd gone to sleep already, or if he was over there feeling self-conscious about his gift. She hoped not.

By the second chapter, she'd forgotten all about him. By the third, she was reading as fast as she could, her fingers starting to go numb where she gripped the pages.

It was all there, laid out like a map of every year of her adult life. The honeymoon phase, when their connection had been positively electric and she thought no one had ever understood her like Brad did. The slow buildup of angry arguments that moved to criticism, then intimidation, and then violence. The way he always had some excuse why he didn't like this friend or that friend of hers, reasons why she needed to cancel plans. Why he wanted her to spend all her time at home, just with him. Why, after her car accident, he never wanted her to go back to work, because he wanted to take care of her.

She had thought she didn't have friends anymore because she was kind of boring, and because she always seemed to upset people. But here in this book, she could see how Brad would set up situations for her to fail, then blow up at her when she inevitably did. How, after she and Brad moved, her friends used to say they'd called, but Brad swore they hadn't, and she'd believed him and thought they must have been lying.

In chapter seven, she saw how his genuine remorse and fear that she'd leave him would lead to his apologizing and being so painfully sweet. Just like he'd been back when they first got together. How that would make her feel guilty and ungrateful for being angry with him.

Suddenly, her whole life made sense. Everything that had felt confusing and shameful was laid out in this book. Bullet points one after another because it had never been that her luck had gone bad: everything traced back to things Brad had done to her. Ways he'd manipulated her and isolated her and hurt her because of what was wrong inside him.

The book knew everything because it wasn't just their marriage, it was a *pattern* that happened to other people. No different than if she had diabetes and she'd finally gotten a diagnosis that explained every strange thing her body had been doing.

It was a revelation, and at the same time, it was deeply, harrowingly humiliating.

How had she become such a cliché that this book could explain her whole marriage without the authors ever having met her?

It wasn't as if she'd been following a manual, or even that Brad had. They'd just been groping along the best they knew how in an imperfect world. She knew neither of them had meant to end up here on that day so long ago in the courthouse when they promised to love and honor each other.

She poured another whiskey, thinking about it. Staring at the dent in the wall where so many people had opened the motel door just a little too hard. There were other people, just like her. So many that books were written about them, for them. So many people, ashamed of what their lives had become and all thinking they were alone.

The whiskey burned her throat, and tears slipped unnoticed down her cheeks. But when she blinked, the wall in front of her came back into focus, and she remembered that Jack was on the other side.

It had happened to him, too. He'd recognized things about her, because he'd been through the same. It pierced her straight in the heart to think that he'd been hurt, back when he was helpless and small. He'd had no one to bring him a book to explain what was happening to him.

She wondered if he'd eaten the pizza before he went to sleep. She hoped he had.

Out of respect for the fact that he'd given her the book, she began to read again, and that's how she found chapter nine.

Because of the manipulations of your abuser, you will begin to doubt your own instincts. Anything that is healthy or in your best interest will trigger doubt because for so long, your abuser taught you that none of that was allowed. Now, what's right will feel *wrong.*

The book dropped into her lap as memories overwhelmed her. And they weren't of Brad.

"*You're a good man.*" It's what she told Jack.

Neither of them had been able to believe it when she said it, because for so long, it had been beaten into them that they were stupid, and careless, and didn't deserve any better than the hell they were living in. That day, neither of them had read chapter nine, "Self-Sabotage."

Mari closed the book, capped the whiskey, and set her alarm clock for very, very early.

The glowing numbers 4:45 were the first thing he registered, before he heard another soft knock on the door and remembered what had woken him in the first place. Jack threw off his blankets and staggered to his feet. He was fully dressed in wrinkled clothes, his head that particular kind of heavy and fuzzy that told him he'd been drinking. No nausea or headache, though—the water and pizza Mari had left him had taken care of that. Embarrassment crawled through him at the thought that she'd been so kind while he'd been such a mess.

He shoved a hand back through his hair and caught a thumb on the rubber band dangling from his half-unraveled bundle of hair. With a curse, he yanked it free and finger-combed his hair once or twice more to get the worst of the knots out. It fell over his bleary eyes, and he knew he must look like boot-kicked shit, but he didn't dare take any longer to open the door—just in case it was Mari.

He didn't want her to think he didn't want to see her.

"Yeah, hey, hi," he said as he pulled the door open. Stuttering because it *was* her: blue eyes as clear as truth and silver-highlighted hair shining in the light above his door.

"How are you feeling?" she said, her voice pitched so soft and low that even if he'd had a pounding hangover, it wouldn't have hurt his ears.

"Hey, listen, I'm sorry about last night," he rushed out. There was a good damn chance she'd come here to tell him she never wanted to see him again. If it was the last thing he ever got to say to her, he needed it to get said before she walked away. "It was pushy as shit, giving you that book and whatever else I said last night, I'm sorry for it. I'm a jerk when I'm drunk."

"No," she said. "You're not."

He was already starting in on more apologizing, but that stopped him, confusion freezing his tongue.

"When most men get drunk, they get cocky, or mean. You were . . . sweet." She took a big breath. "Jack, would you like to go out with me?"

He stared at her.

"On a date," she clarified. "That kind of going out."

Hey, you want this? It had been Leroy's favorite game, to dangle whatever Jack wanted most, to promise it was hidden somewhere, and that if he could find it, he could have it for good. Jack was good at finding things. He learned to follow the prints his brother's shoes made in the dirt of the forest, or even the scuffs in the dust of the kitchen floor, so he could figure out where the prize was hidden.

Of course, what he found wasn't always what was promised. Sometimes it was a spider, or a snake. A Polaroid of Leroy's butt. One very memorable time, he'd found nothing at all, but Leroy had followed him out into the forest and swiped his pants, running away laughing that Jack would have to walk home bare-assed or not at all.

But no matter what game Leroy ended with, first—always first—Jack had to admit he wanted something.

Jack blinked away the memories because Mari's face was starting to fall while he just stood there, processing her question. He tried to swallow but his dry throat stuck hard, so he simply nodded. Slowly, as if that would keep the ax from falling now that he'd set the old game in motion.

Hey, you want this?

He nearly flinched, but no hand reached out to smack him. Instead, she smiled. Just a tiny bit at first, but when his mouth twitched a small curve in response, hers softened even further. They stood for a long moment, the question asked and answered but neither of them willing to part just yet.

Jack coughed to clear his throat and swiped some of his scraggling hair out of his face. "Tonight?"

Her eyes widened. Shit, that was too pushy.

"Or tomorrow. Next week's fine. Or this weekend," he blurted, watching her face after every option, trying to decide what she wanted him to say.

"Maybe . . . tomorrow?" she asked. "I'd love to go tonight but I need time to dig up something to wear."

To wear? Ah, fuck, what was he going to wear on a date? All he had was work shit and maybe a T-shirt.

"Tomorrow, yeah," he said, before she could think he was turning her down. He'd figure out the clothes thing, even if he had to drive all the way to LA. He worked a lot and spent very little. He had plenty to cover some clothes, even if he factored in whoever he'd have to bribe to tell him what the hell kinda pants and shirt women liked these days.

Mari touched the doorframe of his room, her fingers curling softly as she smiled. Goose bumps rippled all under his slept-in clothes, and he had to pull his gaze away from her hand, yank his mind away from wishing it was him she was laying her hand on.

"I, uh . . ." He wanted to say something nice. Something to get her to smile and make her understand he was happy that she'd asked him. Jack did not, however, know what that might be. "Tomorrow," he said stupidly. "Yup."

Mari's eyes sparkled, crinkling at the edges as her smile grew. "Tomorrow," she agreed.

It was Jack's new favorite word.

19

Priceless

Tomorrow was not turning out as well as Jack had hoped.

He'd used his second day of suspension from work to buy clothes for his date. Though it had been weird to try shit on and gauge how it looked in the mirror, instead of just checking the sizes and heading for the register. Today, he'd showered right after work, and now he was struggling with his hair.

At some point along the way, it'd gotten pretty long. When it started growing into his eyes, he bought some rubber bands and had been using them to fist it out of his face. However, he'd never tried to put it back in a way that looked presentable.

A long ponytail made him look like a beatnik, and combing it into a high ponytail looked absurd. When he left it down, it flattened helmetlike to his head, then poufed out at the bottom like a skirt. He was starting to get a headache from glaring at himself in the mirror, and the front of his hair kept tangling in his eyelashes and tickling his lips.

Grunting, he snatched up his multi-tool from its battered leather case. He grabbed the bunch of his hair that was the most in his way and put the knife to it. Unfortunately, he used this blade all the time and it was due for another sharpening. After half pulling, half cutting a chunk of his hair out, he put away the knife blade and flicked out the saw blade. This snagged and yanked at his hair, but it cut a damn sight faster.

His vision cleared, and Jack was feeling a whole lot better about everything until three fistfuls of hair had been hacked away and he looked up.

Most of his hair hung long, in its helmety-frizzed-end style. But now a fringe of shorter hair covered his forehead and stopped in a ragged line just above his eyebrows. He looked like a girl.

An ugly girl.

Jack slammed the saw blade onto the bathroom counter. He'd known he was going to blow this date in a spectacular fashion, but he thought he could at least handle the getting dressed part.

Throwing a glance at the clock, he ground his teeth. Would an hour be enough? It'd have to be. He leapt for his keys.

Jack wasn't coming.

Mari left her motel curtains open once she was dressed so she could watch for his truck to pull in without having to peek through the gap. She sat on her bed because it had the best view. Sitting down would wrinkle her borrowed dress, but she couldn't very well stand in the middle of her room waiting for him to show up, or she might cry.

Waiting for a man was bad, but waiting for a man while wearing a bright red dress was infinitely worse.

Especially when she had to keep reminding herself not to bite her lip or she'd end up with Valentine's-red lipstick on her teeth instead of her lips.

Why had she worn lipstick? She wasn't the kind of person who could pull it off. Lipstick on an older woman just looked desperate, as Brad had said when he'd found her one last stashed tube.

Mari pushed off the bed and went to the bathroom, ripping out a tissue to wipe all the bright, hopeful crimson off her lips. When she was getting ready, Rajni had trimmed the last dye-stained two inches off her hair and it was all her natural color now, swirled up in a twist that she had thought made her silver streaks look pretty, almost like highlights. Now they just felt conspicuous.

How awkward it must be for Jack, trying to avoid a date when they lived in the same motel. He couldn't claim he'd had to stay late at work when they'd left together an hour and a half ago. At least he had the grace to stay away so she could pretend to believe whatever flimsy excuse he came up with. She wasn't sure she could have stood it if his truck were parked out front and she knew he was just on the other side of the wall. Ignoring her.

She threw away the stained tissue and sagged against the sink. After reading chapter nine, she'd been so sure that her doubts were just self-sabotage. That the steady safety she felt in Jack's presence was the correct instinct and the rest was all just baggage from Brad.

Seeing him be a little bit nervous around her had even boosted her confidence until she was bold enough to ask him on a date. She hadn't bargained for them being good enough friends that he would feel bad about telling her no and would agree just out of politeness. Apparently all that nervousness had just been because he could tell she was more into him than he was into her and—

A flurry of knocks came on her door, pausing and then slowing down to a more measured pace in the middle. She frowned. Ricky had moved out after Jack fired him, and none of her bio friends would show up here without calling first. Could Jack have been in some kind of accident?

An image of his green truck with a smashed-in grille flashed through her mind, and she hurried for the door. When she opened the door, she didn't recognize him at first glance. Once she did, she couldn't look away.

"Sorry. Wasn't gonna be late, but tried to cut my hair and fucked it all up. Haircut place had a line and couldn't—didn't wanna . . ." He threw her a desperate look. "Shoulda done it yesterday, not made you wait."

His man bun was gone, and his face appeared achingly naked. This new style set off the height of his cheekbones, the sharpness of his jaw, and the catlike tilt of his hooded eyes. With his long hair, he'd been ruggedly handsome, but without it, he looked like something she should paint with tiny brushes onto high-quality canvas.

"Yes, right! I mean, it's not a problem. The cut is . . . well, goodness." She swallowed. Sweet God, she was babbling and she couldn't even look him in the eye. Even in the air-conditioning, a sudden flush of heat had prickled sweat across her body so she could feel every inch of her skin. How could a dress this short be so stifling hot?

He grimaced. "You still wanna go? I could wear a hat."

She blushed. He'd clearly noticed how distracted she was by his appearance, but when she made herself meet his gaze to apologize, he appeared as embarrassed as she felt. She realized he'd jumped to the wrong conclusion.

She reached out and squeezed his arm. "I liked your long hair, but the new haircut looks great. Just in case the stuttering didn't give that away." The stunned look on his face whooshed all the nervousness back out of her body.

She understood this man. They were born-again virgins at dating, to be sure, but she wasn't wrong about him. She was going to stop giving in to all those slippery little impulses to believe the worst.

Chapter nine, she reminded herself.

She scooped up her purse—borrowed, so tiny her room key practically poked out the top, but sleek and cute—and smiled at him. "Ready?"

He nodded, and looked anything but ready as he led the way to his freshly washed truck. She couldn't stop stealing glances at him. He wore a black button-down shirt that was loose at the tucked-in waist but stretched perilously tight across his muscular shoulders, plus jeans so new they still had the shelf-folded creases.

"We're not taking the bike?" she teased, just to break the ice.

"You want to?" He paused next to it, his expression lifting in a way that looked almost boyishly pleased. "Probably need pants, though." Reluctance entered his voice, and when she glanced at him, she caught him looking at her dress.

"Next time," she said, and his gaze flew up to hers. She smiled.

The drive lasted awhile, because he took her all the way to Palm Springs, the biggest town for miles.

They didn't talk much on the way over, but they did share a laugh when they noticed they were both humming along to an old Eagles song. His seat covers were creased oddly, and she snapped a price tag off the edge, then tucked it into her purse before he noticed, so he wouldn't be embarrassed. She felt a little bad that he'd bought clothes and truck seat covers just for the date, but it put a light, kind of whirly feeling in her belly, too.

By the time they got to the restaurant, she had to search for her borrowed high heel on the floorboard. Without thinking of it, she'd kicked one off and curled her leg underneath herself like she had the last time she was riding in his truck with him.

There was an awkward moment when he came around to open her door but she'd already opened it. She paused and nearly closed the door again, and in the end she hopped down while he just stood there, his hands sort of half-up like he wasn't sure what to do with them. She laughed it off, her cheeks feeling rosy from more than the desert heat, and took his arm to go inside even though he hadn't offered it.

His arm was scorchingly warm through the fabric, and she wondered if black hadn't been the best choice for the Mojave Desert. It looked incredible on him, though, so she didn't say a word. Maybe men could suffer for their looks now and again, too. God knew her borrowed heels were pinching something fierce. Rajni had gone begging for her to every woman on the project, and Ivy was the only bio who'd packed a dress that fit Mari. Unfortunately, her feet were a half a size smaller.

At the door of the restaurant, she remembered to wait so he could open it, but was distracted as soon as they walked inside. The place was all slick black marble and open spaces, the glasses on the tables these strangely space-age cylinders of flawless crystal. Blue lights spotlighted each table from above, and techno music pumped through the restaurant, just low enough to allow for conversation.

The waiter looked barely out of high school, with a haircut that might very well have cost more than Mari's last paycheck. His smile was slick as he ushered them inside. "Welcome to the Blue Loft, and thank you for dining with us this evening. Party of two?"

"Got a reservation," Jack growled, his voice so rough it came out sounding like an insult. "Wyatt."

"Ah, yes, of course. Your table is all ready for you." The man retrieved two leather-bound menus and led the way.

When they got there, Mari slid gratefully onto the backless bench seat and eyed the vase in the middle of the table. It had a . . . flower-like object in it. Made of some supershiny swoop of plastic. She was studying it with so much puzzlement she missed the waiter's leaving. Jack already had his menu open, so she did the same. And then nearly had a cardiac event.

"What's wrong?" Jack asked.

Her eyes jerked up. Had she let out a sound? "Ah . . . just . . . are you sure this is where you want to go? I'd be totally happy to go someplace different, if you were," she hurried to add. "We haven't ordered yet."

His scowl lines deepened. "Nothing on the menu look good?" He flipped a page, scanning. "It sounds weird, but it's pretty normal stuff under all that. They got steak. We can go, if you want. Just, this was the place the internet said was the best food."

"The internet?" she said faintly.

"Yeah, you know, the food place thingy. Yapp."

"Yelp?"

His scowl was moving into grimace territory. "Yeah, that one. Bunch of people said the food was good."

"Right, but the only thing I could order in good conscience is the side of guacamole," she said in a low voice, with a rueful smile to let him know she was in this with him. "I don't need anything this fancy, honestly."

His facial expression was now something best described in terms unique to extreme weather warnings. "Order what looks good. I make a decent wage. Don't spend it all on drink or boats or anything. Can afford it. It's fine."

"I know you don't," she teased. "That whiskey I lifted off you wasn't even that good."

"They got better whiskey here, if you like that. Saw it online." He flipped to the next section. "Here it is. Back page. I'm driving, have what you want."

She hesitated, and he looked at her squarely for the first time since he'd picked her up.

"Wanted to take you someplace nice."

Mari hoped this dress was tight enough to contain her, because she was definitely melting, starting with her heart and spreading to every other part of her.

"Okay," she whispered, and Jack's gaze dropped to her lips. It kept doing that. There must still be a lot of pink left from the lipstick she'd wiped off.

"Here." He took her menu and pulled the parchment page of entrées out of the leather holder, then ripped it all the way down the edge.

Mari squeaked, her hands flying to her mouth. "Jack! What are you doing?"

He wadded up the line of ripped-off prices and stuck it in his jeans pocket, then passed her menu back. "Get what you'd like. Rest of it doesn't matter."

Mari took it with a wobbling smile that threatened to burst into something embarrassingly large. Instead, she cleared her throat and made a concerted effort not to spend the whole date beaming at Jack.

"So, Kipp seems like he's really gotten his act together this week. I think you finally scared him into working more than he talked."

"We don't have to talk about work stuff," he said. "We can talk about, uh . . ." He glanced around. "Whatever."

She reached across the table and laid a hand over his. It gave her a double thrill: the touch of his skin and the rush of her own boldness, made even more intoxicating by the fact that she was pretty sure he didn't mind.

"Jack. All of this is lovely, but you don't have to be a different person just because we're on a date. It's enough that you wanted to come here with me, that you wanted to make this . . . something." She hesitated, but nothing could feel like a risk right now, with this man. Not when she had his seat cover price tag hidden in her purse. "It already feels special. It makes *me* feel like something special."

His head was ducked, stealing glances at her with his fingers tense against the table as if he expected her to lift her hand to smack his any second. But he didn't hesitate at all to say, "You are." Then the tiniest of pauses, just enough to let her know he thought twice before he said, "Especially in that dress. Look beautiful. Are beautiful. Even not in the dress." His eyes flew wide. "Not like . . . *not* in the dress. Just, like, in anything. Is what I meant."

"Um, thanks," was all she said, utterly losing the battle against beaming.

The waiter chose that moment to come back, and Mari gave Jack's hand a quick squeeze before she took hers back.

"Oh no, what happened to your menu? I am so sorry, ma'am, just let me run over and get you a fresh copy."

"I'd rather stick with this one, if it's okay," she said, laying a protective hand over her torn, price-less menu. "I like this one better."

20

A Ride

Mari had discovered something. The more she smiled, the more Jack talked.

So, by the end of dinner, her face was fantastically sore, her ears hummed with the sound of his gravelly southern drawl, and she'd barely remembered to eat a bite of her delicious citrus-infused chicken.

". . . And I was so sure I was gonna impress my big brother by bagging a deer before hunting season ever started. Instead, I ended up mowing lawns all summer to pay the vet bills on the neighbor's Jersey cow."

She burst into giggles, covering her mouth in chagrin. "Oh, I shouldn't laugh, I shouldn't! That poor cow."

Jack grunted, taking a slug of his soda. "My aim was a whole lot sorrier than that cow was. Barely managed to wing her."

"Was that why you switched from hunting with a gun to a compound bow?"

"Nah. Just shot one at the range once and it fit my hands." He paused, his eyes flicking up to hers. "Felt right."

She was disappointed when the waiter interrupted—again. She'd never been so frustrated by good service. He picked up the already paid bill and told them to take their time, but Jack shifted in his seat like he felt bad occupying a table when they were already done. It was the same probably baseless guilt that always nagged at her in restaurants, so she smiled and said, "You ready to go?"

"Uh, sure," he agreed, but somehow she got the feeling he meant just the opposite. No matter how much she told herself it made her a petty, egotistical person, she liked that very much.

Jack kept his eyes on the road as he drove them home. The waiter had looked at him a little oddly when she ordered wine and he insisted on a Coke, but Leroy had wrapped two trucks and a borrowed Honda Civic around assorted trees in Alabama. He swore he drove better when he had a little drink on, but Jack had never seen him wreck a car sober. Then again, Jack had rarely seen him sober.

Either way, he wasn't taking the slightest of risks with Mari in his truck. He only let himself glance over when he stopped at a light. She was messing with the radio, her shoes kicked off and legs curled up underneath herself. That dress of hers was about the best thing he'd ever seen: red as tulips and nipped in at her tiny waist, flared out so it danced around her knees. A neckline that swung round and came down to a little point, showing the slightest shadow of cleavage that was driving him to distraction.

He loved the dress, how it made her look like a pinup with her long, elegant neck and upswept hair. But he loved even more how she always curled into his truck seats as if she were home on the couch. It made him especially glad he'd covered the duct-taped rip in his seats before she rode in his truck. The whole drive over, he'd been stiff with worry that she'd move the wrong way and hear the duct tape crinkle. It was still under there, still trashy as shit but veiled for the moment.

Now . . . she looked so comfortable he somehow doubted she'd recoil even if she did hear the tape crinkle. They'd had a whole conversation about that once, about how they both liked old trucks better than new ones.

"It's green," she said.

He frowned, wondering how she'd known he was thinking about his truck.

A horn blasted behind him, and he came back to the moment with a jolt, hitting the gas. So much for attentive driving.

The motel came up too damn soon, its dusty facade looming like his father's scowling face, announcing the end of any fun being had.

Jack took as much time parking as he could get away with, then busted ass to get around the truck so he could open her door this time before she did. She waited, and accepted his hand to hop down. She made the jump lithely, but wobbled the landing in her red high heels. He touched his other hand to her waist because their joined grip didn't seem like it was going to be enough to keep her from rolling her ankle.

She looked up, but she didn't move away. Jack had been debating for the whole date if it would be okay to kiss her when they got back. Mostly, he'd decided it was safer not to try. But now . . . now he wanted to so damn bad.

He leaned in. So slowly it could have been awkward, just so she had every chance to push him away or even change expression to indicate this wasn't something she wanted.

She held perfectly still. Her eyes were so warm and soft, with this light to them that looked a little like hope.

At some point he lost track of the caution of leaning in and kind of melted in around her, his hand cuddling farther around her back as their lips came together. Her mouth was just as forgiving as her gaze, welcoming him until he never wanted to be anywhere else.

Somewhere, dimly, he knew he ought to keep it short. It was just their first date. But he kept coming back for just a tiny bit more, one last touch. And then her tongue teased at his and he wanted to feel exactly what she was doing there so he leaned in more. His hand that had been clasping hers found her neck instead and the line of her jaw was terribly small and warm. He brushed it with his thumb while she kissed him, stroking her like he could soak up that much more of being with her.

The curve of her breasts thrilling his chest was his first clue that he'd pushed her back against the truck, and he hurried to step away. "Shit, sorry. I washed the truck, but your dress . . ."

Her eyes were a little hazy, but they focused at his words. "Oh no, did I stain it?" She twisted to try to look behind her. "Can you see?"

He tried not to look at the curve of her lower back sweeping into her rounded little bottom, his gaze scouring the fabric instead.

"I borrowed it from Ivy, and I don't want her to be mad at me," Mari fretted.

"It's all right. Ain't stained." He brushed a little dust off the hem. "You ought to keep it, though. Ain't no way it looks better on her."

She snorted. "Have you *seen* Ivy? She's about twenty-five with green eyes like a mascara model."

"She the drill sergeanty one? One always going on about every bird for miles?"

"Ivy has an avian specialty, yes."

He humphed. "Didn't think she'd have a reason to own a dress like that, much time as she spends with those bird books."

"Well, you shouldn't judge. She's very good with birds, but I hear she's a heck of a dancer, too." Mari looked amused. She glanced at her motel room door.

There was no logical reason for them to do anything other than go back to their rooms, but he did not want to do that. He just stood, refusing to even introduce the topic.

"You know, it's early yet," Mari ventured.

"Yeah," he agreed. "Sure is." Jack had no notion of what time it was, and he could not possibly have cared less. "Wanna go someplace?"

The notion of "someplace" was pretty vague in his head, but he figured there were a whole lot of places all bundled up on this planet, and if pressed, he could find one to take her to. Especially when the alternative was going back to his dingy little room alone. Always trying to remember that he wasn't back in Alabama, and Leroy wasn't going to stagger in with his pupils blown wide and start stacking the furniture against the doors.

Mari was looking at his bike, her gaze running longingly over it in a way that made him shift his weight and fidget.

"You know, I could change into pants," she said. "If you wanted to take me for a ride."

The blood revved in Jack's veins. He was not in favor of her changing out of that dress, but he was very much in favor of taking her out on the bike.

"Yup," he said. "You go change and I'll get you a helmet. Back in five minutes, maybe less."

She raised her eyebrows but didn't ask. He liked that she trusted him, even if it was just something small, like being able to find her a motorcycle helmet on short notice.

"See you in a minute." Her fingers brushed over his arm in farewell as she turned toward her room. He grabbed his helmet out of the truck toolbox, jumped on his bike.

He didn't have a spare helmet. No reason to, when no one had ever ridden on the seat on the back. But Ron, the project supervisor, was even more into bikes than Jack. Ron had three or four different helmets in the construction office a few blocks away. Never could decide which one made him look "cool" enough, a trait Jack had always scoffed at before, but now was grateful for.

Mari was waiting outside when he got back. He handed her his helmet, because he knew it was clean and had never taken a serious impact, and he didn't know much about Ron's helmets. She already wore jeans and cowboy boots, but he wrapped her up in his lightest leather jacket. "Safer," he said. "Know it's hot, but it'll be all right once we get going and there's a breeze."

"I feel like an astronaut," she said, her voice muffled until he flipped up the face shield of the helmet. Inside, she was grinning hugely.

"You look real tough," he promised.

She mimed flexing her biceps under the oversized jacket, and he snorted out a laugh.

"Easy there, killer." He pulled on Ron's fancy helmet and straddled the bike. His heart pumped like he'd been pushing the triple digits on the speedometer, and he hadn't even hit first gear yet.

It was too soon for him to even think about going home with her. He never would have asked; he felt guilty and worried every time he ever even thought it. But when she swung on behind him, her thighs coming up tight beneath his, his muscles flexed all in a rush like he was ready to thrust. He wanted to wrap her in his arms, hide her under him. Strip off every bit of fabric she was wearing so he could kiss the precious skin beneath.

Basically, he was losing his mind.

"Hold on," was all he said as he booted the kickstand up and started the bike.

She took him at his word, holding on not just at his sides but wrapped all the way around to where his abs flexed under the leather jacket he'd thrown on in a nod to safety—mostly in case he got distracted enough by her touch to lay the bike over.

He wanted to roar out of the parking lot, his fist eager to crank the throttle. Instead, he made himself take the acceleration slow and smooth, letting her get used to the open air and balance of the bike. Her fingers clung tightly to him for the first few starts and stops, but once they got out on the desert highways, she warmed up right along with the engine. Melting over his whole back and resting into him, letting him lean into the curves, and mirroring his movement like they'd been riding together for decades.

He revved the engine and finally let it roar. She pressed against him, seemingly eager for the speed. He wondered if the growl of the bike massaged all the way down to her bones the way it did for his.

It was heat and speed and the thrill of promise for something exciting. Just out of reach but undeniably there.

The light around them deepened until the sky was a midnight blue, the first few stars sparkling at the edges. Jack flicked on the headlight and checked the gas gauge, but when the turn came up for the motel, he veered the other way and took the long way back.

If sex had ever been as effortless as this ride, thrilling and warm all at once, he might have been crazy enough to ask her if she wanted to come back to his room. But it wasn't, at least not for him. Even if he had gotten so lucky that this incredible woman actually liked being on the back of his bike, it was all going to come crashing down if she started hinting toward wanting more.

Jack hit the next gear and let the engine howl, but it couldn't drown out the sound of tomorrow bearing down on them.

21

Losing Your Head

It always started out innocent.

They'd share dinner in the driveway, she'd pack her stove and cooking supplies back into her truck while he washed the dishes, and then they'd settle into Jack's room in time for their favorite home renovation show. She always sat on his bed, so he did, too.

Some nights he held off for an hour, sometimes only five minutes. But eventually he'd crack, edging his hand closer to hers so his knuckles nudged her own. Or maybe leaning over to press a quick kiss to her cheek. And that was all the invitation she needed.

He'd have been happy if all he got was any one of those small touches. If the back of his hand could simply rest against the heat of hers until they fell asleep against the wall, he'd probably have dreamed about nothing else all night. The idea that he could lean over and kiss her smooth cheek and she *let* him? Well, he wasn't anywhere near used to that.

But Mari . . . she was fierce. The hand holding, the times when he put his arm around her, it seemed like a heated energy would swarm up in her as soon as he got close, and she wasn't able to sit still anymore without her lips finding his. Her knee slipping up onto his thigh. Her breasts nudging closer, pressing more deeply into his chest with each breath she gasped. It didn't take him too many days to consider that maybe she was just waiting on his first touch, to tell her it was okay to do what she really wanted to be doing.

So he started reaching for her sooner.

He was most comfortable starting with a kiss, and he loved her lips. They touched him nicer than anything he could remember. It was so perfect he would almost get disappointed when she moved on from there . . . but then as soon as her tongue found his, he'd forget all about those innocent little closed-mouth touches and growl into her. His hair would end up as thrashed as hers, even though it was shorter now. His shirt would ride up as they'd slip lower on the bed. The sheets always got bunched and clammy with heat, the bedspread shoving annoyingly at their ankles.

Their legs . . .

Somehow they'd always get tangled up, couldn't seem to lie side by side without his knee pushing between hers. As soon as he became aware of that, of the demand he didn't mean to be making on her, he'd pull it back. But then she'd end up kneeling half over him, her inner thigh rubbing his until his cock would do its best to bend his zipper teeth out of shape.

For hours, she'd come back to his mouth. Even when her favorite show about rehabbing farmhouses came on. Even when she was out of breath. Even when he hadn't shaved and her face grew red and chapped from his five-o'clock shadow. It seemed like there was a spark in her that kept getting bigger the more they tried to rub it away.

Jack decided maybe her ex hadn't been too good at kissing.

Not that he figured he was. Hadn't had much practice. Kissing was just what you did to keep from having to look at each other when you were getting ready to hook up.

Of course, he hadn't done a whole hell of a lot of that, either. He wasn't great at spending time with women. Didn't know what to say, or what really he was supposed to do with them. He took them out, sure, any idiot could do that, but they didn't seem to have much fun just staring at him across a table or a bar.

Jack couldn't blame them—he wasn't much to look at.

Back when Vernon had been alive, Jack used to go to his house for dinner on the regular, and he remembered how his old foreman had acted with his wife. They'd been married fifteen, maybe twenty years. They were always talking soft and low, or joshing each other and laughing together. He envied that, but the girls Jack dated never seemed to find him funny.

So he ended up with the kind of woman who just wanted a quick ride now and again, maybe somebody to fix her sink when it leaked. That worked okay for a while, and he figured the more sex he had, the better he'd get at it. But instead, he seemed to get worse.

Then again, like Leroy had always said, Jack was good at one and only one thing, and that was disappointing people. Even when they didn't expect hardly anything at all.

The exception appeared to be Mari, who seemed to think he was rather good at kissing. She must have had odd standards, because she thought he was funny, too. Sometimes, when it was just the two of them, he even *felt* like he might be funny, as if the world were a little less heavy than usual and it wouldn't hurt to attempt a joke.

Mari was a strange woman all around because he could talk to her. She seemed perfectly happy to chat about animals they'd seen that day, and the best way to refinish a floor, and all sorts of things about Alabama and his bike.

Right now, though, she wasn't doing much talking. They were to the part of the night where he'd slid halfway down flat, his head still kinked up against the rumpled pillows and her knee between his. She had rolled up on her side to kiss him, and he was deeply, thoroughly distracted by how her hand had found the bare skin of his stomach.

His skin felt like he was clocking a fever of 130, maybe higher. The sheets clung to his back and Mari's hand was cool and slim. Different from his heavy body in a way that made every movement of it the most interesting thing he'd ever felt.

Unfortunately, it was also calling up a restless energy that normally made him slam the door open and kick-start his bike to ride until the wind whipped it all away. He wasn't about to go any-damn-where at the moment, so instead he cupped a hand around the back of her neck and pulled her in tighter, using his teeth against her lips for the first time, his tongue getting more demanding with hers. Tension tugged under the skin of his belly, pulling from where she was touching over his bare hip bone and thrumming all the way up into his shuddering heart.

His dick had gotten thick and hard, shoved up against his jeans so that it was starting to feel almost good. He broke away from her to gulp a breath, and even that tasted hot. The AC rattled away in the background, but it might as well have been in the next county. Mari only lasted one breath before she came back for more, her lips not sweet anymore but slightly swollen from beard burn as she pressed in for a dueling, groaning kiss that left his thigh muscles twanging.

She was practically on top of him now, one breast pressed against his chest and the other tormenting his clenching biceps on the arm that was sandwiched between them. He could feel her flat, soft belly against the back of his hand and the warmth of her leg thrown over his. He shifted without meaning to, jumpy with all the parts of her he could feel. That ratcheted up the heat between them a couple of extra degrees as the center seam of her jeans rubbed brightly across his leg.

Her hand slipped under his shirt. *Under*. His abs flexed, and he didn't mean to thrust up against her, it was just a reflex because of how high was her hand going and where was she going to touch him and, fuck, his heart was starting to flail and could she *feel* that?

Jack was about to come out of his skin, but he didn't want to draw back to catch his breath because then she'd stop touching him, and he desperately wanted to know where she was planning to put that hand. Instead, he took out all his agitated energy on her mouth. Normally, he let her lead, but somehow in the firestorm of his disjointed thoughts, he forgot about that.

He hauled her toward him. Now it wasn't just her hand caressing him, it was all of her. The taste of her was everywhere, along with her soothing, smooth scent that he'd gotten so used to lingering on the pillow next to his when he went to sleep alone. She was making tiny panting, whimpering sounds in between snatched breaths. He could feel the hard points of her nipples through her shirt and bra, and it drove him wild.

Now she was the one writhing, rubbing their bodies together like she was twitchy, too. Her leg clamped down over him and her lips fell away from his.

On sheer instinct, he tightened the muscle of his thigh, boldly pressing harder where she was rocking herself against him. Her breathing stuttered and stopped, the nails of her hand digging into his bare chest.

Jack did not move.

Her hips jerked, her center grinding down on him for just an instant that he liked way more than he probably should. His cock was twisted all up in the band of his underwear, doing its level best to tear his belt straight open. He needed to adjust so bad he was getting lightheaded, but he didn't dare disturb a thing right now when she might be about to—

A breath hiccupped out of her, and then she started breathing again, sagging off-balance down against his shoulder.

Instinctively, his arm went around her, gentling from her neck down onto her back as he pulled her into more of a hug. His trapped arm tingled from a lack of circulation, and he guided her to lie on top of it anyway because that brought her as close into his side as possible. The room seemed quieter, and uncertainty thrummed in his head.

"Did you just—"

She hid her face in his neck and let out a breathless laugh. "Oh my God. I'm ridiculous. I'm so sorry. Clearly I've been out of the swing of things for so long that all it takes is a little kissing and I lose my mind entirely."

Their legs were still tangled, and he shifted, rubbing the inside of his thigh against hers.

She'd . . .

Just like that?

With her pants still on?

Had he . . .

No. Like she said, it'd just been a long time. He was so close these days that he practically lost it every time she bent over to look into the bushes. Besides, she probably hadn't been taking the edge off every night like he had.

She still wasn't looking at him, the languid softness of her body turning to something more self-conscious and motionless, so he moved his head enough to kiss her cheek. It landed just in front of her ear, and when she didn't move to kiss him back, he stroked one hesitating hand down her back. Usually, all it took was one touch to let her know he was in for whatever. Right now, maybe it was gonna take a little more.

He remembered the cold shame that followed when you shot off on your own. Hadn't happened to him in years—just the first couple of times he was fooling around. Once with Jayci Mead playing doctor behind his daddy's shed when they were really too old for that game. Which wasn't really about doctoring. It was mostly her bossing him into doing all kinds of things he wasn't too sure about until the very end. Probably she'd just been mad because when he came, it hadn't been one of the things she'd ordered him to do.

The second time it happened was the first time he had sex, a couple of years after Jayci Mead. Both times, the girls had started out happy and ended up disappointed, and he took off. He did not want Mari to take off. He didn't want Mari to feel any of the things he'd felt on those days. Which was a big part of the reason he was leery about taking this past kissing.

He moved more strongly this time, shifting her fully onto his chest and wrapping both his tingling and his awake arm around her in a solid hug. He kissed her hair where her head rested timidly against his shoulder. "We can watch the TV for a while if you want," he whispered. "But just so you know, I want you to do that again. Soon. Tonight, if you want. Liked it."

He could feel the line of his cock caught between them. Huge and obvious. It wasn't so embarrassing right now, though, because maybe it would be a hint that she wasn't the only person getting excited.

She let out a little laugh that hitched in her throat. "I just . . . keep losing my head with you. I'm sorry."

He craned his neck but couldn't reach her, so he rolled them onto their sides, still holding her tight. His elbow dug into the mattress, and the pins and needles in his arm turned into swords and sabers, but he didn't give a shit. Ducking his head, he kissed her real soft. Wanted to give her that nice calm feeling she gave him sometimes.

Except one tiny kiss wasn't enough. He wanted another, then he stole a third. Then he remembered he'd meant to say something comforting, but instead he went back for a fourth kiss because he loved, just positively fucking *loved*, the idea that she lost her head with him.

"Like you this way," he finally managed, his voice all fucked-up and growly. "Like you—" He got stuck there, casting about for the words to explain how she was so much different than other people, but it didn't matter because she must have finally caught his green-light cue. Her lips collided bruisingly with his.

She pushed him over onto his back, and his pins-and-needles arm subsided into blessed numbness even as his dick became absolutely, definitely not numb.

Jack decided then that maybe it didn't matter if he was garbage in bed. Maybe he'd found the answer—messing around seemed to be their golden ticket. He was perfectly happy to dedicate the rest of his life to figuring out more ways to make her feel good. As long as he kept his pants on, he might not even screw this up.

22

Bunny Hugger

"Oh my God," Rajni sighed on the other end of the phone. "He caught a baby bunny for you?"

Mari shifted in her seat on her motel bed, grinning into the empty room. "Yup. It had fallen down one of the foundation holes for a new tower, and he found me in tears because I couldn't catch it. So he unbolted one of the boxes off the side of the crew truck, and used that and a shoelace to trap it. And then he cut the bottom off a can of LaCroix to make it a little water bowl. Because he was worried it was thirsty."

There was a moment of silence. "I think I just had a cute-gasm. Is that man still single? Because if you're not gonna hit that, I'm sure going to. Maybe he can catch me a shrike so I can tame it and teach it to skewer me lizards on cue."

Mari laughed at the mention of the desert bird and its odd eating practices. "You are a deeply disturbed woman."

"Yes, but I could be a deeply disturbed woman with a cool pet-skewering bird."

"Also, what would Leo think of you stealing my boyfriend?"

"He doesn't get any say in the matter!"

"Did you guys break up?" Mari caught herself before she tacked on the word "again."

"He's got that jealous thing going again and I'm not into it. He—"

A beep interrupted Rajni's rant. "Hey, can you hold on? I've got another call." She pulled the phone away from her ear to see who it was, and froze.

It was area code 262.

Wisconsin.

She hadn't seen that area code since she fled the state. No one back there had her new number.

Brad couldn't have . . . there was no way. The phone wasn't even registered under her real name. But if he had . . .

Her voicemail was just a generic recording. If he didn't hear her voice, maybe he'd think it wasn't her number. While she stared, her heart pounding, the call went to voicemail. She waited, not even breathing, but whoever it was didn't call back. Slowly, her fingers loosened. If it was Brad, he'd never stop calling. Never give up once he'd found her. Must have just been a wrong number, or a telemarketer.

"Sorry, just a marketing call," she told Rajni. "What were we talking about?"

"Can't remember," the other woman said. "Though, hey, I've been meaning to text you but when I went to do it, I didn't have enough service. I was going to ask if you put in your résumé for that job walking triangles in the Chocolate Mountains?"

"Oh wow, it's already time to start worrying about the next job, isn't it?" Mari sighed. "I heard we'll be done with this project in four weeks."

"I heard three."

"Yeah, but Jack said that the foundation crew has been having a lot of trouble getting the concrete to set up in this heat. They poured a whole truckload of ice into the mix yesterday and still didn't hit the temperature right. Had to rip out the footings on Tower 1195 and start all over again, so he thinks the concrete thing will buy us an extra week."

It was the closest they'd come to talking about what they might do after this job was over. Mari had brought up how soon it was all ending, and Jack had rushed to explain at least three reasons it might last a little longer. It was sweet, how earnest he'd been. She knew it was too early for promises, or to even consider prioritizing a relationship over the jobs that would carry them in different directions in a few short weeks' time. But a pang twisted her stomach every time she thought about living someplace where Jack wasn't just on the other side of the wall.

"*Buy* us an extra week?" Rajni laughed. "Like I'm dying to stay? It's hot as hell's sweaty armpit up here and I'm ready for a research job with just us bios. I've had enough of these environmentalist-hating construction workers. I'll dump ice into the concrete truck myself if I have to."

"It might come to that. I heard that Chocolate Mountains job was already full, but I'll send my qual forms just in case. Lord knows my bank account needs the work."

"Good. It'll be fun to camp out with you again. I say we make Tuesdays ladies' night. Me and you and Ivy and Lisa can find a spot off by ourselves and let the guys fart themselves to sleep once a week."

"I suppose it's not a coincidence that you chose Taco Tuesdays." Mari laughed. "Smart woman."

"Hey, the guys don't just love me for these rockin' legs, sweetie. It's all about the brain. But speaking of tacos, I've got to make dinner. Talk to you soon? Don't hesitate to call me if the Beastmaster does something cute."

"Will do." She hung up with a smile still lingering on her face. Why had she always assumed Rajni didn't want to be better friends? She was a riot.

She glanced at the clock and her smile faded. It was getting late and Jack still wasn't back. When her boss had stopped by to ask her to trap the rabbit, an offhand comment had led to Marcus betting Jack that he was faster on an impact wrench than his crew. Marcus managed to beat the apprentice, and Kipp, and gave Gideon a good run for his money. He didn't come within a mile of matching Jack, but the bet had been that the biologist couldn't beat anyone at all.

As a result, Jack was over at Marcus's right now, changing out a loose belt on his Toyota to pay off the debt. She'd missed Jack at dinner, but counted it an evening well spent, because the men seemed to be getting along much better. Jack didn't seem to have many friends, much like her when she'd first gotten here. The difference was, other guys weren't as likely to do what Lisa had and drag her into the circle despite her worrying that no one wanted her there. Hopefully, right now Marcus was doing the same thing for Jack.

Still, there was only a half-hour's worth of shows left before they flipped to reruns for the night, and she got a little pang that they wouldn't get to hang out. Of course, it was just one night. She'd so quickly gotten used to sharing her evenings with someone who made her smile.

For just a second, she thought of the yellow cottage, and the rest of the interpretive team that would be living beside her if she decided to take the job. Maybe that wouldn't be so bad. On this job, making friends seemed to be coming easier to her than it ever had. Like something in her that had been bracing for their disapproval was finally starting to loosen its guard. But then, she couldn't imagine liking any of the interpretive team at the park as much as she liked Jack. And a national park held few jobs for a construction worker.

She caught herself checking the parking lot for his truck again, and swished the curtains determinately closed. She was being silly, and she had plenty to do.

Her microwave needed cleaning, after all. The motel maids never remembered that part, so she set to it with a vengeance, and after that she did a load of laundry in the rusting washer next to the ice machine.

She was just getting ready to go move it over into the dryer when a knock sounded at her door.

She answered, the smile that rose to her face so automatic that she couldn't have stopped it if she tried. Jack smiled back from the other side of the threshold, a little bashful.

"Hey. Thought maybe I'd, uh—stop by and say—anyway, I'm back." He shifted his weight, the paper grocery bag in his arm crinkling. "Not that you asked, or—"

She pushed up onto her toes and kissed him softly on the lips. "It's nice to see you. Have you eaten? Want me to make you something?"

His eyes were hazy after the kiss, and a second late, he frowned. "You don't gotta cook for me all the time. I stopped by the store on the way home. Got some steaks for us for tomorrow. I can do them on the barbecue out back."

"That thing is full of wasps," she warned.

"I cleared the wasps out last week. Wanted to give it time to settle before I used it." He shot a glance at her. "Can't cook much except on a grill, but I'm half-decent with a set of coals. Probably could use some protein, as many vegetables as you eat."

"Ha!" She caught herself smiling. "Very thoughtful, though I don't think I'm in too much danger of vegetable overdose. Want to come in?"

He nodded, his face lighting.

It was only the second time he'd been in her room. They'd tried watching shows in here, but he kept shifting his weight around and asking if she was tired and what time she went to bed, and no matter how much she reassured him, he still left exceptionally early. It seemed to work better if they just went to his room, where he knew she'd leave whenever she was ready.

What would he think if he knew she'd been considering sleeping over?

"Do you want me to put those in my fridge, or do you want to drop them off in your room?" She pointed to the grocery sack of steaks.

He grimaced. "We can keep them here. Smell of fresh meat is turning my stomach anyhow." He passed over the bag.

"You not feeling well?"

"Yeah, uh, when I got done fixing Marcus's truck, Lisa wanted me to stay and have dinner with them."

Mari cringed. "Why'd you eat it, though?"

"She's your friend, isn't she?"

"That doesn't mean I eat her cooking."

Jack snorted. "Okay, well, next time warn me, and then you'll know why she calls you spouting about what an ungrateful ass—I mean, jerk I am." He sat down on the edge of the bed. "Speaking of, she asked me a truckload of questions about you. I think maybe you need to call her more or something."

Mari raised her eyebrows as she went around to take her spot on the other side of the bed. "Questions like what?"

"Like how you been and how you *seem* and if you're eating enough." He looked disgruntled. "If Ricky's giving you any trouble down at the motel. Told her I fired his ass."

"Oh, I probably should have told her he was gone. I got out of the habit of mentioning him because I didn't want her to worry."

"I almost miss the moron. That new idiot operates a crane like he's playing a bad game of Jenga. Gonna get us all killed."

She winced. "I hope not. Because I don't miss Ricky much."

"Ricky ain't coming back," he reassured her.

He scooted back onto the bed, put his arm around her shoulders. She froze a little at the surprise of it. Had he ever reached for her so casually before? She melted into his side, enjoying having him finally home for the night.

"How many fistfights did you and Marcus get into at dinner tonight?"

"Ah, he's all right. For a hippie. Talked guns, mostly. Bet him a fifty that if the three of us went down to the range, you'd outshoot him."

She pulling back, laughing. "Now why'd you go and do that? I told you I was quieter on the stalk than him, but he's a dead-on shot."

"I got a feeling you can take him." Jack settled her more closely into his side. "We have time for a show before bed?"

For a second, she considered bringing up the topic of the job ending again, but she didn't want to pressure him to put a name to what they had here, or commit to something he might not be ready for. Even if she got lucky enough that he was interested, a lot of her jobs were so remote that it would be the kind of long distance that came with no internet, no mail delivery, and only sporadic cell phone service. And if she took the biologist-in-residence spot, there'd be no place for him there at all. Permanently.

She swallowed away that thought and put on a smile for him.

"Sure, I have time to watch a show. Nowhere else I'd rather be."

23

Ain't a Gazebo

"Ain't a gazebo!" Jack groused at the TV screen. "Any asshole with eyes can see it's a pergola. Idiot Realtor."

"So you know a lot of assholes with eyes, then?" Mari looked gently amused.

"You know what I mean." He subsided, but a moment later the offending structure came on-screen again and he couldn't help muttering, "Pergola."

Mari burst out laughing, and then leaned in and kissed him. Her lips were still shaped by her smile, and the kiss tasted sunny and bright, like her laughter melting into him.

His dick thickened in his pants. He focused on holding her, trying to ignore it. He never used to be so sensitive in that area, but everything about Mari went straight to his head. And not the thinking one, either.

Her scent: so smooth and rich, like a crisp fall breeze with a hint of vanilla lifting it.

Her hair: so shiny and soft, usually swept back and leaving her face open in all its delicate beauty.

The curve of her waist: how his arm always seemed to slip into the nook of it when they were lying together.

She could never kiss him for long without it getting more urgent, little gasps huffing out between kisses. Even now, her body squeezed closer to him as if it had goals of its own while Mari was distracted by his mouth.

Jack had no idea what always got her worked up so quickly, but it didn't do a whole lot to help the situation in his pants. When her hips began to curl against him, he pulled back just enough to speak, their foreheads still tilted together.

"The other day, when you . . . I liked it. Sexy as hell. Wanted to try . . ." His fingers trailed along the waistband of her jeans, his heart pounding almost painfully at how soft the skin was right there. At how his hand was already beneath the hem of her shirt and she didn't seem to care for him to move it. "If you think you might want."

It'd probably have been easier to just try to touch her instead of thinking of how to describe what he'd like to do and forcing himself to say it out loud. Except if she didn't want to, he didn't want her to have to push him away.

"Yes. I'm not exactly sure what you're asking, but yes." Mari smiled, cupping his cheek as she stole another kiss.

He huffed out a self-conscious chuckle, his head whirling at her answer. He thumbed the button of her jeans, not undoing it but just tugging at it a little. "You know. If I could get you to . . ."

"Yes." The word came out breathier this time. She started kissing him again, urgently enough that he had trouble keeping his thoughts straight, much less managing the button and zipper on her jeans without looking.

He tilted her, laying her down on the bed next to him and smoothing his thumb down the side of her face. His other hand flattened on her belly, his fingertips just brushing the elastic of her panties. His cock snapped fully erect in a surge that left him light-headed, and he had to brace an elbow against the mattress. She made a tiny throaty sound, and he realized she was waiting on him, that she wanted more, crazy a thought as that was.

He edged his hand into her panties, little by little. He wasn't breathing. There wasn't a lot of room in there for him—his hand was too big. The zipper of her jeans scratched at the back of his wrist as she arched up against him. She was so wet. Slippery and warm and not lying still at all. Probably it'd been a long time since she'd gotten much relief in this department, except for the other night. The thought gave him new purpose.

He might be no more good in the sack than he was on a dance floor, but if she was deprived enough to get there without even taking her pants off, he figured he might be able to muddle through.

At first, he didn't try anything fancy, just cupped his palm gently between her legs and kissed her mouth for all he was worth. That got her quaking and straining against the heel of his hand, which did terrible things to his oversensitive dick.

His fingers kept dipping into where she was slick and warm, and so he let them stroke her just a little bit. When her breathing started coming in fits and starts, he relinquished her lips and lay his head on her chest. Cuddled in just under her chin, his cheek against her breastbone, he could hear her heartbeat and he followed it like he was hot on a trail, shifting his hand here or there to get it to speed while she clutched his shoulders.

When she started pushing up against his hand, he followed a hunch and held firm for her to pleasure herself, petting her down below. Before he could believe it was happening, her whole body clenched taut and her fingernails dug into him through his shirt. Just like last time, she stopped breathing for so long he started to worry before she went slack against the bed.

Damn, that had almost been . . . easy.

Something in his chest lifted, and he fought against the unfamiliar twist of hope. He took his hand away, carefully untangling the band of her underwear and smoothing it flat again, zipping up her jeans even though he couldn't quite manage the button while he was on his side, his other arm out of commission.

Maybe that was something he could do for her again. Say, every single night for the rest of his life.

"You good?" he murmured, laying a small kiss on her neck. Even all the way up here, her skin was flushed and warm to the touch.

"What are you buttoning my pants for?" She rolled his way, and kissed his lips searingly. "We don't have to stop. Not if you don't want to."

Hold on, she'd thought they were going to—his train of thought crumbled apart when her hand landed on his thigh and climbed up to the thick ridge of his erection. When she rubbed her palm over him, he felt the coarse texture of the denim clear through his boxers, and it was the best damn thing in the world. He'd been studiously ignoring his own reactions but that . . . felt too good to pass up.

Vaguely, he was aware that she'd asked him a question. Or said something, or . . . something. She stroked him in long, firm strokes, his cock flexing eagerly against her hand. His jeans were so fucking tight at this point that he might need to cut them off. Then, miraculously, they loosened and his erection leapt to fill the gap, throbbing from the pressure it'd been under for so long now. Heat was the next thing he registered. Heat and smooth skin as her bare hand stroked over his bare—

Jack bolted upright, nailing his head on the headboard.

"Whoa, are you all right? Did I hurt you?"

"No, nah." He shoved an agitated hand at his hair, but it was mostly gone, the shorter style just a soft brush against his palm. "Felt . . . Fuck," he said, because she was still wide-eyed and startled. "Good. Real good."

She smiled at that, scooting back up and curling against him as her hand descended back into his boxers. His jeans were flapping open where she'd unzipped them and halfway down his ass thanks to his idiot jumping move. He gulped, his head thick with arousal. It was hard to think, and then she grasped his erection. Except her fingers were too small and they couldn't fit all the way around him, and she made a quiet, very female sound.

"Well. You're ah—well. Goodness."

At that, his erection flagged. "Yeah, uh, sorry." He scooted back, her hand coming out of his boxers. "Know it's big. But it's all right. You ain't gotta—it's okay."

Mari blinked. "Did you just apologize . . . for your dick being too big?"

He attempted a smile, because he knew she was trying to joke, but it slumped miserably off his face. Girls pretended sometimes that it didn't hurt, but he could tell. It was all over the way they shifted or squirmed or got all tense but while making lots of noise so he'd think they were done so he would finish. He couldn't stand the thought of Mari pretending he wasn't hurting her when he was. He jerked his jeans up, buttoning them fast so he didn't have to see the humiliating flash of his underwear.

"I like just—" He gestured toward the still-open button on her pants. "I like messing around with you. We can just do that. None of that other stuff. That'd be fine with me."

She sat up next to him. "Are you saying, never . . . ?" She looked puzzled. "Jack, you're big, yeah, but you're not . . . I don't think it's *too* big." She laid a hand on his leg. All gentle, not like she was trying to get his pants open again. "We can take it slow the first couple of times." She ducked her head, trying to catch his eyes. "I trust you not to hurt me."

He looked away, at the TV that was still playing. "Yeah, uh."

Didn't she get it? He was *trying* not to hurt her. They could mess around and he could take care of his business after she left, like he had been. But she was looking at him like she wanted to talk him out of it. And he wanted to let her, but on the other hand . . . he *hated* it. The way he could tell when they were ready for him to be done and just get off.

He cleared his throat, staring down at the ugly pattern of the bedspread. "Might not be so easy as all that. Wanted you to know so if . . . Don't want you to think it's you. It ain't. It's me."

He'd always been messed up about that stuff, even as a kid. In a flash, he remembered the slash of pain across his back from his dad's belt, the wet streaks on his thigh from what he'd been doing when his father walked into his room. *Don't you ever let anybody see you diddling your dick again. Jesus, boy, what's wrong with you?*

"Jack, it's okay." Her voice was quiet, soothing. "We don't have to do anything like that if you're not comfortable. Did you like it when I was just touching you?"

He frowned at her. Couldn't she tell? "Yeah, of course. Feels great. Just, the rest of all that usually doesn't turn out so good, so you don't gotta try. That's all."

"What about . . ." She bit her lip, color flushing over her cheekbones. "I never used to like it, but lately I keep thinking about . . ." She huffed out a breath, laughing at herself. "Listen to me, I'm shy as a teenager." She leaned forward and whispered something in his ear.

Jack nearly went cross-eyed. Heat rushed into his pants so quickly that his cock got all twisted up, and he had to jerk a quick adjustment to his britches. "Yeah, uh, course I'd like that, but it's not something you have to . . . but I guess if you *wanted* to . . ." He stared at her, curious, but the blush on her cheeks was pretty and excited, and she did not at all look like a woman who was doing him a favor. "You can do whatever you want," he declared.

She wet her lips. "Really?"

"You don't . . ." He could not believe they were having this conversation. "I mean, you wouldn't ever maybe want . . . have you ever thought about doing that . . . in a car?"

Her eyes widened. "How did you know that?"

Jack shoved a hand over his face. He was starting to sweat. Jesus Christ, the woman was into blow jobs in *cars* and she wanted him and he was telling her no. Hell, maybe his whole too-slow problem wouldn't be a problem with her. Seemed like he spent half of the time he was with her trying to hold back from shooting off with his pants still zipped.

But he still didn't want to hurt her. It had probably been a long time for her, and he *knew* Mari. Even if it hurt, she'd be so worried about his feelings she might pretend that it didn't, and he didn't like that one tiny bit. Then again, if she was already having fantasies about blow jobs, that kinda thing would be safe enough. Except . . .

He shook his head. "No. Nah. Better not try the car thing. Ain't no place private enough, and no way am I risking somebody seeing us."

She smiled wickedly. "Jack. I'm a biologist. I know lots of places people never go. You just give me a couple of days to pick out a spot."

24

First-World Problems

Mari walked into the coffee shop, and slung her purse onto the table so hard it slid across and nearly fell before Rajni caught it.

"You are not going to believe this."

Rajni squirmed in her seat, a smile lighting up her whole face. "Oh, I cannot wait. I've never gotten an 'Urgent, must meet tonight' text from you. FYI, other people just text 911."

"You can text to 911 now? Why would you want to type in an emergency?"

"No, no, you text *me*, but you say 911 and it means—you know what, never mind. What am I not going to believe? And how come you're not telling it to Lisa?"

"Lisa's sweet, but she can only keep a secret from anything that doesn't have ears." Mari took a chair and leaned in close to the table, dropping her voice. "This is incredibly personal and I don't care how funny you think it is, you cannot tell anybody in your entire life, not even on your deathbed."

"Got it." Rajni nudged a big ceramic mug across the table, wafting vanilla-spicy deliciousness into the air. "Did I mention I already bought you a chai?"

"And you know that a chai is enough to buy every secret I have, including my PIN number and blackmail pictures of me with a bad perm. But this isn't about me." She didn't blink, holding the other woman's gaze hard. "Swear to me on your truck, Rajni."

"Sweetie, you are just about to piss me off. You think you can't trust me?"

"I think I wouldn't trust anybody with this, if I didn't need help too much to figure it out on my own."

"I swear on my truck," Rajni said levelly. "And I'll get some to-go cups. If it's that way, we shouldn't be talking about it in public."

She led the way to the parking lot, and as soon as the doors on Rajni's truck closed them into the cab together, Mari said it.

"His dick's too big."

"You're freaking—" Rajni exploded into a peal of laughter. "No it is not! And I can't tell anybody?"

"He won't have sex with me because he's worried he'll hurt me."

Rajni lost it, her truck seat creaking as she howled with laughter. "Okay, okay, no . . . but is it really that big? C'mon."

Mari couldn't look her in the eye. "Um, maybe?"

Rajni stopped laughing. "You're freaking kidding me. He catches bunnies for you, takes you for rides on his motorcycle, looks at you like he wants to curl up in your lap and purr, *and* has an enormous dong?"

Mari's mouth twitched with a guilty little smile she couldn't quite hold back. "And he's been making me coffee in his French press every morning because he knows how much I hate the stuff the motel gives us."

Rajni rolled her eyes. "What I wouldn't do for your luck. So when he told you, what'd you say?"

"Told him we could just do other things. I don't know, at the time I was so horny I wanted to cry, but I figured he'd take that the wrong way. C'mon, I figured if anybody would have any idea what to do, it'd be you." She widened her eyes, not above begging. "Because if we try and it doesn't work, he is never going to sleep with me again. I'm serious, I know this man. If he thinks it'll hurt me, he'd rather die a virgin."

"He's a virgin, too!" Rajni clapped her hands over her mouth.

"No. *No.* But you know what I mean." Mari wiped sweat off her forehead. With the windows rolled up, it was stifling.

"Yeah, yeah." Rajni started the truck and hit the AC. "No, I know I laughed, but some folks have a real deal with all that. I had a boyfriend once, a fisherman from Maine—well, anyway, if it's honestly too big, there isn't much you can do except get real good with your hand. Mostly, if it's big but still within reason, it's not too tough. Little lube and warm yourself up first. Have him get you off two, maybe three times before you start. Loosens everything right up, won't be a problem."

"Okay." Mari cleared her throat. "Good. So that's settled." She fanned her face, hoping the heat in the truck would provide an excuse for how flushed she'd gotten. "How's your week going?"

Rajni leaned back in her seat and started to laugh all over again. "Let's just say we've all got problems. And we all wish we were having *your* problems."

Mari leaned into Jack's work truck, slipping a plastic bag full of brownies up onto his dashboard. It smelled like him in here, and she took a deep, deep breath. She hadn't seen him much since he confessed his little "issue" with sex. At work yesterday, sure, but he'd been busy, and then they'd missed dinner together because she'd taken Rajni out for emergency chai and even-bigger-emergency advice.

Today, he'd been distant. Not rude or mean to her. Just . . . holding back.

"You need something?"

The gravelly southern drawl caught her off guard and she jumped, nearly hitting her head on the doorframe.

"Mmm, maybe to be a little bit sneakier?" She turned with a rueful smile. "I was hoping you'd be too busy on the tower to see me in here."

He glanced past her into the truck. "So's that mean I can't eat those brownies because I'm not supposed to see them yet?"

He sounded so disappointed that she caved immediately. "No, go ahead." She stepped aside so he could get past. "They're an equal-opportunity bribe."

"Bribe?" he said through a mouthful of crumbs, the first brownie already gone. He frowned. "For what? Whatchu need?"

She batted her eyelashes, then felt ridiculous. "I found a spot. Out in the desert, like we talked about. Very private."

Jack blushed so hard and fast his skin went more purple than red.

"Uh, yeah, yup. All right. Tonight? Or, uh, whenever you were thinking is fine."

She leaned in closer, dropping her voice to slip it under the roar of an approaching large-engined truck. "Tonight. Definitely tonight."

The bag of brownies hung in Jack's hand as his Adam's apple bobbed.

Behind them, a truck shut off and Mari blinked, coming back to earth as she worried that she hadn't checked the construction area for tortoises before they pulled in. Then again, she'd cleared that area not three minutes ago when she walked over with the brownies. She turned, scanning, but didn't see any animals nearby. It was too hot midday for most anything to be out anyway.

The truck door opened and Rod stepped out and hitched up his pants, surveying the construction site with an air that reminded her of English nobles in old BBC miniseries. Behind her, Jack made a brief, derisive noise.

Rod sauntered over to them. "Hello there, little lady. How's the afternoon treating you?"

She fought off an eye roll, having a quick debate with herself about the best way to set this guy back on a professional track without making an enemy.

"Her name is *Mari*," Jack snapped.

"Thanks, Wyatt. If I need any other introductions, I'll call you."

Rod stared past her and she didn't have to turn to know the two men had locked eyes, or that Jack's would be creased at the corners by his scowl.

"Your crew doing okay over there without your supervision?" Rod said after a long, uncomfortable moment.

"Figured you were here to talk to me." Jack spat off to the side. "There ain't any other foremen around."

And even Mari knew Rod didn't bother to talk to any of the regular workers.

"Actually, I'm here to talk to your biologist." He smiled at her, and the hairs on the back of Mari's neck rose.

"So talk," Jack grunted.

Rod gave him a look, flicked his eyes pointedly toward the tower.

"Crew's fine." Jack didn't budge.

The supervisor laughed. "Oh, that's right. I'd heard rumors you two were very special friends."

She held her breath. She'd worried it was a conflict of interest, for her to keep monitoring his crew. Even wondered if she should ask Marcus to reassign her, but her boss hadn't seemed concerned so far. Out in the desert so far from an HR department, rules about employee fraternization were rarely enforced. But if Rod decided to kick up a fuss, he might be able to get her in trouble even if Marcus didn't care.

"Don't worry, Wyatt. I'm not planning on hitting on your old lady." The emphasis on the word "old" was just a breath. So subtle she couldn't have said for sure if he'd really meant it that way. Except the word scraped along her bones like sandpaper, and she knew, damn it. Men like him never did anything by accident.

She pretended to hear something, turning to the imaginary sound in such a way that she ended up directly between the two men, because she knew Jack. He'd been doing a lot of work on his temper, but she was pretty sure none of that work was going to hold him back if he thought Rod had insulted her.

"I think I hear Joey calling you," she told him. "I can handle this. I'll come get you if it ends up being something that might affect the crew, or our schedule." She smiled at Jack with her back to Rod so he couldn't see the edge of steel in the outwardly cheerful expression.

The corner of Jack's mouth twitched upward toward a smile, and she knew he had read her expression just fine. His eyes still looked unhappy, but he ducked a nod. "All right. Be just over there if you need me."

He gave Rod a look and there were no amount of polite or professional words that could have disguised what it was: a warning from one large, aggressive male to another.

He walked away, the baggie of brownies disappearing into a pocket on his tool belt.

"I've been hearing very good things about you," Rod said, before her attention had fully come back to him.

"Is that so?" She adjusted her hard hat to cover the subtle tension that gathered in her. Men like him complimented for two reasons, and it was always the follow-up that'd tell you which it was. Either they were about to hit on you, or they wanted a favor.

She didn't care for either option.

"Wyatt's crew started out with the second-worst environmental compliance record on this transmission line, and now they have the best. It's very impressive, the uh . . . difference around here since you started." He smirked.

Ah. So it wasn't sexual, then. Too bad. That would have been easier to shut down.

"Their record has improved because Jack put a lot of time into training his men to follow the rules." Mari folded her hands neatly in front of her. "It doesn't have a thing to do with me—you could put another bio on this crew tomorrow and get the same results."

"You see, I'm glad you think so, because I agree."

She did not like the sound of that.

"My son's crew has been paying a lot of very expensive environmental impact tickets lately. I think they could use a little of your . . ." He paused. "Extra-special treatment."

Only because she'd spent years getting slapped for her expressions did she manage to keep her reaction off her face.

"Like I said, that's not me." The only thing she did differently was how she explained the rules to Jack so that he could see the reasoning behind them and really understand how they protected the animals. That's when he started enforcing them himself instead of making the bio try to ride herd over his whole crew.

"Good. Then you won't mind that I had you transferred to Junior's crew."

Her balance quivered at the words "had you transferred." Her new life felt so precious, she had to remind herself he couldn't take it away. Not the job, not Jack. Not even the fact that she was assigned to this particular crew, actually. A man like Rod, though, was probably riding on the certainty that she'd give in to his orders, regardless of how valid they were.

Once, she would have.

She matched his unblinking stare. "You can't have me transferred. I don't answer to you."

Joey trotted up. "Kipp thinks he saw a rattlesnake."

She didn't look away from Rod. "I'll be there in a moment."

At least twice a day, Kipp needed her to come over and check because he thought he'd seen a rattlesnake. He'd yet to be correct.

She didn't intend to be rude to Joey. It was just that everything about Rod made her want to drop her eyes, and she wouldn't let herself do it.

She'd fought back so many times with Brad, but he'd always pushed back even harder. Yelling, then screaming, the violence escalating until she gave way. Until she learned never even to try. The way Rod was testing her now made her feel like the early days with Brad, like if she gave a single inch, he wouldn't quit until she was broken at his feet.

"Oh, I have the authority," he said. "I talked to Marcus's boss, and he felt just fine about it."

Her next breath stuck in her throat. It wasn't that it was the end of the world to work on a different crew. She couldn't work with Jack forever, and she'd see him at night. It was just that she didn't want to do what Rod wanted. No matter what it was.

"Jack said to tell you he thinks Kipp might be right about the snake this time," Joey persisted.

She turned to look at the anxious-eyed apprentice. "Tell Jack not to worry. I have it all under control."

Her voice was calm, even though she wasn't totally sure if she was lying or not. She understood all too well what Rod was expecting of her by transferring her to his son's crew. He wanted her to look the other way when his son broke the rules. If she didn't do it, she'd lose her job and therefore her ability to pay the medical bills that gained more interest by the day.

If she did do it, she'd lose her integrity, and with it, her fragile self-respect.

Rod waited until Joey retreated, and then he said, "Of course, if there's a reason you'd rather stay on this crew, I can let your boss know all about that."

He looked pointedly to where Jack was standing, staring across the job site at Rod and Mari. When Jack saw Rod's head turn, he looked away.

So did Mari.

"That won't be necessary," she said to the dirt between them.

Jack had been right. "No" wasn't a word you were allowed to say to Rod.

25

Best View in the Desert

"You sure this spot you found is—"

"Yup."

"You sure you, uh, still feel like . . . Because you ain't gotta—"

"Jack. I'm sure."

Click. Click. Click.

The turn signal clicked until they made the turn, and she tried to fight back a smile at how nervous they both were, like teenagers rather than adults in their forties.

Tires hummed on the road, so much louder when they weren't bald.

"Just . . . don't expect anything spectacular, okay? I've never been all that good at it."

"I don't think there is any *bad* where that's concerned. But just because I said there was no sense in trying to go all the way, don't want you to think I was fishing for this instead."

"I know."

"Mari."

"No, it's not that! Really. It's fine. I don't want you to worry."

Click. Click. Click.

"Don't pull over." He was definitely still pulling over, maybe even turning around. She laughed. "Oh my gosh, you're so sweet, sometimes it still surprises me. I'm nervous, but I'm fine, really. Don't pull over."

His hand inched across the seat. It didn't quite make the whole journey before she met him in the middle. She laced her fingers together with his, and then the cab of the truck was quiet again.

Mari gave him directions, and eventually he had to let go of her hand to shift, and to wrangle the steering wheel as the dirt roads they bounced over got increasingly rocky and less traveled. The sunlight slanting in the windows was finally starting to ease in intensity, and she clicked the AC down a notch. They were close now.

She'd been looking forward to this time alone with him all day; clinging to it, really, after the tension-filled, short conversation with Rod. She hadn't yet told Jack that Rod was going to transfer her off his crew. She'd have to tell him later tonight, because the change was coming tomorrow, but she really didn't want to see his expression when she admitted that she'd given in. Not that she had had a real choice, but somehow that only made it seem more like a failure.

What Mari wanted was just to forget about terrible, pushy men and concentrate on the one she was with, who was kind and uncertain and twice the man his boss would ever be. She wanted to think about consummating her fantasy of driving Jack wild with her mouth. Except now that they were so close to their goal, she was remembering that in real life, she wasn't the seductress she could be in her imaginings.

How was this going to work? Maybe she was supposed to undress. A blow job in a car was something he'd fantasized about, too, she could tell. But she wasn't sure he could stutter his way through an explanation of how he pictured the logistics. Should she kneel on the seat, or maybe try to get down in the footwell on her side . . . The stick shift was in the way, that was for sure. But didn't men like the on-the-knees thing?

Brad had, but sometimes she wasn't sure if that was just because he knew it hurt her kneecaps. Or because he could yank her hair more easily from that position.

She ran a hand through her hair, thinking of how many times she'd thought of shaving it down to her skull.

It was funny—she'd been having so many dirty thoughts about doing this with Jack. About using her tongue to make him gasp. About running her hand down the whole, impressive length of him. But now that she was so close to getting her fantasy, she was remembering how little she'd liked it all the times she'd done it in real life. The way her jaw would get tired and she'd wish for a break but couldn't take one. The way Brad always finished, but a minute later he'd be telling her all the ways she'd done it wrong.

"It's right here," she said, spotting the boulder she'd chosen as a landmark, tucked down in a small valley, along the faintest side track off a little-used four-wheel-drive road. On a midweek night when the rowdy weekend crowd wasn't likely to even consider going dirt biking.

Jack parked, and just like that it was time. And she still wasn't ready. Suddenly her heart started fluttering, stumbling over itself with its own speed. Her throat tightened, her scalp screaming with the phantom pain of her hair being gripped and pulled.

"Mari?"

She inhaled a long breath and took hold of her courage with both hands. This was her present, not her past. She was safe, and this had been her idea, and in this new life, her choices were supposed to be her own again.

"I don't think I want to—"

"Okay." His agreement tripped out before she was even done, and something soothing and nice flooded through her tensed chest. She peeked up from his dashboard to his green eyes. "Thought it was weird," he confessed with a rueful twist of a smile. "That you'd wanna."

"No, I do." She fumbled, not sure how to explain her contradictory emotions. "I really do. Just . . . not right now, I don't think."

"Yup." He glanced around. "Wanna go back or . . ."

"It's nice out here. We might as well watch the sunset, since we came all this way," she suggested, trying to salvage the night.

"Yup."

They both looked out the windshield, where the pinks and oranges of early sunset streaked the sky, framed in the rising curves of the small valley they were parked in. The spines on the cactus caught the sun and made a glowing halo that was almost romantic.

Inside the truck, the only sound was the rush of the AC. Mari felt guilty leaving the truck idling—emissions and all—but they'd roast for sure without air-conditioning. Even with twilight coming on, it was topping 90 degrees.

Two empty feet of truck seat separated them. Jack didn't say a thing, just watched that sunset like it was his job. Mari bit her lip, relief and tension warring within her.

"Can I, um, come over there?" Even her murmur sounded too loud in the silent truck.

"Yeah. Course. C'mere." He raised his arm in invitation and she scooted over, nuzzling into his side with a noiseless sigh. "You all right?"

She tucked her head in under his chin, his collarbone warm beneath her cheek. "Mm-hmm." It was okay. *They* were okay.

They could fool around another time, and she was glad she hadn't ruined her own fantasy by trying to do it on a day when her head wasn't fully in the right place. She hadn't really thought Jack would protest her saying no, but it was nice to know he wouldn't take it personally and get weird about it, either.

While they watched, the shades of the sunset began to deepen, like they were settling into their true colors, and it was utterly beautiful.

Jack ducked his chin and kissed Mari's head. Her hair was soft and tickled his nose. He liked sitting out here with her. Hell, maybe his fetish with cars and shit wasn't even sexual, because even cuddling in a truck was turning out to be better than he'd expected.

She turned a little and kissed him back, in the bare scrap of skin above the first button of his shirt. A quiver ran through him, and she laughed.

"Ticklish?"

"Yup," he agreed instantly. It was better than the truth, which was that he was basically a teenager where she was concerned. He was half-mast hard and his heart was speeding at even that tiny kiss, which was miles away from his mouth or any more-sensitive parts.

Her free hand stroked over his ribs, patting nicely against his buttons. "I like this shirt."

"You do?" He'd got it three for ten dollars at Walmart, all different colors of blue plaid. It wasn't what Leroy would have called a "gittin' laid shirt."

"I do." Her fingers started to toy with his first button, and he had the notion that perhaps she hadn't bought the ticklish explanation after all. Her lips rose, touching his throat this time, and he considered if it'd be worth it to pull away for long enough to turn up the air-conditioning.

Instead, he just started to sweat.

"It's such a nice sunset," Mari murmured.

"Mmm. Yuh-huh." His eyes had fallen closed, but he didn't think she could tell from where she was cuddled down into his side. His ribs on that side were tingling, every gentle brush of her body waking them up all over again. He could feel the slim curve of her shoulders, her long, pretty back. His hand curled into her waist, holding her into him.

His chest loosened, and it took him longer than it should have to realize the sensation was one of his buttons. Now he was afraid to open his eyes.

Her cheek skimmed the exposed skin, and he stopped breathing. Two buttons, three. Shit. Hell. Unborn illegitimate son of a—

"Mari!" he blurted and she paused.

"Mmm?"

His eyes had popped open, and he was rather discomfited to note it wasn't even close to full dark yet. "Maybe I oughta—" he mumbled, not sure what he meant to say.

He worked hard, kept fit, but his chest wasn't anything to write home about. Scattered with tattoos as faded as his jeans, and most of them were crooked because his cousin Wicket hadn't often been sober when he was in the mood to get his tat gun out of the closet. Even when Jack was twenty, he'd never had one of those stomachs like you saw on women's paperbacks in the grocery store, like six dinner roll tops poking up in individual bulges.

"I can stop," she whispered. "I kinda felt back in the mood, but it's okay if you didn't."

"No! Nuh-uh, you don't have to stop." He paused, but before he figured out how to explain the situation he was having, she kissed him again. In that hollow, hard spot between his nipples. Damn, that felt good. And when she undid another button and kissed that spot, too, he forgot all about abs and grocery store books.

"Jack . . ." She wiggled in protest, and that's when he realized his hand had clamped closed over her side with all the strength of years of climbing towers.

"Sorry." He let go, then rubbed the spot in case he'd hurt her. She gave a little shiver he recognized and the corner of his lips kicked up. "Ticklish, huh?"

"Not a bit." She tipped her head back and gave him a smile so wicked that he suddenly remembered it'd been *her* idea to drive all the way out here so she could get in his pants.

And, okay, she'd decided she'd rather not, but he certainly wasn't opposed to the chest kissing that had started up. He petted her back more softly now, letting his palm stroke over her bare skin where her shirt started to pull up.

That seemed to only make her more enthusiastic about uncovering more of his chest.

Jack was starting to think this sex thing, much like the conversation thing, was just not the same with Mari as it had been with other women. She and Jack seemed to maybe have similar taste in stuff. Or maybe it was just that everything she did appealed to him one whole hell of a lot.

He got bolder, letting his hand slip up under the back of her shirt. When she arched her spine and let out a little huff of breath, he wandered lower, past her belt line. To her pocket. He faltered a little but she pressed closer and his hand ended up filled with the delicious curve of her ass.

She had slipped sideways to where she was almost lying in his lap now. His shirt was unbuttoned and her position the same as all his fantasies. The sight of her lit up something in his chest that felt halfway between pride and some crazed, masculine energy that demanded to be released. It was *Mari* here with him. So much more impressive than all those faceless fantasy women.

He hauled her up to his mouth, a growl building in his chest that he didn't fully understand. That fevered aggression that always seemed to take her over had infected him now, too, and it made him want to use his tongue. On her mouth, her breasts, her . . .

His brain got a little foggy, possibly because she was letting him support her weight while her hands had snuck inside his shirt. His belt buckle had loosened, and her kisses had gotten hotter and more out of control. He became very bold then, whispering things to her and nipping at her neck just beneath her pretty little ear and the wink of her tiny earrings and she was saying yes. *Yes, yes, yes* into his ear. A lot of things happened then.

One of them involved her losing her pants, which apparently talked his shirt off as well. His fantasies about trucks had taken a sharp, interesting turn, and Mari was all on board with his whispered idea of what he wanted to do to her.

A few grunts and his too-wide shoulder honking the horn later, he got his back to the driver's door, and stretched out across the bench seat with Mari spooned between his legs. Her head lay against his shoulder, her bare legs pale and pretty against his new seat covers.

His hands found their way back to what was becoming familiar ground between her thighs. Mari's went to her own buttons, opening her shirt and popping her front-clasp bra so that he now had the best view in the desert.

And it didn't have a thing to do with sunsets.

26

Fantasies Fulfilled . . . Kind Of

Jack had Mari's delicately curved body draped all down the front of his, and even in the limited space, she felt amazing.

She shifted against him and made a sound. It wasn't a moan—Mari wasn't a moaner. Mostly, she made these tiny sounds in the back of her throat, changes in the way she breathed. They'd only messed around a few times but he was already starting to sense patterns in her noises that told him when to lighten his touch, when to go deeper. Easy as following tracks in fresh snow.

Goddamn, but this was easier now that she wasn't wearing pants.

He liked the position, too, except that he was getting all worked up from being able to watch what his hand was doing to her. His other arm was hugged tight across her waist, keeping her securely on the narrow seat. At least until Mari took his wrist and moved his palm up, unambiguously, to her breast. Jack made a sound. It might have been a moan. Damn, he hadn't known he was a moaner.

That made her make a louder sound. Shit, by the end of this, they were both gonna be moaners.

She was so fucking wet. He had no idea women could get this wet, and it did something crazy down deep in the base of his skull. His hips kept rolling against her back, twitching forward when he wasn't paying enough attention to keep still.

Mari arched her back and reached behind herself to pop his pants open.

"Hey," he rumbled. "I'm fine. Just lay back and let me take care of you."

"I'm just giving you a little more room. It's got to hurt."

It did hurt. The confines of his now-too-tight jeans, not to mention the door handle digging a bruise into his spine. But Jack was used to pain, and it wasn't much penance at all to pay for having an armful of mostly naked Mari.

"Ain't nothing," he said, but she opened his zipper for him anyway. "Let me know if I'm crushing you."

His cock was free. Swollen as all hell and rubbing against her back with only a thin layer of cotton boxers between them. "Uh-huh," he tried to say, his throat all tight and scratchy. Sweet God, that felt like heaven. He loved fooling around in trucks. He loved *her*.

He blinked and stopped moving at the thought, the way it'd just snuck up on him like that. But then Mari curled her hips, rubbing restlessly against his palm in a mute protest at his sudden lack of movement. He went back to exploring which parts of her were soft, and which were slick, and which made her shiver when he brushed a fingertip across them. He was just working out a rhythm of pressing and slowly circling when a spasm jerked through her and her legs clamped closed around his hand.

She wasn't a screamer any more than a moaner. When she finished off, she just got real, real quiet and stiff, and he was learning if he got quiet along with her, he could almost feel the pleasure bolting through her nerves.

He hugged her into him, his hand drifting to her silky inner thigh when she relaxed again. Kissed her head two or three times, because he really, really liked it that she let him do that for her. Especially when she wasn't wearing pants.

She shifted, hitching herself a little higher up in his lap, which just rubbed on his too-sensitive cock, and he bit back a groan.

"I want to hold you," she whispered. "Inside me. Would that be okay?"

He blinked, trying to sort out the words she just said. "Uh . . . what?"

She reached around behind herself and gave his shaft a squeeze, like this was something they'd done a hundred times. "We don't have to do anything. Move or anything. I know you're worried about that. I just . . . want to feel you."

"Don't wanna hurt you."

She laughed gently and turned onto her side, nipping a little playfully at his pectoral muscle. "I'm so wet right now I'm pretty sure nothing could hurt me."

He couldn't breathe. Wasn't sure he wanted to. "Don't have a rubber."

"I do. No glove, no love, remember?"

He chuckled, remembering their conversation about gloves and tortoises.

Mari pulled his head down and kissed him, then caught his eyes from so close that it felt private, safe to talk about anything. "We can stop if you're worried. I only want to know what it would be like. Just for a minute."

He could feel one of her nipples brushing his chest, and she was so pretty, her eyes so earnest. "Uh . . . uh-huh. Yeah, all right."

She answered his stuttering, grunted answer with a brilliant grin, and crawled out of his lap and across the seat to dig in her purse. He was so distracted by the view he almost forgot to toe off his shoes and shimmy out of his jeans. After a second, he shoved off his boxers, too. It was nearly dark out, but getting naked still set his heart to pounding.

That, or maybe it was the shadowed desert spreading out around them, the steering wheel that kept barking at his elbow.

In his fantasies, they were usually in traffic, with people all around who could see what the woman in his car was doing to him. But this was better. The impulsive, adolescent nature of making out in a truck in the middle of nowhere. The way the narrow truck seat seemed reckless and experimental: like trying out what felt good was all that mattered and not as if he needed to perform some three-part symphony of a seduction.

He half smiled. "Wait, you brought condoms?"

"Bought some last week." She threw a laughing glance at him before she went back to digging in her purse. "Then had to go back and exchange them, because I wasn't entirely sure you were going to fit in the size of the first batch." She procured a foil package and scooted back into his lap. "First time I've ever gotten turned on by running errands."

He laughed, taking the condom. "You serious?"

"Dead." She passed him a small plastic bottle of lube and gave a happy little shimmy in his lap. "Buying a different size was kind of fun."

A laugh rumbled deep in his throat at her gleeful reaction.

This was usually the point where his excitement started to wane in response to the nerves about getting to the sex itself. But with her so near and the vanilla scent of her smoothing the air, his cock was so hard it hurt to even roll the condom over his swollen tip. He wiped his palm on his leg, the lube leaving a slick spot. Then he scooped her back into his lap.

The additional weight made his neck kink and the truck door dig even harder into his back, but his dick was between her legs now, prodding at a place that made his heart pound in his ears. He didn't want to fuck this up, didn't want to spoil how perfect this night had been.

"Just put it in so you can feel me, right? Because I'm not much good at everything that comes after that."

"Nothing else unless you want to," she said. "But if you get any dirty ideas you want to try, just let me know." She turned her head and kissed his neck, and he could feel her smiling. He chuckled again. She was a strange woman, but if she wanted him just to put it in, he'd try. Couldn't drive him any more out of his mind than he already was. He positioned himself and nudged inside, having to put a little force behind the thrust to make it work. Her breath hissed out and she wiggled, tipping her hips up and then back.

"Can I flip over?"

"Uh-huh, but, Mari, if it hurts—"

She pulled away and laid a finger over his lips when she turned in his lap. She was smiling, though, her eyes twinkling. "Don't even take away my birthday right now. I'm just fine." Her voice was light and teasing, and when she took hold of his erection, his hips twitched and yearned upward. She shifted and urged him flat on his back on the seat. His back eased in a happy rush at the change.

She braced one knee in the crease of the seat beside him. To fit, she had to drop her other foot to the floor of the truck. It was an odd position, but she didn't seem to mind, and as soon as the tip of his dick felt the slick warmth of her, he didn't mind, either.

She started to sink down on him, wiggling a little until she got the right angle. Her forehead creased and her eyes squeezed shut. She braced one hand on his shoulder and he caught her hips. "Mari, don't if—"

"It doesn't hurt," she gasped, taking a little more of him. "It feels . . . I really don't know if I could explain it to a man. It's a lot. But a really . . . *good* lot."

He held very still, uncertain and slightly unnerved by how great it felt. One inch at a time, he sank into the heat of her, the tight clasp slick and . . . safe? That was crazy. His sex brain was getting unhinged. But it really did feel like that, like they were hiding together someplace nice and he didn't ever want to be found.

The creases in her forehead had given way to soft sighs and a strange look that he liked very much. He flexed his legs, just enough to bump up into her, and she gasped and then grinned. "Almost there," she whispered, and gave a quiet squeeze that he felt all along his length.

Jesus.

His thumbs rubbed at the creases of her hips, holding her so she didn't have to keep her whole weight on her legs as she adjusted. When she slid the last part of the way, it felt so good his eyes fell closed. *Don't move*, he reminded himself. She just wanted to feel it. That's it.

He could feel it, all right. Feel every beat of his heart pulsing blood up through his erection. Feel how tight she was all around him. Feel that, even now, without his fingers strumming at her, she was wet as fucking hell. She gave a quick squeeze, clenching deliciously around him. Sweat broke out across his forehead.

Maybe he'd just never had it so slow before, so he could concentrate on every little thing, but he couldn't remember sex ever feeling this . . . fancy? That wasn't the right word, but he couldn't think of a better one at the moment.

"You okay?" His voice came out sounding hoarse.

Somehow, their eyes came open at the same time and hers looked dreamy, almost startled. She smiled at him. Just a little, but it was enough.

She shrugged off her open shirt, untangled the straps of her bra. The fabric tickled his knee as it slipped onto the floor of his truck. She leaned forward, and he stole a kiss before she gasped against his mouth and flexed around his cock all at the same time.

"Ooh, that angle is . . ." She moved and his arousal pressed deeper, into a place that made her breath flutter and his speed up.

"Is this all right?" Mari whispered. "Should I stay still?"

"God, no," he growled, then remembered himself. This was her experiment, not his. "Can move however you want, if you like that."

He clamped his teeth shut, fighting against the instinct to thrust. Wasn't no point in rutting away. Nothing good ever came of it anyhow. This was just about her. And she was shifting around, tiny sounds falling from her lips whenever she found a particularly good angle. He could watch her like this all day. He could tell he wasn't hurting her; maybe because she was in control, or just because she was so worked up from all their playing. Hell, she seemed to be kinda . . . enjoying herself.

Slowly, her little movements evolved into a jerky kind of rhythm as she found a place that felt good to her and kept coming back to it. Even those small up and downs were shivering pleasure all up and down his shaft, and a groan wound tight and silent in his chest. Fuck, at this rate he wasn't going to be able to drive back to town without staggering out in the desert and having a private moment first.

Her hand laid against his jaw and her hazy eyes came open again. "This okay?"

He nodded. "Like watching you. Like you—" He didn't know how to say it without sounding crude.

Jack liked her using his dick to make herself feel good. Fucking loved it, actually, but it didn't seem like the kind of thing you should say to a woman.

Her nails curled against his chest, steadying herself as she bucked backward. She kept thrusting herself onto him, going for this one little spot that made her twitch and clench when she found it. The next time she tried, he clenched his ass, presenting his cock even more fully. She squeaked and quivered, and triumph burst deep inside his chest. One of his legs slipped off the seat and he used it for leverage, pushing the heel of his foot against the floor so he could arch upward. Not far—just an inch or two. But it seemed like it was enough because Mari's rhythm had sped up.

She was moving faster and jerkier, his movements combined with hers seeming to work just right for whatever she was trying to do. He loved the unconscious clench and flex of her muscles as she chased that elusive feeling, her lower lip disappearing between her teeth as her eyes closed and brow furrowed and she worked her hips over him. His cock was getting wet, sliding in and out of her when she rocked now, and he caught himself watching that, too.

That seemed too personal to stare at, so he closed his eyes and just got lost in the feeling of her. The swell of her hips under his hands and her soft, nice skin, and how crazy lucky he was that she'd picked him to do this with. But now she was starting to rock so quickly he had to stop moving and just brace, his abs flexed and dick thrust up while she lifted and then shoved herself back toward the root of him in a quick, frustrated little—ah. There.

He felt it when she started to peak. The rush of heat and the waves of clench and release, massaging him now that he was inside, locking the swollen head of his cock deep inside her with this crazy tension that felt like . . . damn. She wasn't quite finished yet but he was starting to quake and he needed to, needed—

"Mari, can I move, will I hurt you—"

She made a sound and thrust herself down even more tightly on him.

"Yes," she gasped, the word so tattered he barely recognized it, but her nails were biting his chest and the sweet sting of pain just—his hips burst upward in a frenzy of movement. He surged all the way to sitting, his arms locking around her waist and face hidden in her neck, one foot on the floor slammed down so he could rail up with all the power in his body. Hammering into her as the friction went from slow and slick and tiny movements to long, mind-bending thrusts and then nothing but *heat.*

He yelled. Incoherent and loud, into her neck as he held on to her and came and came and came, his cock shooting so hard his body trembled all the way down to his toes.

"Fuck—bas—damn—" He started to curse, then swallowed the ugly words down so they wouldn't get all over her. His mind kept convulsing in bright, fisting knots of pleasure even after he stopped babbling out any sounds in response to them. When it slowed, he found himself hugging Mari and shaking, while her lips left small kisses at his temple.

Her neck was damp and he didn't know if it was sweat or if his eyes had maybe been watering from the force of all of it. He wiped a hand quickly over her skin before she noticed, shoving his knuckles across his eyes when he pulled away.

"I'm okay," she said before he could speak. "When you started to move, it felt crazy good, and I think I came twice instead of once." She grinned, then laughed. "I've never said that word out loud before." She snorted, then laughed some more. "I'm sorry, I don't know why that's so funny right now."

He chuckled, too, just because he felt all light and spinny, and damn it, he felt like laughing. He felt like lying down and dying happy and also drinking about a gallon of water. "Dang. You thirsty?"

"Are you kidding? God yes. I think I brought something." She turned, and they both hissed at how that jarred him where he was still inside her.

There was a little fumbling then, for him to pull out and her to get to her purse, and him to tie off the condom and ditch it out the door. He glanced at her, feeling guilty for littering but having no God's honest idea what to put the used thing in to get it back to town. Sure as fuck wasn't going in his jeans pocket.

Mari passed him a water bottle. "I won't tell Captain Planet if you won't."

He meant to talk to her, tell her he hadn't meant to go for full-on sex, ask if that was as amazing for her as it was for him. Figure out a way to find out if she'd ever felt *that* before, because what the holy shit?

But instead, he snickered at her Captain Planet joke, and then a snort escaped, and then he started to really laugh. And just kept on going because it was a good day, and laughing felt fan-fucking-tastic.

27

The Stakes

Dinner was tense. Though not because they'd had sex yesterday.

Jack had kissed her cheek—out in the open in the parking lot!—when they'd gotten home from work today, and Mari didn't think he seemed any more self-conscious than normal. More like . . . distracted. He kept leaving tasks half-done and he had to ask her to repeat herself twice, and that wasn't like him.

She smiled to herself as she loaded spices back into her milk crate. Once, not so long ago, it had been normal for the man in her life not to care what she had to say. Now, it was odd enough to catch her notice.

In between his distraction, too, he asked all about her first day on the new crew. How Junior was. The other workers. She didn't lie, exactly. Just downplayed how long the argument had been over how they dealt with the hydraulic leak on-site. And forgot to mention how many crude comments she'd pretended not to hear. Or the three times she had to request that Junior call her by her *name*.

"So they, uh, following the rules okay?" Jack asked, picking up the topic yet again. "Not pushing you to look the other way on nothing?"

"We're getting by." She hoped the casual words covered her unease. It was only a matter of time before they did something she'd have to write them up for, and then Rod would know she wasn't going to be his puppet. She wasn't sure what he'd do, and frankly she didn't want to know. But she couldn't go against her professional integrity, and she absolutely refused to let that crew do anything to threaten the animals she was there to protect. Even if there were only a few weeks left of this job.

Mari swallowed, and pushed her anxieties away, because there was no sense in getting Jack more worried than he clearly already was. Some things you couldn't compromise on, and you just had to pay what it cost you.

She waited for him to fold her camp stove and pointed at the nook she wanted him to slide it into, in the back of her truck. "How are things on your site? Getting twice as many towers built now that Kipp's not trying to talk to me all day?"

He snorted. "He's almost as bad with following Lisa around."

"How's Lisa doing, by the way?"

"Ain't cried once." Jack hefted a water jug back into her pickup. "Maybe she got on meds or something since last time."

Mari held back a laugh. Most likely, Lisa wasn't crying because Jack wasn't growling at her for enforcing rules that nobody had ever bothered to explain to him. He wasn't much for following rules he didn't understand.

"She said she volunteered. Even asked me to dinner again tonight at her and Marcus's." He dodged her a fast glance. "Told her my stomach wasn't feeling too good. You better not tell her I lied."

"Wouldn't have been a lie if you'd eaten her cooking." Mari slammed the tailgate quickly, before the sun-scorched metal could burn her palm. "So I think we can let that one slide."

"Did you tell her to be nice to me?" His voice darkened. "Wasn't like it was hurting my delicate little feelings for her to hate me, before."

She locked up the truck, waving away a stray bee. "I think she's curious about you, since I told her we were together. Plus, she said

Marcus always pretends to know more about cars than her, but you knocked him down a peg or two when you agreed with her about that transmission thing."

Her last comment was interrupted when her phone rang in her pocket. Hotaka had said he might stop by this week to borrow her ratchet set, but he hadn't said what day. But when she checked her phone, the botanist's name wasn't on the screen. Her heart jerked, then started to race.

It was area code 262.

Wisconsin.

Again.

"Probably a telemarketer," Jack offered, glancing from her face to the number displayed with no contact name. "Can just send it to voicemail."

But if she did that, she wouldn't know if he'd found her. She hit "Accept" and lifted the phone to her ear, only to feel chilled all over again by the silence. "Hello?" She pitched her voice low so it wouldn't sound like her, and said it twice, but there was no answer. She hung up with a gusty exhale. Ridiculous, to get so jumpy over a simple area code. Tens of thousands of people lived in that area. For all she knew, Brad had moved since the divorce.

"Telemarketer," she said. "You can always tell by the delay before the recording clicks on."

"You okay?" He was giving her a strange look, and she scrubbed a hand over her face, knowing she must have gone pale when she saw the caller.

"Takes more than a telemarketer to scare me, mister." She set off toward their rooms with a determinately casual stride. "Your beers or mine?"

"Mine." Jack moved around her to unlock the door to his room, but once they got inside, he kept fidgeting around with different things and seemed to forget about heading for the minifridge. Distracted again.

"Something on your mind?" She touched his arm, bare beneath the sleeve of his T-shirt.

His eyes came up to hers. Tumultuous with more thoughts than their simple conversation should have brought up. They were such a bright, piercing green that her breath got all tangled up at having their full focus on her. And then he came to her, his hands cupping her neck, his mouth coming down on hers harder and faster than the careful kisses he'd risked so far. Mari didn't think they moved, but suddenly the thin, sun-heated door was at her back, his thick chest closing her in.

Jack was not distracted now.

Upset, maybe. Intense, definitely. But he was kissing her with such tortured, begging rasps of his chapped lips that she could only cling to him, her arms trying to hold softly enough to comfort him because she didn't dare stop him long enough to ask what was wrong.

Every time she thought he might be pausing, he came back for more, until they were both panting and her nipples had gone sensitive and peaked beneath her shirt. He leaned his forehead against hers. "It's good. Having you back. Here, I mean. Not off on Junior's crew."

She laughed breathlessly. "Well, hello to you, too. I would have put in for a transfer weeks ago if I'd known I'd get this kind of welcome at night."

"I just . . . Be better if I knew you were okay, but . . . Dunno, it's dumb, but—" He seemed to give up after his third try and kissed her again. Hard and long and sweet, until one of her hands was fisted into the side of his shirt and her pulse throbbed hazily in her temples.

"It's not dumb," she said, when he finally relinquished her mouth. "Can I . . . would you let me try something?"

He nodded, his rough thumb skimming along her cheek. He kissed her forehead once, quickly, before he pulled away. Like he was saving up that little touch for later.

Her heart squeezed a big, painful beat at that, and she took his hand and tugged him toward the bed. Didn't even bother turning on the TV to pretend that's what they were doing. Instead, she started unbuttoning his shirt. Deliberately, not with the cramped frenzy of getting them both undressed in the cab of his truck yesterday. But slowly, with the time to enjoy the strong chest emerging beneath the gapped fabric.

He got tense, shifting his weight from foot to foot like he wanted to pull away, but wouldn't. She was confused until she saw his big shoulders hunching forward, and recognized the movement. It was the way her body always caved in on herself when she was insulted. It was the hideous self-consciousness of your own shortcomings.

The last button came free and she slid her hands up his chest, across those glorious shoulders.

"Look at me." Her voice came out low and private, more a murmur than a whisper, and his eyes startled up to hers. "I don't think you know how you look to me."

She let her hands crest his shoulders, pushing the shirt off so it fell to the floor behind him, her palms traveling down his back, even when she felt the ridges and roughness of old scars. She'd glimpsed just the edges of them once, beside the new burns from the metal of the tower, the bloody rip from when a drill had slipped the other day. None of it seemed to get much more than a wince out of him, and she couldn't imagine being so impervious to pain.

It was respect for that toughness that glowed in her eyes now, and pure desire for the strong body half-bared in front of her. She pushed up on her toes and kissed one shoulder, a bit of mischief darting through her. "After all the time I spent staring at these shoulders at work, I deserve to see the rest of the package."

When her heels came back to the ground, his eyes were confused and a touch wary, but longing echoed underneath.

Those scars hadn't all come from work, she knew that. At least some of them must have come from what was done to him as a child. But the depth and breadth of the healed wounds just made her feel . . . powerful. Because he'd risked worse than those to leave whoever had done that to him, and he'd been brave enough to do it anyway. After all that pain, all that humiliation. And she had, too.

It was the stakes they'd faced, slashed across both their skins in marks that would never fade or smooth. And yet they'd both stared down that cost and stolen back their lives for themselves.

She was fucking proud.

Of him. Of herself.

That made the sight of every scar thrill desire deep in her belly. Like the roar of a motorcycle, the whistle of wind at the edge of a cliff. Danger, denied.

It was sexy as almighty hell, and she knew he saw it in her face as she pushed him down to the bed and crawled up over the top of him, taking out the ferocity of her feelings on his lips.

She pinned his big wrists to the bed, and his muscles flexed, all those years of swinging a heavy hammer corded tautly beneath her grasp. But he didn't flip her over, just stayed put and let her take charge of the moment. The fly of his jeans bulged, nudging the inside seam of her shorts.

Mari dipped to kiss his neck, which shuddered with his ragged breathing. He smelled like soap from his after-work shower, tasted of just a hint of salt from cooking tailgate dinner in the desert heat.

She got lost in kissing his chest, in touching all the muscles that she'd already admitted to watching for so many hours of her workday. It was intoxicating, to be the one allowed to see him like this, to touch him and feel him tremble in response when he avoided everyone else's hands.

She wanted to keep doing this, for years. To go to sleep with him and wake up with him and know that no one else could see him naked but her. But Mari was used to wanting and never being able to have, so she pretended just tonight was enough. That she didn't need a plan, or a future. And his body was very nearly distracting enough to make her actually forget those things.

By the time she got to undoing the button and zipper of his pants, it wasn't so much a decision as it was a craving.

She still checked in with him, letting the heat in her body burn from her eyes when she looked at him. He nodded without her having to figure out how to ask the question. His Adam's apple bobbed. His jeans hit the floor.

Mari undressed herself after she undressed him, and Jack wasn't sure if she did it because she knew how much he wanted to see her, or simply because she didn't want him to be alone in his nakedness.

He only managed to choke out a sputtered sound that quickly turned into a groan when it became clear what she'd wanted his pants off for. Her mouth was hot and wet and hungry on his cock, her hand sliding down his shaft in sweet consolation when she couldn't take him all.

After yesterday in the truck, when she changed her mind about doing this, he hadn't dared hope she'd ever want to. Now, he could hardly think past the pleasure.

What he did know was that heat was surging up through him, tension pooling in the root of him, the muscles in his hips begging to thrust. The head of his cock was so sensitive that when she sat back a little and ran her tongue from base to tip, he flinched and made a strangled sound, tingles blanking out his thoughts.

He didn't know how that was possible, how release could just be nipping at his heels after a few short minutes of Mari when sweaty, awkward hours with another woman had never once gotten him excited this fast.

He started swearing, fumbling for her shoulder to hold her back so he wouldn't get it in her mouth when he went. She looked up at him, her hand still curled protectively around his shaft. "It's all right. You don't have to stop."

His eyes damn near fogged over from the heat, but desire was driving him now, and the longing pulled words from his mouth that he wasn't sure he'd have ever been able to say otherwise. "Would you want—"

"*Yes.*" She moved up over him, then grimaced. "Except my condoms are in my purse, in my room."

"Bought some this morning." He threw an arm out and—thank fuck—made it to the nightstand without having to move, digging out the plastic-wrapped box and a bottle of the same brand of lube he'd seen that she had bought. She took over condom duty, and he reached down to pet her and help her catch up to his raging level of arousal. His fingers twitched when he found her slippery instead of dry, and his forehead creased.

She laughed softly at his surprise, her face bright with a smile. "I like it, doing that to you. Didn't used to. I think I do now."

Her hand wrapped around the length of him, her palm smooth with lube, and he thrust up into her grip, his head falling back on the bed. Hellfire, he wanted to fuck like a demon right now. Wasn't wholly sure he could trust himself with her in such a state. He started to sweat as she rolled the condom down over his sensitive tip, then slicked it with more lube sliding beneath her tight grip.

"You gotta stop me. If I go too hard or deep or—you gotta," he insisted.

"I will."

"And don't pretend, if—"

"I won't."

"And we can stop if—"

This time she quieted his words with a gentle kiss. "I don't want to stop."

She took his dick inside. She had to wiggle to get it to slide, and then she held tremblingly still while he pushed up, slow so it'd be smooth on her, biting the shit out of the inside of his cheek to keep control over himself. He tasted blood and his head whirled until he remembered to breathe, and he'd never felt so good all at once in his entire born life.

Her breath was stuttering a little, too, and he stopped only halfway in. The part of his shaft left out in the cold throbbed and ached, and he tried his level best to ignore it. "You all right?"

"I, uh . . ." She laughed breathlessly, her eyes closed and face flushed. "My ex wasn't quite so, um, fulfilling in that area. This is . . . very nice."

His dick fisted harder, and blood rushed hot in his chest. It shouldn't feel so good, to hear that her husband had a tiny prick. It probably made him a caveman, but he enjoyed the idea that her ex hadn't filled her up the way he could. His hands flexed on her hips and he arched, gave her more.

"I can take it all," she whispered achingly. "I like it deep." Her lashes fluttered as she sank down onto him, her small breasts trembling with the movement.

Deep.

The word roared silently in his chest, like it was some kind of key twisting in him, unlocking things he probably shouldn't be thinking. Definitely shouldn't be feeling.

Her legs flexed as she rose up. "Last time, you let me do what felt good to me." She braced her hands on his shoulders, her eyes soft on his face. "I want to know what it's like when you do what feels good to you. Please? I'll stop you if it's uncomfortable."

He grunted out a breath, his heart beating so wildly he could barely hear her over it. She wouldn't ask for that if she knew how far gone he already was. He could barely stay still right now. Slow was totally beyond him, and the pressing, arching exploration she'd done? Utterly impossible.

Gritting his teeth until he was sure they'd crack, he flexed his hips.

Just enough to rub the head of his cock deeper in her. Even that was enough to make blackness shudder in his vision.

"Mmm," she hummed. "Can you . . . a little harder?"

Fuck. Hell. Jesus's sandblasted sandals.

He rolled her onto her back and withdrew from her body, hovering for a stretched second before he powered back in. She gasped, knees coming up and toes curling hard into the blankets, nails biting the scars in his shoulders. He did it again, living on her stuttered gasps. Going faster when her head fell back.

He couldn't find one thing so far that he liked that she didn't seem to like even more. Her knee had jerked up toward her chest with his last movement, so he wrapped his arm around it. His next slide in went even deeper, like they fit better this way, and he nearly whimpered.

Mari's fingers clenched, trembling where she gripped his arms and urged him on, and the leash on his control went ragged. He forgot about the long, smooth strokes to satisfy her the way her ex couldn't. Instead, he jerked against her in tiny hard jabs so he didn't have to leave her body but could still find that spot that locked him in deep. The one that wrung low noises from her throat and made tingles run down his spine and gather heat in the muscles of his legs.

How could she feel this wet through a condom? How could she manage to grip and fist his cock the way she was, and *damn*, was she doing that on purpose, or was that just what happened when she liked the way he was fucking on her?

He was breathing through his gritted teeth now, every beat of his heart like a shout as he powered into her just to feel her clench and wriggle and *ah God*—

It took him without warning, like a waterslide gone steep so everything just dropped out from underneath him and pleasure burst through his body. More and more and more of it, so he might have yelled, startled by the force of it. By how long it went, picking him back up when he thought he didn't have any more left.

He fell unevenly onto his elbows, the hard motel mattress biting into them. "You—" he gasped out. "Did you?"

Mari blushed pink and glanced away as she nodded, the smile tugging on her lips so damn cute that he had to kiss her even though he couldn't half catch his breath yet.

"Ungh," he said, not sure what word that was supposed to have been, but pretty fucking pleased about his entire state of affairs at the moment. He pulled out of her and flopped over onto his back, lungs heaving to catch up.

She curled into his side, and it took him a lot longer than it probably should have to finally get his heart rate to settle down, and then to work up the motivation to get rid of the condom. But when he came back, she settled right onto his shoulder like he'd never left, and kissed his collarbone, making his heart jump.

"I like the truck," she said, "but I think I like the bed even more."

He gave her a squeeze, not bothering to hide his grin.

After a while, he couldn't help but start to think about the situation, and he must have tensed up or something, because her head tipped back.

"What is it?"

"Just . . . why do you think it works so much better with you?" He gestured at himself. "Ain't no smaller."

She chuckled. "Um, I think with you, I'm usually excited enough that things are just . . . easier."

He considered that. He usually hadn't messed around as much before sex with his few other women. They hadn't asked for it, and he'd been afraid to try anything they didn't initiate. But with Mari, he knew she liked him using his fingers on her, and the more she wriggled and panted, the longer he wanted to do it. It just seemed to make things more awkward, with other women, when he'd attempted different ways of touching them.

"Didn't know what I was doing before," he admitted. "Didn't know how to ask. It's easier, with you. To know what you like."

Now she really did laugh. "It seems as if I like everything, when you're doing it. So yeah, it's probably easier." She kissed his jaw. "Don't be shy to ask about things, if you're curious. I might blush, but I'll also probably have a really good time answering your question."

He grunted, rubbing slow circles on her lower back because it cuddled her farther into him and made her get all relaxed feeling.

"I like that you're comfortable with me," she whispered into his neck.

"I, uh—" He hugged her naked body against his side, his throat scratchy all of a sudden. "Same thing. Like that, too. Want you to be okay."

What he wanted was for her to always be where she was right now: her little breasts pressed against his ribs, her skin warm against his while both their bodies hummed with the pleasure of what they'd just done. Far away from all those other filthy workers and their eyes following her. Far away from Junior, and anything hurtful he might say to her when Jack wasn't there to put a stop to it. He wanted her to stay with him, pretty much forever.

He wasn't entirely sure how to make that happen, but he was thinking on it. A lot.

28

Bad News

"Would you please sit down?"

"I don't like it."

"You don't have to like it. It's my job, and that's that."

Mari tried to keep the sigh out of her voice as Jack kept pacing her motel room. He hadn't been able to settle all evening. Actually, all week since she'd been moved off his crew, though it had gotten worse every night. Couldn't focus on working on her truck, or his own. Just got in her way trying to help with dinner.

He'd finally given up pretending it was an accident that they ate dinner together every night. Now, he paid for the food and she cooked while he caught up on all the long-overdue maintenance on her truck, then they cleaned up together. It had felt like a pretty good routine, until this week.

"It ain't about you just doing your regular job. I was in the office this week when Rod got the stack of tickets Junior's been racking up all week. He blew his fuck—his damn lid. And your name was signed at the bottom of every one."

He paced past where she sat on her motel bed, the agitation roiling through him too clearly for him to stop moving.

"Besides, I don't like you all alone with them. They ain't a good crew."

"They're lazy. That doesn't make them dangerous." She folded her arms and gave him a knowing smile. "And I'm hardly alone, am I?"

She'd been reassigned to Rod Jr.'s crew on Tuesday. On Wednesday, Gideon had shown up to their morning meeting as well.

"Wyatt got very concerned about being overstaffed on his crew," Gideon had told her.

She'd laughed and rolled her eyes, but then at lunch, Gideon had come to sit with her in the scanty shade of her truck.

"You don't have to babysit me through lunch, too, you know?"

"You're better company than they are." He had ducked his chin and given her a wide-eyed look. "Please don't make me go back. As soon as they find out I'm gay, they all assume I'll be overcome with lust for their balding, sweaty selves. Watch me like I'm a lion just itching to pounce."

She had choked on her laugh. "Okay, okay, I wouldn't subject you to that. But seriously, what is Jack doing, sending you over here? I worked on construction crews for a lot of seasons before I started on his team. It's hardly my first day alone with workers."

Gideon had taken a thoughtful bite of his sandwich. "It's going to really put his crew behind schedule, being a man down. Rod keeps track of their production like it's the Super Bowl scoreboard."

"That's what I'm saying! Rod's going to get him in trouble for transferring you, and for what?"

Gideon had given her another slow, sidelong look. "I've never seen Jack care about anything more than he cares about building fast. Or keeping his job."

Thinking back on that conversation, she hunched her shoulders, prickling all over with emotions she didn't want to be having. It was simple vanity, enjoying a thought like that. And terrible, too, because what if Jack really did lose his job because he was trying to help her?

For all that she'd argued with him, she didn't want to be transferred, either.

It wasn't like she enjoyed going to war with Junior's crew about every environmental regulation. Not like she enjoyed being called "little lady" and constantly correcting how every conversation seemed to come back to something about her body. Not like she enjoyed how they laughed like it was a joke when she told them to knock it off, and treated her like she was uptight for not laughing, too. Or how they wouldn't actually shut up unless Gideon went after them for it.

Not like she didn't see the shadow of a bruise not quite hidden by the edge of Gideon's beard, or the way he didn't have a single friend on his new crew. Her fault. Her fault, too, probably, the guy who'd had to leave work to see the medic because he'd "tripped" over behind some pallets.

"It's a construction site," she told Jack now. "No better or worse than any of the others I've been on."

He threw her a black look. "I know how it is. Worked on them all my life. I don't like you dealing with it on a crew where the foreman ain't got your back."

She tried a different tack. "C'mon, though. You have to admit it's funny. Rod only put me on that crew because he assumed I was fixing your crew's environmental compliance record to look perfect. He hoped I'd do the same for his son, and instead I'm writing tickets so fast I ought to be doing it on hemp paper."

Jack shoved both hands back through his hair, the movement too quick now that he didn't have long hair to yank at.

"Get it?" she teased gently. "Because hemp grows faster, and that way I wouldn't use any trees? Never mind. Anyway, if Junior spent as much time building towers as he did breaking laws, we'd be out of a job already." A little pang twisted through her. They were nearly out of a job as it was, and it seemed like she would spend the last two weeks of it seeing Jack only in the evenings.

"Ain't funny. You think he's going to just pay those fines and that'll be it?" His eyes blazed. "You didn't see how Rod got when he saw those tickets. I'm talking to Marcus tomorrow. Get you moved off that crew."

Her back straightened so hard she wasn't even touching the pillows behind her anymore. "What, so you think I'm making those violations up? Any other bio would be writing him up as much as I am, so moving me isn't going to get Junior out of trouble or calm Rod down."

At least any bio would if they didn't fold to all the intimidation he tried when he wanted them to let it go "just this once." It was Junior's favorite phrase, "just this once," and it always reminded her of Rajni's "one and done." Which was why she hadn't let him off on a single ticket.

"Rod's gonna blame you for the trouble, not his boy." Jack shook his head. "Spread out the blame some, let the other bios make him mad."

She narrowed her eyes. "You hate me being over there at all. It's not just about Rod, or you wouldn't have sent Gideon. He couldn't do a thing for me against Rod unless it came to a fistfight, and that doesn't seem like Rod's style."

Why had she been flattered that Jack sent Gideon to watch over her? Brad used to have people watching her, too. Everybody from his buddy who worked at their grocery store to their accountant. If she so much as nodded at another man on the street, he'd hear about it. And here she was getting all starry-eyed over a guy who was basically doing the same thing.

"Gideon can keep the other workers from grabbing at you. Junior sure isn't going to stop them."

"I'm perfectly capable of slapping a hand away if it comes to that, which it usually doesn't. You've worked on enough construction sites that you should know it's mostly talk."

"Rod's not mostly talk. He's deep down mean, not to mention sneaky as hell. And you're right, Gideon wouldn't be able to slow him down worth shit. Rod's been covering up for that son of his forever, but with biologists watching all the time, he can't hide all the slipups before management sees them. When it comes to a head, I promise you it ain't his kid he's going to blame for the problem. I don't want you being his goddamn scapegoat."

She knew he was having a hard time with the change in crew assignments, and she hadn't meant to get upset, but now her temper was rising in spite of herself. "So what, just because we're dating now, you're never going to let me out of your sight?"

She'd been through this before. Protective became paranoid, and that turned into the kind of forced isolation she was still trying to break back out of.

"You ain't—" Jack blasted out, then stopped himself and dropped his voice. Even quieter, it lost none of his intensity. "You ain't listening. You don't know what he's like."

"What's he going to do? Suspend me? He can't. Not without Marcus's permission, and Marcus knows exactly what that joker is like." She shot off the bed, unable to sit still anymore. "I'm not just going to stay in whatever tiny box you decide is safe, Jack. You're my boyfriend, not my father. I lived for months—God, *years* now—alone in a truck in a desert. I think I can probably take care of myself without your help, thank you very much."

His eyes flared and he scowled furiously. "Fine. You do whatever you damn well please. What do I know, anyhow?"

"Oh, thank you so much for your *permission*!" She could barely hear Jack, because Brad's words filled her whole memory.

You think you can just flaunt yourself all over town, doing whatever you please?

That had been when she wore a tank top in August, and Brad made sure she couldn't wear anything but long sleeves again for weeks.

Mari's voice was quiet when she spoke again, quivering along with the tears that blurred the edges of her vision. "I don't need a man to tell me what to do, and I will never be treated like a child in my own life ever again. I thought things were going to be different with you, but God knows I've been wrong before."

He cursed, his hands knotting into fists that made the muscles stand out all along his arms. "Mari, please don't cry. Listen, I fucked this all up—"

"Yes, you did." She cut him off, thinking of chapter seven, "Apologizing." They were always sorry after. But it sure didn't mean they wouldn't do the same thing over again if you gave them the chance. "I think you'd better go."

He stood very, very still, his eyes flicking between her face and the floor like he had to see her but couldn't quite stand to hold her gaze. But when she stormed over and threw the door open, he went without her having to ask him again.

And the worst thing about it, worse than the click of the closing door or the gaping silence from his side of the wall, worse than the sobs that racked her after he left . . . the worst thing was that she didn't think either of them were surprised that everything that seemed so perfect had fallen apart after all. For people like them, it always did.

29

The Call

Jack didn't sleep much that night. For hours, he could hear Mari crying through the wall. Every sniffle, every scrape of a sob tore at his insides like a steel-toothed brush. He'd done that. To her.

His brother warned him that he had a talent for disappointing people, but this was worse than that. Through the wall, it sounded like despair. She'd had such a bad run of it with men, and after this, he doubted she'd ever have the heart to try again. Nobody would get to see her slow smile, or the twinkle she got in her eye when she wanted to make a dirty joke. He'd ruined that not just for himself, but for every other man in the world.

The shitty part of it was, he couldn't see a way to do it differently. Every time he thought about ignoring his instinct to protect her and just leaving her to face Rod on her own, he came up against a flat refusal, like a dog hitting the end of its leash and a concrete wall at the same time.

He. Could. Not.

It wasn't that he didn't trust her. He'd match Mari's brain against Rod's and bet every cent he'd ever seen that she could outthink that old buzzard before she'd even had her coffee in the morning. And she was a flawless biologist. No way could Rod catch her in a mistake, because she never really made any.

But Rod was meaner than her, in a way he doubted Mari could fathom. Rod was like a varmint that got into your garden. You could put chicken wire three feet underground, build the fences up to the sky, electrify those fences and line them with traps . . . and Varmint Rod would sneak in your bedroom window just to piss on your pillow. It wouldn't win him a single vegetable to eat, but he'd do it anyway, out of sheer cussedness.

Jack couldn't abandon her to whatever Rod might do to her. Not even after she asked him to. Not even if she wouldn't speak to him again.

He understood that she didn't want to be watched or be told what to do. He probably should pull Gideon back off Junior's crew. Mari was right—Gideon couldn't save her from Rod's wrath. Mari could deal with off-color remarks, and if somebody got handsy, he bet she could kick their asses the old-fashioned way. With so many witnesses, it wouldn't go further than that.

Maybe she would let him apologize for being bossy. He really hadn't meant to take her choices from her, and after her ex-husband, he could see why she'd be fully fed up with that sort of thing. He thought maybe there was still a chance she liked him enough that they could work it out.

But every time he heard her take a ragged breath, doubt sank its teeth deeper into him. He'd heard crying his whole life, through cheap walls and doors, muffled into thin pillows and sometimes dirty laundry when there wasn't anything else.

His brother had taken him from his dad so they could have a fresh start, but it didn't turn out all that fresh. It still smelled of Bud Light and dust and a little mildew. He still got yelled at, still caught the occasional fist. After they left, he never felt the cut of a belt again, but he wasn't entirely sure that was an improvement.

He loved Leroy more than he loved his dad, so it hurt more when he yelled. As a kid, Jack would have preferred the belt to disappointing his big brother.

Jack flipped onto his side and balled a fist in the rough sheets, yanking them up over his head to try to block the sound. They carried the reek of heavy bleach in an attempt to hide their stains, and there was little comfort to be found there.

They'd left their dad to try to have a different life, and fucked it up. He'd left his brother to try to be better, and fucked that up just as bad. Maybe lineman work paid a little better than the shit they'd done back home, but he'd still landed in a motel with half its neon sign burnt out, listening to a woman's grief over his poor choices.

When Mari hiccupped, it broke what was left of his heart.

He wanted to do what she asked, but with Rod, and any other danger she might run into . . . how could he not try to protect her? The problem chewed on him even after her crying quieted. He lay there for hours, staring at the wall between their rooms and wishing he were a different kind of man. He didn't even realize he'd fallen asleep until the trilling of his phone woke him up.

It jolted him out of a restless dream of searching the Alabama woods behind his old trailer. Leroy had hidden something back there, and Jack wanted it worse than he'd ever wanted anything. But he couldn't find it and there wasn't a track in the woods for him to follow. Not a deer, not a rabbit, or even a rat-faced possum. The forest was eerily empty, like he was the only man left alive.

His ringtone blasted out again, shaking him out of the dream forest and back into his desert motel room. He yanked his phone out of his jeans pocket, jerking it back to his face.

"This is a collect call from Lancaster County Correction Center, from Inmate—"

The recording broke off for a confusingly long pause, and then

Leroy's voice burst jovially onto the line: "Your smarter, better-looking big brother! Pick up, you dumb—"

"Do you accept the charges?" the recording interrupted again.

Jack fumbled for the button to accept the charges and sat up.

"Morning, you dickless wonder!" Leroy sounded damn cheery for somebody who was sitting in jail. That wasn't a good sign. The worse things went, the harder Leroy tried to prove how little he cared. Now, if he'd been pissed off, that'd mean things were running just about normal. "It's been a coon's age, hasn't it? How the hell are you?"

"Where you at?" Jack groped for the switch on the lamp. "There ain't no Lancaster County in Alabama."

"I'm not in Alabama. I'm residing in the great state of Nebraska. Listen, I need some bail money, and don't even try to tell me that cushy lineman job of yours ain't paying enough to cover it."

He grunted. It had been months since he'd heard from his brother. He'd half wondered if Leroy had one drunken car crash too many. But no, of course he was fine and just wanting money.

"Yeah, let me get a pen. I'll find a bond place over there and call them on my way to work. You better fucking pay me back this time."

"Now is that any way to talk to your only kin? You ought to at least come pick me up. You really going to make me take the bus like some trash?"

"Leroy, you're in *Nebraska*." Jack staggered to his feet, jerking up the twisted waist of his pants as he squinted around his room in search of a pen. "I'm in California. I know you weren't hot on school and shit, but they ain't exactly neighbors."

Any other time, he would have just quit the job and gone. But that was before he met Mari.

"Yeah, see, here's the rub." Leroy dropped his voice. "I can't just make bail and walk on outta here. I'm in just . . . well, just a wee tiny bit of trouble. Some assholes got it in for me, and if I buy a plane or a bus ticket, they'll find me. I need a ride, little brother. Something they can't trace to somewhere they can't trace."

"Leroy, you can't skip town, or we don't get our bail back. Collateral and fee's one thing, but I ain't got five grand or so to spend on keeping you from getting your ass kicked by some guys who are probably kicking it because you rightfully owe them money. Just like you owe me." He scoffed. "Hell, you probably owe me more than you owe them."

"Come on, now, has your big brother ever let you down? I'll come back for my court date! Just need to lay low until then. Let them forget all about me. Then you'll get your bail back, no problem."

"Uh-huh. When's your court date?"

"Two weeks."

Jack nearly choked. Two weeks? The job would be over in two weeks. He couldn't babysit his stupid brother to make sure he showed up for his trial. Mari wasn't even speaking to him right now, and they hadn't made any plans for after the job, even before their fight. He couldn't disappear now, or—

He couldn't even stand putting the possibility into words.

"You really gotta think it over? You owe me, kid. I pulled you outta that hellhole and raised you up myself, when I could have left you to take Dad's shit all the way to eighteen, just like I had to."

The words were so familiar Jack could have recited them from memory. It was Leroy's trump card, worn around the edges from being played so often. And maybe it was true. The worst scars that ripped up his hide were from his daddy, not his brother.

Maybe it had been better to walk to school hiding bruises instead of blood. His brother always said he'd saved him, and Jack figured there was a whole world of worse past catching the occasional punch.

But sometimes he thought Leroy had just wanted to live someplace where everybody had to walk on eggshells around *him*, not vice versa. Because once they'd moved out, Jack still had to keep his mouth shut.

Do his homework outside because the sight of schoolbooks always seemed to piss Leroy off, especially if he was coming off a bender. Said if he didn't need to finish school to get by, neither did his brother.

Leroy interrupted his thoughts, his voice dropping even lower. "Listen, Jack, I ain't asking. They busted my arm, I'm in a cast. I can't defend myself in here, much less out there. I need you, brother. Got nobody else I trust right now, with the kinda guys that are after me."

"Shit." Jack's breath hissed out as he grabbed clean clothes out of his suitcase. "I'm coming. You fucking owe me, asshole." He hung up.

He threw clothes into his suitcase, nabbed his French press and his toothbrush. He'd only meant he'd go pick his brother up, not that he'd stay with him. But as soon as he heard himself saying he'd go, he knew this might be the only thing that saved his chances with Mari.

It was too early to call her, but he didn't dare go over there in person. If he saw her pretty eyes all red and swollen from crying, he'd hate himself so much he wouldn't have the guts to ask her to take a chance on him, no matter what he tried to change about himself. Jack's stomach lurched at the thought of what he was going to do, but he snatched up his phone anyway. The alternative was never seeing her again, and he was too much of a coward to face that.

He heard it ring in his ear and through the wall. Once. Twice. Was she staring at the screen, hating the sight of his name? What if she—

"Hello?"

"Mari." He exhaled it like a prayer, his chest expanding in a way he couldn't describe, just at the sound of her voice.

"Jack, I don't want to talk to you. Not yet and certainly not at four thirty in the morning."

Her voice sounded crisp and certain, not the least bit sleepy.

"And while I'm telling you how things are going to be, let me add one more tip. The whole persistence song and dance, where you call and send flowers and follow me everywhere I go until I give you another chance? I don't care what movies you've seen it on, because Brad saw all the same ones. That is the opposite of romance, in my opinion. If there is going to even be a chance of me forgiving you—and I'm not saying there is—but if you even want a *chance*, then you'd better back off by about a mile and give me the respect of waiting for me to make my own choices. About you, about Rod, about everything. I'm a grown fucking woman, and if you can't treat me accordingly, you have no place in my life."

Hearing Mari swear made something hurt behind his eyes, like he needed to cough or sneeze, or possibly something far more embarrassing.

"I understand, and I will. Shit, Mari, I'm so sorry you even have to say that to me. I just, I needed you to know that I lo—"

The words came pouring out of him, and the only reason he stopped in time was that his throat caught. He hadn't meant to tell her how he felt. He'd been keeping that locked way deep down for a while now so he wouldn't pressure her or scare her or come across as one of those guys who fell too fast.

Except that he had. Fallen so fast and hard he was all but picking chunks of sidewalk out of his teeth. But he couldn't tell her like this, when she was angry at him. She'd think he was trying to soften her up.

He took a breath and switched gears back to facts, not emotions. "The only reason I'm calling is—"

"Is to show me you'll promise one thing and immediately do the other?" Her voice was so sharp he could have cut himself on it. "If you respect my ability to make my own choices, then prove it. Back the hell off and let me make them."

She hung up.

He hadn't told her about his brother or that he had to leave. He hadn't even gotten out a decent apology. But there was one thing he could do: exactly what she asked. Leaving would prove to her that he would give her space and respect her choices. The idea of leaving her to face off with Rod alone made him physically ill, and more than a little dizzy.

But maybe being halfway across the country was his best bet at not sticking his fucking nose into it and pissing her off again. She could handle Rod. Mari was tough, and she was asking him to believe in her. If she'd forgive him, he'd do anything, no matter how much he hated it.

He grabbed his stuff and let himself out, a pang going through him at giving up the room next to hers. He'd call her later when she was busy at work and leave a voicemail so she knew where he'd gone and that he was available by phone, when—if—she felt like talking.

The suitcase went into the truck and he yanked out his ramp to load his bike. He couldn't think about all the terrible what-ifs. Right now, he needed to get his ass to Nebraska before his temporarily crippled brother got himself killed.

30

A Little Help from Friends

When she arrived at work, Mari was still so upset that she didn't even react when Marcus told her she'd been transferred from Junior's crew back to Jack's. She wasn't surprised, since she definitely hadn't been looking the other way on his son's transgressions, like Rod had implied she should. Hopefully, now he'd realize he was out of options and was going to have to get his jerk of a progeny to follow the rules like everyone else.

At the moment, she didn't much care what Rod did, except that today was clearly not the best day for her and Jack to be stuck on the same construction site. When she left the morning meeting for Junior's crew and headed across the construction yard to Jack's crew, Gideon went with her, even though Marcus didn't have the authority to reassign him. She glanced over.

"Aren't you going to get in trouble for changing crews without orders?"

"Nobody on Junior's crew likes me enough to care," he told her with a wry smile and a quick shoulder squeeze. "Besides, Wyatt's going to need me to catch their productivity back up to quota."

Except, of course, Jack wasn't running his crew that day.

His truck was already gone when she'd left for work, so he couldn't be late. Either he was avoiding her after their fight—which was pretty immature, in her opinion—or it had something to do with Rod. His company was paying thousands of dollars in environmental impact fines, and if her second hasty transfer in a week was any indication, Rod wasn't happy about it. The last time he hadn't been happy, Jack was home all day with only Jack Daniel's for company.

Where was he this time?

What made it all even worse was that when she caught a glimpse of Rod at the construction yard this morning, he hadn't looked upset. He'd been . . . smiling. That couldn't be good.

When she got back to her truck and checked her phone, she got her answer, in the form of a voicemail from Jack. She gritted her teeth. "Seriously?" They had one fight and not only did he skip work, but he called her again when she'd explicitly told him not to. He wasn't acting anything like the man she'd thought he was.

"Lesson learned. Again," she whispered fiercely to herself, as if that would make the knowledge stick better this time.

But she still pushed the button to listen to the voicemail. Just in case this had something to do with her crew transfer, or with Rod being passive-aggressive because he'd lost his corrupt little gambit to cover up his son's crimes.

It was only a few words, Jack's gruff yet uncertain voice telling her he had to deal with a family emergency. Wasn't sure how long it would take. Might not be back for a little while, but she could call him anytime she wanted.

Right. She hung up and nearly flung the phone across the truck cab. Jack didn't have any family. He'd told her what his dad had been like, that his brother wasn't much better and he didn't even know where Leroy was these days. The only "emergency" he had was not wanting to face her.

She jumped out to check under her tires, then cranked the ignition to head out to the site. You could learn a lot about a man by how he reacted when you were mad at him. Brad would turn it around on her, make everything her fault and get loud and mean. Jack, apparently, ran away. But then, the two men had always been opposites. Brad tore her down and Jack put her up on a pedestal like she was better than him when she wasn't hardly, tried to protect her like she'd never had to deal with jerk bosses at work before. She wasn't sure either approach was healthy.

Pulling into that day's construction site, she squinted against the rising sun to make sure the dirt was clear where she wanted to park. Though, at least she knew from their fight that even when Jack was deeply frustrated with her, he wasn't the least bit violent. She hopped out of her truck to check the site before the crew got there, scanning the ground absently as her thoughts tumbled and twisted inside her head.

Maybe he hadn't come to work because he was giving her the space she'd asked for, and then some. It would bug him all day, knowing his crew was working without direction and potentially screwing up whatever plan he had for this tower. For a man like Jack, who took such pride in his work, taking a sick day would be nothing short of excruciating.

She caught a frisson of warmth rising in her and pushed it aside. There was nothing cute about what he'd done, bossing her around that way and talking about interfering in her job. Nothing a man did in apology was as important as what he was apologizing for, she reminded herself. It was one of the lines she'd underlined in chapter seven. Of the book *Jack* bought her.

She hugged her arms over her chest as she watched the crew trucks pull in. He'd tried to help her heal, in the only quiet, fumbling way he knew how. That should count for something. But did she want to forgive him out of old self-sabotaging habits, or because she really believed he wouldn't try to control her again in the future?

Rajni's pizza trick was memorable, but telling a good man from a bad one was far more complicated than food. Mari wasn't sure she'd survive choosing the wrong man twice.

For the next few days, she walked a rut around the construction site, so distracted that she'd have to check a patch of dirt two or three times before she could be sure there wasn't a lizard on it, or fresh tracks anywhere. Jack never came back to the motel, so either the family emergency was real, or he was giving her space. One moment, she'd decide to forgive him, and in the next she was convinced that was the worst choice she could make. She thought about how he used to explode into shouting the first time anything went the least bit wrong. And then she thought about how terrified he'd been of hurting her in bed, even a little bit.

On the third day, when her phone rang in her pocket just after lunch, she scrambled to get it out and peek at the screen. Maybe it would be Jack . . .

That was ridiculous. She'd told him not to call, so she shouldn't go hoping he might. But when she saw the 262 area code, she relaxed. It was that same unfamiliar number from Wisconsin that had called before, which was a double relief because she was afraid that if it had been Jack, she might have answered. And also because it meant she was on some telemarketer's automated dialing list after all.

"Please put me on your do-not-call list," she said firmly, as soon as she answered.

"Mari?"

She knew that voice.

Electricity jolted up through her whole body, and she flinched so hard she stumbled back into a bush.

The phone jumped out of her hand and she couldn't hear anything, couldn't see. She'd had this dream a thousand times but she was awake now, Brad's voice real and terrifyingly familiar even after all this time apart.

Her cell phone. He'd called on her cell phone. No one back in Wisconsin had her number. After the divorce, she'd changed her number. Hell, changed phone carriers just so he couldn't find someone who remembered he was her husband and give them some story about needing to be let into her account. She was six states away from the town where they'd once lived together, and there was no way on earth he could have found this number.

How much time did she have to get away? She couldn't remember if he'd sounded angry or apologetic. Was he *here*?

She dropped to her knees and scrambled to find the phone. Stupid to have dropped it when she *needed* it to find out exactly how much trouble she was in. She shoved her hands into the dirt, trying to feel if it had gotten buried in the dust somehow, but then spotted it under a buckhorn cholla. Heedlessly, she jammed her hand in among the spiny branches of the cactus and snatched up the phone, but the line was closed. Somewhere in the bouncing on the ground, it must have hung up on him.

It was stupid, and so careless, to have dropped the phone like one word in that voice was as terrifying as all the monsters in the world. Now she had no idea where Brad was or how much he knew. If he could find the phone number, he could find her. She had to get away from here.

"Mari, are you okay?"

She looked up, her eyes wide and heart pounding, but it was just Gideon, frowning down at her with concern. Of course he was worried; she was acting like a crazy person. She rose to her feet, dusting the dirt off her hands and trying to blot away the dots of blood welling up from the cactus spines.

"Fine," she gasped. "Dropped my phone."

"You're not fine," he said. "And you're bleeding. Let's get that hand cleaned up." He took her arm and turned her back toward her truck, but then hesitated. "You're shaking . . . Mari, who was that on the phone?"

She closed her eyes, fighting the rising panic that tried to steal her breath. Lying wasn't an option because she couldn't stay at work the rest of the day anyway. He might know where she was right this instant.

"My ex," she said, the word barely audible between the tiny, gulped breaths that were all she could manage right now. "He found me. I need to get out of here."

"The fuck?" Gideon tensed, glancing around them. But outside the busy construction site, nothing moved. The dust on the dirt access road was still, water droplets already dry from where the water truck had passed half an hour ago. "Did he say he was here?" The lineman's hand rose to the hammer in his tool belt, but Mari shook her head.

"But he found my number. It was under the same fake—" She broke off, but it was too late to cover. "The same fake name as my motel room," she said, avoiding his eyes. It was a crime, the ID she'd bought off a guy in a greasy bar outside Las Vegas.

"Okay, but you can look up phone numbers pretty easy on the internet. Motel records aren't on the internet, so he might not know where you're staying. Is he a stalker type?"

"Worse," she whispered through bloodless lips.

"All right," Gideon said levelly. "Well, I'm a brown belt in aikido, and we kind of specialize in wiping the floor with big-ego'ed, ham-fisted idiots who like to hit girls. But I say we move you out of that motel just in case."

Out of the motel, hell. She'd been planning on more like out of the country this time. But no, driving away would only trap her more, because she needed money. Her last check was gone, to the motel for last week's bill and to the medical bill collection agency to stave off another hike in her penalty rates. The money in her wallet wouldn't last her until she could get a new job. She'd need to stay until the next check, which was an endless week and a half away. But she couldn't stay alone, exposed to anything he might do if he found her.

She could go to Jack. In a fight or not, all she'd have to do is call him and he'd never turn her away, she knew he wouldn't.

But no, that would be worse. If Brad found her with a man, there's no telling how far he'd go, and what if he had a gun?

Marcus and Lisa's house, then. Except Brad was so jealous there's no way he'd believe she and Marcus were only friends. Marcus would be in as much trouble as Jack. More, because he wasn't as good in a fight.

Mari hadn't realized Gideon had started guiding her along until they arrived at her truck. He lowered the tailgate and urged her to sit on it, muscling out her water jug so it sat next to her.

"We can move you into the Best Western tonight," he said, turning on the water spigot and letting a gentle stream of water run over her dusty, blood-speckled hand. "Wyatt's crew takes up most of the third floor, and we'll get you a room right in the middle." He smiled at her. "If your ex feels like facing down a whole dirty-brawling lineman crew, he's welcome to come over anytime."

She just blinked at him. Did they really like her so much? Gideon, and the crew? She couldn't imagine why any of them would put themselves out for someone who'd only known them a few months. All she'd done was move a few snakes, nag them to check their tires. She cleared her throat, blinking back tears and trying for a light tone. "Wow, brownies buy you a lot around here, huh?"

"Good people aren't so common that I take them for granted," Gideon said mildly. He turned off the water and patted her hand dry with one of her dishtowels.

"It's not just the motel, though. Brad has construction experience. He could show up and blend in here, maybe even get hired on one of the crews." She had to swallow several times just to finish, folding her arms so her shaking hands were stuffed out of sight in the crooks of her sweating elbows. She'd forgotten, somehow, what it was like to be afraid. It had been a constant for so many years, but somewhere along the way in her new life, she'd fallen out of the habit. The fear tasted all the more acrid now for being unfamiliar.

"Listen, you're safe here," Gideon said very gently. "If you've got a picture of this guy, we'll pass it around, make sure everybody knows what breed of asshole to keep an eye out for. I know you think the crew is only nice to you because of Wyatt, but these guys adore you. Even if Wyatt was gone, even if I was . . ." He shook his head. "I'd like to see somebody try to hassle you on this job site." His light eyes gleamed and a laugh coughed out of her, her vision blurring with sudden tears.

"Thank you," she managed in a choked whisper.

"Not necessary. If you need anything, anything at all . . ." He shrugged. "Just say the word and it's yours."

"Maybe . . ." She bit her lip. "Could you come with me tonight to get my stuff out of the motel, just in case my ex is there? If it's not too much trouble? Jack and I are . . . not really getting along at the moment."

"That doesn't mean he wouldn't help you out if he knew somebody was giving you a hard time," Gideon said. "I know he lacks a little something in the charm department, but I've been following him from job to job for a while now. He's a good man." He gave her a wry smile. "I'm sure you'll be surprised to hear it, but there aren't that many foremen in this business that take kindly to an openly gay lineman. Alabama redneck he might be, but Wyatt doesn't give two shits about anything but your work ethic. And when it comes to you, well . . . ten bucks says if you move into the Best Western, he picks up his bags and moves right along with you as soon as he gets back."

"Oh, I can't move in there." If Brad found her near any men, there was no predicting how far he'd go. Not to mention that she couldn't afford it.

The lineman didn't look pleased with this pronouncement. "Do you have someplace else safe that you can go?"

"I—" She started to lie, and then realized she didn't have to.

She could move in with Rajni. With a guy like Brad, her .45 was a better bet than even the most effective set of fists. And if they needed numbers, Rajni's ex-boyfriend lived right down the street, where he shared a rental with Hotaka.

Warmth started to seep back into her, like the desert sun had come out from behind a cloud. She had options. Not even just a single person who would help her if she asked, but many. The last time she could have said that was high school, before she married Brad.

"I do," she said. "I do have a place to go." And then, in spite of everything, she managed a small smile, too.

The rest of the day went so slowly she could hardly stand it. Every time a truck went down the access road, she felt like her skin was freezing and then burning, prickling like a sickness until she could see that it wasn't Brad coming for her. She'd turned off her phone, but now that he had her number, he was probably calling. Calling and calling. He never gave up when he wasn't getting what he wanted. He'd be angry that she was ignoring him. Whatever clue he had to her whereabouts, he'd be following it. The flowers and apologies would be gone after the third call, maybe the fourth.

After work, Gideon followed her back to the motel, and as soon as she pulled in, her heart sank at the sight of Jack's still-empty parking space. The curtain on his room was open, too, so she could see the sterile furniture that was all that was left of the place where they'd spent so much time together. Three days was way too long to just be giving her space to cool off. She doubted Rod would give him more than two days off, this close to the end of the project, so he must have quit.

The only family he had was the brother who used to take his fists to him. Either the family emergency was a lie to cover how he was taking off on her, or he'd chosen his abuser over her. Neither option was promising.

That was it, then. She didn't need to sort out how she felt, whether she should forgive him or even *could*. He was gone, and that told her everything about how disposable their relationship had been to him.

She glared at his empty room, her vision blurring a little with angry tears. "I didn't do what you wanted and so you just took off?" she whispered to her empty truck. "Well, damn you, Jack Wyatt. Damn you to hell."

Gideon knocked softly on her window then, and she blinked away tears and made herself get out. Escaping Brad was what mattered now. Survival and keeping herself safe. There was no time to think about what could have been or the way something deep in her felt like it had started to crack as soon as she realized Jack's absence wasn't temporary.

Gideon did a gentlemanly job of pretending not to notice her occasional swipes at watering eyes and quietly helped her move all her clothes into her truck. Waited for her to pay the last couple of days of her motel bill. Flirted with the guy at the cell phone store so he'd change her number *and* throw in a new phone upgrade.

In the process of moving her mattress from her truck to the nook they created behind Rajni's couch, he made pretty good friends with Rajni, too, and they had a great time laughing over beers about old kung fu movies they all loved.

By the time Rajni closed the door behind him, Mari was almost feeling normal again. Except for the cold space under her ribs that throbbed with Jack's name. She clearly wasn't in the right frame of mind to make major life decisions right now, but she missed him. Nothing would have been so comforting as a half hour of a home renovation show on the mussed coverlet of his motel bed. Him mumbling an offer to get her another beer even though he never allowed himself more than a single one.

If his family emergency was real, what had happened to his brother? Was he being good to Jack?

"Hey . . ." Rajni's soft voice interrupted her thoughts, and Mari's chin jerked up. Her friend smiled. "I'm glad you called."

Mari smiled back. "Thanks again for letting me stay."

"Please. You know I'm just doing it hoping I get to take a shot at that asshole." She winked. "I've always wanted to bag a trophy douchebag."

"Oh, I don't know that Brad'd make much of a prize, alive or dead," Mari joked.

Rajni perched on the arm of the couch, the curve of her hip graceful under her yoga pants. "You know, I don't know why we never hung out before. I thought we'd become friends on that first job, but you never called to catch up or anything when we moved onto the next one, so I figured I wasn't really your speed."

"Hey, no." Mari pressed her lips together. "I'm just not so good at—" She stopped and corrected herself. "Brad didn't much want me to have friends. And after all those years, I felt so rusty and awkward I wasn't sure anybody would want to be around me."

"You hung out with Lisa." Rajni pretended to pout.

"That's because Lisa invited *herself* over."

They both laughed.

"Yeah, she isn't exactly shy, is she?" Rajni caught sight of the clock. "I better head for bed. But, Mari?"

"Hmm?"

"It's gonna be okay," she said softly. "All of this. So don't worry, okay?"

Fresh tears prickled Mari's eyes, and she could only nod.

Her new friend disappeared into her bedroom, and Mari reached for her cell phone to set her alarm clock. But it vibrated in her hand and a text message from Marcus popped up on her screen.

Double check - is this your new number, Mari?

She rolled her eyes and texted back an affirmative. It was so like her fussy boss to be checking her number at eleven o'clock at night. She'd called him and Lisa earlier to fill them in on the situation and the new number, and had barely talked them both out of showing up at Rajni's place. But the last thing she needed was more worried people to set off her own anxiety. There had been no sign of Brad yet, but she wasn't sure how long that could last.

A new text popped up.

I'm really sorry, know this is a bad time, but I need you to meet with me a half an hour early tomorrow.

Mari frowned.

Sure. Is this about Brad? Did somebody see him around the site?

The three little dots popped up to show he was typing, then disappeared.

Then appeared again.

Then disappeared.

Her fingertips went cold and started to tingle. Somebody had seen him, hadn't they? Or worse, what if he had tracked her down and he was at Marcus's house right now, forcing him to text her and it was a trap to get her to the construction yard when it was dark and deserted and— .

It's not about Brad. A crushed tortoise was found. I'm sorry, Mari, but it was at your tower site.

31

Stored Like Spare Cheese

Jack did not care for Nebraska.

Part of the reason was his black eye. He hadn't had one in years, and he didn't remember them hurting this bad. Probably he was getting soft in his old age, as his brother had helpfully suggested several times.

Since it was Leroy's fault they'd gotten jumped, he'd blacked his brother's eye, too, just so the dickhead could see how it felt. Wasn't his finest moment, punching a guy who had one arm in a sling, but Leroy wasn't exactly on his good side at the moment. If it weren't for his poor life choices, Jack's eye wouldn't be all swelled up. His bike wouldn't have a bullet hole in it, and they sure as shit wouldn't be living in a Cheesy Charlie's pizza warehouse.

Jack knew how to fix a lot of things on a bike, but not a bullet hole.

He shifted on the concrete floor, fighting not to itch his head. That was another thing he'd forgotten since leaving Leroy's trailer and Alabama behind—how itchy his hair got when he couldn't wash it. This time, it wasn't an unpaid water bill that was the culprit, though.

He tossed a glare at his brother in the dim light of their one flashlight and clicked on his phone. The battery was down to 8 percent. It'd probably die before the workers in the front of the warehouse left for the day and he could get to an outlet to charge it. Leroy knew a guy who worked in the warehouse, who'd snuck them into this far back room where they'd be safe from the assholes who were after him.

It had a bathroom—well, a drain, which was about as good as it got when you were on the run. But they had to be quiet as hell so the other workers didn't figure out there was more living in this warehouse than roaches and pizza yeast. Unfortunately, quiet and Leroy never had seemed to exist in the same place for long.

Jack thumbed his phone again, staring at the battery icon and trying to remember how long 8 percent might last.

If Mari called this afternoon, he'd miss it.

Not that it mattered. She'd had four days to call, and she had chosen not to. He'd fucked up something fierce when he stuck his oar in about her being on Junior's crew.

"Stop checking that phone like a girl that just got her first training bra," Leroy said. "We've got nothing to do but sit here with our thumbs up our asses. You think we wouldn't have heard it ring?"

"Guess you can shut the hell up, since you're the reason we ain't got nothing to do," Jack said. "If you'd paid those pricks back, we'd be waiting on your trial in your apartment right now. Eating real food, not that gas station shit." He jerked his chin at their two shopping bags of canned hams and Slim Jims, a few bags of jalapeño Doritos thrown in for "the vegetable group," as Leroy put it.

"I would have paid them back all nice and square if the coke hadn't gotten stolen before I could turn around and sell it."

Jack scoffed, looking away.

"What? Not my fault I got robbed, could happen to the best of us. Even angelic little you, Jackie-O."

"You robbed your own junkie ass," he bit off. "And the guys you owe aren't dumb enough to buy that story, either, or they wouldn't have shot up my bike."

"You oughta be thanking me for helping teach you a valuable lesson," Leroy said. "Don't drive a getaway truck with a motorcycle in the back. Too recognizable and it makes a bigger target."

"Blocked a bullet meant for your thick head, so maybe you can shut the shit up about what I drive when I'm saving your ass."

Jack was really thinking that of the two, he would rather have the bike. Especially since his phone battery was down to 7 percent and he was looking at another ten days before he could deliver his brother to his court date. Ten more rounds of this glorified closet all day and sleeping out in the warehouse at night, using bags of powdered pizza dough mix for pillows.

"Aww, your panties are just in a pinch because of this girl. I'm sure she'll call, kid. Prize like you? What woman wouldn't want you?" Leroy said it with a straight face, but he couldn't keep the chuckle out of his voice.

Jack turned the phone over in his hand, nearly dropping it because the case had gotten oily with days of sweat. He rubbed it against his jeans.

Maybe for Mari, this was the best thing that could have happened. Leroy could mock all he wanted, but the kind of man Mari deserved wouldn't be trespassing on Cheesy Charlie's property to hide from drug dealers. What was he going to tell her about the bullet hole through the back of his motorcycle?

Decent guys didn't have bullet holes in their stuff.

His shoulders hunched as he tried to block out whatever Leroy was rambling on about. She'd smiled all the time when they were together. It had been her idea to have sex. Her idea to . . . do what she'd done with him in that motel room last week. Surely she wouldn't have done all that if she had just been biding her time before they could break up.

Maybe she was still pissed at him and hadn't listened to his voicemail, so she didn't know why he hadn't come to work. Maybe if he called her and got her to pick up, he could apologize and explain in person.

It wasn't like this was his mess, anyway. He wasn't the one who owed money to a gang. Though it would probably be his money paying them off, once they could figure out a way to contact them without fighting their way through another ambush like the one blocking the street between the town and the prison.

Jack chewed the inside of his lip. Until their argument, Mari had liked him. He was pretty damn sure. He could still remember the soft glow she'd get in her eyes when she looked at him. Fuck Leroy, and all his "real men don't have to call, let the ladies come to you" shit.

He hit the button for her number and turned his back on his brother.

Three electronic tones sounded in his ear. *"I'm sorry. This number has been disconnected or is no longer in service."*

He pulled it away from his ear and frowned at it, but no, he'd dialed directly from his contacts, so he couldn't have put in a number wrong.

"Hey, when a phone's battery goes dead or it's shut off, do you get the out-of-service message?"

"Nah." Leroy bit off a black-ringed fingernail and spat it across the closet. "Goes to voicemail. That your first phone, or what? Let me give you a little tutorial: you push the buttons with the numbers on them, then you talk into the bottom, and the phone sex lady talks out the top end."

Jack didn't even hear him, pushing to his feet to pace around the racks of cleaning supplies.

Her phone hadn't given that message before, when he'd called to leave a voicemail.

His stomach twisted sickly. She'd never answered, and she'd never called him back. He could picture her staring at her phone screen and sighing when his name popped up again, hitting "Ignore."

He was the guy blowing up her phone who couldn't take a hint. Harassed her enough she changed her number. Probably that's how she had to get rid of her ex, too. She'd said he would never give up and leave her alone.

"What you PMS'ing about over there? Did she yell at you and hang up, or just plain old change her number?"

He glanced over at his brother, really looked at him for the first time since he'd picked him up at the jail. He was gaunt except for a little pooch of a belly straining a wifebeater undershirt that had a swipe of jalapeño-flavored powder at the hem. All the lines in Leroy's battered face lifted as he chuckled, because of course he knew what Mari had done. That's what women always did to shitbag guys like the Wyatt brothers.

And would Jack want it any other way? Would he want her wiring him money to pay off drug dealers, or straining to hear him whisper into the phone because he was hiding in a storage closet?

Would he want her to take a guy back who'd made her cry the way he had?

Jack shut off his phone.

32

If the Boot Fits

There were three men in the construction office trailer, and her.

Mari wore her best white blouse, buttoned all the way to the top, khakis, and her hiking boots because she didn't have anything else, though she'd carefully wiped all the dust off them.

Marcus, in cowboy boots, jeans, and one of the western shirts he always wore.

Rod, in well-cut chinos and a smile that made her sick to look at.

And a barrel-chested man with dramatic chops of facial hair and a bolo tie. He was apparently the representative from the power company, and Rod's boss. She'd only ever seen his name before on the signature line of her paychecks: Stanton Davis. It sounded like a brand of cowboy boots.

Stanton Davis was currently going down the list of the evidence against her.

Pictures of the deceased animal, printed from Marcus's phone into surprisingly sharp eight-by-ten glossies. A baby tortoise only the size of her palm, smashed into the center of a tire track with its shell cracked into pieces.

The traffic report log of all people who entered and exited that access road that day, kept by the biologist who monitored the road.

Her report, stating that she worked at Tower 2123 that day, and that she cleared the area of all biological resources and observed no fatalities.

When he was finished, Stanton tapped the edges of the papers together, then gave Marcus a slight nod.

It had been six days since she and Jack fought and he disappeared. Three since Brad had called her, and two since that first awful meeting when Marcus told her that he had to suspend her while they investigated. Sympathy in his eyes when he said he hadn't believed it, so he'd gone out and seen the tortoise's body for himself. He'd been so sure it wasn't her crew, that he'd find someone else had been on that site. But no one else had been, and now her friend had no choice.

Marcus turned to her with tight lips and sad eyes. "I'm sorry, Mari, but I'm going to have to let you go. I'll need your access pass and any company equipment you've been using."

It took less than five minutes to lose everything she'd worked for since the divorce.

The job, all the friends she'd made. Any hope of paying her medical bills. She'd already moved out of the motel, which was the only half-assed excuse for a home she had.

At least Jack had left before he could see what she'd done. How thoroughly she'd failed the only job she had on the construction site: to protect the animals she loved. He would have been so surprised and so disappointed.

She could still remember how carefully he held the tiny tortoise he'd found under his own tire. If he'd been at work, *he* probably would have seen the tortoise she'd missed, and it wouldn't be dead.

The day it happened, she'd been so distracted, thinking about Jack and then with Brad calling out of the blue . . . She' checked all the tires, she was sure she had, but she'd been rushing. Maybe she'd glanced past the tortoise and not even seen it. Had it been *her* tire? Had she even noticed the bump when she ran it over? It was so small . . .

She'd always been absentminded when she was stressed. Had misplaced her keys a thousand times, living with Brad, even after he installed hooks by the front door for her. She thought she'd changed the oil according to the sticker on the windshield, only to find the car was choking and the numbers on the sticker were different than what she remembered . . . She'd been like this for years. How had she thought she could handle a job with so much responsibility?

Brad wouldn't have been surprised at her failure. She always figured he'd be aghast if he knew her new career. How it all hinged on her being attentive when he always accused her of being thoughtless to the point of stupidity.

"Have to say, I'm starting to wonder if we shouldn't revisit which company we're contracting for our biology work." Rod gave a concerned look to Marcus. "We chose to use experienced personnel specifically so you could save us the sort of take fine we're about to pay out *because* of one of your people."

"I do apologize, sir," Marcus said, his voice so uncomfortable it didn't really sound like him. "Mistakes do happen, though, and even the best biologist can miss tortoises. In fact, before California tightened its regulations, many projects didn't impose a fine for takes smaller than one hundred fifty millimeters, because the statistical probability of finding those animals is so low. That's nearly twice the size of the tortoise Mari missed."

"Doesn't matter what used to be," Rod said. "It matters what the regulations are holding us to now. Are you saying none of your people can be relied upon to spot the tortoises we're not allowed to run over?" He pursed his lips and looked to his boss. "If this is the kind of carelessness we can expect from this company, perhaps we need to discuss the tickets this girl has been passing out like Tic Tacs. If she can't see the animals she's hired to find, can we trust her judgment about what is or is not a violation?"

"I assure you—" Marcus started in, but Mari didn't even hear him. All she heard was Brad, laying into her for losing the keys again.

But in the book Jack had given her, it said that abusive men often set up situations to make it appear their victim had messed up, to justify their own anger. And now that Mari thought about it, she realized she had never forgotten an appointment, never forgot to *do* something. She just got confused when her keys weren't where she remembered leaving them, didn't get milk because they had a full carton, found the door unlocked when she swore she'd thrown the bolt last night.

And how easy would it have been for Brad to move the keys, pour out the milk, unlock the door?

Looking at Rod right now, with the tiny gleam of triumph behind his fake-worried smile as he argued with Marcus, Mari remembered her life with Brad so, so well.

She waited for an opening in the conversation, but the men were leaning forward to argue across her as Stanton slouched in his chair behind the desk.

"Excuse me," she started, but they just talked right over the top of her. Brad used to do that. Interrupt her and interrupt her until she couldn't remember what she'd started to say in the first place.

Mari stood up.

"I want to see the pictures." She pointed to the file in front of Stanton. "I remember where every person was parked that day, and I at least want to know if it was me who hit the tortoise."

"Mari . . ." Marcus winced. "You're responsible for the site, so technically it doesn't matter if it was your tires or one of the work trucks. It won't affect . . . I'm still going to need to let you go."

"I understand. I just want to know, for myself." She couldn't get that *pop* sound of a crunching shell out of her mind. She'd never heard it in real life, but she could imagine it far, far too well.

Stanton nudged his chair back a touch. "I might duck out, if you're okay to finish this up, Rod. I need to get back to the main office."

"You'd better stay," Marcus said. "The file and the pictures need to go back to the main office with you to be included in the report to the BLM."

"It'll only take a second," Mari promised, covering her twinge of guilt at his impatience by snatching the photos off the top of the file. "My truck was to the left of the driveway to the access road. The two crew trucks were on the right side of the pad." As soon as she saw the concrete abutment next to the tortoise in the first picture, she frowned. "But . . . this is underneath the tower." She looked up at the men in the office, appealing to Marcus because he spent the most time on-site, so he'd know. "No one parks under the tower when the crew is working. It's too dangerous—one dropped screwdriver could shatter a wind-shield."

"Listen, honey," Rod said, "that turtle didn't run over itself. Somebody must have parked under the tower. Trust me, if those damn linemen could do what they were told, I'd be out of a job. Here, you don't want to look at those, you'll just get upset."

He reached for the photos, but Mari hung on to them. He even started to exert pressure, trying to tug them out of her grasp, but when she didn't relent, he finally let go, his jaw twitching with tension.

The pictures *were* hard to look at, with the crushed animal and the tire track in the dirt right over the top of it. The tracks looked wider than those of her Toyota, each mark cleanly pressed into the soil by the tread of a tire so much newer and more aggressive than anything she could afford.

She looked up. "I want to see the road traffic records."

"We already went over that in the investigation that took place before this meeting," Stanton said. "There was no one out of the ordinary, and no one else on that road that would have stopped at that pad except your crew and the mobilization crew that came to move the crane—the ones who found the dead tortoise. We already told you everything it said in the summary I gave."

Her skin prickled with the scrutiny of everyone in the room. Stanton checked the time on his phone, and she knew they all thought she was being ridiculous. But if once, just once, she'd thought to mark the level of the milk with a pen before she went to the store, she wouldn't have had to wonder if she was crazy. Not once did she ever have enough faith in herself to think that Brad might have poured it out, because he always looked at her with that crushing combination of disappointment and pity. Just the way Rod was looking at her now.

"It's evidence against me. I want to see it."

"She has the right," Marcus said.

Stanton shuffled through the papers and passed over the records, creases deepening at the corners of his frowning mouth.

"I looked at them, too, Mari," Marcus said in an undertone. "Nobody strange went through."

She scanned down the records, and it only took her seconds to find what she'd expected.

She put her finger on the name and slid the paper into the middle of the desk. "That's who ran that tortoise over. Not me. Not my crew."

All the men leaned in to see, and when Stanton recognized the name, he frowned even more deeply. "If we need to call security to escort you out, Ms. Tucker, we will. We investigated, and you were at fault. Wild accusations aren't going to save your job."

Fear fluttered in Mari's belly, and she started to feel like she wasn't getting enough air, but she set her jaw and refused to let them see how close she was to a panic attack. "Really? Why was Rod on that road, then?"

"It's my responsibility to oversee all the tower assembly crews. That's what being the assembly manager means, in case you don't understand the term." His manicured nails drummed on the arm of his chair.

"We were the only crew on that section," Mari said. "The next assembly crew was down at 2144. The only reason you would have had to be on that section was to come to the tower we were at, to check our work. So you were the last person at Tower 2123."

Marcus pulled out his phone, and she caught a glimpse of the report-uploading software as he scrolled quickly to the date of the tortoise fatality.

"There's no need to get hysterical," Rod said. "I know it's upsetting to be fired, but you'll get another job. Not as a biologist, certainly, but you'll need work. To show you there are no hard feelings, I'll even write you a reference if you'd like to try for a secretarial position at the offices of our construction company. But if you go making accusations toward your superiors, I don't think anyone's going to be too interested in hiring you."

"She's right," Marcus interjected. "The next closest assembly crew under Rod's supervision that day was at 2144. He was on that road after Mari's crew left and before the mobilization crew found the tortoise."

"Those are your tire tracks," Mari said to Rod, her heart beating stronger and more certainly now. "Both of the crew trucks have bald tires. One of them blew out on the freeway last week. The tire it got replaced with is used, too, and barely has enough tread to hold the rubber together. Three of my truck tires are bald, and narrower than this. But your truck has those brand-new off-roading tires. I bet we could even match the tread to this photo. Measure the width."

"So, what, we're supposed to believe you're some kind of tire specialist?" Rod scoffed. "Look, binge-watching *CSI* isn't going to do anything but go straight to your thighs. I suggest you stop trying to sound like an expert when we all know you're just a disgruntled *ex*-employee." He raised his eyebrows at Stanton. "How about that security guard?"

"I'm a tracker." Mari sat back in her chair, crossed one leg firmly over the other. "And those are your tracks."

"Of course you would say that! You're trying to save your own ass."

She couldn't help but notice that his volume was climbing. Stanton hadn't reached for his cell phone to call security, if he even knew the number of the rent-a-cop who patrolled the construction lot during the day.

"It's not just the tires," she said. "I know that tortoise. It was about a seventy millimeter, wasn't it, Marcus?"

"It's kind of hard to tell when it's *flat*," Rod said.

Mari flinched, but only a little. "That's the only tortoise that surveys found anywhere near Tower 2123. Its burrow is two hundred meters away from the construction area. That's pretty far for a little guy like that to move, especially in triple-digit temperatures. But if you check my report, I checked on him and logged him as being in his burrow, face out, at . . . I think around two that afternoon."

Marcus snatched the rest of the papers off Stanton's desk and shuffled quickly. "Two fifteen."

"So if the tortoise was found at four thirty, that means he moved two hundred meters when it was 103 degrees, in two hours and fifteen minutes." Mari gave a look to Marcus, because those numbers would mean nothing to the workers.

"It's nearly impossible," Marcus said. "Two hundred meters is very far for a tortoise that size, and most of them won't leave their burrows when it's over 95 degrees. If they did, they'd stop at the next shade they saw."

"That isn't the only tortoise in the desert," Rod said. "You can't even prove the dead tortoise is that same one. What, are you going to say you recognize his hairdo?" He laughed.

"No, but his burrow is on the GPS maps that we all have access to, including you. I bet if you went there right now, he wouldn't be in it anymore." Mari's stomach churned, because recognizing that tortoise meant something very, very ugly. It helped her case, but even so, it wasn't something she wanted to think about. "What size shoe do you wear, Rod?"

He rolled his eyes. "Look, if you think I'm going to listen to some girl get all PMS-y and try to blame her mistakes on me, saying she can recognize a road-killed tortoise and—"

"Were you at that tower that day, Rod?" Stanton interrupted. "You were on the road, okay, that doesn't mean anything. So where did you go? You didn't stop at that tower, did you?"

"No! I was just driving through. Taking the access road to Tower 2144 to see my other crew, like you said." He threw a glare at Stanton. "Not that I should have to explain myself. I was doing my job. If she'd done hers, we wouldn't be here."

"Tower 2144 is closer to your office than Tower 2123," Marcus said. "To get to Mari's tower first, you'd have to leave the yard, get on the freeway, get off on the far exit, and come back around the long way. And according to the road traffic records, you were going the wrong way for that to be the case." He looked to her. "Mari, what were you asking about shoe size?"

"If we went out to that burrow right now," she said, "I bet you there would be two sets of tracks to and from it. Mine, from checking when we were working that day. Size seven and a half, Merrell hiking boots. And his. Red Wing work boots like most of the linemen wear, size . . ."

She tilted her head to look at his feet, gaining confidence now that she had Marcus on her side. The facts on her side.

She was right and she damn well knew it. No tortoises had been harmed until he put her on his son's crew, looking for a free pass, and got a double handful of citations instead.

"Looks like you're maybe a size eleven? Not much chance of another worker being that far from the construction pad, not with the schedule you keep them on."

Rod surged forward, not leaving his seat but getting right in her face. "Listen, you little bitch—"

She held his eyes, lifting a hand to hold Marcus off when he jumped up to get between them.

"Go ahead, hit me. I know you're dying to. I know you're capable of it." She stared Rod down ferociously. "You carried that little baby tortoise all the way from its burrow in that heat, put it under the tower, and ran it over."

She blinked away the angry tears in her eyes to sort through the pictures in her lap, and when she found the right one, she put it on the desk for Stanton to see.

"And after you ran it over, you backed up and did it again, to be sure it was dead. Look, you can see the turnaround marks right here. You didn't even hit it by accident and then try to shift responsibility. You killed it on purpose, so you could frame me because you were mad that I wrote up your son."

His nostrils flared and goose bumps jumped out along her arms, a warning trilling through her because she damn well knew when a man was about to get violent, and that's what he looked like. But she didn't back down, because she'd had worse. She'd had worse, and she wished she could have fought for herself back then the way she could now.

She wasn't stupid. And she wasn't wrong.

"Do it," she said, rising and leaning right into his face so their noses nearly bumped. "Slap me. I am dying for an excuse to hit you back."

"That's enough, Rod," Stanton snapped. "Ms. Tucker, will you please wait for us outside?"

Ten minutes later, Stanton Davis came out, alone.

"I'm going to need you to sit tight until we sort this out, ma'am. Rod will be remaining in the office, and security will be coming to make sure neither of you have any contact with the other or leave the premises. Marcus and I will be going out to check those tire tracks, as well as to check for those boot prints you alleged. Decisions about your job status are on hold for the moment."

"Thank you," she told the executive, keeping her voice calm even though her blood was still running hot from the confrontation. She was so not in the mood to sit still and wait.

Andy from lot security let himself into the trailer, gave her a bashful nod. "Mari."

"Hi, Andy." She smiled at him as he went to the coffee machine to pour himself a cup.

Marcus came out of the office, and when Stanton turned to go, Marcus gave her a conspiratorial wink, a smile starting to brighten his face. "His boots were a size smaller than you guessed," he said. "Turns out old Rod wasn't as big as he looked."

The two men left together, and she let out a long breath.

When she'd fought with Jack, she was just sliding back into her old patterns of not trusting her own judgment. She'd compared Jack's protectiveness to Brad's spying because experience had taught her that a man would only watch over her because he wanted to control her, not because he truly wanted her to be safe. All along, Jack had been right that Rod was dangerous. But he'd been wrong that she couldn't handle it.

She'd won.

They'd confirm it when they got back, but she already knew. The last two days she'd been jumping at her own shadow, because even with her number changed so he couldn't call, she could feel Brad somewhere near. Every night, Rajni took her out in the desert so she could practice shooting her borrowed .357 pistol. Though even her increasing accuracy with the gun hadn't given her the rush of confidence that winning this battle had.

Before, she'd only ever mustered the courage to fight with Rod when she was shielding someone else: Jack, his crew, or one of the desert animals. Even when she left Brad, she'd been in such a bad place that it was less to protect herself and more to protect him from the consequences of what he might do.

But today, no matter how hard Rod had tried to intimidate her, she hadn't backed down, and she'd fought for *herself*. Because she hadn't done anything wrong, and she deserved to be protected from that jerk every bit as much as anyone else. A smile crept onto her face and Andy smiled back, assuming it was for him.

She gave him a nod, and his folding chair creaked as he took up a spot outside the office where Rod still waited.

She was dying to fly back to the motel and tell Jack that she'd done it, that after all this time, it was she who was finally going to get Rod rightfully fired. But he wasn't there.

Taking out her phone, she scrolled to Jack's name. It glowed up at her, the simple, familiar letters as comforting as a warm breeze. Their fight had been silly, a hard moment they could have gotten through easily if they'd talked it out after they both calmed down. Except, in the end, he hadn't cared enough to stick it out.

It had taken her so long to get to a place where she felt valuable enough to fight for herself, and she deserved a man who knew that, too. Who could stand up for his own worth, and their relationship, and not run away the first time things got hard.

Sure, she'd changed her number since he left, but even *Brad* had cared enough to track down her number, and it'd be far easier for Jack, if he wanted to. All he'd have to do was ask Marcus, or Gideon. Any of the biologists on the project. And yeah, maybe she was being ridiculous and holding a double standard by expecting him to track down her phone number, but what it came down to was that she was done loving men more than they loved her. Finished with soothing hurt feelings while her own ached in silence. If she was going to risk her heart on anyone ever again, it would be on someone who was willing to risk theirs right back.

She clicked off the phone and turned it facedown in her lap.

33

Left Turn

Jack's fingers tapped against his steering wheel, and he took shallow breaths, because even after two showers and a long stint in the laundromat, he couldn't stop smelling the raw pizza of their warehouse hideout, and it pissed him off.

"Ain't you even gonna come in and give me morality support during my trial?" Leroy asked.

Dough. Garlic.

Jack gritted his teeth.

Tomato sauce.

"No." He lost the battle to keep his mouth shut. "And damn it, it ain't 'morality support'!" Not that he had all that much morality to lend, but even if he did, likely it'd just bounce right off Leroy. "It's 'moral support.'"

"'Moral' is just the singular of 'moral-i-t-y,'" Leroy argued, standing on the curb but still not letting go of his truck door. "Same thing. Either way, ain't very brotherly of you to just go off before my trial's even started."

Grated processed cheese.

Every breath reminded Jack of where he'd spent the last two weeks of his miserable life. Sitting around Cheesy Charlie's warehouse with only his silent phone, loud brother, and regret-filled thoughts for company.

He'd finally managed to pay off the guys Leroy owed without getting either of them shot, and babysat his brother until his court date so he couldn't skip bail. Jack was ready to shake the stench of this place off his boots, but he didn't really have anywhere to go.

He missed his crew, sad a bunch as they were. Missed having a new tower to puzzle out every few days. He missed the scent of brownies baking in the open air of the desert, and the little inhalation of breath Mari took whenever a house with a particularly nice porch swing came on one of their TV shows. The closer the calendar drew to the end of the power line job, the itchier he got. Once that job back in California was over, he'd never know where to find Mari again. Which was the point, damn it. He wasn't good for her. Had made her cry and upset her so much she'd changed her number.

"C'mon," Leroy said. "Pony up for a better lawyer for me and I'll be out of here by this afternoon. We can grab a couple of cold ones, wildcat around for a little bit." He grinned. "Ain't nobody out there who can have more fun than the Wyatt boys on a tear."

Jack ducked his head, picking at a loose thread in the lacing on his steering wheel. He didn't have anybody waiting for him, not anywhere. The only person who wanted his company was standing outside the passenger side of his truck.

"Forget all about that pretty little piece who changed her number," Leroy coaxed. "I'll introduce you to a real woman. You wouldn't believe how crazy these farm girls get out here, and they're a cheap date, too. Twenty bucks' worth of blow will set you back less than dinner and a movie, and they'll do a hell of a lot more for it."

Jack coughed to clear the bitter, greasy taste from his mouth. This was what he came from. This was what Wyatts were always like. It was also why he'd left, the first time and every time since. Because this had never been the kind of man he wanted to be.

"Gimme your phone."

Leroy frowned. "What?"

"Gimme your damn phone! I'm going to put an app on it," Jack muttered. "So I can send you money next time you need, without having to drive all the way to goddamn Nebraska."

"What happened to good old Western Union? Can't the government trace those apps?" Leroy groused, but passed over his phone. Jack hit a few buttons and tossed it onto the passenger seat. He didn't meet his brother's eyes.

"You better go. Judges don't like it when you're late."

"You're leaving, just like that? Download some app and wash your hands of me, when I'm your only kin?" Leroy pocketed his phone, his tone starting to turn ugly. "Don't forget, you owe me, kid."

He always said that, but these last couple of weeks, Jack had started to think it might be the other way around. After they left their dad's house, his lawn-mowing money used to pay their bills, or at least whatever part of their bills ever got paid. And for all his talk of being the protective big brother, this was far from the first time Leroy had left Jack's face bruised up, just like it was now. Left him scared and full of regret and wondering how he'd managed to screw up so bad. But he wasn't a kid anymore, and this wasn't *his* mistake.

He used to think he had no choice but to take his brother's shit because no one else would ever care about him. Until Mari had.

He could still remember pulling into the parking lot at night and smelling spaghetti from her tailgate kitchen, knowing without having to ask that she would have made extra for him. How his crew had started to joke around with him a little bit at lunchtime. How Mari's hippie boss had invited him to stay and eat a truly terrible dinner with him and Lisa even when Mari wasn't around.

In his life out in California, people actually *enjoyed* his company, and the last two weeks with his only family felt more like a visit to a version of himself that no longer existed.

"Paid your bail. Paid your way out of trouble. Don't owe you shit," Jack growled. "If anything, you owe me. Hell of a lot of money and two weeks of my life back."

Leroy clucked his tongue. "Now, if you'd see your way clear to loan me a little more so I could hire a real lawyer instead of one of those public defense idiots, I might be able to shake these charges so I could turn over some real cash. Pay you back quick like."

Once, the hint that his brother truly wanted to spend more time with him would have swayed Jack. He'd have bitched and moaned, but he'd have parked the truck and walked into the courthouse beside Leroy.

But now, he knew that the ask had everything to do with Leroy being scared of going to prison, and absolutely nothing to do with any real affection for Jack.

He was starting to wonder how many times he'd ended up feeling like a piece of shit just because Leroy's misery needed company. Jack had never had too many friends, but that hadn't always been true. He used to play with the other kids plenty until Leroy had started smacking them around for their lunch money. It might have been that far back that he'd started assuming people didn't really care to be around him. It wasn't just about Mari. It was about him and every person he'd ever pushed away, and it all started with his brother.

Now, finally, he knew who really deserved to be alone. And it wasn't him.

"Turn loose of my door or I'm gonna drive off, and whatever happens to your hand is on you."

The oily smile on Leroy's face twisted, and a petulant scowl replaced it. He hurled the door shut and leaned back and gave it a kick. Judging by how the truck rocked, that'd leave a dent, too. Jack hit the gas so hard smoke poured off the tires as he sped out of the lot.

He'd seen the charges against Leroy. There wasn't any way his brother was shaking that rap, but with his debt paid to the local gang, he'd be safe enough both in prison and once he got out—safe as Leroy could be, considering the trouble he stirred up everywhere he went.

And with that, Jack was done.

Instead of downloading a money transfer app, Jack had deleted his own number from Leroy's phone. Thanks to his job, he had no permanent address, and Leroy didn't know his email. He'd never be able to find him again.

Leroy could only poison the new life Jack had built. Now, when they were both okay, was the time to make that clean break. He should have done it a decade ago, honestly, but he'd always thought his new life was a fluke, or luck. Had thought he was no different than his brother, deep down. But that wasn't true. He'd worked hard to change his life, made his own choices that led to a good paycheck and comfortable life. Leroy's choices had led them to sleeping under shelves of Cheesy Charlie's dough with a matched set of black eyes.

No matter what happened with Mari or the future, he was done letting Leroy's choices fuck up his own.

Jack broke the speed limit as he passed the lot full of cop cars behind the courthouse, and kept pushing it until he was all the way across the city and looking out onto open Nebraska prairie. Then he pulled up to a stop sign and let his foot sit heavy on the brake.

A week after Jack left, Rod had called and said he couldn't hold a foreman spot open for him when the project was ending so soon anyway. As of tomorrow, the job would be over, and Mari would disappear with it.

It weighed on his mind that she'd never called back. It didn't seem like her, as forgiving and even-tempered as she always was about everything. Also, would she really have changed her number just to avoid his calls?

He stared at the red sign on the side of the road.

He could still remember what it felt like when she looked at him. The way he could *tell* she liked him.

Jack's hand closed tighter over the steering wheel. That hadn't been a lie, and one stupid argument didn't erase it. There had to be some other reason she hadn't called, and he was going to find out what.

Maybe Mari was hesitating, too, not sure if he really wanted to talk to her when she hadn't answered his voicemail right away. Hell, it took him some time to cool down from a good fight, so it wasn't like she didn't deserve the same. He'd been assuming she'd want to be done with a guy like him, but everything he'd been ashamed of led back to Leroy's choices, not his own. He'd grown into a decent man, in spite of everything, and Mari had been the first to treat him like he was worth caring about.

It had just taken him a little longer to believe the same.

A horn blared behind him, and instead of continuing in the same direction, he took a hard left toward California. Back to Mari. By the time he got there, the job would be over and she'd be gone, sure. And her phone was shut off, okay.

But in a great big world chock-full of people, they'd somehow stumbled into finding their perfect match in each other. There was no way, after all that, that they wouldn't find their way back to each other—no matter how many lost phone numbers and state lines fell between them. It was just that simple, and he believed it with the kind of faith he used to reserve only for death, taxes, and hard luck.

Because life, it turned out, wasn't *always* cruel. Not even for a Wyatt.

34

Last Days and Second Chances

Mari parked her truck in front of Rajni's apartment. Checked her rear-view and her side mirrors, then craned her head to scan the cars along the curb. There was a blue sedan she wasn't sure she'd seen before, but when she checked the list she now kept in her glove box, the blue sedan was scrawled in near the bottom of the paper. Everything was normal.

She popped the list back in her glove box and slammed it, then unlocked her doors and went around to the passenger side to retrieve the cookie sheet she'd had to use as a serving platter for her cake. The words "Happy Last Day!" had been eaten down to just "Ha" by Jack's ravenous crew—well, Gideon's crew now. She'd barely saved the piece she'd promised Rajni. First to go were the pieces with her piped-on depiction of a lattice tower. With her dollar-store decorating tools, it had come out more like the Eiffel Tower than a power line, but her linemen seemed more smug than offended by the comparison.

The cookie sheet got juggled onto one hand as she fumbled with her keys and hurried up the sidewalk. The buttercream began to melt as soon as she took it out of the shade, and it'd be a puddle if she didn't get inside quickly.

A man's voice spoke up behind her. "Mari?"

Fear punched the center of her chest, and she whirled around to put her unprotected back to the locked door. The cookie sheet went flying, hit the browning grass of the yard, and cartwheeled. She barely heard the jangle of her keys dropping from her nerveless hand to the scorching concrete beneath her feet. She couldn't hear, couldn't smell, couldn't think or breathe, because every cell in her body was focused on what she was seeing: her ex-husband's face.

Brad was thinner. Clean-shaven like he never used to bother with except on Sundays, and wearing a new shirt buttoned all the way to his throat, though he was already sweating through it at the armpits.

He winced. "Sorry. I didn't mean to startle you. I planned to talk to you on the phone, see if you'd be okay with meeting up with me. Except at first I was afraid to say anything when you answered, in case I scared you off. And then after the last time, the number stopped working. I wanted to tell you, if you needed help with the phone bill to get it turned back on, I could give you the cash." He bent down and flipped over the cookie sheet, scooped the cake back onto it despite the dirt and dead grass now matted into the top. He stood up and offered her the tray.

Her arms didn't feel like they were attached to her body, electricity racking all her nerves in a soundless shriek of DANGER DANGER DANGER. She did not take the tray.

Brad started to fidget, wiping his hand along the seam of his pants and leaving a long streak of blue frosting and sandy soil. He'd always done that, wiped his hands only along the seam as if that would hide the stains. She remembered the *sshht* of thousands of sprays of stain remover, scrubbing the fabric against itself to get the stains out of his pants. When her hands were bruised or her fingers broken, it had been so hard to grip the fabric hard enough to rub.

"You didn't come back to the motel you were staying at," he said, his voice slower and softer than she remembered, as if he was worried he'd startle her into fleeing. "I thought the PI was wrong about what you were driving, or I'd have found your new place sooner." He smiled, a little lopsided. "You always hated pickups. Said they were hard to park."

What kind of private investigator didn't check for restraining orders when they were hired to find someone? She wished she could scream at him, whoever he was, rip away his stupid investigator's license, and throw the pieces back in his face.

Taking her shocked silence as assent, Brad came closer, and all her muscles balled tight.

Maybe she should take the cookie sheet from him. It was light, but she could use it as a weapon. Smash it into his face to blind him or shove the edge into his Adam's apple. She wasn't allowed to carry weapons on the construction site, and she was safe enough with the crew around her, so her borrowed pistol was locked out of reach inside the apartment. The restraining order wouldn't protect her. It only allowed her to press charges more easily once he'd done his worst.

She had no idea when Rajni would be home. It was the last day on the project, and all the crews were doing different mop-up tasks, so there wasn't an official clocking-out time. Organizationally, things had gotten more than a little chaotic since Rod had been fired for killing that tortoise to frame her.

She shifted her weight toward her truck, preparing to make a run for it.

Brad raised his free hand, palm out. "Hey. Look, you've got every right to be nervous, but I'm not here to hurt you, I swear. We can go somewhere more public to talk, if that would make you more comfortable. That's what I'd planned on in the beginning, before your phone got shut off." His eyes narrowed, studying her. "It did get shut off, right? Or did you shut it off?"

Her breath caught in her throat. It sounded like a question, but it echoed in her mind with the *snap* of a trap. He'd ask these things, all innocent and supportive sounding, but if she admitted she'd done it to get away from him, he'd be hurt. The hurt would twist to anger, and the anger would break her bones.

Brad shook his head. "I'm sorry, that's none of my business. I didn't come here to interrupt your new life. I just wanted to say I'm sorry. For everything, all those years." He swallowed. "For breaking the promise I made when I asked you to marry me, that I'd never be like our messed-up dads."

A different kind of pain bit into her, and she hated it twice as much. She snatched the cookie sheet from him, swooped up her keys, and wished for the thousandth time that Jack hadn't taken off after their argument.

She couldn't hit hard enough to punch Brad's face the way it deserved to be punched, but Jack could.

"You owe me that apology," she said fiercely, recklessly. "Because you *lied*, Brad." Her voice cracked and she nearly yelled what came next because she hated so much that he could still affect her. "When you promised you'd keep me safe, you lied your ass off."

His eyes glistened, shiny suddenly with tears. "I know," he whispered. "I wanted to be better, and I messed up over and over again. You deserved better than that, Mari-baby."

She twitched at the old nickname. He hadn't called her that since she was in her twenties. She looked away and scoffed, her nails scraping metallically over the baking sheet when her hand tightened.

"I've heard it all before. 'I'm sorry, I'll change, everything will be different.' Well, guess what? Everything is different, because you're finally out of my life. Now you can leave, or I'll call the police *and* my friend with a very large gun who lives here *and* my two friends with large biceps who live down the street." She'd never threatened him before, not ever, but instead of fresh fear, all she felt was strength welling up through her.

She'd faced off with Rod in his own office and she'd won. She was done crumbling in the face of a man's fury. Maybe it was all the sleepless nights, trying not to miss Jack. Maybe it was the empty feeling in the pit of her stomach from the job ending that was making her reckless, but she just didn't care anymore if Brad put her in the hospital for standing up to him. Right now, all she wanted was to able to look at herself in the mirror without shame.

But instead of the familiar flare of anger, his face stayed embarrassed. "I knew you wouldn't believe me, not at first. That's why I brought proof." He reached into his pocket and pulled out a thick wad of folded-over slips of paper. He held them out, but she just glared at him.

"Receipts," he said. "From my therapist. A different receipt for every week I've attended. Over a year now. There's . . . there's been a lot to work through, and it hasn't been fun, but I've done it. For you. Mari, I never realized how empty my life was without you. I hate what I did to you, and I want our life back. But different this time, better."

She glanced down, curious if he'd tried to forge the receipts. They were signed, though, with a signature that tilted left when his always scrawled right. Printed with an official-looking logo and a name. She leaned in just a little to see. Steven Partridge, PhD.

She nearly laughed. Of course it was a man. He'd never respect a female psychologist.

"Anger management classes, too," he persisted. "Every Tuesday night at the Methodist church. I graduated the program after six months, but I went back for another round because I figured, more couldn't hurt, right?" He took a step closer. "I could have tracked you down months ago. But I wanted to wait until I was sure the therapy was going to help. I'm sober, too, got my six-month chip, and both my sponsor and my anger management coach said you can call them to verify. I didn't want to come to you until I had proof. Listen, it wasn't all bad. Remember when we took that trip to the beach and made love so long that we missed dinner and all the restaurants were closed?"

He smiled, and it made him look young again, like the teenager who used to sneak in her window late at night just to kiss her.

"And you made us a picnic from candy bars and one sad little orange from a gas station that you squeezed over the candy bars to make them orange chocolate. Remember? Or when you had the flu and I tried to make you chicken soup from scratch and gave you food poisoning on top of the flu." He grimaced. "Actually, never mind that. Don't remember my terrible cooking." He patted his waistline. "I've been meaning to start working out again, too, but I've already lost plenty of weight just from eating my own cooking." He let out a small, tentative laugh, but she didn't join in.

She remembered that flu, how he'd carried her to the car to get to the hospital for an IV, because she'd been so sick. But even so, they'd laughed and laughed about his horrible chicken soup.

She tilted her chin up, really looking at him for the first time since he got here. He did look different. Tired, skinnier. More earnest. No trace of the anger that he'd always carried around like a thick cloud riding on his back. He *had* changed.

She knew it all in a second, like a shift deep in her gut. No one had known him longer than she had. No one, not even her parents, had spent as many years by her side as he had. She knew something was different this time, not because of the therapy receipts or the sobriety chip, but because she knew Brad.

All she had to do was nod her head, and everything would be easy again. She wouldn't have to live every day under the scalding desert sun, sweating half to death when she tried to sleep in her truck when it was still 99 degrees at midnight. And he'd fought for her. Hard enough to track her across half the country even after not seeing her for years.

She could go back to their little ranch house with the blue bistro set on the back patio. For as much as Jack seemed to occupy her every thought, she hadn't heard from him in two weeks, and she didn't know if he was even still in California. He'd disappeared like a dream she'd had about the kind of man she would want if wishes weren't as fickle as fate.

But Brad was real. He was right here and he'd always take her back.

He'd been quiet for a long time, watching her think, but now he spoke. At just the right moment, because he knew all her expressions as well as his own. "Come home," he whispered, and it was his voice that put her over the edge.

It wasn't the right voice. Wasn't that gravelly sweet Alabama drawl she'd give anything to hear again.

She stepped back. "That was never my home. And I'm happier here." She gestured to the expanse of desert, stretching out beyond the spare few houses.

Hurt flashed in his face. "I know you're angry, but—"

"If you'd really changed, you wouldn't have followed me," she interrupted. She hadn't interrupted him in probably twenty years. Had never been so stupid, even with her lawyer at her side during the divorce proceedings. "After I disappeared to get away from you, any decent person would have known that was THE END in capital letters."

Jack's absence ached like a phantom limb. How many times had she debated calling him? But even when her resolve wavered, the facts remained. He was gone, and that was his choice. He hadn't chosen her.

She straightened, and focused on the man in front of her.

"I'm glad you're getting help, I am. Any woman in your future deserves that much from you. But whatever kind of better man you want to turn yourself into, you're going to have to do it alone. You've used up all your second chances with me."

She turned her back on him, the fear returning to thrill coldly up her spine at the vulnerability. But she needed this moment, needed them both to see she could still be the strong, new version of herself even when her past had found her.

"You lied, too."

She left her keys dangling from the apartment lock and turned around. "Oh, really?"

"You said if I signed the divorce papers, you'd give me another chance. But you took off instead, and now, you won't even have a damn coffee with me. Won't give me five minutes of your fucking precious time after I've spent months, hell, *years* doing everything you ever wanted to make myself better for you." His sneer didn't quite cover the little-boy hurt in his eyes.

"Yeah, I lied. I would have said anything to get you to sign those papers. But seriously, Brad, what made you believe a woman who promised to give you another chance only *if* you'd give her a divorce?" She arched an eyebrow.

"What makes you so much better than me, huh?" He jerked a long step closer to her. "You've made mistakes, too, Mari. I'm doing all the apologizing here, making all the amends, and you just give me that holier-than-thou look like you've never so much as forgotten to put a dollar in the collection plate on Sundays."

In chapter eleven of the book that Jack had given her, it said that men like Brad often looked for victims who were used to being poorly treated, anyone who could be convinced to accept their behavior as normal. Mari lifted her chin and stared him down, her whole body calm and still, like in the early days on Wyatt's crew when she wanted Jack to know he couldn't fluster her.

She wasn't an easy target. And when her hands wanted to shake and her eyes wanted to drop and her heart tried to climb out of her chest, remembering how much Brad's big hands could hurt if she pushed him . . . she just remembered the feeling of Jack's scars under her hands. The bumps and textures that reminded her of what he'd risked when he tried to leave the abuse.

Freedom didn't come for free.

She knew that, and she was terrified but willing to pay whatever toll she had to in order to get through this, to convince both Brad and herself that she wasn't his property anymore.

"You gonna hit me?" she murmured.

She honestly didn't know the answer. She knew he was capable of killing her. But she didn't know if he would. If the person he was right at this moment would cross that line.

He ducked his head and stuffed both hands in his pockets, the carefully hoarded therapist receipts making a crumpling sound. "No. I've changed, Mari. That's what this is all about. That's why I'm here. If you'd spend just a little bit of time with me, I'd prove it to you. No strings, no obligations. If you change your mind and want me to leave, I will."

"I want you to leave," she said without hesitation. "Right now. And if you want to do something for me so bad, pay all the medical bills I racked up from all the times you hurt me," she said. "That would show me you've changed. I still won't come back, but it would ease my mind to know that other women might be safe from you."

She let herself into the apartment, her heart racing in the tiny scrap of a second before the door latched and she flipped the dead bolt. It had been so incredibly risky to face him down on her own. She should have run, screaming for any help she could muster, just in case.

Mari whipped around, nearly sick with adrenaline and fear and pride, and crammed her eye up to the peephole.

It magnified the view of everything outside, so she flinched when she saw Brad's face in the fish-eye view, his eyes beginning to glisten. The cookie sheet bit into her ribs as she tried to lean even closer, to be sure what she was really seeing.

The first tear broke free and disappeared into the deep creases beside his eyes.

"Mari," he whispered hoarsely, his shaking hand stretching toward her until it hit the door between them. He leaned into it, as if he couldn't quite stand on his own.

Her throat clamped closed. The last time she'd seen him cry, it was when his father had stabbed him in the hand with a fork, for reaching for the last piece of chicken without permission. He was fourteen.

She'd comforted him that time, and washed his wounds, but this time she was the one causing his pain. In his slumped shoulders, she could see so clearly the boy he'd been, and the hopeful young man she'd married.

Her free hand curled around the doorknob, and it wasn't until she felt the cold metal that she realized she was doing it. She hated when people were upset with her; she couldn't stand to hurt anyone. She felt sick when his shoulders started to shake.

It would have been a thousand times easier to turn him down if he'd punched her.

But then again, Brad knew that. Knew *her* and all her soft spots. He was using them against her now, as clearly as if he'd used her hair to drag her down the street and into his car. After all, if things had been all bad between them, she'd have left him ten years ago.

It had never been the threat of violence that held her. It wasn't as if she was safe even if she didn't try to leave. Fear, even extreme fear, could be faced. Bones could be healed. Scars could be endured. It was his love that crippled her. And it was the good times that kept her doubting herself until it was almost too late.

Mari closed her eyes.

She leaned her head against the door and listened to the quiet huffs of her ex-husband crying on the other side. Slowly, the fingers of guilt eased their grip on her heart. It didn't really matter if his tears were genuine or calculated. Either way, they were a lure that would only draw her back to a place she never needed to be again.

When she heard his footsteps shuffle outside, she ducked over to the window to make sure he wasn't about to take a run at the door. Instead, Brad's back filled her view, retreating down the sidewalk.

Holy shit. He'd listened to her. He was walking away.

She just stared, clutching the cookie sheet to her chest with every emotion of seeing him again catching up all at once.

She could hardly believe he'd just listen and stay gone, but what if he did? She walked slowly into the kitchen, setting down the cookie sheet with a clang of metal that sounded loud in the empty house.

The job was over. She and Jack were over. She could move back into her pickup and hike and read and listen to the empty wind until she found more work, but the thought of the solitude she'd once craved now stuck in her throat like a sob. On this job, she'd finally found the friends she'd always wanted, and it had steadied something in her, shifted something about the person she thought she was.

The whole time she'd believed no one liked her enough to get close, it turned out they were worrying the same about her. She wondered how many other potential friendships she'd let slip away.

Not only that, she'd stopped feeling guilty for every man who got mad at her, and figured out what was beneath all that shouting: insecurity and fear. For decades, she'd let men like her stepfather and Brad and Rod make her feel like she spoiled everything, and she could never have a home with people she cared about. But she was done waiting for other people's approval before she could have the kind of life she'd always secretly dreamed of. Probably, it had been there for the asking all along. Just like everything else.

Mari slipped her hand into her purse, took out her phone, and made the call.

"Hi, Harriet," she said. "Have you filled the biologist-in-residence job yet?"

35

The Yellow Cottage

The wind was calm today, the sun gentler than usual. Mari couldn't have asked for a more beautiful day as she threaded her way through the Joshua trees alongside the national park employee.

"We're so glad you changed your mind about the position." Harriet smiled. "It's been surprisingly hard to fill. We wanted someone with experience with all the desert species we run across here in the park, but all the desert biologists we've talked to have been very hesitant to sign the one-year commitment."

Mari smiled back. "We're a nomadic bunch, it's true." She nodded toward the yellow cottage. "Do you mind if I take a look around? It's been a while since I've seen the place."

"Of course. I'll be in the office whenever you're ready to sign the paperwork. Take your time."

She waited a second for the other woman to start walking away before she turned to face the cottage. A lizard darted across the porch steps, and she tried to ignore how washed out the place looked in the flat midday light. The last time she was here, it had been nearly sunset, and buttery light had poured out of the windows like a beacon. Now, the glass looked flat and translucent, neutrally gray except where it caught the light of the sun and beamed it harshly back at her.

Mari ignored the wisp of pessimism and marched toward the steps. It felt odd and fancy to be dressed in her best white shirt, no hard hat or safety vest in sight. Her slacks clung in places her cargo pants never did. One of the other employees must have commandeered the rocking chair since she was here last, because the porch was bare, and narrower than she had thought. The door was unlocked, and opened with only a slight creak. It was clean, though, the stale ghost of Pine-Sol stinging her nose.

The house was smaller than she remembered, too. It had a nook next to the kitchen with a table and chair, an armchair tucked in a corner that was really too small for it so it partially blocked the doorway. And then the bedroom, a bare mattress standing white and square in the middle of the room.

Two rooms and silence.

It was too much like the moment after Brad left Rajni's apartment, when Mari tried to think of what was next for her, and came up blank. But this was her life now. It wasn't perfect, no, but it was a good job, and more importantly, a place where she could build a community. It was the first place she'd ever had that could be just hers, and nothing inside its walls had to please anyone but herself.

She headed for the kitchen, determined to recapture some of the daydreams she'd had of pumpkin pancakes and zucchini bread. Crackling brown roast chickens and brownies that were gooey in a way that was nearly impossible to achieve in a solar oven.

All she found were a few mouse turds in one corner and a skim of dust across the plain Formica counters. The oven was missing one knob.

Mari stood alone in the center of the room, an odd emptiness growing under her skin.

This place had represented everything she finally dared to dream of, but now it seemed like the "before" picture in one of her HGTV shows. Before the family moved in with their cozy furniture and made it a home.

It hadn't really been the solid walls and electrical plug-ins she'd been hoping for, after all. It had been the *soul* of a place where there was love, and people, and safety, and a house wasn't any of those things. It was just a house.

It was more than what she had now, sure, but it wasn't enough.

But what other choice did she have? Her friends were mostly unemployed now, surfing and living on bean burritos, passing time in their trucks and sending out résumés on free Starbucks Wi-Fi.

Mari reached into her purse, either to call Rajni or maybe to just take a second look at the dancing leprechaun GIF that Gideon had sent her for luck this morning. She wasn't quite sure yet. But instead of her phone, a tiny square of paper nudged her fingers, and she drew it out. It was the price sticker for Jack's new seat covers, the ones he'd bought special for their first date.

Her knees trembled and she sank down onto the armchair in the corner, hardly noticing when dust whooshed out from the cushion. Every time the thoughts rose in her head, she slapped them away, but she couldn't stop remembering, not really. How bashful he'd been on that first date, with his too-fresh haircut and clean truck, and seat covers with the tags still on.

She'd stopped herself a thousand times, but she was weak in the moment and she let herself click her phone on and open her pictures. She had only a handful of Jack: working on his bike, climbing a lattice tower. One of his Good Mood Scowls where his eyes were twinkling a little even as he grumped at her for taking his picture. She even had one terribly awkward selfie of them on his bike on their last day off together, both of them with helmet hair, sweaty foreheads, and shy, ebullient smiles.

A pang twisted in her chest.

She'd never felt like this about anyone, not even during her most infatuated early days with Brad. That pull to be near Jack, and that settled feeling, like she could truly rest once they were side by side. Not to mention how bold she became in bed, his shyness somehow bringing out her wild side . . . Mari flushed and glanced toward the bedroom, but the bare mattress quelled the heat rising in her veins.

She clicked off her screen, because it was pitiful to pine like this. He hadn't wanted her enough to try, and that *hurt*. The memory squirmed in her belly. Maybe she wasn't special enough to be worth fighting for. Or maybe she'd been wrong to tell him he couldn't interfere in how she did her job. She didn't want to believe those things about herself anymore, but the empty spot where Jack used to be screamed for an explanation. As hard as she tried to tell herself this was his fault, that didn't feel true, either.

What felt true was that things shouldn't have ended between them so fast, and she didn't quite know how they had.

Mari flipped her phone over in her hand, feeling its smooth edges. Once, just once, she'd believed that what she wanted was hers for the asking. She'd made the call, and she got everything she'd asked for. But a permanent job and a cute little yellow cottage weren't actually what she'd wanted after all.

She wanted a *home*. And this wasn't it.

Maybe if they'd hired Rajni or Hotaka for the botanist position, she'd have felt better, but she doubted it. What she wanted was Jack, peeking shyly around the corner into the bedroom, and grousing about the wiring to hide how much he liked the place. But Jack built things for a living, and this was a national park, set aside from the relentless growth and development of the rest of the world.

Tears clamped her ribs tight over her lungs, and she hiccuped but didn't cry. She'd told herself she deserved better, that she wouldn't chase a man. That if he wanted to talk to her badly enough, he'd find her number. But none of those things mattered as much as holding him again. Making sure he knew that when she told him to get out that night, she'd never meant for it to be for good.

She'd wanted him to fight for her, but he'd actually shown her more respect by doing as she'd asked when she demanded he give her space. She'd been hurt and expected him to somehow mind-read that she needed space, but also needed reassurance that she meant as much to him as he did to her. She'd been wrong, and the thought of him out there somewhere, lonely and hurting, was harder to swallow than her pride.

His number was still in her phone, but no semi-awkward phone call could cover everything that had happened since they'd been apart. Or the total insanity of trying to snatch a future together when they were both unemployed and qualified only for the kinds of jobs that moved to a new place every few months. Plus, Jack was the actions-speak-louder-than-words type. Which meant if she wanted to see whether what they had could be repaired, she needed to do it in person.

Mari grabbed her car keys.

36

Scent of a New Life

"Mari Tucker has never had a room here."

The twentysomething kid on the other side of the motel desk had a fat head, a skinny neck, and nose hairs nearly as thick as said neck. Jack figured there ought to be plenty of room inside that head for a brain cell or two, but so far that wasn't looking to be the case.

"Not a room for tonight," he explained patiently. "But *before* today. Say, last week." The job had only ended yesterday, but perhaps she'd gotten laid off early.

The kid clicked the mouse for his ancient desktop computer. *Click. Click. Click.*

"Nope."

Jack fought the urge to smack his hands down on the counter.

"Listen, kid, you remember me? Lived here for weeks, gave you more of my hard-earned money than this place deserved?"

The kid nodded.

"Well, I happen to know Mari lived here, because I lived here. She was in room 106. Stayed here for months. Probably moved out sometime last week."

"Oh! Why didn't you just say so?" *Clickclickclickclick.* "Denise Trinity. Room 106, all paid up. She moved out two weeks ago, though, not last week."

"Denise Trinity? That can't be right. Are you sure you didn't write it down wrong?"

The kid gave him a disgusted look. "She signed it that way, too, so no, I didn't write it down wrong every single time she paid her bill."

Jack chewed the inside of his lip. There were only a few reasons to use a fake name, and if rule-loving Mari was doing it, it had to be because of her ex. His pulse picked up. Had the ex shown up and she'd had to run? The clerk said she'd checked out right around the same time her phone number had stopped working. Jack had already been to the only phone store in town, but they'd been very protective of her private information. Hadn't told him a thing, unlike this ass clown.

Jack grabbed the kid and hauled him halfway across the counter. He yelped. "Hey, that hurts! What's the—I told you what you wanted!"

"Ain't anybody ever told you motel information is private?" he growled. "Don't you ever—and I mean until your last pitiful day— ever give a lady's name or information to some asshole who comes in here asking questions about her. This is the kind of place a woman goes to hide from assholes." He dropped the kid, who slid back to his feet and rubbed his belly from where it had scraped over the edge of the counter.

The clerk scowled at him. "Don't go getting pissed at me for telling you when you were the one who asked."

Jack threw down one of his business cards. "Call me if you ever see her again, unless you want me to get pissed for real. You hear?"

"What happened to protecting ladies from assholes?"

He ignored that and strode out of the motel office.

Mari had told him not to call her, not to chase her down and try to win her over with persistence. But he knew how uncertain she could be, and there was a good chance she was just too shy to reach out after the blowout they'd had. Jack thought they deserved one more chance, more of one than they'd had in that rushed early-morning phone call after their fight. If he was being honest, he thought *he* deserved one more chance. He'd never pressure her, though. If she still wanted him to go, after all this time to cool off and think things through, then he'd go.

But before he gave up, he'd make sure she knew beyond a shadow of a doubt that she was wanted. That he'd do anything and give everything to give her the kind of life she deserved.

To do that, he needed to find her. He could call the crew, ask them when she'd stopped coming in to work or if they knew where to find her, but he didn't expect Mari would have confided in any of them. No, he'd wanted to find her on his own and avoid the stomach-curdling embarrassment of telling somebody else she wasn't speaking to him. But if her ex might be involved, if she might be in trouble . . . he couldn't wait.

He pulled out his phone and called the only person who might know how to find her.

Don't yell.

Don't yell.

Do not *yell.*

The reminder pounded through his head with every thump of his boots against the sidewalk as he approached Marcus's rental house.

Two days ago, when he'd called and asked for Mari's new number, Marcus had said no.

But then, that was his job. Jack would do more than haul the lead biologist over a counter if he thought Marcus was giving out Mari's phone number to every yahoo who came asking. But Lisa was Mari's friend, which meant her boyfriend, Marcus, probably knew about the whole ex issue. With any luck, that made him more cautious where Mari was concerned.

So Jack had checked into the Best Western and spent two of the longest days of his life asking around town, trying to find any lead on where Mari had gone or what her new number was. He'd gotten nowhere, and now he was all the way back to Marcus, who he knew had the information he wanted, if he could just ask in the right way to get it.

Unfortunately, Jack was not the best talker.

He'd never put much effort into being persuasive, because if his childhood had taught him anything, it was that if he was talking? Nobody was listening.

His crew listened, sure, but they were paid to. Convincing Marcus to give him Mari's number would be better done man-to-man, he knew that much. But now that he was standing in front of the biologist's door, he had no idea what more he could do in person than he could do over the phone.

But the urgency of finding out if Mari was in trouble drove him past his own doubt, and he lifted his fist and knocked. At least his black eye had faded, because that probably wouldn't have helped his case.

Marcus opened the door and eyed him warily. "Uh, hi, Wyatt."

Apparently he wasn't the only one worried about how he'd handle this situation. Fair enough, he hadn't built the best reputation as calm and collected over these past few years. But this was important.

What would Mari do in this situation?

Make small talk, probably. Which was easier for her because everyone liked her. She knew little things about everybody's lives and always asked about them.

"Uh," Jack said. "So how's that belt working?"

Marcus glanced down toward his fly.

"On your truck!" Jack yelped. "Actually, never mind the belt." He already knew it was working fine; he'd put it in himself, and there wasn't too much that could go wrong with a brand-new belt. "How's Lisa?"

Marcus relaxed. "She's fine. Off talking to one of our contacts in Vegas to see if we can't pick up some more work, while I wrap up this job. I have to admit, I kind of thought you were going to yell at me for not giving you Mari's number."

"Ain't gonna yell at you," Jack muttered. "I need to talk to you."

"Better get in off the porch, then."

Marcus led the way inside, and even in here Jack couldn't get away from the smell of pizza ingredients lingering in his nose. Like hiding in that warehouse was going to follow him for the rest of his life, reminding him how low he'd gone for a brother who didn't deserve it.

"Sorry the place is a mess," Marcus said. "I'm in charge of the packing, and Lisa's not going to be so fine anymore when she sees what a crap job I did. This place came furnished and all our stuff got mixed in with the landlord's stuff." He led the way to the kitchen. "I mean, how the hell are you supposed to tell your spatula from a rental spatula?"

"Don't matter. Spatula's a spatula. Landlord ain't gonna care unless you put it through a window."

"No, but Lisa will. Want a beer?"

"No, thanks, I'm fine." Then something occurred to him. "Let me see the spatulas."

That brow went up again. "Mari said you were some kind of amazing at tracking, but I don't think even you can spot the difference between our spatula and a rental."

"Bet you fifty I can. Actually, never mind the fifty. If I'm right, you've got to help me."

"I can't break employee confidentiality," Marcus said. "And even if I could, I wouldn't when it comes to Mari."

Jack nodded. "Good. I didn't want to hit you."

Marcus looked confused, but when he started to speak, Jack just gestured toward the kitchen drawers. The other man turned and dug out two spatulas, holding them up. Both were black rubber, about the same length, and both scratched from long use.

"Yours is the one on the left, with the three slits in it."

"Okay, but you could say either one and I'd have to believe you. It isn't like I know the difference."

"Night I came over for dinner, Lisa kept talking with her hands when she was cooking. Waving that thing all round in my face until I thought I was gonna lose an eye. It's not a thing a man forgets."

Marcus chuckled. "Okay. Fair point. Now, how can I help you that doesn't require giving you Mari's new phone number?"

"Do you know where she's at, know if she's okay?" Jack took a step forward. "You said on the phone that she worked to the end of the job, but the motel says she checked out weeks ago. With that and the number change, I'm thinking her ex is giving her trouble again. Plus, she was staying under a fake name. Think that guy might be more than annoying, if you catch my meaning."

"Damn, you are some kind of tracker, aren't you?" Marcus dropped the three-slit spatula into an open cardboard box. "The ex-husband was giving her trouble. She moved in with Rajni, and he still found her there, but Mari dealt with him all on her own."

Jack's blood slammed up into his ears and he went light-headed for a second, his fingers tingling into numbness. "Where is she?" he whispered, hospital beds and heart monitors threading through his head. He knew what it cost you to run away from a guy like that. His daddy had caught him trying to run away and live out in the woods, when he was nine. Ripped a pole out of the tent he'd been living in and beat him half to death with it.

"Mari's okay." The other man's hand landed on his shoulder and gave it a squeeze. "He didn't hurt her, and we've all been watching out in case that was to change. But the guy seems to be finally taking no for an answer."

Jack was so dizzy he didn't even knock away Marcus's hand, because he was pretty sure it was the only thing holding him up.

"Need to see Mari." The words came out raw and unplanned, and

Jack fought back a wave of nausea, a burn behind his eyes. She could have been in a hospital bed. She could have been dead. He was off rescuing his brother, who would never have returned the favor, when he should have been here.

Marcus let go of his shoulder and winced. "What happened between you two? She wouldn't talk about it, and I don't really feel comfortable sticking my nose in without knowing."

Jack wasn't in the habit of airing his dirty laundry to hippies he barely knew, but right this minute, he'd tell Marcus anything from his bank account number to the truth about how he lost his virginity if it'd help him find Mari.

"We argued about Rod. I didn't like her being on Junior's crew, was afraid Rod was gonna pull something. She said she could handle it. I got mad, wouldn't listen. Dumb." He shook his head. "Thought she changed her number to shake me off, but now I'm maybe thinking that was about her ex."

Marcus was giving him a funny look. "You were right about Junior's crew. It was a whole big thing. Rod killed a tortoise—dug its burrow up with a shovel, brought it to the construction site and ran it over, then tried to frame Mari for it."

"He killed a *tortoise*? That fucking—"

Marcus held up a hand. "Easy. Mari wouldn't take an ounce of his shit. She figured out it was him and managed to prove it, too." He grinned. "Rod lost his job, and Junior didn't last a week after the interim manager saw his crew's performance."

Jack snorted, a little tickle of pride coming in to soothe his panic. "Well, fuck. She handled him, just like she said." Got the jerk fired, which was more than Jack ever thought was possible. It made him sick to think of that dead tortoise, though, and how upset Mari must have been. "Turtle . . . wasn't one of the little ones, was it?" She was even more protective of the juvies.

"Yeah. Wish I could say it wasn't." Marcus sighed. "Anyway, the job ended and Mari got hired on as a—well, I can't tell you that part, but she got a new job. Somewhere. She's probably already headed out. Have you tried apologizing?"

"Called to try but she'd already changed her number." Before, he'd been so sure it was all him, that she changed her number not because her ex had found her but that she was avoiding him because he'd messed up. But then, that wasn't like Mari, was it? She was so gentle where he was concerned, always kinder than he expected. "I can't . . ." He paced away, paced back. "Can't just let her go without trying. She's . . . I just never figured . . ."

He swallowed down all his stuttered words and looked the other man in the eye.

"Ain't nobody like her. Never will be again. Can't fuck this up, man. Can you . . . help?"

He damn near choked on the question, but he'd beg if he had to. Shit, he'd cry if he thought it'd do any good. Wouldn't be all that hard, either, thinking of how Mari could have landed in the hospital without him here to give that douchebag ex the beatdown he had coming. Jack's knuckles tingled just thinking of it.

Marcus's face had gone solemn. "She's special, Mari is. You're right. Look, what if I call her, tell her you're here and worried about her, maybe put in a good word for you?"

"Now? Could you—I mean, would you mind calling her now?"

"Sure. Just maybe don't . . . um, stare at me like that while I'm calling, okay?"

Jack cleared his throat. "Uh, right. I'll wait outside, then. Just get me. When you're done. If she answers. Maybe leave a message, though. If she doesn't."

Marcus's lips twitched. "Yeah. Of course I will. No worries."

Jack hauled his ass outside, pacing all the way to the curb by the time the door swung shut behind him. Would she answer? The more he thought about it, the more he thought their fight hadn't been all that terrible. He really didn't think she'd be so mad at him that she wouldn't want to talk. She'd always smiled so much, when they were together. He thought . . . hell, it felt like bad luck even to think it, but he was pretty damn sure she liked him, that she was maybe even a little bit serious about him.

He'd been good to her, and if he got a second chance, he'd be even better. His whole life, his dad and brother had laughed at the idea that a woman would ever want him, but he never knocked women around like his dad had. Or manipulated them, stole their money, and cheated on them like Leroy had. He was kind to women, and if he didn't always know how to make conversation with them, well, there were worse faults.

He clenched his jaw. He and Mari were good together. No matter what Leroy said, he didn't think she had changed her number to avoid him. If she hadn't called to give him her new one, it seemed likely it was just because she was as uncertain as he was when it came to dating.

Probably if he hadn't freaked out and gone running off to Nebraska, he and Mari would have made up the afternoon after their fight. He would have found the right way to explain that he never wanted to order her around, that he just wanted her to be okay, was all. Even if he had to write the words down on paper and move them around until he got them right, he would have figured out how to explain it a better way than he had that night.

If he'd just stayed and tried to work things out, Jack probably could have spent the last two weeks watching HGTV and laughing and kissing Mari and eating her delicious brownies with one hand happily bandaged from caving in her ex's ugly face, and everything would have been hunky-fucking-dory.

His phone rang. He whipped around to see if it might be Marcus calling, but the door to Marcus's rental house was just coming open, like the guy was emerging to tell him what Mari had said. Which meant this could be her right now. Jack skinned a knuckle on his jeans as he ripped his phone out of his pocket. Unfamiliar number, California area code.

"Is that you?" he rushed out. "Listen, I'm so fucking sorry . . ."

"Good!" a male voice exclaimed. "You should be, considering what an asshole you were to me a few days ago, and twice as sorry considering I'm even calling you now, which I shouldn't, because as I said, you were an asshole. Also, it's against motel policy. I think. Actually, you were the one who said it was but I'm not even sure we have a privacy policy so you were really out of line yelling at me about it."

Jack frowned. "This the motel?"

"What, you don't remember assaulting me and cursing me out over a woman whose name you couldn't even remember? You kept saying she was Mari but she was *definitely* booked as Denise—" The kid kept prattling on, but Marcus had come out of the house and was shaking his head.

"Went straight to voicemail," he whispered, like he didn't want to interrupt Jack's call. "Cell phone service is iffy where her new job is. I'll try her again later, and yes, before you even ask, I left a message."

Jack nodded.

"C'mon back in and have a beer when you finish your call," Marcus said. "I'll try her again in a while, okay?"

Marcus went back inside, but suddenly Jack found it too exhausting to stay on his feet, and he sank down to sit on the stoop's single step, the concrete oven-hot through his jeans. Mari told him she'd gone months without cell service. She didn't have any family left, and usually the service was so bad that she said she'd just turn off her phone and be done with it until the end of the job. How was he going to find her if Marcus couldn't get through? If it took months, what if she moved on, found somebody else during this job? Anybody with half a brain would kill to get with a woman like Mari.

In his phone's speaker, the motel kid was still talking.

"Anyway, when she came in asking about you, I remembered her face. And really, I don't get why you seem to care so much about whether she called herself Denise or Mari or whatever, or why anybody would care in the first place if a motel knew your name. It's not like I'm going to google you and invade your privacy by reading your blogs ranting about why Twitter should be blocking *Game of Thrones* spoilers and—"

"The fuck did you say? Denise?" Jack's forehead crinkled, and he could hardly think through his headache.

"Yes," the kid said. "She said her real name *is* Mari and wanted to know if you'd left a forwarding address, and I said you hadn't but you left your card, and she made me dig it out of the garbage heap of the owner's desk, which took forever but I did it because she seemed really nice and I don't know why she'd be looking for you, because you're very much *not* nice, but she said—"

"She was there?" Jack rocketed back to his feet. "When? How long ago'd she leave?"

The kid sighed. "This is cute and all, or it would be if you weren't kind of a dick, but I'm starting to get the feeling you're not really listening to me. Do you want to just talk to her?"

"*Yes.*" He remembered to add "thank you, uh . . ." He had no idea what the kid's name was. It'd been on his name tag, idiot had said it out loud and it was . . . he had no idea. He really needed to start being a nicer person like Mari, who remembered people's names, if he was going to—

"Jack?" Her voice came across the line. "Is that really you?"

His tongue stuck to the top of his mouth, and his vision blurred.

She laughed softly. "Oh my gosh, you came *back*. And Wayne said you were looking for me here?"

"Uh . . ." He could barely force his throat to make a single, scratchy sound. He scrubbed furiously at his eyes but even though his fingers came away wet, his vision didn't clear.

"Jack, is that you? Say something."

"You okay?" he forced out hoarsely. "You all right?"

She laughed, tight and high pitched. Not her normal easy, soft laughter. "Well . . ."

"Is he there?" Jack shot toward his truck. "Your ex, did he come back?"

"How did you know . . . He was here. But that was days ago. It's over, I'm okay."

She exhaled shakily.

"Listen, you were right about Rod. I was just touchy because of my history with Brad, and I cooled down pretty quick but I was so upset that you just left like that, and I was being stubborn, wanting you to call first. But then I tried to move on and got that job with the park service and the yellow cottage and I hated it and no matter what I tell myself to do, I just couldn't stop thinking about you, wondering where you were. So I came back to see if the motel had a forwarding address or something, even though I wasn't totally sure you wanted to see me. I couldn't believe it when the guy said you'd been here earlier this week, and I meant to do this in person but I got so nervous I let him call you first, just to test the waters and—"

"I'm sorry I love you," he blurted out.

There was a soft sound on the other end of the line. Like a broken breath, or a word that didn't quite make it out.

"I mean, I'm sorry about what I did. Never meant to piss you off, and I never want you to feel like I wanna control you or keep you down." The feeling of being held down filled his memory. Claustrophobic and familiar, and he didn't have all the words to tell her he knew what it was to be trapped. He would sooner peel his own skin off than make her feel that way. "And I love you. Wanted to tell you every day but figured it was always too soon. Feels too late now."

The phrase "I love you" sounded so unfamiliar that it was like he didn't recognize his own voice. He tried to remember the last time he'd said that out loud. It must have been before his mother died. Which explained why it sounded so strange, since he'd never said it since his voice had dropped into a man's lower register.

Her breathing stuttered on the other end of the line, and he turned in a circle, looking up at the brutally clear blue of the desert sky, the phone pressed so hard to his head that it was creasing his ear.

"It's not too late," she said, her voice breaking. "Can I see you?"

"Coming right now," he said, leaping in his truck and cranking the ignition with his left hand so he wouldn't have to move the phone from his ear for even a second.

"I'm sorry, hold on. Marcus keeps calling on my cell and I'll call him back later but I probably need to just turn my ringer off because it's so loud. Jack? Are you still there?"

"I'm here." He took a breath, his heart beating wildly. "Sorry for what I done, sorry I left, sorry I didn't listen to you when you said you could handle Rod. Marcus says you kicked Rod's ass."

She laughed again, all sweet and soft, and how had he ever thought a woman like that would hold a grudge against him over one argument? She had a heart bigger than the whole earth, far as he could tell.

"Sorry about that tortoise he killed, too. Can't fucking believe it." He cut off a Honda and accelerated down the street.

"I wish I'd really kicked Rod's ass," she said. "I just filled out a whole lot of paperwork and took a wild guess at his shoe size that paid off. Would you believe it, when I figured out what he'd done and told everybody, he tried to say I just had PMS?"

"He probably thinks PMS is a TV station, man's so stupid," Jack growled.

"Anyway, you've got nothing to apologize for," Mari said. "I should have listened to you. I thought he'd try to bully me, or make a lot of off-color remarks. I never dreamed he'd go so far in trying to punish me for reporting his son, when Junior was clearly breaking the law, and wow, Marcus is calling again. Maybe I'd better take this. Something might be wrong and—"

"It ain't," Jack interrupted, running a yellow light that was looking pretty damn red. He hoped it still counted as yellow if it was yellow when you first saw it. "He's calling because I was at his house, pretty much begged him to get ahold of you for me. Helped him with a spatula."

"A spatula? He can't fix his own truck, and now he can't work a spatula, either?" Mari laughed. "Oh! Is that you pulling into the lot?"

Jack threw down his phone, stomped the parking brake, and left the truck in the middle of the parking lot. He couldn't concentrate on lining up with painted lines when *she* was coming out of the motel office, heading for his truck with a walk that turned faster and faster until she was nearly running. He jumped out of the truck and dashed to meet her, but right before they got there, he stopped dead and threw his hands up, not willing to risk even catching her by the arms.

His eyes scoured her face—not a dark blue smudge on it. Nothing swollen or cut . . . "You hurt? Did he hit you, shove you around?"

She was wearing a tank top, and he knew just the spot where the fingertip bruises showed up if someone grabbed you to keep you from running away. He hadn't wanted to hug her and risk hurting her, and if he caught her arms to stop her so he could look, it would have squeezed right over the tender places her ex might have left.

Mari shook her head, tears shimmering in her eyes. "Brad never laid a finger on me. In fact, he apologized. He's been going to therapy, said he's changed, and I think there's a chance he really has. He left when I told him to leave, and made a big down payment on my medical bills this morning. Sent a screenshot of that and a gas station receipt from six hundred miles east of here."

The words ran over and over through his head on hyperspeed. Her ex reformed, got better, and she still hadn't gone back. Instead, she'd gone looking for *Jack*.

He took the last step forward so fast that he knocked her off-balance, but his arms were already closing around her, so he caught her without even trying and hugged her straight off her feet, his face tucking into her neck, her scent surrounding him like the softest, sweetest moment of his whole life. It washed the Cheesy Charlie's warehouse smell straight out of his memory.

Her slender arms bruised his rib cage and the nape of his neck, she was holding on so hard. Dampness touched his scalp where her face was pressed but he didn't mind because she was laughing, all scratchy and kind of sobbing like, but she sounded happy. Because of him.

"I love you," she whispered. "I've been so in love with you, and the more right it felt, the more scared I got that anything this good had to be a trick."

"Ain't a trick. I'd kick the fuck out of anybody who ever tried to trick you."

She started to laugh again, her shoulders shaking against his chest, and he realized he should have said something romantic, but couldn't come up with anything to say but the truth.

His voice came out hoarse against her hair. "Never should have left. Never want to leave you again, Mari. Please," he said. That was all the vow he could think to make. "Please."

And she kissed him so long he forgot it'd ever been a question.

37

Keystone Species

The sunset sky was all yellow and orange, clouds catching the colors and stretching them out across the sky. The roof of the truck radiated heat through the seat of Jack's jeans, but perched atop the cab, Jack and Mari could see for miles. He propped his boots on the windshield and tightened his arm around Mari's waist so she'd lean back even more fully against him.

They'd gone back to their spot, way out in the desert. This time, she'd been very much in the mood to make all his blow job fantasies come true, but he'd made her stop before he finished because he couldn't stand waiting one more day before making love to her again. Judging by the sounds she made, he hadn't done a half-bad job of it, either.

He was feeling pretty fucking smug.

They'd gotten dressed again to climb up to the top of the truck and watch the sunset, but he barely saw the colorful sky streaking out all around them.

"It's sad, you know," he said.

She frowned, tilting her head back to look at him. "What?"

"That you tracked me down before I could track you down. I'm supposed to be the tracker." He squeezed her a little. He couldn't seem to get enough of hugging her, holding her, since he got back.

"Well, I'm a determined woman."

"Damn right you are. Every man in our company had been wishing Rod would get knocked off his pedestal for years, but all of us put together couldn't make it happen. I was only gone a couple of weeks and you had it checked off the list just like that."

Mari smiled, but her expression looked a little distracted as she stared out over the desert.

"What?" He nudged his knee against her thigh.

"You know why we go to so much trouble to save tortoises?"

"Because there ain't that many of them left?"

The little buggers were cute as hell, but he was pretty sure nobody was funding biological monitors just for cute.

"No. There are plenty of at-risk species that don't get much help," she said. "Tortoises are sort of a keystone species because they dig burrows, which are used by snakes and owls and all these other species. They spread the seeds of native grasses and plants around so the vegetation thrives wherever there are tortoises. You hardly ever spot a tortoise anymore, but where they're around, the whole desert looks different. I was just thinking it's funny, how one little thing can change so many things."

She paused for a long moment, her fingers toying absently with a fold in his jeans.

"Just like me. I was different when I was with Brad than when I was with you. Now, I have my own money, a job I'm proud of, and I do it well."

"Had that before you met me."

"I did," she said. "But now I also have friends. I dress different, eat different, jeez, I noticed the other day I even walk differently. I laugh, just, all the time now." She turned a bit to look up at him. "It's not like you did any of those things for me, told me how to dress or introduced me to my friends. But you change one little thing, and so many ripple effects come of it that you never could have expected. You didn't give me my new life, but you gave me hope."

He had no idea how to answer a declaration like that, one that made his chest fill and fill until it felt as big as if he'd breathed in the whole damn sky. Like he might bust with all the happy locked up inside him. Instead, he just kissed her cheek, and she looked over at him and smiled.

"Maybe hope is a keystone species."

Epilogue

"You don't think it's too small?"

"Are you kidding? I love it."

"Ain't anything special." He kicked the tire of their new fifth-wheel trailer. He'd bought the most premium model he could find, but now, seeing it next to Mari, it didn't seem half good enough. Especially since he knew she'd given up a permanent job with a house to be with him.

"It's better than anyplace I've ever lived in." She bounded inside. "Look at those gorgeous countertops!"

"AC, too," he offered. "Central, so it vents in every room and you don't have to throw your pillow under the window unit come August."

"That's going to be important, until I get certified to work with some nondesert species." Mari ran her hand over the creamy paneling. "It's really beautiful. I can't believe how big the bathroom is, and this kitchen is a dream. Huge upgrade from my tailgate, and I can even bake in here. Are you sure it wasn't too much money?"

"I make a good wage," he growled. "If I'm gonna live in a trailer again, it better be a damn nice trailer." He shook back his hair—getting long again already—and squinted at the complicated panel for lighting and climate control options. "I'm not having you living in some shithole with tinfoil on the windows and a hose poked through the wall for a shower."

He didn't want to risk the chance of the smell of a pizza warehouse creeping back into his nose. This was his new life, his choices. He liked the hell out of all of them, but he wanted to make sure Mari liked them, too.

"Heck, when I was living in my truck, I didn't even have a shower." She grinned, dropping to bounce on the thick cushions of the leather couch. "This is practically a palace. And it feels like *ours*."

Her quiet smile made his chest feel tight, like it was growing too big for his ribs, and he glanced down and cleared his throat, trying not to grin like a dope.

"Well, it'll work for now, anyhow. Give us a home to take with us. Plenty of power lines being built through the desert to LA and Las Vegas. That'll keep me busy until you get certified for those other species like you were telling me about."

"I love the Mojave Desert, but honestly, I can't wait. Then we can travel all over the country, see the mountains, the rivers, the coasts . . ." She tugged him onto the couch next to her. He didn't put up much of a fight. "Besides, there are fewer tortoise jobs all the time."

"If you ever get tired of moving around, just say the word," he insisted. "I can work local distribution lines anywhere. I don't have to build. Don't need to bust my back lugging steel into my sixties like Vernon did."

"I could get a job with a local fish and wildlife department someday," Mari suggested. "Maybe somewhere with some big shady trees . . ."

"House with a porch." He'd build her a porch swing, buy her some cushions for it so she could sit out there as long as she liked on nice days.

"I could take some time off, too," she said. "If you ever get a job somewhere they don't need biological monitors. Money's not so tight now that my bills are caught up."

Brad paid the medical bills he'd given her, sure. But her ex only lasted a few weeks before he broke his word and showed up again, begging her to come home. Once he saw Jack, he stopped the Mr. Nice Guy act and came back with a gun. They'd already alerted the police and had him on the restraining order violation, but it was the pistol that sent him to prison. Still woke Jack up in a cold sweat some nights, to think how close they'd come to bullets flying before the cops showed up.

"You shouldn't have had any medical bills to pay!" he grumbled. "It'll be a cold day in the devil's jockey shorts before I give that prick any credit for paying off those bills when he's the only reason you had 'em to start with."

"Oh, I don't give Brad any credit. But it's sure nice to have *my* credit looking better." She gave Jack a soft smile, her blue eyes glowing the way they did so often now.

He shook his head with a laugh. "You've got to be the nicest damn person ever born. Give Gideon a run for his money."

"Oh, Gideon isn't that nice. Don't you remember what he said about that referee's mother when the Packers lost last Sunday?"

Jack chuckled, and she kissed him, her hand finding his and toying with his fingers.

"You're too good to me. I can't help but tease."

"Ain't too good. You had to take out the trash yourself last week because I forgot."

"You're still upset about that?" She snorted. "Are you going to buy me a trailer every time you forget to take out the trash?"

"Nope. Only gonna buy one, that way you've gotta stay in this one with me." As soon as he said it, he realized it sounded bad, like he was going to make her or something, but she laughed like that was so far from their reality that it could only be a joke.

After they'd found each other again, she never took that biologist-in-residence job, or the survey gig in the Chocolate Mountains. Instead, she'd come to monitor a job he took building power lines near Vegas. No matter how often he checked in with her, she never seemed to mind having followed him to that assignment. His whole crew had pretty much come with him from the last job, even Kipp and Joey the apprentice.

Mari wasn't always the bio on his crew, but he was pretty sure she ran interference for him with the other bios because they were all real good to him. Explained the reasons for their weirder regulations, which he appreciated. He tried his best never to yell at work anymore, tried to talk soft and let people figure shit out on their own like Vernon had, but every now and again he slipped up when someone did something really stupid.

After the Vegas job ended, he'd shown her a list of all the places that needed linemen, all mapped out inside the boundaries of the desert tortoise habitat he'd found online. She'd picked their next job and he'd applied, and bought a ring on the drive there. Took him five months to work up the courage to ask her, and only then because he'd found the ring moved from one side of his underwear drawer to the other.

She hadn't left him after finding the tiny velvet box, and had made his favorite dinners for the next six consecutive days, so he'd figured it was a pretty safe bet to ask her.

Turned out, that had been a correct assumption.

That ring glittered on her finger now as she braced herself on his shoulder to swing a leg over his lap and straddle him. "I'm going to have to stay in this RV with you, huh? Well, we've all got problems." She kissed him with a smile curving her lips. "I sure like mine."

Much later, when their clothes had migrated to the floor and the AC was working overtime to catch up, Jack was thinking about their conversations about what made a home, both today and when they first met.

He stroked a hand over her silver-streaked hair, hugging her closer into his chest. "Just so you know, I don't care if we get a house or not. Or when." He laid a kiss on her forehead. "With you, anyplace feels like home to me."

Acknowledgments

For the last ten years, I've worked various desert biology jobs that helped inform the details in this book. For the first four of those years, my husband and I lived year-round in the ancient Toyota truck that you can see in the background of my author photo. For the rest of that time, we had a home base but still lived between three to nine months of the year in our Toyota or cheap motels like Mari's.

When it comes to the details about desert animals, or bio life, or the tasks and dangers of lineman work . . . it's all as real and accurate as my own experience can make it. A few details have been changed to protect the insiders of turtle club, though none of the people in the book are taken from real life. Lineman work really is crazy dangerous and some companies are careful and care about their workers and some companies don't, to the extent that it's literally criminal. As far as the specific laws and rules referenced in this book: some laws are federal, some come from the state, and some guidelines change by the job, according to the restraints of the Biological Opinion written by the supervising agency. Some laws have changed already since this manuscript was written. I based the specific regulations on a power line job I worked several years back, but I'm sure some inaccuracies or mistakes have crept in.

Desert tortoise populations were documented as declining more than ninety percent in the twentieth century, and continue to decline at a staggering rate, despite efforts to set aside more land for them, and vast improvements in translocation protocols. If you'd like to find out more about how you can help, go to the Desert Tortoise Council's website at deserttortoise.org.

The first person I need to thank in these acknowledgments is my husband, for being my partner in this crazy life. Not many couples can hike five meters apart all day, huddle in a truck bed all night, and cook outside in fifty-mile-per-hour winds, without eventually killing each other. You're the best roommate on earth, and you're not allowed to die. Ever.

All my gratitude and awe go to my incredible agent, Naomi Davis of BookEnds Literary, who blows my mind anew every year that we work together. I can't believe how great you are at making all my writerly dreams come true, over and over again. I will never forget you calling me while I was in a motel room by the sea, to babble about how much you loved this book. Or my husband blushing while he told me to lower my voice because our conversation about Jack's "attributes" might be scandalizing the motel neighbors.

My eternal thanks to Kristine Swartz, for giving this book a home and a team of incredible professionals to bring it to the world, and for protecting my vision for the characters. I love how you're willing to let me go there with my books, even about tough topics. Sorry again for Jack's foul mouth. We can start the swear jar on the next book.

Flavored ChapSticks and fruit baskets to Jessica Mangicaro, Jessica Brock, Dache Rogers, Brittanie Black, and the rest of my hardworking team at Berkley, for being the bearers of good news, and the wizards behind the curtain working tirelessly to *produce* that good news. All publicists and marketing people go directly to heaven. It is known.

Hugs and crooked cakes to Katie Golding, who has been there

since my very first fanfiction, weathering every celebration and disappointment with me, and living in my phone to keep me company when my husband is gone and I'm alone in the desert for too long. I love you, girl. *Almost* as much as I love your incredible books. ;)

I owe peach muffins for life to Gwynne Jackson for reading and voting on approximately one billion versions of the opening to this book. Your steadying presence and unwavering kindness are a constant inspiration to me. The sea otter pics don't hurt, either.

All my love to Sandra Lombardo of Reads and Reviews, my books' godmother, who gave lovely notes on this story and is there to support every one of my works. Thanks for always sending great reading recs and fangirling over books with me.

Special thanks this time to my workshop partners at the Pneuma Creative Meditation and Revision Retreat: Heather Demetrios, Lyn, and Shelly. Thanks for helping me dig deeper into Mari's character, figure out a better climax, and make her goals more concrete. That retreat week was magical (Ingrid, I love you!) and I have to give a special shout out to the amazing Highlights Retreat Center in the Pennsylvania forest, and to German Chef Lady and her very inspiring story about four-leaf clovers.

Peanut butter cookies and all my heart go to Margaret Torres, who still has no idea how much her enthusiasm breathes life into my muse.

Blankets and hand-warmers and love to Rhylaigh Richler, who has been a light in every tunnel I've ever been in.

Thanks to Sarah Bailey for her excitement about this book and all her very useful notes, and for being my musical soul sister.

Blown kisses to my collective fiancé, the Berkley Art Department. I proposed marriage to all of them collectively for the gorgeous cover of *Unbreak Me* and I was forced to declare my undying love to them again when they nailed the cover for this book *on their first try*. Considering I'm that author who asks for "just one more tiny adjustment" approximately 436 times for every cover, that is a feat worthy of temples and marble statuary.

Big love to my wonderful family and my mom, who is the world's most hardworking publicist, and a killer bookkeeper. Thanks for all the spreadsheets, Mom!

To my fanfiction readers, whose love and support got me into this writing career, and whose reviews and belief in me have revived my rejection-crushed heart for far more than its allotted nine lives. God bless you, every one.

I do realize these acknowledgments are eight hundred years long, but I can't finish without giving a wave of my sun-gloved hand to all my fellow tortoise biologists. I've been to a lot of countries, on a lot of continents, and tortoise bios are by far the strangest, most independent-thinking, competent, and kind individuals I have ever encountered.

You all have squinted through sandstorms, slogged through rain, and sweated—endlessly sweated—with me. We've twisted our ankles in the scree fields of Mt. Doom, and staggered through the Valley of Fun. You've made me laugh when I was too tired to see straight and invented birthday presents and parties for me when we were oh so many miles from any store. Most importantly, you taught me how to keep searching without ever giving up, despite thousands of hours of finding nothing, because on the 10,001st hour, sometimes there's a tortoise! That was truly the best preparation for a writing career that a girl could ask for.

Tortoise work has been hard, but it's afforded me the freedom to build a life better than my wildest dreams. I am infinitely grateful for that, and for all of you.

Author's Note

This story deals with some very tough themes, about types of abuse that happen every day in America. I worry that too much popular media shows both abusers and survivors as easily dismissed caricatures, not as people with complicated motivations and a few unhealthy habits that don't always serve them, just like the rest of us. To be clear, I don't think anything ever excuses or justifies abuse, but I also think portraying abusers as cartoon villains of unrelenting evil makes it difficult for observers to grasp why it's so difficult for survivors to leave those relationships. I tried, with the research methods at my disposal and my own observed experiences, to make this a more accurate picture of what some people have endured. However, no one story can encapsulate all the different ways abuse can be experienced, or all the different reactions people have to it, and I don't pretend this could ever be universal.

If you're reading this as a survivor, I know what you went through was entirely unique to you and no story could quite capture it the way it happened. Still, I hope that you found strength and validation in these pages, and I pray that nothing I've written causes you any additional hurt.

If you're reading this and any part of Mari's old abusive relationship is sounding too familiar to you, you can call 1-800-799-SAFE (7233). No matter how hopeless or impossible or just plain complicated your situation is, there *is* help available for exactly that and to get you safe. You don't have to face this alone.

Breathe
the Sky

MICHELLE HAZEN

Questions for Discussion

1. If you were going to be a wildlife biologist, what animals would you most like to work with?

2. Did you see any ways in which Mari's and Jack's experiences of abuse make it easier for them to connect with each other, even though it might have made it more difficult for them to connect with other people?

3. Both Mari and Jack struggle with how to follow their hearts, when so many of their instincts are habits driven by years of abuse and insecurity. In your own life, how do you tell when to follow your heart, and when your first impulse might instead be self-sabotaging, produced by old bad habits?

4. Both Mari and Jack feel in some ways unworthy of having a home and family, but their longing for it shows in their fas-cination with home improvement shows. Do you think hav-

ing a physical space is essential to the concept of home? How much or how little do you think this contributes?

5. Mari's ex-husband uses tears and reminders of their good times together to influence her. Did you expect him to use emotional manipulation tactics or more physical intimidation? Which do you think would have been harder to resist, if you were in that situation?

6. Some of Mari's conflict with Jack comes from her worries that his shouty temper could be a warning sign that he could later become abusive or violent. What are some warning signs of an abusive relationship? How can you tell the difference between when someone's simply angry, and when they might be dangerous?

7. Rajni's test of a good man in "Pizza Doesn't Lie" might seem oversimplified at first glance. But what does her example define about the difference between a healthy and an unhealthy relationship?

8. At the end of the book, Mari says hope is a keystone species, because its existence changes everything around it for the better. What are other "keystone species" in a relationship?

Michelle Hazen is a nomad with a writing problem. Years ago, she and her husband swapped office jobs for seasonal wildlife biology gigs, and moved into their Toyota truck. As a result, she wrote most of her books with solar power in odd places, including a bus in Thailand, a golf cart in a sandstorm, and a beach in Honduras. These days, if she's not hiking or scuba diving, she's probably writing fan fiction, watching *Veronica Mars*, or driving an indefensible amount of miles to get to a Revivalists' concert.

CONNECT ONLINE

MichelleHazenBooks.com

❑ MichelleHazenAuthor

🐦 MichelleHazen

Ready to find
your next great read?

Let us help.

Visit prh.com/nextread

Penguin
Random
House